TRAM

GREG GARDINER

Melbourne Australia

Greg Gardiner c/- Intertype Publish and Print
Unit 45, 125 Highbury Road
BURWOOD VIC 3125
Australia
www.intertype.com.au

Ordering Information:
Quantity sales. Special discounts are available on quantity purchases by corporations, associations, and others. For details, contact the "Special Sales Department" at the address above.

Tram/ Greg Gardiner. —1st ed.
ISBN 978-1-7640856-6-3

Contents

PROLOGUE: 1888 7

1. Portrait of a Tram 11

2. Five Years... 21

3. Kangas & Orcas on the Number 72................................ 25

4. Myths of Origin.. 35

5. Route 78: The Shopping Mecca 41

6. The Star Witness 49

7. Route 75: Typo on Flinders Street............................... 59

8. The Tramways Act 1883 67

9. The Marvellous Engineer.. 73

10. South Melbourne Beach 79

11. Route 64: Looking for Engine Houses 87

12. A Visit to Gog and Magog 97

13. The Gripman 101

14. Central Park on the Number 5.................................. 107

15. At the Workshops 113

16. Grand Junction.. 119

17. The Language of Route 58.. 123

18. The Terminus 133

INTERMISSION 141

19. Network Evolution 149

20. Trams, Trusts & Acronyms... 153

21. Route 16: Reveries 157

22. A Royal Commission & an Act of Parliament........................ 163

23. Alex Cameron's M&MTB 171

24. Body Politics on Route 67 177

25. Transport Wars.. 185

26. An Existential Ride on the Number 57................................... 193

27. A City's Identity: The W Series... 203

28. How to Drive a W Class Tram.. 209

29. MCG Trams 219

30. Love & Grief on the Number 11 223

31. This Connie Life... 233

32. Fashionista Trams 239

33. Invasion Day.. 243

34. The Coup.. 249

35. Route 19: The Joyce Barry Revolution 253

36. Out West on the Number 82 263

37. The Major-General.. 271

38. Clarrie O'Shea & the Union 277

39. Public v Private: From a Z to a G 283

40. Six O'Clock Closing on the Number 6................................... 291

41. Route 59: The Cars that Ate the City......................................297

42. Beyond Tram Lines 303

43. Route 96: Tracks to St. Kilda 307

44. Visiting Aunt Bea on the 109..317

EPILOGUE: 2040 331

BIBLIOGRAPHY 335

ACKNOWLEDGEMENTS...347

AUTHOR'S NOTE

This is a work of creative non-fiction, combining history, memoir and imagination, a form that allows the author a certain freedom in representation. It should be noted though that everything to do with trams and tram history is based in fact, and is as accurate an account of the Melbourne tramways as I have been able to create, based on my research, personal experience and discussions with former tram workers and experts. Any mistakes in this representation are my own. Please note that no recording devices were used in the development of this work, and any resemblance between fictionalised characters and living persons is purely coincidental.

In memory of my parents, Betty and Chris.

PROLOGUE: 1888

I can just make out the tram approaching up the hill in Bourke
Street. It's a wet, blustery night and I recognise the tram by the
glow of blue light, blue signifying that the tram is bound for Nicholson Street. The light is created by blue glass set over kerosene
lamps, located in the tram car's bulkhead, and the front car's dome.
As the tram pulls near I can make out the lettering which confirms
the route – 'Nicholson St.' I board the tram with a step up and sit in
the tram car out of the weather. The oil lamps set at either end of the
car provide interior lighting for passengers and crews at night, and
shed a soft yellow glow. The floor is wet from the previous passengers, and my dripping umbrella adds to the mix. The bench seats are
made of beautifully grained wood, and the whole interior is hand
crafted, elegant and brand new. The poor gripman, the driver, is out
in the open lead car – called the 'dummy car' – wrapped in a large
black raincoat. No-one will be sitting out there with him tonight.

The tram turns left at Spring Street and stops outside the Princess
Theatre, the newly built Second Empire edifice, said by the proud
inhabitants of the city to be the rival of the Paris Opera. A large
crowd of theatregoers are waiting for the tram and, as it arrives, they
rush on to claim a seat. This group are well dressed and highly excited, the men sporting tall hats and tuxedos, the women in shoulder to
heel dresses, jewellery and silk shawls. They've just been to the late
night performance of Gounod's *Faust*, starring the ineffable Nellie
Stewart, the queen of the Melbourne stage, in the role of Marguerite.
A free-flowing discussion of the performance – its singers, music and
stage sets – is carried on across the tram benches and by those stand-

ing. Someone out of sight starts to whistle an aria from the show and, when finished, receives a round of applause. The show has been running for two weeks and clearly some theatregoers have been more than once. The men and women all appear to have had a few drinks, their faces gleaming. The lamps throw shadows this way and that across the space. I look down to a vista of polished shoes and high heels. The tram sways from side to side as it goes along and those standing brace themselves by holding onto leather straps hanging from a rail attached to the ceiling. One man lights a cigar, only to be told by the conductor to put it out, which the man does by stabbing the cigar against the sole of his shoe, creating a small shower of sparks. The conductor has been pushing his way through to collect the fares, his bell-punch dinging as he does. Outside the gripman is sounding the gong to clear the road ahead.

As the tram trundles up Nicholson Street the passengers start to disembark in pairs and small groups, and by the time we approach the terminus at Park Street only a handful remain, and the chatter has ceased. It's raining heavily at the shunt, and the conductor dons his raincoat to join the gripman in reversing the cars so that they can head back the way they came. Before departing back into town the conductor shakes his raincoat out at the door, and folds it away under one of the seats. The tram car now looks like a deserted stage set.

The conductor doesn't bother to collect my fare, but instead takes a seat on the bench at the end of the compartment. From here he gazes out the window, but at what it is hard to tell. The glass windows of the tram reflect its interior and the half images of the sole occupants, just myself and the connie. He looks tired and is probably at the end of his long shift. I'd like to chat to him about his job but he looks ill disposed towards conversation. He's young, I'd guess early twenties, and his face is unlined and innocent. In the soft interior light of the tram his face shines forth like some portrait by Rembrandt – a slightly peevish face, with its upturned nose and narrow mouth, his eyes now half shut, utterly a face of this world. He won't talk but I'm happy, and why wouldn't I be, I'm travelling in a tram run by cable, co-

cooned in the night, a small lit capsule passing in its share of time and space.

1. Portrait of a Tram

The MRI emits a series of loud other-worldly noises. I'm lying in a long coffin-like tube, ears covered with headphones, eyes masked. During the procedure the spectral voice of the operator occasionally asks me how I'm doing. When the sounds of the machine momentarily recede, classical music pours into the headphones. The sound of the machine is enormous, at the point of unbearable, but the counterpoint between the two soundscapes is strangely compelling. The classical music is staid, predictable, of a tradition. The machine music is metal, bold, experimental. Inhuman. But aren't there voices too within the staccato strips, words that are continuously repeated? Is this a foretaste of the algorithmic music of the future?

After the test is concluded I sit in the small waiting room, waiting for the all clear to leave. I'm at the Epworth hospital in Richmond, a vast complex of rooms, corridors and levels, so crowded and confusing that I had gotten lost looking for the imaging centre. This is my umpteenth test over the last few weeks, following a series of blinding headaches – scans, blood tests, doctors prodding and probing. I've never liked 'medicine' or its smell. I'm not a doctor person and visit them as infrequently as I can, but the headaches and the dizziness had started to worry me so here I am at the mercy of the experts. My sole companion in the waiting room is an ancient man in a wheel chair, who has plastic tubes inserted into his nostrils, the tubes running down to a cylinder of oxygen at the back of the chair. He is breathing heavily and his legs, which stick out from a hospital smock, are swollen and red. Part of me wants to get up and pull the rucked up smock down to cover them. He has rheumy eyes which he dabs continually with a handkerchief.

Appearing to sense my presence for the first time, he swivels his head around in my direction. It becomes apparent from this angle that the old man is blind. In a soft, scratchy voice he asks me if the machine next door is as bad as it sounds. I tell him that it is, but that it will be over quickly (which is definitely untrue). 'I really don't know why my doctor has ordered this test', he says. 'It's a mystery to me why you would do tests on anyone of my age', he continues, 'I mean, I'm 92, I've got angina, diabetes, emphysema. What's the point?' As he speaks there is a half smile playing on his face, as if his situation – old age, his mortality, the mysteries of modern medicine – is faintly amusing to him. His voice is husky and febrile, his speech punctuated by frequent sharp inhalations. But he's clearly up for a chat, and apropos of nothing he goes on to tell me how as a child he played in the back streets and lanes around the Epworth when the hospital was little more than a suburban house. To pass the time I ask Walter – his name is on a tag on his smock – to tell me more about those days.

'Oh gosh, it was so very different back then. Yes. When I was a lad they delivered milk every morning by horse and cart. Draught horses, very beautiful in their way, ponderous and slow with massive hooves. You could hear them clip clopping on the cobblestones. Depression years, you know, and then the war. There were very few cars, particularly in the war years when we had rationing. In fact in those years there was very little of anything, either to eat or to do. I don't mean we were hungry, not at all, our family was okay, but it was a basic existence. I still remember men going around on bicycles selling all manner of things for the home, yelling out their wares as they went. Goodness.

'I spent a large part of my youth riding around on the city's trams. I'm old enough to remember the cable trams, they were rickety old things, and slow as a wet week. They were all gone by the '40s. You know it was a lean time but I wasn't unhappy as a boy. In those days at night you used to be able to hear a rain storm approaching, with the rain rumbling down on tin roofs in the distance. I loved thunderstorms, floating stick boats in the back lanes, skipping yonnies across the river. Little things like that.'

A long pause. The old fella has actually nodded off. A nurse enters the waiting room, checks the old man's oxygen bottle and, waking him up, tells him that it shouldn't be long before he goes in. When the nurse leaves Walter resumes his story as if there'd been no hiatus.

'You know I remember during the war the trams were overcrowded with men in uniform, Australians and Americans. Sometimes they fought each other. The Americans were so smart and lively compared to our lads, and the girls really went for them. One night, you see, I was on my way back from some scavenging trip and caught the tram home, hiding behind the Aussie soldiers to avoid paying the fare. At a stop in the city a group of GIs got on, laughing and smoking, hair oiled, uniforms crisp and stylish. The Aussies started making jibes at them and before my very eyes in seconds the two groups were at each other. Have you ever heard the sound of a fist smashing into flesh? Oh my lord. Anyway, the fight spilled out into the street and it was mayhem, but with all the soldiers off the tram the connie pulled the cord and off we went again. The connie was a woman I remember, a big blond woman. She guessed I didn't have the fare but let me travel on.'

Walter begins to cough. There's a water stand in the corner and I fetch him a drink in a plastic cup. His hand shakes as he raises the cup to his mouth but he manages to get most of it down. He's quiet for a while – perhaps ruminating somewhere in the corridors of memory. But then he reemerges. 'I was a dreamy child I suppose, the opposite of my father who was an accountant. But he tolerated me sufficiently well to take me on fishing trips most years. We camped all through the eastern rivers and lakes. I got to know the different species of fish, their colours and shapes, and the places they were most likely to be running in different seasons. Let's see – we caught bream, flathead, perch, mulloway. One year we caught King George whiting, oh yes, and trevally and garfish in such numbers we had to throw them back. The lakes teemed with fish in those days. When it was still you could see them swimming in big schools underneath the boat. I loved the shapes they made under the water, the way they moved together and, when we landed them, their wonderful, subtle colours. I have never seen those shades of yellow, grey and silver anywhere else. They were so strange, so beautiful.'

Another long pause. Is he asleep again, or just casting back in his mind? Walter says suddenly, 'Are you still there?' I reassure him that I am, and he resumes:

'In the evening my father would make camp, setting up a Tilly lamp, and cooking our catch on the fire. He had bought me a sketch book at some stage and a set of HB pencils, and I spent the time before dinner drawing the fish we had seen or caught that day. I found that sketchbook after my father died. He had kept it in a box of papers at the back of the wardrobe. My father wanted me to follow him into accountancy. He said I could continue to draw on weekends, but should have a steady job to get ahead in life. I tried accountancy with a local firm run by a friend of my father's, but I wasn't cut out for it. My numbers never added up, pretty important don't you think! I lasted a year and then I did what I'd wanted to do all along. I knew where my passion lay – I'd been drawing and sketching for years by then – and applied to the National Gallery Art School. He was very angry with my decision, called it irresponsible and immature, and we didn't speak for many years.

'Hmm, yes. So I got in to the Gallery School on my third attempt. The Gallery was very conservative. Our teachers, all men mind you, were mostly figurative painters, as distinct from their Sydney rivals who had taken up expressionism. But you see, I liked what John Brack and others in the – what was it called, ah yes, the Antipodeans, the Antipodeans – what they were doing, for a while I copied them. But I got tired of that too. I loved drawing but as soon as I had paint on a brush, I wanted to experiment. I became addicted to the work of the Americans, Pollock, Motherwell and Rothko. I had a bed-sit studio at the back of a house in Fitzroy, and I took to all night painting sessions, getting up late in the day, coffee and cigarettes, splashing the paint around, diving into the canvas like it was the sea.

'Actually, you see, I took up swimming to make my upper body stronger so I could paint for hours and hours. I would climb into my painting like I would step into the pool, immersing myself in strokes, turns, kicks. Canvas after canvas poured out. I had to build a loft in the bedsit to store them. I painted layer on layer, sometimes a first layer was completely obscured by later ones. This added mystery to the whole process for me, these hidden layers of form and colour. I was making several paintings in one, I was crazy for it, but really, did I know what I was doing?

'I kept playing you see. I wanted to fuse things, the figurative and the naturalistic, with layers of abstraction. Sometimes the figurative layer would emerge in a corner or as a single section of the canvas, as if the canvas had been meddled with there, or the artist had simply failed to paint over a section of what was an unfinished work. I liked the idea of the finished and the unfinished you see. Some of my paintings look like some strange patchwork quilt. In the morning I would fall into bed exhausted, but extremely happy. Most of it was rubbish of course, but I kept at it for several years solid like that, and finally got an exhibition. Well, well, the critics were not impressed – I was an amateur, a copyist, or worse, a poser! But they sold, much to my astonishment. One of my bigger canvases from the exhibition sold straight away and turned out to be very popular. Actually, it now hangs in the National Gallery, you might know it, huge thing.'

Walter is taking some deep breaths and I wonder if this conversation is now wearing him out – dangerously. I don't want to have an nonagenarian's death on my conscience. But he rallies again. There's a line of saliva running down his chin which drips onto his white smock.

'For the biggest one I drew a perfect replica of a green tram, you see, not just any tram but the one I'd spent so much of the war years on, the number 48. I drew it not as a whole but as a series of panels, each panel showing a different part of the tram – a wooden seat, a doorway, the roof, the tram pole, the front of the tram, running board – you know, a kind of mosaic or puzzle. In amongst these panels I painted, as silhouettes, a series of passengers – standing, sitting, hanging on to straps. Aussie soldiers, slouch hats. It was a bit of a joke that, trying to one-up Brack, I suppose. Anyway, then I painted layers over the tram panels, swirling waves through which the tram could be seen below, almost like it had fallen to the bottom of a pond or sea, and broken apart down there. You could just make out the tram number in one of the corners. As soon as it was finished I thought it was total kitsch and wasn't going to put it in, but the gallery owner saw it and insisted.

'To my utter surprise my father came to the exhibition and wandered around inspecting the canvases. He wouldn't have had a clue what he was seeing, but well, I shouldn't be unfair – he did come and that was extremely pleasing to me. He didn't say much, only that my paintings were truly memorable, a phrase that could cut both ways of course, but said without a trace of irony. Irony was not my father's style.'

At this point Walter looks like a balloon that the air has escaped from, crumpled and shrunk. His eyes are shut and his breathing laboured. It's been a bit much and I'm feeling guilty for not interrupting him earlier. The breaths are long and difficult and his head is nodding. I won't wake him. He is mumbling in his sleep now, something about 'being there momentarily'. Interesting old man, wish I could've heard the rest of his story.

The radiographer who did my MRI comes in and tells me I'm good to go. I ask her if she found anything unusual but all she's prepared to say is that the specialist will review the film in the next few days, and his rooms will call me. Going down in the crowded lift I have a sudden memory of visiting the gallery decades before as a school student and seeing the tram work that Walter had talked about. I didn't understand it then, and I'm not sure I completely understand it now. But who would've thought that there was a connection between trams and fish?

*

Two days later I am back at the Epworth, at the rooms of Dr Bun, the physician who had ordered the MRI. The rooms have large ceiling to floor windows with city views. From my last appointment with Dr Bun I'd learnt that he had no interest in small talk, or long talk for that matter. The physician has a large, bulbous face, deeply lined and grey, yellow teeth and a comb-over of motley strands of thick hair. Dr Bun addresses me by my surname – no-one has done this since schooldays – and throughout the appointment his gaze is on the screen in front of him, or set just above my head and to the right, at some feature or point on the wall that he apparently finds more compelling than his patient.

Dr Bun is also a bit of a mumbler and he's doing that now with the screen in front of him. He abruptly swivels it around at an angle so that I can view a series of coloured images. Dr Bun explains, with a cough, that the MRI has revealed a significant lesion in my brain that is 'of concern'. He points to various locations in the images that are highlighted. He says that the images explain my recent bouts of dizziness and headaches. 'At this stage, I can't rule out the probability that you have cancer, a brain tumour. But we, my colleagues and I, will review all of the tests and determine how to proceed.' He looks down solemnly to the papers in front of him. Despite the elevation of the medical suite from the roadway, and the thick windows, a faint hum of traffic is finding its way into the room, and in the silence that follows his statement, I hear a tram bell ring, a single muted note in the distance. For some reason I start thinking of an old episode of Law and Order in which Lenny, the detective, discovering a body in a lift shaft says, 'always take the stairs'. Is this the brain tumour talking?

The physician is speaking again about a biopsy to determine what kind of lesion it is. According to Bun, this procedure has 'minimal risk'. He looks up from his notes and, staring at that point above my head, asks if I have any questions. It sounds more a rhetorical than an actual question and there is a strange time lag between his words and my apprehension of them. Basically I haven't heard anything much since he uttered the word 'cancer'. Bun is continuing, and I catch a few phrases. 'Obviously we will take it step by step, no reason to panic at this stage.' 'It is far too early to be talking about worst cases.' 'There are unfortunately no guarantees.' 'There are many outliers in this business.' 'You are otherwise healthy, only in the early stages of old age.' 'Remain positive.'

I now gather a thought and ask Bun what the survival rate is for this kind of cancer. He becomes evasive and tells me there are too many factors to give a precise figure.

'So please tell me an approximate figure.'

'An approximate figure...'. Bun says this as if it had never occurred to him to make an educated estimate of a patient's life expectancy. 'Well', he says at last, 'the data does show that for most people at your age a tumour in this region will provide a one in five chance of survival after five years, give or take. Give or take. But I need to stress that this is general data not a precise estimate.' He nods several times.

Five years. Christ.

Dr Bun is now standing up with his hand outstretched. I stare at the hand and momentarily wonder at the meaning of this gesture, until I gather he wants to conclude by shaking hands. This is perhaps a worryingly human move on his part. When I grip his hand it is like holding a patch of old leather. I turn and look up at the wall area he's been staring at throughout our exchange, expecting to see a wall clock but there is none – just a circle on the wall in a different shade to the rest, suggesting that at some point there was likely a clock there. Old habits are hard to break. I pay the massive bill and head out. Dr Bun's staff will contact me soon with my biopsy appointment. I've been in his rooms for less than 20 minutes. I take the tram towards the city and get off at the Fitzroy Gardens and wander into them. I sit on a bench under a large spreading Moreton Bay fig tree. Its leaves are creaking like old doors in the hot northerly wind, but under the tree it is dark and relatively cool.

2.   Five Years

It's been over six months since I sat in the rooms of Dr Bun, watching him watch the imaginary clock above my head. The biopsy was positive for a malignant cancer and, after a 'conference' between Bun and unnamed medicos, it was determined that the best 'way forward' would involve surgery, combined with radiation therapy and chemotherapy. A partial removal of the tumour was performed – it being too dangerous to remove all of it given its embedded position in the brain – followed by weeks of radiation and months of chemo. Happy days.

Following these various assaults to my being, the tumour has significantly dwindled ('less than a golf ball, but bigger than a marble', says Bun) and I have no secondaries. The chemo in particular was dreadful, cycles of intravenous drugs followed by days of vomiting and diarrhoea and total lassitude. The words now are watch and wait, although in Bun-speak this becomes entangled with statistical in-and-outliers and references to the powers of positive thinking. I do my own research, and while it's clear that I am not dead yet, Bun's original estimate looks pretty on the money – five years looks okay, anything beyond that is in the lap of the gods.

...We've got five years, stuck on my eyes
Five years, what a surprise
We've got five years, my brain hurts a lot
Five years, that's all we've got...

Thank you Ziggy!

So, dear reader, what's going on here? So far we've had: an opening scene in which a crowd of theatre folks board a late night tram; an old man with a rucked up smock recalling fishing and painting days; a scene at the physician's; and, well you've just read the last bit so I don't need to repeat it. You have no doubt surmised that this work has something to do with trams. The story will start at a very early point in my life when I could not yet walk (more on that later) and takes us through to these, potentially, last days on earth (for me). But how did this come about? Aren't there enough books on trams already, making any contribution to the genre by me redundant?

A few days after receiving my biopsy result, I told work that I would be taking 12 months leave of absence on medical grounds. My boss, a man 20 years my junior, expressed his concern when he learnt the reason for the request, but didn't appear overly distressed by the news; he was no doubt already thinking of how he could reorganise the team with me out of the way, and the money he would be saving with a senior member of staff not on the books. When I walked out of the building later, with a box of useless things under my arm, I realised that I probably wouldn't be going back there.

As I said, the chemo was the worst part of my treatment and it took months to regain a sense of balance and energy. Fortunately, apart from my eyebrows, I didn't have any head hair to lose, so my appearance hasn't changed much, not that that matters. I have plenty of vices but vanity isn't one of them. I am fairly non-descript, a characteristic that has done wonders for me over the years. I excel at the appearance, if not the reality, of mediocrity and have been dutifully rewarded with a cohort of boring, yet well paid jobs. Employers tend not to like spectacular, it shows them up. People like to tell me their work gossip too, sensing that I am a safe vault for their secrets, or simply lack the cunning intelligence necessary to exploit them.

When I got the qualified 'all clear' from Dr Bun I was still months away from any potential return to work, and had zero desire to do so. Divorced, single, my overachieving children living overseas – a son living in New York and a daughter in London – and my sister living in

the far north of the country. Apart from an ancient Aunt I had no relations in the city. Clearly family wasn't going to be the centre of my
waking days. Friends suggested I take up a language, or do yoga. One
friend urged me to become a bee-keeper, a challenging role for someone living in a one bedroom flat in the inner city. And then there was
travel, of course. Almost every year I worked I took holidays overseas – there was a stigma attached to staying at home. You didn't go
to Rosebud or Lorne, you went to Siem Reap, Sicily, Tokyo. You came
back and told stories to your workmates and then settled back into
cloistered life.

None of this well-meant advice was appealing and I didn't have
the energy to travel overseas. The chemo had really knocked me, and
the idea of cramming into flying buses made my stomach turn. Spanish had defeated me on more than one occasion, and yoga made me
anxious. I would need a project though to fill my days. It wouldn't do
to just sit around moaning and bemoaning at the TV.

I played around with several ideas over my months of convales-
cence. What about the crime novel I was always going to write when
I retired? Or, a biography of my famous ancestor, Oliver Cromwell?
How about a travel book with personal anecdotes? However, none of
these ideas developed; none of them grew any flesh as it were. Then I
found recurring amongst my ruminations the memory of the time I
sat with Walter in the waiting room at the Epworth and his description of his early life, the rides on the trams and his painting of the 48.
Gradually a more fertile idea took shape: a project about trams. I liked
them, had always liked them, but I didn't know much about them,
except that they had been part of my life from the beginning. I was
attracted to the powerful image of Walter's tram portrait, with its
fragments of the tram glimpsed through the watery deep. Perhaps
travelling in the topography and history of my city's trams would reveal unexpected routes and destinations... .

The idea gelled. I decided to spend a month or two travelling the
city's trams, to revisit some of the journeys and places of my childhood and youth, the period before my first and subsequent cars. Like

everyone else, I'd always accepted trams as simply part of the city's furniture, as a familiar and ubiquitous part of the streetscape. How did this system come about and who was behind it?

As the project took shape, I also imagined myself as a latter day Andrew Urban, conducting *Front Up* style vox pop interviews with total strangers. Given my reticent nature this was the most challenging element of the whole idea. Me, talk to strangers? On the other hand, as I've mentioned, apparently I have the ability to attract people's confidences, so perhaps this could be put to good use. What genre would this work be? At this early stage I had no definite idea: a biography of a city and its trams, leavened with childhood memories, add in some history and stir? Obviously, trams are essential public transport, but I wanted to find out more about them and their history. My first task would be to ride around the network, take the routes I've never taken. Then, see what happens, what emerges. Loosen up a little. Talk to people. (Yikes!)

In my usual pedantic way I worked on a plan that would see me traverse the city's tram network from north to south, east to west, starting with the lowest numbered routes and working my way up, covering every inch of the system.

It looked like a great schedule, except it too closely resembled the type of project plan I'd been constructing for over a quarter of a century. I needed to make the project something to enjoy rather than to slave over. I decided to randomise the travelling part of the project. I had a map of the network, not to scale, with neat coloured lines with numbers attached to them. I would get up each day, close my eyes and stab the map with a pin; the nearest route to the pin that I hadn't yet travelled for this project would be the trip for the day. And I'd also do something I'm really good at – research.

Sound exciting? Yes, dear reader, perhaps the prospect is not as enticing for you as it is to me, but bear with me, this ride(s) might turn out to be more interesting than either of us would anticipate.

3. Kangas & Orcas on the Number 72

I climb out of the heavily chlorinated pool at the City Baths, and head for the showers. Fifteen laps will have to do today – it's more than I've done for months. I have always enjoyed coming to these Edwardian baroque baths, with their highly articulated façade of red-brick and cream touches, and the interior of wooden galleries, and skylights. When it rains the thrumming on the tin roof mixes in with the slush of many arms plowing through water.

Outside I stand in the cold at the Victoria Parade stop waiting for the 72 tram to Camberwell. The day is without sheen or gloss. An ordinary day. Things, human and otherwise, are occupying their usual place, doing what they do. People walk, trams pass, buildings stand. Boring and comforting. I board the tram which travels down Swanston Street, the mock-Doric temple that is the Shrine of Remembrance in the distance. The 72 shares Swanston Street, Princes Bridge and St Kilda Road with other trams pursuing other destinations: the number 1 to South Melbourne Beach, the 3 to East Malvern, the 6 to Glen Iris, the 16 to Kew, the 64 to East Brighton, the 67 to Carnegie, the 5 to Malvern. It is the busiest tram thoroughfare in the city, and trams frequently bank up behind each other as they crawl along picking up and dropping off their passengers. I was born at one end of this street, to the north in Carlton, and if I 'own' any part of the city it is this zone and its endless commotion.

I am on my first journey of the Tram Project (as I've named it), and this journey from the city to Camberwell is highly familiar. It's ironic that my first pin stab of the tram map should land next to this line, which I travelled for much of my childhood and teenage years. But, it's been years since I took it, and it combined well with a trip to the pool. At 16.8 kilometres, route 72 is one of the longer tram routes in the system and takes over an hour to travel from terminus to terminus. The route is shaped like a horseshoe; the first leg runs south through the city from the University of Melbourne, before turning east at Commercial Road, running along Malvern Road to Gardiner, and from there northwards to Camberwell, terminating at Cotham Road. The first leg is old, really old, with cable trams running this section in the 1880s. The east leg to Gardiner was constructed in 1915, and north to Cotham Road was completed in 1918. How many hundreds of thousands of people have travelled this route over the last 100 years?

We pick up speed as we enter St Kilda Road, the wide boulevard lined with elms. I'm riding in a D1 Class tram, a low-floor three-unit articulated tram imported from Germany in the early 2000s. The D1 class has been rated the worst tram on the system for comfort and ride. I don't really care today. I'm happy someone else is driving. We pass the modernist icons of the Performing Arts Centre and the National Gallery, with its blank grey wall. When the Premier of the day, Henry Bolte, was asked by journalists why the National Gallery had such a grim façade, lacking any windows, he replied that the curators didn't add windows because they needed the hanging space. (This comment was made not long after Bolte had ordered the hanging of prisoner Ronald Ryan, the last man executed by the Victoria criminal justice system in 1967, so it didn't go down too well.) On the opposite side of the road sits the flower clock in all its splendour, today planted up with bright marigolds and begonias.

Soon we're passing Victoria Barracks, an institution founded in the early years of the colony. The barracks have a chequered history. The first bluestone building on site was constructed by British Imperial troops, after their massacre of miners at Ballarat in 1854. Today men and women in dull green uniforms file in and out of the Barracks' bluestone gate. The War Memorial commands the eastern hill, as the tram approaches the Domain Interchange, where the 58 tram to Toorak crosses. Apartment and office blocks, products of different architectural eras and styles, form a bulked mass on each side as the boulevard curves its way south. The sun has come out. My city always looks finer in the sunlight.

The tram turns into Commercial Road and runs past the Alfred hospital. The Alfred was originally built in 1870, and named after the British Prince, who the locals had the temerity to attempt to assassinate on his short visit to the colonies a few years before. Most of Webb's original Queen Anne structure has gone the way of Whelan the Wrecker. Soon enough we are at the stop opposite Prahran market. People pile in with the trolleys, bags and back packs, laden with supplies. They have the look of tired, satisfied hunters returning from a successful foray into the wilds.

Commercial Road becomes Malvern Road after Chapel Street, and the tram is coming up on the Francis Street stop. It was at this stop that my mother and I caught the tram every week to travel to Camberwell to visit her parents, who had retired from the country to live in the suburbs. The route was numbered 7 then but was exactly the same. We would leave our small one-bedroom flat in Prahran midmorning and the tram would ferry us in a wide arc through the east to Parlington Street. My grandma was my mother's step-mother, her mother having died when she was a girl. Until this was explained to me I found it strange that my mother called grandma by her first name. Queenie was a big presence, big breasts, big laugh. She wore pearls and long dresses, and had a habit of ruffling my hair and pinching me, behaviour I overlooked because of the bowls of ice cream topped with passionfruit she gave me on each visit. My grandpa, Percy, a squat man with a small moustache, rolled cigarettes with one hand and rarely spoke.

At the stop a young woman on crutches enters the crowded tram, and hobbles her way to the rear where I'm sitting. Her knee is encased in a plastic splint and she sits sideways on the only available seat. Having had my share of knee problems I'm curious what her injury is. Torn cruciate ligament playing basketball? Meniscus injury? She must be a mind reader, or else I've been staring too obviously, since she says without preamble that I won't be able to guess what the injury is, since it's so rare in someone her age. 'I've managed to tear the lateral quad tendon off my knee', she says, 'and two weeks ago I had it surgically reattached.' She says the surgery and aftermath had been fine but when she tore the tendon it was excruciating – she felt like someone had shot her in the leg. I ask her how she did it, and she explains that she had been surfing and the break was working across a reef and she'd come off her board at the worst spot, cracking her thigh against the rocks. She had no control at that point, couldn't organise her body to stand or swim, her board was still attached to her leg and being thrown around in the surf. Fortunately one of the others who were out there saw what was happening and got her into shore.

I haven't said much so far, simply nodding and trying to look empathetic. The tram has stalled behind traffic. We both stare out the window. There's a tall, thin man being dragged along the street by a huge dog, wearing a studded collar. While he can't be heard, he's clearly yelling at the dog to stop, which is having zero effect. His face is contorted and bright red, while his arm looks like it's about to be yanked out of its socket.

I ask Claire – she tells me her name later in the journey – what she likes about a sport that is so obviously dangerous. She replies that there isn't usually any danger in surfing, or not much if you know what you are doing. Usually, she says, the swell is up over enough of the rocks so that you can 'bail' without hurting yourself.

'Yeah no, surfing is awesome, I just love it. I'm not afraid out there, just really excited. Paddling out on my longboard, can't wait to get to the backline with the others. It's like an art you know, especially now I've switched to a long board. It is so much more buoyant than a short board but it's harder to manoeuvre. You need to really dig your heels and toes in, use your knees to turn. But it's kind of graceful

I guess, yeah, on the longboard, it feels like you're closer to the original Hawaiian boards.' She says that as a surfer you look closely at the sea – you want to know if the wind is onshore or offshore, how the breaks are working, whether the sea looks messy, or the swell is either too big and too small. She uses some words that elude me – 'knarly' and 'super-rippy' – but I'm loathe to interrupt her to ask what they mean.

The tram is tracking along Malvern Road, passing the 'ong' roads: Kooyong and Orrong. The sun is still out and the streetscape shines with an almost iridescent green. The scene is bourgeois and familiar. Where they haven't been torn down I recognise individual houses, the odd hotel, shops and stores. Some businesses just keep on going don't they? I ask Claire how she got into surfing.

'My Mum taught me when I was young, like really young, three or four. She was, still is, a mad surfer. Crazy for it. She's surfed all around the country and some big breaks overseas. So I grew up with surfing. Whatever we were doing as a family there was always a chance that she would suddenly pile us in the car and head down the coast for the day. We hadn't surfed together for a few years but recently she organised a trip to New Zealand for the two of us. We stayed on the Coromandel peninsula – have you been there? Beautiful. We surfed every day for hours, checking out all the best beaches along the coast. One afternoon, this was so cool, we were in a rolling swell in a big bay with not much happening and then about 100 metres from us three orcas suddenly breached; two adults and a juvenile. For the next hour we paddled behind them as they slowly crossed the bay, blowing and lolling in and out of the swell. I was full stretch on my board propped up on my elbows, the sea was a real dark blue that day, and the orcas' black and white was so sharp and clear, like the most beautiful pattern, as if they were some kind of sea sculpture. And their movement was so beautiful and powerful, they looked fearless, like the bay, the sea, belonged to them, which I guess it does. We're really only interlopers out there.'

'Interlopers, but it sounds like you really feel at home out there. Have you ever thought of competing?'

'No, I'm not good enough to be in comps. God, watching Molly Picklum is amazing. She does stuff that I've never seen anyone do. She just tears it up, totally fearless. So, no I'm not in that class at all. I don't really want to be to be honest. It would take the fun out of it for me. When you are out there you have the energy of the whole sea with you. I mean on my board riding a wave I feel really alive. It would ruin it for me if I was doing it for points. Of course you want to be good at the skills you need: to manoeuvre, shifting your weight, cutting back across the wave, the art of it I guess, all of that, and all the time you are on something that is alive itself, that is bearing you along, that is this one wave you are on and endless at the same time. The sea is strange and beautiful, always changing. I like being part of the surf community too. Lots of girls surf now, the guys can still be idiots out there, but you know, you can ignore them, and most of them are fine. Compared to the sea being on land is kind of boring you know. I really don't like walking. Don't laugh, it's true. Anyway, you should give it a try if you've never done it. Plenty of people your age are out there now.'

Your age. Yes, I am discernibly, craggily that age.

Malvern Road has finally reached Burke Road where we turn north through the Gardiner station interchange, one of the ugliest such intersections in the city, dominated by concrete, pylons, on and off ramps and the freeway beneath. I recall how this interchange was once simply a set of railway gates, operated by a gateman in a small structure to the side. My mother and I would often have to wait here on the tram while the trains passed in each direction. A string of shops opposite has been demolished. Without the impediment of gates, the tram now heads up the first of Camberwell's hills.

I'm thinking of another question to ask her when Claire asks me what I do. I've been so engrossed in her story that I've completely forgotten my mission. I give her a brief outline of my tram project. Listening to myself it sounds dull and nerdy, which of course it is, but

Claire doesn't appear to take it that way. She tells me her grandfather had been a tram driver and he used to tell her stories when she was young. When I ask her if she can remember any of them she looks away for a moment or two before replying. She says, 'Yes I remember one of these stories, I mean I never knew whether his stories were real or not, what's that word, apoch-something?'

'Apocryphal.'

'Yes, that. Well, the story is he was driving late at night out on the hills near Wattle Park, you know the park up on Riversdale Road, when he sees something on the tracks ahead. So he slows down, it's really late and there are no cars around, and realises that it's an animal of some kind just sitting there and if he doesn't stop he's going to run into it. So he stops and as he's doing so he sees that it's a kangaroo which is now staring straight into the tram lights. He calls to the conductor – he had to tell me what a conductor was – and the two of them stare in disbelief from the cabin at the kangaroo, still there caught in the lights. Finally my grandfather rings the tram bells and the kangaroo turns around and jumps away right down the middle of the tram tracks towards the tram terminus, with my grandfather following behind for quite a long way before at some point the roo turns sideways and bounds into the bush. My grandfather said that when they got back to the depot and told their story no-one believed them. And then he would say to me, with a smile on his face, but you do, don't you Claire? And I wouldn't know what to think. Is that the sort of story you are collecting?'

It sure is Claire, it sure is. Just after Toorak Road Claire says goodbye, gets off the tram and hobbles to the kerb.

The tram heads up the hill towards Camberwell Junction. On the journey with my mother all those years ago I loved this part of the trip. Sitting up the front as we slowly chugged up the slope, cresting the hill and the huge vista opening up ahead and below, the tram flying down the tracks, the screech of the brakes as we pull up at the Junction in a cloud of dust. Can you believe that once there were no traffic lights here, where six roads and three tram lines intersect?

Now, in my German D1 we sit at the Junction, waiting for the lights to change as the 70 to Wattle Park and the 75 to the city cross in their opposite trajectories. The 72 takes us on up the hill through the shopping centre north towards Kew. I notice that a few of the shops are shuttered, but Sofia's Pizza is still here, as is the Palace Hotel and Curry House. The Palace is on the west side of Burke Road. Why? Because the east side was 'dry', subject to prohibition. Yes, strange as it may seem in this city of inebriates, a vast swath of the eastern suburbs, starting in Camberwell, was once free of the pernicious influence of alcohol. The wealthy of Camberwell, poor things, were forced to drink their Grange reds at home.

As we near Canterbury Road I'm thrown back 50 years to school days. I would take the train from school to Gardiner and catch the 72 to my then girlfriend's house, just off Canterbury Road, near the church on the corner. Her house was a large sprawling Edwardian, totally unlike the suburban cottage I lived in then, with an attic full of dust and cobwebs, a mattress and an old record player, where she and I would spend our afternoons listening to Dylan, Donovan, smoking Drum, and (close your eyes dear reader) having premarital sex. From the attic, you could hear the bells of the W class trams in the distance.

I never spent the night there, getting home much later in the evening and usually missing family dinner. My excuses for lateness ranged from the elaborate to the feeble; football practice, theatre rehearsals, social club meetings, study, a friend needed to talk to me urgently etc. etc. I'm sure my parents knew what was going on, but these were the days of 'propriety' and 'what would the neighbours think' so nothing was ever said. I heard years later that my girlfriend got married, had many children and moved to the country. Good for her.

No, I don't think I will take up surfing. Despite what Claire said, it sounds ferociously dangerous to me – not just rocks that can smash your head open, but those anti-social white pointers biting off legs and arms. We've reached the terminus at Cotham Road. I cross the intersection and wait for the 109 from Box Hill to take me back to the city. I notice an old iron tram shelter on the other side of the intersection, coloured bright green and fronted with scrolled fret work. I look up the Heritage database on my phone, and there it is, one of a dozen surviving tram shelters built in the early 20th century. This one is very early, circa 1913, and it has a drinking fountain too, although it's unclear of what vintage. The 109 arrives and I get on. When we reach Swanston Street, I will have gone full circle.

*

Parlington Street. Caught up in memories of attic days and Dylan, I'd missed the stop just past Canterbury Road where my mother and I used to get down to visit my grandpa. I recall climbing an old almond tree in his backyard, which was planted up with veges and fruit trees. I would sit in the tree and eventually grandpa would escape from inside and stand next to the tree – supposedly keeping an eye on me but actually taking time out to smoke a ciggie. I always liked the feel of this man despite the fact that he never said much to me. So I would perch there amongst the almonds and he would puff away – the tobacco smoke drifting up to me in the tree, a smell I've always ever after associated with him.

As I travel back to the city I'm stung by another memory: Parlington Street in the early 1960s, the lounge room of Percy's single fronted weatherboard, and from the dining room there's the sound of a woman crying and she's been crying for a long time, a keening sound mixed with sobs that goes on and on and which is accompanied by other voices that are making soothing noises and the situation is one which I don't really understand except that grandpa went into hospital shortly after Queenie went into hospital but neither of them has come out. My mother is distraught and my father has brought me here to sit in the lounge although I don't understand why he thinks this is better for me since the sound of her crying is distressing and I would rather be in the room with her and maybe me being there would help her to stop crying or at least make her feel better. Eventually some family friends come to the lounge and announce that they are taking me with them to their home where I will stay for some time, although the amount of time is not specified. Shortly after we leave.

This was the day my young mother became an orphan.

4. Myths of Origin

L et's go back, way back to the beginnings.

The crawler has made it through the open front door, across the verandah and onto the lawn. There's a front gate leading to the street that someone has left ajar. He spies this and heads towards it. In the background there is a woman calling his name, but he ignores this and pushes forward. He's not a very good crawler. It takes him a long time to get anywhere, what with his plodding this-leg-now-that-leg style, but it's effective. He hasn't been through this gate before on his own. What's on the other side? Well, it's a busy road, with cars, trucks, bicycles, pedestrians and trams. He goes through the front gate and crawls onto the footpath and smells the air. At this preverbal, prewalking age he resembles more of a hamster than a human. He definitely doesn't know the potential danger he's in if he proceeds any further. Behind him the calling of the woman has become more insistent and shrill. She can't find him in the house. He crawls forward and makes it to the 'nature strip'. Fortunately there's not a lot of traffic around – it's mid-morning in the city in the 1950s – so the risk factor is not as high as it could be during peak hour. On the other hand, if he does get out onto the road there's still a chance he could be squashed like a melon by an unobservant driver. He has succeeded in getting his front paw down into the gutter and is working on manoeuvring the rest of his body down there without falling flat on his face. Finally he's got all four limbs onto the road and is proceeding to cross. Inch by inch he crawls along the bitumen.

At this point God intervenes in the shape of – yes, you guessed it – a tram, or more specifically a tram driver. The driver has spotted the errant child heading onto the road, and pulled his tram up to a sudden halt. The driver steps out of his cabin, crosses the road and scoops up the little grommet, no doubt to the amusement of the conductor and passengers inside. Right at this moment my mother comes streaming, and screaming, out the front gate. The trammie is smiling and laughing and giving me a good old cuddle. He hands the squirming baby over to its mother, who is thanking him profusely in a kind of gibberish brought on by anxiety. The driver is still laughing as he reboards the tram and heads off down the road. No doubt a good story back at the depot.

Now, question: Is this story true or apocryphal?

My mother was a big one for stories, and I grew up surrounded by them. Stories about her childhood in the Mallee, her five brothers and sisters, her Pop, the war, the Depression, camping on the Murray River, her cycling tours, her first football match at the MCG, her first boyfriend (who drowned at Cape Schank), how she met my father. Stories that were retold, embellished and embroidered, depending on how many drinks she'd had that afternoon. She would be preparing dinner, cigarette going in the ashtray, long neck beer open, and telling me, her cook's assistant, one of her short or tall tales. One of these tellings was the tram story. She told it pretty much as I have related it here, although, as I say, her stories were true myths in that while their core remained the same, they constantly evolved and changed, depending on her mood and inventiveness. I had, as a child, no reason to doubt this story, but then I never doubted any of the stories she told me. I liked being inside them as she told them, even if it was the tenth telling. It was like being in a word bath, warm and soupy.

What do I think now? It would be odd if she'd made up a tale in which she is depicted as a mother who can't keep track of her baby, has left not only the front door, but the front gate open. It isn't exactly flattering from her perspective. On the other hand, it could be made up. I discovered later in life that my mother's stories could indeed be inventions; versions of events that other family members or friends either contradicted or had no memory of at all.

Of course, stories don't need to be literally true to be important. This account of my tram saviour reminds me of those Greek myths in which the hero, as a child or baby, faces a mortal threat to their life and survives, in the process acquiring formidable powers. Clearly this doesn't apply in my case. But like all good origin myths it does set the scene for what will come. In my case, trams would be threaded into my story from the start.

Incidentally, and apropos of nothing at all, I would also like to know what happened to my childhood set of blond curls, depicted so often in photos featuring my mother and me. There are dozens of these photos of mother and son: they are, in that archaic 1950s and 1960s photographic style, reminiscent of Madonna and child portraits, with the participants staring soulfully into each other's eyes. Blond child and dark Madonna, a true primal pair. Even before the chemo my curls were a distant memory. My mother often remarked upon this; 'How strange', she would say staring at my thin pate and gathering baldness when I was in my twenties, 'to think you once had such a glorious head of blond hair Grego, and now look at you. Such a pity you take after your father.'

*

One hundred and twenty years earlier, another crawler is bruising his knees shuffling across the bare floorboards of his parents' house in Holden, USA. Born the year before this domestic scene in 1833, Francis Boardman Clapp is the son of Oliver and Mary Clapp (née Boardman). Holden is a small town (pop. in 1840, 1,800) in the county of Worcester, in the Commonwealth of Massachusetts. The Clapps are descendants of Puritans, who fled England in the early 17th century due to their persecution by Church and State. The very first Clapps, all six of them, arrived on the *Mary and John* at Nantasket in 1630. Over the next decade more than 20,000 Puritans would join them.

Oliver Clapp, one of 12 siblings, is a merchant, and the family is a member of the Massachusetts middle class, not wealthy by today's standards, but keen on industry, stability and getting ahead. Why are we in the Commonwealth? Because this is where our tram guy is from. Francis Clapp – I discover – is the man who plotted, planned and designed and eventually created our city's tram system, thousands of kilometres from where he was born. He's my hero too; imagine if the city didn't have trams – I could well have ended up road kill that morning in the 1950s.

Let's peek into the future and shuffle forward from 1833 to 1882. The crawler is now a middle aged man and he's sitting in the ornate surrounds of the Legislative Council Committee Room (LCCR) of the Victorian Parliament in Melbourne. Clapp is there to give evidence in support of a Bill to establish a tramways system for the city. Clapp is the star witness to present before the Select Committee and his testimony is crucial. The Select Committee recommend that the Bill go forward, and in 1883 the *Melbourne Tramway and Omnibus Act* is passed by both houses of parliament and becomes law. Building the cable tram network commences in 1885, and Clapp is in charge of the whole enterprise. He's the mastermind and creator of the city's tram network.

How did Clapp's translation from small town America to cosmopolitan Melbourne come about? And what kind of values did he bring with him? We don't know much about Francis' childhood. He would have been schooled, either in a private college or in the Massachusetts public education system. Both were liberal and progressive, supported by a community that embraced education as part and parcel of doing good for God and for society. Clapp's heritage is important. As descendants of the original Puritans, the folk of New England looked to the light on the hill.

Francis is brought up in a home where frivolity is frowned upon, hard work and belief in God embraced, and every day an opportunity to do good works. For Puritans and their descendants life is a serious proposition. You may not know if you are part of the Puritan 'elect', predestined for an eternity with the angels after your death. But you sure as hell were not going to ruin your chances by slacking off in this life. Puritans believed in their special covenanted relationship to God, valued equally charity, self-reliance, moderation and prosperity, individual freedom and hierarchy. Christian names reflect their Old Testament world view. In a wondrous work from 1876, *The Clapp Memorial,* the names of the descendants of the Clapps on the *Mary and John* are recorded: Hopestill, Supply, Jehiel, Eliphaz, Preserved, Mindwell, Increase, Charity, Seth, Silence, to quote just a few.

The Puritans of the New World developed a distinctive culture, which deeply influenced the ethos of American values. With their belief that material prosperity was not inconsistent with religious devotion, the Puritan world view would fit well with America's nascent capitalist culture. Puritans were vehement in their belief in the rights of a people to self-government and like so many towns in Massachusetts, Holden formed and supported peoples' militias in the Revolution. The Puritans called King George the 'Whore of Babylon'.

When Clapp turns 20 in 1853 and turns his back on home and the United States, and crosses the Pacific Ocean to Australia, he does so armed with a particular world view – he's ambitious, hard working, self-confident and full of hope. Francis is joining the thousands and thousands of men (and some women) streaming into Victoria from across the globe and they are all coming for the same reason – gold. But Clapp doesn't disembark at Port Melbourne and head to the diggings. Instead he joins the Cobb and Co. coaching company in Ballarat, which had originally been established by four Americans, and serviced the Melbourne to Ballarat run. Four years later in 1857 Clapp heads a syndicate that buys out the company. He extends the company west and south, to Geelong, Hamilton, Warrnambool, and right out to Penola. In the process he becomes the largest mail contractor in the colony of Victoria, with annual subsidies of 22,000 pounds, a massive figure in the 1850s.

Let's stop here for a minute. I'm reading about a guy who at just 24 years old has already become a minor magnate in the colony. He's driven, calculating and smart, one of those men about whom it is said they 'don't suffer fools gladly' (which can be a euphemism for being an arrogant bastard). Regardless, Clapp bears within him the industry and character of his heritage. He's not wasting a minute of God's time on earth. He's going to make good works happen, and they're going to be big.

Sorry, I have to leave the Clapp story at this point. I've got a tram to catch.

5. Route 78: The Shopping Mecca

The previous evening I stabbed my map with the pin and came up with route 78. It gave me time to do some reading about the route before coming out here today. The 78 is a lonely child, preferring its own company to congregating with its siblings in the CBD. It runs in a straight line from the terminus in North Richmond to the terminus in Balaclava, at 6.5 kilometres one of the shortest routes on the system. The tram has no curves or turns to contend with, it simply trundles along Church Street in Richmond, crosses the river at Prahran, and continues along Chapel Street to Brighton Road. So it's a pretty unremarkable journey – which travels through one of the most remarkable streetscapes in the city.

The southern section of route 78 is old; Clapp's cable trams ran to Brighton Road down Chapel Street from 1888. Travelling from the city along St Kilda Road, they turned left at Toorak Road and headed into Prahran. Cable was important for Chapel Street as we shall discover. In the 1920s the 78 line was electrified and extended along Church Street north to Victoria Street.

It's mid-morning and I'm sitting in the tram at the northern terminus waiting for it to depart. It's a warmish day, all the windows are open and a light breeze is flowing in. I notice a sign on the pub opposite – 'Waiting for a tram? Happy hour everyday from 4.30–6.00pm'. Yes, you might consider that given the length of time I've been sitting here. Today it's an A1 class tram which has seen better days. The A1s were built in the 1980s, so this tram could be upwards of 40 years old.

Happy birthday tram! The second in the A series, the A2, were the first trams to dispense with poles connecting to the power grid, and instead used pantographs. All the A1s were later converted. The pantograph is a square contraption that sits on the roof and has at least two advantages over the pole. The driver doesn't need to change poles at every terminus, and the pantograph can't, like the pole, come off the grid, an event that occurred more often than it should have – usually because the driver was going too fast round a tight corner, or across a heavily wired intersection. You would recognise the A1: boxy-shaped, not pretty, but reliable and does the work. The As (and the Zs) are the smallest trams on the network.

A woman smoking a cigarette leans into the tram and asks the few people on board when it is leaving. When no-one responds she goes up to the driver and repeats her question, filling the tram with smoke. Apparently the answer from the driver is positive, since she chucks the cigarette out a window and slumps down into a seat. Shortly after we take off. The tram heads south down Church Street. There's a large block of housing commission flats on the right side, a sprinkling of cafes and hairdressers, the Citizens Park, and a police station, outside of which a policeman is eating a burger. A couple board the tram with a large pram, from which gurgling noises emanate. The tram crosses Bridge Road, home to the 48 and 75 travelling east and west, and crawls up Richmond Hill. Outside the bluestone St Ignatius Church a large crowd mills around, the men dressed in black and the women, unusually for a funeral, in tones of lilac and pink. A hearse sits to one side with its rear door open. A large number of the party have grey hair and many of the men are bald. The sun is now well and truly out and the bald heads are shining. At Swan Street a 70 tram crosses heading to the city.

As we progress south large demolition sites appear where wholesale clearances of buildings have occurred, some acres in size. A signboard on one announces that it is a 'New World Workplace for the Employee' and has the title, 'Industry Lane'. Other sites are for apartments, celebrating their locations with names such as '600

Church Street'. How innovative. These razed blocks expose the bare earth in grey or brown clumps seeing sunlight for the first time in over 100 years.

We cross the Yarra River, dull green and flanked on its north side by a freeway. An old poster stuck on a pole on the river bridge says, 'Legalise LSD'. The Yarra has always been a boundary. The land south of the Yarra, which I'm entering, was originally the territory of the Bunurong, who camped, hunted, fished and held corroborees here for thousands of years. The land was covered in wattle, river gums and swamps. Before white settlers developed an interest in the area, the colonial authorities set up an Aboriginal mission, including a short-lived school for Aboriginal children. In the 1840s the area was subdivided for development and the Bunurong were shifted to a reserve down the bay at Mordialloc. They have not ceded any of their traditional lands.

So, in all likelihood, my A1 tram is now snailing along, or adjacent to, what were originally Aboriginal tracks and paths through Prahran.

Chapel Street is not as I remember it. Tall blocks of apartments, their ground floors housing cafes and restaurants, fashion retailers, and upmarket furniture stores line this end of the street. Dozens of people are eating in the outdoor areas along the pavement. The tram travels slowly – over the whole trip it rarely gets much above walking pace – and I can see what everyone outdoors is eating. Enormous American-size plates of food are being devoured – burgers and chips, king prawns with chips, sausages with chips, chips with chips and tomato sauce.

At High Street a young guy gets on and sits opposite me. The tram has been under-populated for much of the journey but is now starting to fill up. The young guy is talking loudly on his phone as he gets on and continues in this vein when he sits down. He's arguing with someone. The money just needs to be sent to him, to his account, he says. 'Surely this is not so hard, I've got things to buy, stuff for the kitchen, for the lounge room. You know, the usual stuff you need when you move in to a new place. Come on', he continues, 'at least send me a few hundred to start with, you've got the money we both know that, I don't know why you are being so difficult.' There's a pause while he listens to his interlocutor. 'Yes I know all that Mum', he says. 'I'm sending you my new account details... yes my account has changed, you need to put the money in asap. I'll text you the details. For God's sake just do it will you!' He hangs up and sits scrolling through his phone. He looks sour and petulant, like a child denied a particular toy and I pity his poor mother having to deal with her wheedling son, but then how would I know what's really going on with him or them?

We've reached Commercial Road and this is where I've planned to get off and walk the next block. The Commercial Road to High Street block of Chapel Street is home to some of the city's most spectacular late 19th and early 20th century architecture, survivors of Whelan's wrecking ball attack on anything old. On the Chapel Street and Commercial Road corner sits the extraordinary Charles Moore Read Store with its copper domes, massive Corinthian columns, turrets, pedestals, cornices and oval windows, built in 1914. It's a grand, grandiose thing, built when department stores were the kings of street architecture. I'm walking on the east side of the street, since nearly all the great buildings in this block are on the west side. Next to Moores is the five storey Love and Lewis department store built in 1913. You can't miss it – LOVE AND LEWIS – is boldly announced on the façade in huge lettering in Art Nouveau style. Red brick, grey stone, green windows, terracotta tiles below the roofline, the store tells prospective shoppers that it is unequivocally the height of fashion. Further down I come to the Big Store, an American style emporium from 1902, also five storeys high and built, according to my guide, in Edwardian Baroque. This store sold everything for you and your home – drapery, clothing, boots, hosiery, bedding, carpets, furniture.

I cross the street to take in the fabulous work that is the Prahran Arcade, recently restored to its original glory. Built in 1890, this emporium, designed by prominent local architect George McMullen, was a centre for 29 exclusive shops, a hotel, a ballroom, billiards hall and

Turkish baths. Its opening was celebrated by a banquet in the central arcade for 250 local dignitaries. The arcade is three storeys high and topped with glazed windows and cast ironwork. There were tailors, watchmakers, dressmakers and in the basement, a bakery and ice makers. Other tenants included an 'oyster saloon', the Prahran School of Art, and the Theosophical Society. The façade is opulent – recessed balconies, columns and a pair of magnificent eagles.

Back on the east-side pavement I get a good view of the Colosseum, which was originally built in 1897, burnt down in 1914, only to be rebuilt in the same year. The new structure is a 'paean to early Beaux-Arts style architecture', says the guide, and faces the street with a long series of Ionic columns, pilasters, garlands and ornate balustrading. The early building was the business of Edwin Geach family, a leading Melbourne draper. One of the Geach offspring was Portia Geach, painter and political activist, an important figure in the early to mid-20th century womens' movement.

There are more as you stroll this block – the Osment building (1910), the Maples store (1905), and the Town Hall (1860-1915) is pretty damn good too.

Why have I digressed into the realm of colonial and early Federation architecture, and what's this got to do with trams? Before coming here I'd pored over as many photos of the street from the era as I could find. Over and over again, the iconic buildings of Chapel Street are shown with crowds of shoppers thronging the footpaths, and in the roadway cable trams are trundling past. The cable trams were instrumental in the development of Chapel Street as a shopping Mecca to rival the CBD. Without the trams there would have been few shoppers – remember there are no cars at this point – and thus no basis for investing the huge sums needed to build such splendid creations. Thanks to the regular access provided by public transport the area boomed, becoming, for a period, the most densely populated part of the city.

Time to get back on the 78. I board the next tram at High Street, where route 6 crosses Chapel. The 78 crosses the railway line at

Windsor station and heads to Dandenong Road (home to the 5 and 64). It passes the Art Deco Astor Theatre, built in 1936 and the last single screen cinema operating in the city, and then continues into East St Kilda where churches and private schools grace the roadsides. At the next stop a young woman gets on and sits across from me. She has a baby wrap carrier on her front from which pokes a tiny bald head. She pulls out her phone and makes a call, speaking loudly so it is impossible for the travellers near her not to overhear her conversation, just as had been the case with the young man earlier. I suspect these on-board phone calls are at least partly performative since the callers are completely aware they are in a public space. By the same token, I don't need to be shy about listening in. If it is indeed a performance I should at least grant it an audience.

The young woman is talking to a friend or relative about her boyfriend, who she clearly feels is behaving in an immature way in their relationship. The boyfriend seems not to appreciate that she is a mother with a young child and that this is a very demanding role. She says that since he is not the biological father it will take time for him to adjust to the new role, but she would like him to at least start trying. The boyfriend is also incredibly and unreasonably jealous of her former partner, the child's father. 'I've explained to him', she says, 'countless times, that Timmy's father is going to be around and involved in his life and that's not going to change. I think he's very immature, and I'm not sure he's really up to this relationship, which I want to happen on my terms for once. I just don't think that he really understands the meaning of love.'

The young woman is now silent, listening intently to what I imagine are her friend's views on the subject. After a prolonged series of goodbyes going back and forth the young woman ends the call. I have been staring out the window during her call, but now look up as she rises to leave the tram. Our eyes briefly meet and she smiles broadly. The tram crosses Carlisle Street (the 16, 3, and 3a can be caught here) and I take it to the terminus at Brighton Road – when we arrive I'm the last person on board.

*

Babies and prams. The Chapel Street/Church Street tram and I have history. As the baby 'grommet' alluded to earlier became a toddler my mother took me everywhere by tram. We had moved from the baby-crawling-danger-precinct next to a tram line to a quiet back street in Prahran, about mid-way between what were then the 7 and 8 routes, plying Commercial Road and Toorak Road respectively. As I've already recalled, it was from here my mother – Elaine – and I could easily catch the tram out to Parlington Street in Camberwell to visit grandpa Percy and Queenie. We could take either route to the city or catch the tram running north south along Chapel Street. My sister would not be born until I was well into primary school, so these were days with just the two of us. One of those Chapel Street trams also did a turn to the city at I think Swan Street, but I can't remember. Anyway, my mother didn't have a car so for her getting around town by tram was also a necessity.

We would take her shopping trolley to the Prahran Market and load up with veges and fruit and cheeses, we took the tram along Chapel Street to various emporiums and arcades, many of which are described above, we could catch the 7 or 8 to the botanical gardens, the 8 to visit Uncle Max in Park Street South Yarra (stopping virtually at his door), we went down to St Kilda Road and got the tram to Grey Street where my mother's closest female friend Irene lived. I remember visiting Irene in her ground floor Grey Street flat one day, and my mother knocking on the fly screen door, and when there was no response from inside her calling out 'cooee', a strange emanation that I'd never heard her use before. She pushes open the fly screen door but it's clear that Irene is out somewhere so my mother leaves a note and we leave. It's true – people didn't lock their doors in those days...

As a girl recently arrived from the country my mother didn't have many friends in the city. None of those school or neighbourhood connections that people so often carry with them for years. I've often thought how different our relationship would've been had she been born in Melbourne surrounded by family and friends. My father left early for work – he preferred catching the train to tramming it – and got back late, so there were many hours to fill for a woman on her own with a young child in the 1950s, not the most spectacular period in the city's history. But she never seemed unhappy, in fact, I never saw her happier.

6. The Star Witness

*"Public opinion and the age of progress is such that the people of Mel-
bourne demand something better."*

Francis B. Clapp, appearing before the
Parliamentary Select Committee, 1882.

Terrible headache. Lasted all night, despite four, or was it six
Panamax? I was warned to expect some 'residual' side effects
from the surgery and chemo, even months later. Apparently
rummaging around in the brain with a scalpel can have unwanted
consequences, some of which can be ongoing. Who would've
guessed? I shouldn't complain. I'm walking and talking, perambulating
on God's earth, not under the sods yet. I'm that rare thing in history –
a free human being. Yes, I know all freedoms are relative, but that's
the point. Compared to most people who have existed, and now exist,
I can basically do what I want every day. It's no small thing. The fact
that I choose to spend that freedom riding around on trams – no
doubt, in the view of many, an idiotic waste of said freedom – is entirely on me.

I did promise to return to the story of Monsieur Clapp. We'd left
the young gun entrepreneur in charge of one of the biggest mail
coach companies in the colonies. In 1860 his attention turns to urban
transport – he can already see the writing on the wall for the coach
business with the rise of regional railways – and he tries to convince
the City of Melbourne to grant him a licence to set up a horse tramway. This attempt fails and for the next seven years he is focused on
the mail runs, until, in 1867, he sells the lot and embarks for overseas.

He travels to Europe and America, and, amongst the joys of travel, he is looking for ideas. He returns to Melbourne in 1868 with a big one. In partnership with Henry Hoyt and William McCulloch, and with Council approval, Clapp creates the Melbourne Omnibus Company (MOC), the first public transport system of its type for the city. Clapp's first line opens in 1869 and runs from Spencer Street station to the Birmingham Hotel (1853) on the corner of Smith and Johnson Streets in Fitzroy. Thirteen years later, his empire has expanded to 15 lines running across the city, including routes to Richmond, Carlton, North Melbourne and Brunswick, has 470 employees and carries over 10 million passengers a year.

The omnibus is not a tram. These are four-wheeled coaches that can carry up to a dozen people and are pulled by two horses. The term 'omnibus' is Parisian, at least in its modern transport context. In the 1820s horse-drawn coaches called omnibuses travelled the wide boulevards of Haussmann Paris; the idea quickly caught on in London and New York. It is, of course, a Latin word originally, meaning 'for all'. And in its shortened form it gives us 'bus'. Clapp imports the first carriage from New York, and its superior American suspension gives a smoother ride than earlier carriages. The omnibus is an instant hit. Unlike the city's small, private cabs the omnibuses run to a regular timetable, are clean, well managed, on time and cheap. The trip to the Birmingham costs three pennies, much cheaper than the cab rate. The first MOC journeys are public events, with local papers describing scenes of large crowds, scrambles for seats, and people simply spectating this new invention. Not everyone was happy though. As the *Daily Telegraph* reported; 'Most faces wore a decided smile of satisfaction; but the features and expression of the "cabbies" were long drawn, sullen, defiant, and occasionally fierce.' Clapp's omnibus empire grows eventually to 178 vehicles, 1,600 horses and 11 stables. Sixteen hundred horses? That's a hell of a lot of shit on the roads. (And at 100 pounds a year for general horse maintenance, hugely expensive.)

No, not a tram, and for all his dedication to his omnibus company, Clapp is most interested in a public transport system that travels on rail. 'Interested' is no doubt an understatement. Clapp the Curious is a man possessed of an idée fixée. In all these years operating the MOC Clapp never loses sight of, or his passion for, tramway systems. He believes the tram is infinitely more efficient than the omnibus and that it will hugely expand public transport in the city. He studies demographics, urban growth patterns, traffic demands, potential routes and their impacts. As successful as it is, his omnibus company is a kind of raw template for the system he wants to build. Clapp visits the US and Europe to witness their tramway systems, reads everything on the subject, and appoints agents abroad to keep him abreast of the latest developments. In 1877, after visiting San Francisco, Clapp buys the patents for a cable tram system from Californian Andrew Hallidie, whose cable trams are operating there. And in 1877 he reconstitutes the MOC as the Melbourne Tramway and Omnibus Company (MTOC). Throughout the 1870s Clapp agitates for the introduction of a tramway system to the city but without success.

When Clapp thinks 'tramway' he's thinking of an integrated network of vehicles that are powered by remote steam engines. The style and make of tram he has in mind has two essential components – a front car, known as the 'dummy' car, connected to, and towing the rear car, known as the tram or trailer car. Both cars have four wheels (a single bogie) and both carry passengers. The dummy car drives the tram courtesy of the efforts of the gripman – more on him later – and, unlike the tram car, is open to the elements. Under the tramway is a continuously moving cable, which, through the efforts of the gripman and his attaching levers, pulls the tram along the rails at a regular speed.

Today I'm visiting the parliamentary library in Spring Street. There are documents here amongst the library's extensive resources that I want to see 'in the flesh', as it were, as opposed to online research. I also want to track how Francis B. Clapp was able to convince his contemporaries of the need to dig up the city to install a cable tram system. It's no small ask, and while a number of cities around the world have installed, or are installing cable, it is a frightfully expensive business.

As arranged, I'm met in the Parliament's vestibule by Julia, one of the library staff, who leads me through Queens Hall into the main room of the library. An expert in urban history, Julia is very interested in my project, and as we walk from ornate room to ornate room, she asks many questions, most of which I can't answer. The neoclassical main library room is beautiful – dark mahogany, plush red carpet, an enormous chandelier, fluted columns and pilasters, gold paint. The large French doors are wide open on this warm winter morning – our winters are getting shorter and shorter – allowing the sound of passing trams to float into the space, and a view of the resplendent parliamentary gardens. There is a sense of abundance and calm here and I am taken with envy for the lucky people who get to work in this space.

Julia has been speaking about the library's history, and now she leads me out of the main room, down winding stairs to the building's basement. Various doors are unlocked as we head deeper into the bowels of the building. The splendour of upstairs has given way to utilitarian bluestone – great thick walls that exude a palpable coldness. I'm brought before a series of racks. Julia shows me where to locate various documents, including the committee reports from the 19th century, which are stacked along the wall, and a desk and chair nearby that I can use. She says that the acts of parliament that I had enquired about are kept in the room opposite, the door of which she will unlock before she leaves. She gives me her phone number and tells me to call her when finished and she will come down and collect me. 'Don't try to come back up on your own', she warns, 'we're still looking for a visiting researcher who became lost down here last year. Nice fellow too.'

I settle in. It's totally silent down here. The only sounds to penetrate the bluestone walls come from some hidden pipes, which occasionally gurgle and rumble.

What I learn about Clapp is that he is a guy not deterred by the occasional set back. Through the 1870s, as his omnibus business grows, he is building his case for tramways; agitating and strategising, he lines up stakeholders and goes after them – politicians, councilmen, surveyors, engineers, businessmen, the media. Clapp has what many businessman lack – political acumen. He hobnobs, persuades and cajoles – all in, I presume, his unmistakable Massachusetts twang – and his omnibus success gives him an entrée to the corridors of power. Amongst his early parliamentary supporters is no less a figure than the young Alfred Deakin, a visionary in his own right. Clapp wants progress but many people with vested interests don't – the hansom cab drivers for one. Rather than ignoring those opposed, Clapp meets with them and makes his case face to face, which includes the line that everyone in the city will gain from the trams, including the cabbies. Eventually, the sum of these efforts leads in 1882 to a Bill before the Parliament of Victoria to establish tramways in the city. After a desultory second reading debate over its merits, the private member's Bill (introduced by MLA Duncan Gillies, later Premier of Victoria) is referred off to a House Select Committee, and it is the report of this Committee that I am particularly interested in perusing today.

The Select Committee's role is to review the Bill, hold hearings and take evidence from witnesses. It can recommend rejecting the Bill, accepting it in full, or suggest amendments. I look through the stacks and here it is: the 1882 report of the Committee titled, *Report From The Select Committee Of The Legislative Assembly Upon The Melbourne Tramway and Omnibus Company's Bill*. The Committee is divided between Members supportive of the Bill and those opposed. The witnesses comprise members of the city's elite, engineers, councilmen, MPs, and various hangers on. The report is over 100 pages in length and it will take me the rest of the morning to get my head around it.

There are documents and then there are documents. This is one of those which are fascinating windows into another era – the voices are all contemporary and qualified only by the grammatical ministrations of the Hansard reporters. Of the 24 witnesses to appear before the Committee over eight days of hearings, Clapp is the star, appearing on four separate occasions over the several weeks of the hearings in August 1882. Four appearances? Most witnesses before parliamentary committees get one appearance, give their evidence and that's it, you're excused. But Clapp gets four. He appears as the Director of the Melbourne Tramways and Omnibus Company (MTOC) and his presentations are informed, articulate, concise, and occasionally humorous. Patient in the face of the Committee's objections, repetitions and drolleries, Clapp holds his ground when attacked, refutes the evidence of other witnesses when necessary, produces documents to support his case, and brings in his chief financial officer to give crucial evidence. He produces an actual tramcar to show the Committee, which sits in the parliamentary grounds for their inspection. Also presented are a section of tram rail, and a model cross-section of tramway road.

The Committee's examination of Clapp is a serious business and is conducted accordingly. But there are some lighter moments, such as when early in the hearings Clapp is asked about the advantages for passengers in travelling by tramcar compared to an omnibus. He points to the greater comforts of the bigger tramcars, and their carrying capacity. In an era when the wearing of hats was ubiquitous, the following exchange happens:

> Clapp: The modern tramcars are sufficiently high for a man to walk in with his hat on and stand up.
> Committee: Without knocking his hat to pieces?
> Clapp: Without damaging his hat in any way; and sufficiently wide for two passengers to walk side by side.

Well, men did wear tall hats, and they weren't cheap, so maybe this is not risible at all. When challenged on the advantage of tramways over railways in a populous district Clapp says, 'Better by trams, because it is a populous district, and you take them direct to their homes.' This is not hyperbole on his part. The tramways will have few formal stops in the suburbs, with passengers calling out to the gripman to pull up as they approach their front doors.

Clapp tells the Committee, which is chaired by Gillies, that there will be one standard three pence fare across the whole system, considerably cheaper than the rates for cabs. The tram cars will carry up to 22 people in comfort inside, in a service operating at frequent intervals, to avoid delays on the system. The first tramcars will be imported but thereafter, all the cars and rolling stock will be built in Melbourne as the omnibuses are currently. His bus drivers, who are currently paid more, work shorter hours and have longer meal breaks than their counterparts overseas, will be retrained to drive and operate trams. The workforce will need to grow as the system expands.

Clapp tells the Committee he wants to at least treble the current patronage. The omnibus network has no real capacity for expansion and cannot match demand even now, with passengers left stranded during peak hour. The new system will rapidly increase patronage and grow the city. As illustration, Clapp points to the areas of the city where new houses and businesses have opened along the omnibus routes, property values have shot up, and argues that this will only be enhanced by tramways. As well, roads will be better kept, because the MTOC will maintain the central 17 foot width (just over five metres) of road necessary for the constructing and running of the tramways, and because the trams will run on the rails, not damage the road like coaches.

The roads will need to be dug up to lay the cable and the rails, and this will be disruptive. Clapp proposes to use as much of the material unearthed in the process and to ensure the work is done as rapidly as feasible. The Committee can get very fussy. Exactly how much of the dug up road materials will be used, they want to know, and what proportion will go back to the keep of councils? Clapp assures them that a portion of the unused materials will indeed be returned to local authorities, the exact amount to be determined. He's already approached the relevant local councils for their permission to construct the tramways, and received it.

The Committee is also worried about the push back from what would be referred to today as 'stakeholders'. What of the views of shopkeepers and cab drivers? Aren't they opposed to what he intends to do? Clapp says the shopkeepers were initially sceptical, but have come on board with the success of the omnibuses in increasing traffic around the city, and thus patronage of their shops. They will want trams along their streets. Likewise the cabbies have seen that their business has not declined. The cabbies, Clapp declares, are now 'our friends'.

This sounds all very altruistic, and no-one could doubt Clapp's sense of civic duty. But isn't he a businessman? He's running a private company and has admitted that a tramway is going to be extremely expensive to set up and to maintain. For example, the cost of constructing one mile of cable alone, Clapp says, including the cable, machinery, engine and tunnel is 16,000 pounds. Under aggressive questioning, Clapp admits that he will need to increase traffic six-fold to make the same profit as he is currently (12 percent). His statement is greeted with incredulity by a member of the Committee, who implies that Clapp is therefore no businessman. The following terse exchange takes place:

> Committee Member: Then you are merely a philanthropist – You want to carry six times the number of people and make the same profit, is that your only object in bringing in this Bill?
> Clapp: Our object is to give a better mode of transit to the people of Melbourne, systematise the fares and make money. We do not do it for nothing.

Pressed to explain why he needs this Bill for tramways when he already has a bus system which could be improved, Clapp disagrees. 'Public opinion and the age of progress is such that the people of Melbourne demand something better', he says, casting himself as a champion of the God of progress, and by implication, his interlocutor as mired in the past. Yes, he admits, the system will lose money in the beginning, but will be profitable over time. And there will be immediate savings – the introduction of the 'endless chain', as the cable is called, will dispense with the need for his fleet of horses, which cost over 160,000 pounds a year to maintain (millions of dollars in today's terms). I'm guessing this includes the cost of clearing the mountains of horse shit off the streets every day.

In discussing the housing of the 200 horse power engines that would drive the endless chain, one of the Committee members twigs to the plan that Clapp had all along. Clapp's 12 horse stable sites were chosen with a dual purpose were they not?

> Committee Member: You selected the site, contemplating that the tramway system would supersede the omnibus system – you had that object in mind?
> Clapp: We had.

When Clapp is asked when he could 'commence active operations' of the network if the Bill is passed, he says, 'At once.' And how long would it take to build the whole network, covering the city? No more than five years, says Clapp, and potentially sooner, depending on the labour market.

The Committee query Clapp on his choice of motive power, during which discussion he rejects steam power, 'in toto', as flawed, inefficient and unpopular. By this he means trams that run on their own individual steam engines. As mentioned above, his system will use steam power but generated remotely at engine houses constructed for each tram line, using the old horse stable sites (more on these later).

Ever the forward thinker, Clapp tells the Committee that the latest news from his agents overseas is that, 'the coming motor for tramways was electricity'. It will be more than a generation before electricity is introduced to the city's public transport system.

I get the distinct feeling that Clapp would not have appeared before the Committee unless he had the numbers. Behind the scenes
key figures are no doubt determining outcomes, a process followed in
our dear state of Victoria to this day. The municipal authorities, for
example, are flexing their muscles over control of the proposed system. Whatever the case, by his final two appearances Clapp is clearly
in the driver's seat of this legislative reform. Discussion has turned to
details related to potential amendments – the implication being that
the Committee is going to recommend passage of the Bill. So, he gets
the votes needed for the Committee's support. Although the report
itself offers only a few lines of summary, the amended Bill returns to
the Legislative Assembly where it eventually passes in 1883.

7. Route 75: Typo on Flinders Street

L ast night my mercurial pin landed on route 75, which traverses the same route (minus two city blocks) taken by Melbourne's first cable tram, before running out to the far eastern suburbs. That first MTOC tram started operations in November 1885, and ran from the city terminus at the corner of Bourke and Spencer Streets, down Spencer Street to Flinders Street, along Flinders past the city's docks, warehouses, markets, and the station – the earlier, less grand version of Flinders Street railway station – before continuing on through the city and onto Wellington Parade, and past the Melbourne Cricket Ground (MCG). It then entered Richmond at Punt Road, travelling down Bridge Road to Hawthorn Bridge at the Yarra River where it terminated. The former MTOC headquarters building, still standing, is just off Spencer Street at 675 Bourke Street – a fine Gothic revival design by city architects Twentyman and Askew. A cable tram engine house, also the very first, was built in Richmond on the corner of Hoddle Street and Bridge Road. As mentioned, these steam engine houses, dotted around the city, drive the cables that literally underpin the cable tram network.

I'm catching the 75 near the Spencer and Flinders Streets intersection. The 75's terminus has been extended from the Spencer and Latrobe corner to Harbour Esplanade and Latrobe Street in the Docklands, a once thriving port given over to modern developers with masters degrees in alienation, wind tunnels and glass. The 75 is on its way to Vermont South, 22.8 kilometres from Central Pier, a hell of a long tramway ride anywhere, and the longest in this city. I'm riding in a B2 class tram built in the late 1980s or early 1990s in Dandenong, the first trams on the modern system to be air conditioned. This B2 tram features 'lean' seats in the middle, neither seats nor proper standing room, a marvel of non-utilitarian design. Not the most comfortable of rides, but any tram ride is better than none. Thankfully, lean seating is not universal on the B2s.

Flinders Street is fascinating, despite the loss of the original docks, the Western Markets and other antiquities. On the corner of Spencer and Flinders sits the Sir Charles Hotham Hotel, built in 1912 in Edwardian Baroque style and sporting a wonderful rounded corner turret. Yes, the old dear has seen better days – lots of peeling paint covers the original brickwork – and the building is slated for 'redevelopment'. Down the street is the Waterside Hotel, which is also in the process of renovation. The Waterside is famous for having a six a.m. licence for the wharfies as they knocked off work at the docks, and a history bathed in gallons of beer, betting and fights.

The Immigration Museum (1876) was modelled on an Italian Renaissance Palazzo, with Ionic columns copied from the Erechtheion temple in Athens. First constructed in 1841, it was originally the city's Customs House, and sat right next to the wharves, and was where both humans and goods were checked for valid entry to the colony. Here clusters of sailing ships anchored for decades before Victoria Dock was built. Before they were dynamited out of existence there were river falls here too – they blocked shipping from going further upstream on the Yarra. It was at or near these falls that John Batman's son drowned in 1845.

The Anglicans scored a central city site with the neo-Gothic St Paul's Cathedral on the corner of Flinders and Swanston Streets. The rule of thumb in Melbourne was 10 pubs for every one church, and it's entirely appropriate that opposite St Paul's sits Young and Jackson, a famous swillery that barred women for decades, while maintaining an oil painting of a naked woman above the front bar. 'Chloe' was painted by Jules Lefebvre in 1875, and has hung at Y and J since

1908. It wasn't until the 1970s, after strenuous protests against their exclusion, that women won the right to drink in the public bar of hotels. In a beer obsessed culture this was no small victory.

My favorite work of architecture in Flinders Street is the Forum Theatre, built in 1929 in what is quaintly termed the Moorish Revival Style. When it opened as The State Theatre it could seat over 3,000 people, the largest theatre in the country. It's an outrageous mix of structures, colours and themes – spire-like minarets, copper-domed clock tower and intricate facade, while inside are classical statues (including a copy of the Venus De Capua), gargoyles and a cerulean blue ceiling that lights up as the night sky. It's been a theatre, a dance hall, film festival venue, Christian revival centre and now a live music venue.

Yes, as usual, I've wandered from trams to buildings. Please remember dear reader that the city's streetscape and urban infrastructure is partly a product of the ability of its denizens to move around it with ease by trams. In this context it is no accident that Clapp chose this particular route to open his system. Clapp's trams got people around the city; from rail station to rail station, to theatres, shops, pubs and museums, outside the CBD to the cricket and football, and then on to the growing suburbs. His trams connected people with places, events, other people, and were critical in the flowering of the city. By the late 1880s, sport had become a major element in Melbourne's life. In a city of half a million, the MCG would frequently host more than one in 10 of the population on game days. And it was Clapp's trams that took them there.

I want to have a look at the original engine house, home to the powerful steam engines that drove the endless chain. I get down at the corner of Hoddle Street and Bridge Road, and after waiting for an eternity for the lights to change, cross over to the east side of the intersection. There's no engine house. Nothing, except a small grassy knoll on the corner. No, wait, I find a small plaque on a recessed wall set back from the road. It briefly describes the former existence of the engine house on this site, demolished to make way for road widening in the early 1990s. I turn around and watch the traffic roar up and down the eight lanes of Hoddle Street.

I reboard the 75 in Richmond to take it out to its newish terminus in the eastern suburbs. At Hawthorn Bridge, the tram crosses the Yarra, travels up Burwood Road into Hawthorn, right at Power Street, continues to Riversdale Road and then on to Camberwell Junction. This is a solidly middle-class journey, reflected both in the passengers and the built environment. The cable tram terminated at Hawthorn Bridge, but from there a horse drawn tram took passengers on this route as far as Auburn Road. In 1916 electrification of the route began, and the route was extended along Camberwell Road from the Junction to Toorak Road and then on to Warrigal Road. By 1927 the whole route was converted to electric, and extensions followed to Middleborough Road, then Blackburn Road and finally, Vermont South in 2005.

The failure of the engine house to survive the pillaging of the car authorities has soured my mood. I'm looking at waves of brick and concrete and I'm struck by the endlessness of the city and its suburbs. It just goes on and on – row upon row of houses, apartments, studios, townhouses, shops, businesses, restaurants, cafes. How many structures can a city have before it is unable to remember itself? In becoming a city beyond the comprehension of one person, is it now, in some critical way unknowable?

Meet Barry. The very affable Barry arrives just in time to alleviate my bout of melancholy. He gets on just before Camberwell Junction and sits opposite. He comments on the pleasantness of the day, and says, gnomically, 'you wouldn't be dead for quids'. He's jovial, ruddy and talkative. As we exchange pleasantries, I tell Barry that I'm doing a project on trams, and have been asking people about what they think of them. Does he have a tram story he'd like to tell me?

Barry is delighted. He says that he has been riding trams since he 'was a little tacker', and can't imagine the city without them. 'I did love the green trams more than these plastic contraptions', he says, 'but they are all good. It's just a pleasant way to get around isn't it?

Yes, my first memory of trams would be with my father back in the 1960s. Dad worked as a typesetter at the *Herald*, you know the old grey building in Flinders Street, and on Sundays he would sometimes take me with him. I loved riding down there with him and he would get me a treat on the way back. I must have sat there for hours while he worked at his machine. Do you know how linotype worked?' I tell Barry that I have no idea.

'Fascinating. The operators, like my Dad, had to turn the editor's paper copy into metal type for printing. They sat at the front of these mechanical machines called linotype machines, which were invented in the 1880s, and they had a keyboard that automatically set the type as they punched the letters. Not an ordinary keyboard mind you, this one was arranged with the letters in columns and by letter frequency. They were quick the typesetters. Dad told me that he could type 20,000 letters an hour – incredible when you think about it. I think I can still remember the sequence of the first row down – e,t,a,o,i,n – and you know Dad told me how when an operator made a mistake he would simply run his finger down that row, keep typing and then pull out the mistake later. But sometimes the typesetter forgot to go back and do the correction, and e,t,a,o,i,n would appear in print the next day, or that evening!'

I ask Barry what happened to the typesetters – surely the technology eventually changed? 'It was a shame for all those men when it finished, must have been in the early 80s when Dad was made redundant. One day he had this high paid, skilled job and the next day he was unemployed. The composing room gave way to photocopiers. It really affected our family tremendously. He was within a few years of retirement, but he wasn't really the same bloke after it. It was like he'd been robbed of something precious, as if his whole working life didn't amount to a hill of beans. I'd left home by then but when I went back to visit he'd be sitting in the lounge with the radio listening to God knows what. Such a sturdy man until then. Had no other skills so he drifted from unemployment to the pension. To tell you the truth I found it depressing to go home, so after a while I visited less and less. Mum would ring me up and say when are you coming over and I'd make some excuse. I regret that now.'

Barry and I sit silently for a while and both of us look out the window. The tram is in the reaches of Burwood Highway and passing Deakin University with its blaze of modernism. We are heading towards Vermont South and as the tram travels further east, the road has been widening from two lanes to four, then six lanes to eight. The tram now has its own exclusive lane in the centre of the road, flanked by concrete poles and electric wires. But it doesn't look like a tram road. The view is dominated by a vast river of snaking bitumen covered in scooting cars, their yellow indicators flicking as they change lanes.

I ask Barry where he is headed now. He says he is visiting his mother in a nursing home in Vermont. He goes once a week, although the frequency of his visits probably doesn't really matter. His mother has dementia and rarely recognises him. 'Sometimes', he says, 'she thinks I'm Dad and gives me a list of things to do around the house while she's away on holiday. She told me once that she was in Paris and wouldn't be back for some time and that the group she was travelling with were lovely, except for a certain Mrs Cook who was a real pain in the backside, always complaining and whinging about something. I'm always surprised by these outbursts of hers. Where do they come from? She's never been to Paris. Mum and Dad had their holidays in Rosebud for years, not very Paris-like. Perhaps this is her secret wish coming out, that she'd always wanted to go there. They had planned trips to Europe for when Dad retired but after what happened they never went anywhere.'

The tram arrives at the intersection of Burwood Highway and Springvale Road which is bigger than a football ground, as eight lanes meet eight lanes. The cars scurry across the intersection in all directions obeying the complex series of lights. Barry gets off at the next stop, wishing me well with my project. Nice man.

I know this suburban landscape well having endured it during my teenage years. The tram trundles up the hill to the terminus. According to my tram app it will sit here for 10 minutes before turning around and heading back. In those earlier days, this region of the city lay beyond the tram lines. It had been a series of small farms – fruit orchards and market gardens – before the developers covered it in neat rows of triple-fronted brick veneers. It always felt intermediate to me, an in-between place, unlike the inner city where I first grew up. The suburbs had their own culture of wide spaces, immaculate football grounds, tennis clubs and silent Sundays. You had to drive to the pubs. Some evenings I could hear a roaring in the distance, as if some huge mechanical animal was stirring just over the horizon. I never found out what that noise was – e,t,a,o,i,n.

*

Bibliotheca tramus. When I'm not on a tram dear reader, more often than not I have my head in a book from my growing tram library. I'm finding myself in the company of a long line of tram enthusiasts, experts and aficionados and, increasingly, drawing upon their knowledge, wisdom and stories. I'm sure my nascent library, which includes works by cable tram historians J. D. Keating and J. Cranston, tram fleet experts Dale Budd and Randall Wilson, the tram custodians from the Melbourne Tram Museum (including the prolific Russell Jones), to name just a few, will be well thumbed, or viewed, by the end. (Any source mentioned in the text can be found in the bibliography at the rear.)

I'm getting the hang of listening too. On my journeys, as well as the face-to-face conversations I'm lucky enough to have with other travellers, I'm finding I'm privy to overheard conversations, as you've already seen. Some are no more than scraps of talk, half-heard over the din, others can be sections of a story begun by the discussants before boarding the tram, and which could well continue after they disembark. At other times I hear entire, self-contained narratives. I realise I've previously travelled on trams with my ears shut. Now they're wide open.

8. The Tramways Act 1883

Two days later and I'm back at the parliamentary library. Julia suggests we have coffee together in the visitors' area known as Strangers Corridor, and with a name like that I can't resist. We sit in a plush cubicle with wood panelling in a room that indeed resembles a corridor. Julia tells me that this is where constituents can meet politicians at Parliament, and where lobbyists practice their dark arts. She's very good company and as we drink the watery coffee she tells me about her latest project, which involves digitising the library's rare books collection. It's tricky she says because many of the works date from the mid-to-late 19th century and are very frail. It takes careful handling not to crack their spines or tear pages, but so far they've succeeded in digitising over a thousand books without damaging them. I ask her what it's like to work in such a grand building and she tells me she just loves working there. 'Even after all these years', she says, 'I still get a buzz when I come into the main library in the morning. It's a special place. Crazy at times, with you know who doing God knows what, and the nights can be very long during sitting weeks, but all in all I wouldn't want to be anywhere else.' We chat a bit longer, and I can't help feeling a twinge of envy – here's someone who loves their work and is happy being at work, such a contrast with my own experience – and then Julia guides me back down to the dungeons. I'm positive she has taken me on a different route down this time, but can't be sure. From the upper floors to here the temperature feels like it's dropped 10 degrees.

*

Given the brief time that democracies have occupied in human history, every piece of legislation passed by an elected body of the people's representatives is a work of wonder. But it's not often that a single piece of legislation can have the effect of transforming a city. Allow me to introduce you to *The Melbourne Tramway and Omnibus Company's Act* 1883, an Act to, 'authorize the Melbourne Tramway and Omnibus Company Limited to construct Tramways in the Cities of Melbourne Fitzroy Collingwood Prahran Richmond and South Melbourne and the Town of Hotham and the Boroughs of St Kilda Brunswick Kew Hawthorn and Sandridge and for other purposes.' According to the preamble to the Act, which we've met in its previous incarnation as the Bill, the making of the tramways will be 'of great public and local advantage'.

I've made my way into the room adjacent to where I was two days before, which houses hard copies of the acts of the Victorian Parliament, and there it is – Clapp's Act. There are 64 sections to the Act and four schedules attached at the rear. (Schedules always appear at the rear and usually provide details for an act's implementation.) As acts go it's a slim document of just 34 pages, written in that 19th century style of few commas and long paragraphs. I won't bore you with a detailed analysis, but here's the gist of it.

The Act provides the MTOC the monopoly and powers to construct and operate a tramway system for the city, subject to the agreement and consent of the municipal authorities of the localities through which each route will run. It contains provisions that govern construction and roadworks, protection of utilities, application of by-laws and the appointment of a Tramways Board. In section 22, the Act states that the tram system will run carriages with flanged wheels or other wheels suitable to run on rails. The trams will be powered by 'animal power, or by means of stationary engines with an endless rope running under the road, or by other such motive power except steam locomotives...'. There are provisions covering the financial relationship between the company and local authorities, licence fees, dispute settlement arrangements, composition of the Board, rules for inquiries, and penalties for non-compliance for the various parties.

The Act states that the tramways will consist of a double line constructed in the middle of the road, with a gauge of exactly four feet eight inches and a half (1.43 metres approx.). At section 42 the Act provides for the local authorities – the councils – to get a share in the profits, proportionate to the mileage of the tramway within its boundaries.

They'd thought about fare evasion. At section 35, anyone found avoiding fare payment is liable to a 40 shilling fine (equivalent to over 150 tram fares!). Section 36 permits the physical apprehension of said fare evaders by employees, who can call upon passengers to help them detain the offender and, when convenient, deliver such person to a constable. You can't carry dangerous goods, and can only carry a maximum of 28 pounds of luggage (almost 13 kilos). The MTOC is not required under section 38 to carry dogs.

The third schedule outlines the fares to be paid. There would be a standard fare of three pennies for a single journey on all lines, except in the case of those commuting between Flinders and Spencer Street stations, who would be charged just one penny. Section 41 provides for the punishment of employees who are found drunk on the job, or whose behaviour or actions or neglect endanger the public; up to three months in gaol, with or without hard labour, or a 25 pound fine (about 10 times the then average weekly wage).

There's a surprise contained in section 62. It provides for the restriction of the hours of work for tramways employees to eight hours a day. Any hours above the eight will need to be paid overtime, and a maximum of 60 hours worked in a week. The employer is liable to a five pound fine for each breach of this rule. While some Victorian workers have had the eight-hour day since the 1850s, and an eight-hour day has been part of government contracts since the 1870s, this appears to be the first occurrence of an eight-hour day in legislation in the colony. I do a check of other jurisdictions but cannot find an earlier example of a legislated eight-hour day. A general eight hours act to cover all workers is not enacted in Victoria until 1916, and federally, a 40 hour, five day working week is not legislated until 1948. It may have been the first eight-hour day legislated in Victoria but the MTOC seems to have viewed it as an 'aspirational' rather than literal requirement. I'll come back to this.

The first of the schedules (which are in such a tiny font I'm going blind reading them) provides a template for the construction of the network, enumerating the system's main lines, running north, south, inner west and east , from which sub-branches lead to a multitude of destinations. The city will be criss-crossed with cable tram routes, but it's important to note that this template was refined and amended over the years – starting in 1883 itself with an amending act passed by Parliament with further amendments in 1884 and 1887. The schedule makes no mention of the western suburbs.

Schedule Four is a shock, if such a thing can happen in an act of Parliament. It turns out that the municipal fathers have indeed been working assiduously behind the scenes to put themselves at the centre of this massive project. Not content with providing consent to the MTOC, and the odd body to the Board, this schedule outlines the creation of a new body entirely, The Melbourne Tramways Trust. The Trust will be made up of representatives of all the local municipal authorities involved, will take over all the functions of the Board (which won't now exist) and have all the rights and responsibilities covered under the Act. (Public trusts became a common feature of 19th century administration and were set up by local communities or governments, under strict rules and regulations and with appointed trustees, to manage public assets, such as parks and libraries, for the benefit of the public, rather than specific entities or individuals. Transport trusts were one example of this method of administration.)

Schedule Four goes on to state that the Trust will be empowered to raise capital for the construction costs of the tramways, pay its own officers and employees, and have a share in the profits made by the MTOC. The schedule then stipulates that the whole of the system should be constructed in five years!

The Trust will lease the whole system, once constructed, to the MTOC for 30 years, as the monopoly operator. The Trust will fund the building of the lines, while the MTOC will provide the rolling stock, and the whole will be under the control of the MTOC. I'm sure Clapp knew this was coming, but its addition as a schedule to the Act speaks to some late night meetings over port and cigars in Strangers Corridor at the Parliament. No need to re-write the Act, just whack in Schedule Four, and insert provisions in the Act to affirm the schedule (duly done at sections 52-56).

I don't think Clapp would have been disappointed by this. The capital for the build will be raised by others, and will be his to spend. He gets the city's tramway system to run, maintain and profit from, for 30 years, by which time he will be in his 80s. The construction, design and fit out, the rolling stock, the timetabling, all the operations of the system will be under his control. It's not a bad deal.

9. The Marvellous Engineer

It's obvious that Francis Boardman Clapp likes trams to the point of obsession. They are, for him, not just a mode of transport but a thing of modern beauty, a beauty that combines aesthetics with civic virtue, creating social change and making money. They are inherently interesting and transformative, and present wonderful problems to solve. They engage engineering and urban transport, the law and politics, and for Clapp, they appear to be well worth the 20 years of his life that he devotes to getting them going.

Clapp is a seriously talented entrepreneur. He also has a sound grasp of the technicalities involved in tramway systems having studied them for years. But he is not an engineer and can't design a system alone. In 1883, after the passage of the Act, he hires New Zealander George Duncan to be the MTOC's principal engineer. Duncan is born in Dunedin in 1852 of Scottish heritage, and later attends Edinburgh University where he studies engineering. Returning to New Zealand, he becomes the provincial engineer for the District of Otago and later the partner in an engineering firm. He constructs a cable tramway in Dunedin, which opens in 1881, and is, most likely, the first cable tramway to be constructed anywhere outside the United States. The success of this line leads to the construction of a second cable line to Mornington (NZ) in 1883. Duncan is also building bridges, railways, drainage works and so on, but it's clear that it's cable that really gets him stirred. It's not known how Clapp meets Duncan, although it is quite likely that they travelled together at some stage to investigate the cable system in San Francisco. They were both definitely cable tram obsessives. When Duncan is hired by Clapp he is just 31 years old.

The Presbyterian culture that nurtured Duncan is an important element to his story. Members of one of the oldest Scottish clans, the Duncans who settled in Dunedin in the 19th century were in the main Calvinist Presbyterians, whose religion, like the American Puritans, stressed good works performed in all fields – a protestantism that was strict, demanding and, at the same time, intellectual. The Presbyterian Scots were obsessed with works, including those involving the mind, that could transform the world around them. It was good to change things, to make things, to buy and sell things. Time should not be 'wasted'. In a world that could be measured, weighed and estimated, God was everywhere but not averse to the making of money. Within this theology, God's creatures could develop and deploy their talents, could become educated, and change the world.

One of the great Scots talents developed to change the world for the good was the science of engineering, the most practical and world embracing of all the sciences. An intensely religio-humanist outlook took to engineering as a means for transformation, and the creation of civic good. Knotty engineering problems were, apparently, God's delight. You could spend endless hours, days and years working to design and construct a bridge, an engine, a tunnel, a machine without a moment of guilt. Scotland, with its relatively small population, became a centre of engineering, exporting its talented disciples to the world. And yes, the Scots can be dour on occasion – I can say this since I'm half Scot – but this characteristic doesn't negate the inherent worldly pragmatism of Scottish culture.

In his history of Melbourne's cable trams, *Mind the Curve!*, J. D. Keating notes that by the early 1880s Duncan is a leading engineering authority on cable tram systems. His role in the development of Melbourne's system is crucial. Using the lessons he has learnt from his own and other systems, he sets about making the city a cable system that is innovative, practical and cost effective. He has the luxury, and challenge, of working on constructing a whole integrated system.

Nearly all systems elsewhere have been created ad hoc. Melbourne's will be a first – fully integrated and operational in a handful of years. There are many engineering problems to address in the Melbourne system.

Trenches, pulleys, cables, wheels, steam engines, grip mechanism. Where to site the engine house? What's the maximum length of cable that can be run, and what power is required to drive it? What's the right weight for the dummy car and tram car? How do you stop the cable from snaring on corners? How many corners can you reasonably have on a single line? And so on and so on. Duncan has faced and solved some of these questions in the construction of his New Zealand lines, but Melbourne is more complicated. The city's tram routes will entail multiple locations where the track will curve. Cable tram systems in the United States frequently run in straight lines, avoiding curves, which place strain and wear on the cable and with the ever present danger of the cable jamming or catching. Duncan works on a multitude of technical issues, but it is the resolution of this problem that contributes to making our city's system so unique and functional.

You may remember how I said earlier that the cable tram is pulled along by a cable under the roadway. To explain a bit more: the continuously moving cable rests on small pulleys within a one metre trench constructed specifically to house them beneath the road surface. The gripman operates the mechanism known as 'the grip' with his levers in the middle of the dummy car to clasp the cable and pull the tram along. Stopping the tram depends on the gripman releasing the cable and applying the brakes, while to restart the tram the gripman uses his levers to release the brakes and grip the cable again. (See the photo image of grip mechanism in centre pages.) When the tram is running straight there are fewer issues. But on curves there's the potential for trouble. The Melbourne system will have over 60 curves and corners to be managed by the gripman. Cable is expensive and the continual flexing of the cable on corners can lead to wear and tear. Worse, if the cable is snagged or fouled by the grip it can be severely damaged.

In New Zealand Duncan developed a 'pull curve', engineered to allow the gripman to maintain the grip around the curve without snagging the cable, and some of these were installed in Melbourne. But in most instances corners, curves and intersections would be negotiated without the advantage of this invention. So what to do?

His solution was to design a system predicated on the gripman releasing the cable fully from the grip – called 'throwing the rope' – at a crucial point in the curve to avoid entanglement and allow the tram to navigate the turn without power. This is achieved by the gripman ejecting the cable from the grip with his levers and then using the tram's momentum or gravity to take it forward round the curve. This engineering solution incorporates the idea of a skilled workforce in the design. The gripman had to be strong – letting go of the cable is one thing, but grabbing the cable while the tram is in motion is entirely another. No wonder so many of the gripmen were big footballers, often ruckmen, from the VFA/VFL.

In some other situations the cable had to be released in order to avoid snares and tangles, requiring the gripman to 'throw the rope', rather than carry it through. As Jack Cranston describes in his book, *The Melbourne Cable Trams 1885-1940,* at intersections in the CBD where separate cable lines crossed each other, the gripman driving the tram attached to the lower cable would need to throw the cable, glide over the intersection, then pick up the cable on the other side. A tricky operation but the same principle applied. It was a demanding network that required the gripman to know his route intimately and maintain concentration throughout the journey. Duncan's system gave the gripman agency to competently manage the tram along the whole route.

It would be a tough job. All tram driving is challenging and every tram era places burdens and constraints on the body. In the dummy the gripmen would be out in the open, standing all day, facing the heat of summer, the cold of winter, rain, hail and wind: subject to the endless trundle motion of the tram, and constantly managing the release and hold of the vibrating cable. In a city not yet familiar with traffic rules, people, carts, hansom cabs and buggies were continually getting in the pathway of trams – an accident was literally just around the corner, making constant vigilance one of the key requirements of the job. The trammies worked long hours and had few days off.

Nevertheless, the gripmen would become skilled operators of the city's first integrated public transport system, and, as challenging as it was, justifiably proud of their work. It would be a popular occupation, and the gripmen became, like the trams themselves, an indelible part of the city's identity.

Stories about Duncan suggest he is pretty strait-laced, odd and renowned for his distractedness. The latter quality might stem from his endless mental cogitations on the interaction of curves, wheels, and trams and their underlying physics. One apocryphal story about Duncan, related by Keating, has him jumping up in the middle of a family dinner and racing into his study where he tinkers with a model set of wheels, braces and cables made of string, compelled by a new idea that can't wait. He is that infrequent character, the inventor. After his sojourn with trams, he goes on to create a mining company that employs an entirely new (although unsuccessful) method for extracting gold.

Duncan works on the system across the whole period of construction, refining it and making changes. The introverted Duncan and the gregarious Clapp are the true odd couple of the city's public transport system. They are both migrants with distinctive native accents, and they both live, have families (Clapp seven children, Duncan three) and die in Melbourne. The city which they transformed has failed to produce a single monument or memorial to their work.

10. South Melbourne Beach

Time to go to the beach.

I'm waiting in the city for the South Melbourne tram – recognisable by its predominantly green livery – at the terminus in Market Street. While waiting, a red-coloured tram turns the corner from Collins Street heading down Market Street. It should, by rights, be heading to its normal destination at Spencer Street, having come up from Victoria Bridge to the east of the city. Instead, the crew have slung a makeshift sign over the front of the dummy car that says in bold lettering, STH MELB BEACH, and as they turn the corner, the conductor leans from the tram car and calls out, 'South Melbourne, South Melbourne Beach!' A bunch of people near the corner race to the tram where it has stopped but only a few can get on. The day is incredibly hot and a tram ride to the beach is a highly popular idea. Trams bound for certain city destinations on such weekend days are permitted to change course in the city and head down to the beaches and are often directed to do so without prior notice when demand is high. Fingers crossed the crew knows the way!

The city air is humid and close. It's 1890 and the streets are full of people and objects in every possible manner of movement, and making every possible type of noise. Hansom cabs and buggies, horses and carts, the cable trams themselves, bicycles, drays, men pulling carts by hand. There are the repetitive gongs of the trams, which echo up the streets, the cabs are honking their horns, bicycles ring their bells, men shout out the news from newsstands, shopkeepers call their wares to their customers, people walk along whistling, muttering, talking. People cross and wander down the centre of streets seemingly randomly, oblivious to the danger to life and limb posed by the trams, buggies and cabs that gong and shout at them to get out of the way. It is a scene of organised chaos of the old town that smells, the open drains running into the Yarra River below.

Trams are transforming the city. People pour in and out of the Western Market, rebuilt as an impressive two-storey neo-classical structure in the 1870s. It fills the whole block bordered by William, Collins and Market Streets, and presages in style and substance the later Queen Victoria Market. On this heated day you hear the echoed shouts of the produce merchants through the market's open windows and doors.

Having failed to catch the earlier tram, I'm waiting for the regular South Melbourne tram coming up the short hill to the terminus. Two cable trams arrive bunched close together, a common occurrence in any tram system, where the lead tram is either slowed down by a rush of passengers or has a gripman who, in tram parlance, is 'dragging the chain'; that is, going so slowly that they hold up everyone behind.

The South Melbourne tram is brightly painted in green, the MTOC's choice for three lines: South Melbourne, North Melbourne and St Kilda Beach. All the lines are colour coded for ease of recognition, in part because some in the community are still illiterate. There are six principal route colours – red, blue, green, white, yellow and brown – and the tramway company ensures trams on routes with identical colouring are on separate streets in their journeys to avoid confusion. Night lights follow the colour coding of the tram routes, except for the white routes (amber lights) yellow (white lights), and the browns, a mixture of white (West Melbourne) and red (Windsor-Esplanade).

The painting of the trams is more than pragmatics. At the workshops in North Fitzroy where the trams are being built teams of painters apply their skills to create works of tram art. On both tram cars and dummys, the colours are vivid and striking. The cars have elaborate sign painting, inscribing the main roads and streets traversed by the tram and its destination. The car number is typically painted in gold leaf and scrolls of flowers and leaves are embossed on the sides. The dummy has a white roof, its wrought iron scrolls at the end are often bright blue, and its wire guards can be painted yellow. Combined with the skilled carpentry and polished wooden interiors, the whole effect is one of splendour and exuberance. The cable trams combine ideals of mechanisation, efficiency and the romantic.

The first of the two trams arrives at the Market Street stop and has barely been shunted when the waiting passengers clamber onto the dummy and tram car – not exactly a stampede but a rush nevertheless. I wait for the second tram to shunt, hoping I will thus secure a seat outside in the dummy. But as it turns out, I'm beaten to it by the next group of travellers, clearly seasoned in jumping on trams, who quickly fill the available seating. I get in the enclosed tram car behind and take a seat on the long bench, which faces into the tram. The aisle fills up in seconds and I'm now staring into the waists and torsos of fellow travellers. The tramcar seats up to 22 people and 34 standing, but it feels like there's more on board than that. For such a hot day, everyone looks overdressed, most of the men in suits and hats, women in long dresses with wrist-length sleeves, and their faces are red and sweaty. The conductor boards and pulls the leather cord twice to sound the bell to signal the gripman that it is safe to depart, and with a jolt the tram is off.

The conductor is dressed in the service's light-coloured summer uniform, cap and boots and he is sporting a wonderful handlebar moustache. Several large pins are attached to his jacket and hold thick strips of paper known as 'trip slips'. The slips are divided into squares and coloured according to the fare they represent – such as one or three pennies. The conductor looks hot and harassed but is stoically getting down to the business of issuing fares, which he does with the aid of his bell-punch, and by repeatedly announcing 'fares please'. Most of the passengers I notice have the standard fare of three pence at the ready, and the conductor moves through the tram collecting the coins in his leather pouch. While there are physical tickets that the conductor can issue – through and transfer tickets – the majority of the day's fares are ticketless. As each fare is handed over, he holds the punch against the trip slip and presses down. The punch simultaneously rings its bell – a not unpleasant tinkling sound – which signals the fare and creates a punch out of the slip, known as 'confetti', which is held inside the bell-punch. At the end of the day the conductor will hand over his takings and the bell-punch to the MTOC revenue clerk at the depot. From here rumour has it that the bell-punch is forwarded on to the central MTOC office, where two women, tasked with opening the bell-punch and counting the confetti inside, are the only people in the entire organisation who know the combinations to open every single bell-punch used on the network. (What if they both get sick?) The conductor's confetti needs to match the number recorded in the dial contained in the punch, and the day's takings. If he is short, he will pay the difference and face possible suspension or the sack.

The tram is crowded but the 'connie' is extremely polite, and moves his way through without pushing. I watch the conductor as he gets to the end of the aisle. Having collected all the fares inside, he exits the car and then, while the tram is running, deftly steps down to the road and quickly hauls himself up onto the dummy to start taking the fares up front – a manoeuvre possible because the tram is crawling at a snail's pace.

The tram rattles over the newly opened Queens Bridge, the city's second tram crossing of the river to the south. We head down Sandridge Road and turn left into Clarendon Street where the street climbs a hill – Emerald Hill – although I can't actually see much outside as the town's markets, terraces and shops are obscured by the press of people. There must be at least 50 crammed into the tram car and the air has a rich human odour. People don't wash every day in this era.

Sitting next to me is a large, bearded man with a canvas bag on his knee. Immediately in front of the man are two lanky boys holding onto the leather straps that hang down from the ceiling as the car wobbles from side to side in its journey. The tram is turning a sharp corner to the right and I hear through the tram car's open windows the cry of the gripman as we go around, 'Mind the curve!', the warning to passengers that he is required to utter on sharp curves and corners. We are now heading down Park Street towards the beach.

Across the tram car I can hear different varieties of English being uttered. The bearded man is talking to the boys, who appear to be his sons, in a deep Scots accent, which I find barely comprehensible, while they respond to him in the flat, uninflected tones of the city's native born. I think the man is discussing the boys' participation in an upcoming swimming carnival and is quizzing them about their likely chances. I gather that the boys have been taking swimming lessons for some time, and that the father is keen for them to demonstrate their prowess at the meet.

By 1890 swimming has caught on as a national obsession. Like others on the tram, the father and his sons aren't headed to the beach to swim in the bay but to the baths at the end of the tramway. The Tramways Baths at South Melbourne have been open for some years, since the opening of the cable trams, part of a contingent of baths strung out along the bay between St Kilda and Port Melbourne. The bay's bath houses are essential infrastructure in a city that bans public bathing and with a large proportion of its housing still devoid of bathrooms. People once bathed in the Yarra, but it became too filthy with garbage and effluent. There have been baths on the bay for men since the 1850s, but recently separate baths have opened for women. In the early days men swam nude at the baths but those days have gone. Nowadays it is knee to neck ensembles for everyone. Open sea bathing for adults is still illegal. Cable – the cheapest way to the beach.

The man and his sons will no doubt be holding concession tickets for the baths, issued separately by the conductor to those who ask and included in the price of the tram ride. I take a punt and ask the father how he thinks his boys will go at the upcoming carnival. He lets out a short whistle – an odd vocalisation – and then says he's not sure. Pointing to the taller of the two boys he says that his eldest would hold up well if he can get through the trials, but the younger one is a ways off. At least I think he said that. He's clearly as proud as punch of his boys and enjoying his day out with them. I ask him what his work is and he tells me that he works in an engineering shop in Fitzroy. Apart from his 'ayes', his accent is really unrenderable here, but I glean the following: the work is solid, never more than six days and 60 hours a week, so he has the time to take the boys to the beach. The tram to South Melbourne takes a 'devil of a time' to get to the beach compared to the train to St Kilda, but the crowds at St Kilda are 'fierce' and a day out there is no longer any fun. He can't believe how lucky he is, two strapping sons, a house that he might one day own, and a good job. 'I came out here 15 years ago on the assisted passage', he says, 'and have never looked back.'

The tram has swung left into Montague Street and now enters Victoria Avenue and people are gathering their bags and getting ready to disembark at the terminus. The tram has hardly stopped since leaving the city and everyone on board is clearly heading for the baths or the beach. The bearded man wishes me 'good day' as they get down and he and his boys cross Beaconsfield Parade to the beach. I stand on the corner. Across the parade are the Tramways Baths, an imposing structure, around and into which dozens of people are milling. The pub on the corner, the Bleakhouse Hotel, is doing a brisk trade – the doors and windows are all open and as I pass the waft of beer fills my nostrils.

The beach is crowded. Men are in suits and hats with their trousers rolled up so they can wade in the shallows, while women wear long white dresses, broad hats and carry parasols against the sun. Children paddle in the shallows but none of the adults are in. There are ice cream sellers, and men selling balloons. Families have spread out blankets on the sand, and opened picnic baskets. There is a slight breeze rolling up from the south, which makes the bay a few degrees cooler than the city. The bay is blue and sparkling, a huge water park that stretches as far as you can see. The people on its edge look ineffably relaxed. There are ball games being played, including cricket, kites are being flown, and there is a sound emanating from the beach that is familiar – the unmistakable hum composed of the carry of waves and human voices and summer heat.

*

Fast forward to the 1950s and the tram to South Melbourne Beach now has a number – number 1.

Route 1 travels 13.2 kilometres from East Coburg to South Melbourne Beach and covers much of the territory traversed by the original cable tram to the beach. On hot days in the late 1950s and early 1960s my mother and I would catch the number 1 tram to the beach during the week, spending the morning swimming and then lying in the sun on our beach towels, with no sunscreen or shade. The beach was uncrowded on these week days. My back was a peeling mess during summer. We would get changed in the beachside change rooms, which smelt of coconut oil and urine, and my mother always wore a blue single piece swimsuit. I remember Uncle Max, who I mentioned in passing above, joined us here once and recall him sitting on the sand in his suit, refusing to go in the water, with his trousers rolled up to his knees, his jacket and hat off, puffing on his pipe.

Coming back from the beach the three of us got off the tram and wandered into South Melbourne Market, where it was dark and cool. There was a man selling fairy floss – a sticky concoction seemingly made of air – and I begged my mother to buy me some. She resisted my incessant pleas while Max stood there laughing saying he would buy me some. My mother relented but wouldn't let Uncle Max pay for it. Her purse was coloured red and had a silver clasp that snapped when it shut. She hands the man the money and he twirls the floss onto a stick and hands it to me. One of her expressions to describe something really tasty was 'heaven on a stick', and she says this now with a laugh as the floss covers my cheeks and nose and hands.

11. Route 64: Looking for Engine Houses

T
he city's tram network began in 1885, quickly becoming one of the biggest tram networks in the world, and from 1885 to 1940 used cable as its driving technology. Clapp's boast that he could construct a system in just a handful of years (and as the Act mandates), turns out to be true. At a speed that would astonish today's architects and builders of major infrastructure, Clapp's MTOC creates Melbourne's cable tram system in just six years. Every year from 1885 to 1891 a new route is opened, with multiple routes opening up in most years. Over 46 miles (75 kilometres) of double track is laid, 16 routes are opened (to be expanded to 17 in 1897), and once completed, the system is running 490 dummy cars and 500 tramcars, and operating 11 steam engine houses and 15 tramcar sheds. (A twelfth engine house with tram car shed was built by a separate company to run a line from Clifton Hill up to Dundas Street Northcote in 1890. This line did not join the network until 1920.) Nearly all of the tram car sheds have been demolished.

The endless rope itself is imported throughout the 55 year life of the system. The trams for the first line, running from Spencer Street to Hawthorn Bridge in Richmond, are also imported from the United States, but thereafter all the rolling stock is built in the city, at North Fitzroy.

The world's largest, fully integrated cable tram system is immensely successful. The city's population is booming. Between 1880 and 1889, the population rises over 60 percent from 280,000 to

445,000, and keeps rising. There is, as Clapp predicted, huge demand for public transport and people flood onto the trams as the quickest and cheapest method of city travel. The MTOC is financially highly profitable and I truly wonder at the contrast with modern public transport systems, which frequently run at a loss. To the shareholders of the MTOC, the company pays a dividend of 20 per cent, while in good years the tramways employees enjoy an annual bonus of five per cent on their wages.

So where specifically are the cable tram routes? Have a close look at the map provided in the centre pages. The tram map shows a privileging of tram routes north and east of the Yarra over both the west and, to much lesser extent, the south. The cable routes east – through Richmond, Collingwood, Abbotsford – all terminate at the river. The cable routes north – through Brunswick, North Carlton, North Fitzroy and Clifton Hill – climb the low rise from the city and terminate at or close to the northern plains. The routes south of the Yarra run mostly to the bay, to the port and the beaches – Port Melbourne, South Melbourne and St Kilda. Prahran and Toorak have their routes, and another route terminates in Balaclava at Brighton Road. The city is criss-crossed with tram routes on major thoroughfares and there is a short route to inner West Melbourne.

Why avoid the west? It's been argued that this was due to the impassable marshlands and the rail yards on the western side of the city. Perhaps. It's certainly a long way to run a cable out to Footscray. But it's also possibly due to the prejudiced view of the city brethren about their western suburbs neighbours; by this time the west is seen as unclean, full of the stench of tanneries, abattoirs, foundries, chemical works and the miasma of diseases – tuberculosis, cholera, typhoid – which was all true. You don't live long over there at this time. Fifty tops.

Clapp had wanted to be both the builder and operator of the system but, as we know, things did not turn out this way. The 12 councils, whose jurisdictions were to be traversed by the new system, did combine together to form a trust – the Melbourne Tramways Trust –

to construct the track and build the engine houses, as foreshadowed under the Act. Clapp becomes the operator of the system, leasing the infrastructure back from the Trust under, as mentioned, a 30 year lease. The MTOC is responsible for the rolling stock and the operation and maintenance of the whole system. The Trust spends 1.7 million pounds on the infrastructure, an enormous sum for the period.

Rope. Cable. The endless chain. What is this stuff? The cables imported from the United States are composed of six strands of high tensile steel woven around a hemp core. As explained earlier, the cables, covered in oil, run continuously and invisibly over cast iron pulleys within trenches under the road. A small slot, less than an inch in width (actually 7/8ths of an inch!) in the centre of the rails, allows access for the grip operated by gripman. The tram thus trundles along pulled by cables which are of enormous length. The very first installed cable, for the Richmond line, runs almost 25,000 feet (approx. 7,500 metres).

The cables hum as they run and their humming is only audible when traffic is light or at night when the streets are deserted; they stretch in length with use, they wear out, can get tangled and frayed. Highly skilled teams of 'splicers' are on hand to maintain and repair them, and the days of the laying and threading of the new cables for each new route are communal events, with teams of horses and drays used to transport the cables from the docks, and crowds of onlookers watching as the street is transformed.

There are photos of the city streets being dug up – long lines of ordered mess, piles of earth and materials, concrete slabs, red gum stumps, metal wheels, a huge workforce to dig the trenches by hand, and the cables held together before their laying in massive circular loops, twice the height of a person. In 1885 when the Richmond line works are under way crowds come out each day to inspect the progress of the works that have disrupted their city and caused an endless blow of dust.

*

So, dear reader, you are no doubt busting to know the details of how the cable tram system was actually powered. (Not interested? You have my permission to skip this chapter.) But the answer to the question is simple enough: engine houses. Lots of them.

It's a bright late-winter's day when I go looking for the surviving engine houses, these central sites in the powering of the cable tram system. The night before I had consulted both Keating and Cranston for insights into the development of the city's cable tram engine houses. Many of them have survived into the 21st century, although some are no longer whole buildings but facades, and all have had their interiors renovated and equipment removed. None of the extant buildings announce what they once were by way of official heritage plaque or signage.

An engine house is a stand alone power house that drives the cables at a standard speed throughout the system. In the late 19th century city of Melbourne an engine house typically contains a boiler room and one or two powerful steam engines of 200 to 400 horsepower, which power a huge drive wheel 24 feet (7.3 metres) in diameter. Four hundred horse power is massive (equivalent to an engine size of 6,000 cubic centimetres). The main drive in turn powers two cable wheels, each of 12 feet (3.6 metres) in diameter, and around these the cables pass in a figure of eight formation before being fed to a smaller tightening wheel to maintain the cable's tension. The cables then run underground into the street.

The boilers burned combustibles and the smoke was exhausted from red brick chimneys, which belched black smoke that ruined locals' washing, not to mention the effect on their lungs. The chimneys were extended to a height of 150 feet (46 metres), the steam engines became more efficient, and emissions were less. None of the chimneys have survived.

The role of the engine houses is essentially functional, but they are also works of art designed to impress the viewer, and built at great expense. Styles vary but they are generally built with blue stone foundations, have patterned red and red-brown brickwork and various ornamental features, such as pilasters, turrets and urns, and other neo-classical motifs. All the engine houses have peep holes and window platforms, and at least one arched opening with a handrail, from where passersby can gaze into the interior and marvel at the works within.

I like the stories of the engine houses with all the equipment painted the same dark green, potted plants and shrubs around the spotless floors, and the employees dressed in the same scrubbed uniforms. The ceilings are enormously high and, despite the noise of engine, wheels and boilers, there is a strong sense of order – the engine houses are demonstrations of the 'age of progress', as Clapp called his era, and the power of rationalist enterprise.

I take the 96 along Brunswick Street to the corner with Johnson Street. The engine house is in Johnston Street just down from the Provincial Hotel. This engine house drove the cable along Brunswick Street, north and south, and is now a Coles store. Crowds of shoppers pour in and out its main door. The only thing left here is the façade, nice enough – dark and light brown brickwork, mixed with the occasional cream workings. A few Corinthian pilasters. It looks craggy and 'old', which right now, is just how I feel.

I hop on and off several trams to Northcote to find that the High Street engine house is now a car repair shop. It's big, masses of painted over brickwork, but again no indication anywhere of its history. As mentioned, this site, including the engine house and car depot, was not developed by the Trust and MTOC, but by a private company. The Clifton Hill to Northcote & Preston Tramway Company opened operations in 1890, using both cable car patents purchased from the MTOC and the expertise of George Duncan. The route ran from the Merri Creek bridge in the south, along High Street to Dundas Street in the north. It passed through a number of hands across its lifetime and had periods when it didn't operate, but was largely successful.

The 19 takes me to Brunswick Road, Brunswick. West of the Sarah Sands Hotel sits the engine house that ran the cables north up Sydney

Road and south into the city – at the time the longest cable in the system. It is now Sam's Tyres and Service Centre and the red brick has been covered in blue and white paint with bold red lettering. It's a true wonder to see the correct use of the apostrophe. Sam has fixed tyres on various of my cars. I had no idea his business inhabited an old engine house. I wander in and he comes out to say hello, assuming no doubt I've got some work for him. I explain what I'm up to and he calls over one of his workers. 'Mick knows all about the trams, he'll set you right', says Sam.

Mick does know his stuff. He shows me a circle in the floor near the doorway and tells me that that's where the cables, running north and south, entered the street undergound. 'The cable's gone but the wheels guiding the cables out are still under there', says Mick, 'too hard to dig them out so they've stayed.' Mick then walks me through the building pointing to various features in the walls and ceilings. The roof is incredibly high and now I see that the girders, frames and walls are original. There are the remains of pulleys, wall bracings and other indeterminate notches and grooves that are all steam engine house related. Mick is pretty excited to meet someone who's interested in trams, but our time is brief. He's called away to fix some tyres.

Across Princes Park and along Park Street, North Carlton I find the Rathdowne Street engine house, which runs the cable for trams up and down this street and is now an apartment conversion. This is one of the lines that was discontinued with the introduction of electric trams. The apartments look cheap and dark. They will never have even half the life span of the building they are wedged into. Why did they do this? The short answer is of course money, but there's a larger issue isn't there, to do with how our city treats, or more exactly mistreats its heritage, as if we have heritage to burn.

I'm tramming and walking. I get to the site of the Victoria Parade engine house on the corner of Brunswick Street. It's been demolished and in its place is a shiny new ACU University lecture hall. Down to the St Kilda Road engine house – one of the most important of the whole system given the number of trams and tram routes traversing this road – which became a luxury car sales room after it was decommissioned and is now a boutique hotel. I wander into and around the hotel foyer. In the corner there are several coffee table books and one of them catches my eye, a picture book of Melbourne's early tram network. I flick through the pages – marvellous photos from the cable era. I approach the front desk and ask the 'concierge', as his lapel indicates, what he knows about this book and the history of the building. He confesses that he knows nothing of that, and wasn't aware that the foyer had such a work lying around.

In North Melbourne, the engine house has preserved its exterior and had its interior converted into modern apartments. They look a bit better than the ones in Rathdowne Street. There was a long struggle by locals to stop the development, with various ideas floated about its potential use as a community asset.

The most impressive survivor is at the corner of Nicholson and Gertrude Streets in Fitzroy, opposite the Exhibition Buildings. Built in 1886–87 this engine house drives three cables and operates until October 26 1940 – the last of the engine houses to operate in the city. It is elaborately, boldly designed with window sills and volutes in bluestone, pilasters, piers, bi-chrome brickwork, urns and a sumptuous, corbelled polygonal signal box that sits above the parapet on the building's corner. This building says 'look at me', and this confluence of engineering, art, functionality and frivolity is a telling demonstration of the then city's pride in modernity. I can find not a single plaque, memorial or sign on, or adjacent to, the engine house to indicate what the building was or its significance. I wonder if the heritage authorities are 'hiding' the building in plain sight, in the earnest belief that in doing so, they are protecting it from vandals.

*

The following day I catch the 64 East Brighton tram to St Kilda. This is a Z3 class tram built in Dandenong in the 1980s. I found them ugly then, an unfortunate offspring of a system that was replacing my much-loved W class trams. With its distinctive chiseled front end and retro looks, the Z3 has now, almost 50 years later, acquired a certain nostalgic character and is testament to the stubborn durability of the city's tram fleet. I've come to appreciate them I guess. The tram turns from St Kilda Road into Queens Road and up to Chapel Street (stop 25 if you are interested) where I get down. I walk along Wellington Street to an establishment that calls itself the 'Engine House'. Just inside I meet the manager of this modern open plan work space, converted from the former steam engine house.

Although I had called him the day before to organise my visit, the manager seems under the impression that I want to rent work space. Perhaps I hadn't explained my purpose too well. Clients here can hire desk or bench space, or a sound-proof office; there are multiple businesses in the house. I tell the manager that I'm writing about cable trams, and although I'm no longer a prospective client, he happily gives me a short tour. The building retains some original features such as doors, archways, walls and concrete floors, but the front façade has undergone a facelift at some stage. This is the last of the engine houses to be built, in 1891, and runs the shortest cable route, from Windsor to St Kilda Esplanade. It is also the first engine house to close, in 1925.

It is the only intact engine house to have its whole interior converted to a modern purpose not to do with cars and tyres or apartments. The manager is proud of how well this old space functions and suits its new role. Just inside the entrance there is a poster banner briefly explaining the former role of the engine house and celebrating Francis Clapp as the system's originator. I stand in front of this in astonishment, my face flushed. Finally, someone has remembered him. Outside of the Hawthorn tram museum this is the only such dedication or remembrance of the cable system and Clapp that I've found.

Probably unwittingly, the modern Engine House reprises one of the earlier engine houses' interior features – around the room are plants, pot plants and a vine climbing around a metal stand. There's a gentle buzz of people working at their pcs and laptops. How different this soundscape is to the one that existed in this space 100 years ago.

Boilers, steam engines, spinning wheels, burning fuel, workers shouting above the noise, all combining to create a raucous cacophony. Now the sonic hum of keyboards, pcs and low conversations floats in the room, intense human activity nothing to do with the era of cable, and yet the scene is strangely comforting. Boiled down, everything human is a brief affair isn't it, a short journey to God knows where. Attached to the building is a cafe, where I have a coffee.

12. A Visit to Gog and Magog

I'm sitting in the middle section of the tram with my mother sitting opposite. It's an old tram with three doors open to the elements and the passing world is sharply defined. It's spring, a shining blue day with a light breeze, and my mother is to my eyes very beautiful – dark black hair, deep blue eyes, olive skin. I don't need to look at her to feel her presence – I must be four or five – but when I do she invariably looks back at me. We are on one of our trips 'to town', as she calls it: weekday jaunts, similar to our beach outings, that take us along St Kilda Road into the city on the number 8 tram. She doesn't tell me where we are going, it will be a surprise, a little game she plays, but I really don't care where we end up. These days are always good. I like looking at everything passing by, but also everyone getting on and off. Adults are so strange and fascinating. How do they do it? Getting around on their own, paying for fares, knowing when to get on and when to get off, dressed in such an array of oddities – ladies with feathers or pins sticking out of their hats, men with round hats, square hats or no hat at all, some with moustaches, others with beards (not many of them), others smooth faced. There's a whole bunch of smells on the tram too, from sweet and sticky to sharp and coarse. The passing parade is a fantasmagoria, the city seems endless in its differences and colours, the trams rattling up and down, up and down with a rhythm all their own.

We get down at Bourke Street and wander past huge department stores with showcase windows that are many times my size. They have larger than life models in them wearing the latest fashions. I can't stop staring at them, I'm sure I will catch one of them moving eventually, if I just stare at it long enough. My mother tugs my hand to get me moving again. I like holding her hand. As we go along through the city I see that people take notice of her as if she is some kind of celebrity.

We enter the Royal Arcade. I love the glass ceiling, the bow-fronted shop windows, and the two monsters at the southern end standing guard over the arcade. My mother tells me these characters, Gog and Magog, are ancient Celtic warriors who defended their lands from invasion. I have no idea what they are doing here in Melbourne, but they are impressive, particularly when they strike bells on the hour. The clock that stands between Gog and Magog is the biggest I've ever seen.

From the Royal Arcade we wander down to Collins Street and enter the Block Arcade. I know why we're here. There's a queue outside the Hopetoun Tea Rooms, which we join and wait patiently for a table. My mother and I stare at the cakes in the window while we wait. There's every imaginable colour and shape on display and I want to gobble all of them up. Inside my mother orders tea and scones with cream and jam. Magnificent! This room is perfect for gorging on cake and scones; from the chandeliers, the emerald wallpaper, the mirrors and white and gold china, to the hushed tones of the patrons, the clink of spoons on saucers. Afterwards we do some shopping at Myers, where the scent of perfumes makes me bilious, and then hop on a tram in Swanston Street to head home.

On the journey home I ask my mother about the two monsters in the Royal Arcade. She tells me a story about her ancestors in Scotland who were driven off their farms by some wicked men. Her ancestors had to get on ships and come to Australia. They got here with nothing. She doesn't connect this story with Gog and Magog though, so I'm a bit confused. She tells me not to worry. History is confusing she says, adding that I will understand better when I'm older. We are in the very front seats of the forward saloon and I can look out the window to where we are heading. The tram tracks curve away into the distance.

*

Was my mother's story about her ancestors being driven off their lands true? I've been doing some digging. My mother's mother, Euphemia, was a MacDonald whose forebears came from the Isle of Skye. In the early to mid-19th century the highland Scots were being 'cleared' from their ancient lands and their communities extinguished. The Scots of Skye faced a similar fate in the same period. Crofting families were marched off their properties and tenancies to the coast where they could farm kelp or board ships to unknown destinations. In the late 1840s or '50s one family of MacDonalds arrived in Warrnambool, where they would be based for most of the rest of the 19th century. Were they expelled from their ancestral homes? My mother's story fits the history so it's highly likely. They arrive in Australia having no idea of the country they've landed in, with nothing more than what they could carry with them. Boat people.

And what about her father, Percy Morey? I know a lot more about the Moreys because of the countless stories my mother told about them, and also because her sister gave me a folder of documents about the Moreys before she died. Percy's family had migrated as assisted passengers to the colony in 1853. They were from Devon and described in the documents as 'yeomen', polite speech for farm labourer. The Moreys are recorded as having the ability to read but not write. William Morey and his wife Sarah travelled on the *Earl Grey* with their two children and the trip took 109 days. Sarah was pregnant with her third child and gave birth on the voyage but the baby died soon after and was buried at sea. William got work in South Yarra as a gardener and handyman on a salary of 104 pounds a year 'with rations'.

Decades later the Australian-born Euphemia and Percy meet, either in Melbourne or up country near Wangaratta. They marry in Melbourne in 1906 and have six children, the last one of which is my mother. Her eldest sister is her senior by 26 years. Percy comes from a line of Morey market gardeners in Melbourne, but he decides to branch out and heads to the Mallee in 1910 or 1913 and, after several less than successful ventures, eventually becomes a horticulturist – a 'blockie' in local parlance – growing fruit trees, almonds and grapes, raising chickens, and a milker cow (called 'Bessy'). They make a good living and climb slowly up the ladder of economic security.

Here then are my mother's ancestors. Poor, rural, dispossessed, suffering loss, arriving in a country they'd never even seen pictures of. My mother grew up in a close Methodist household that believed in family, self-reliance and hard work. They were optimistic people, loved family gatherings, camping along the Murray River, playing cards, telling jokes. I know because every year my mother would take me up there on the train for a holiday. My aunts and uncles treated me like a prince while my cousins tortured me mercilessly.

Three of her siblings died before my mother was an adult, but the most profound impact on her came with the death of Euphemia when she was 13. Her childhood was instantly over. On top of losing her mother, she was made to leave school to help run the household. She always hated that she was 'uneducated'. And then, before she had left her twenties, her father dies.

Why am I going on about this and what does it have to do with trams? I'm not exactly sure. But clearly trams and my mother are strangely bound together in my mind, their histories in some measure, for me, intertwined. This at least I'm realising as I go along in this strange project.

13. The Gripman

Today I'm travelling in the Clifton Hill tram, heading out northwards through the city, and I'm sitting out in the open-air car at the front, which as you know goes by the curious title of the 'dummy' car, with the enclosed tram car behind. It's a warm day in early autumn 1891 and I'm perched on one of the wooden bench seats to the left of the gripman. The bench faces outwards and I've got panoramic views of the streets, people and passing parade of the old city in its heyday, bursting with movement and activity. The tram is painted red to signify its route from Collingwood to Clifton Hill and the destination is also painted on the front and sides of the tram. It's a very fine vehicle indeed sir! Running permanently on this route, with its familiar cable tram 'top knot' on the roof in the shape of a miniature pagoda, also painted red and visible from a mile away.

The gripman is standing behind me in the middle of the tram, but if I twist around I can watch as he manipulates the levers that effectively drive the tram. The gripman is tall, broad shouldered, tanned and dressed in a crisp uniform, white shirt and peaked hat. On his hat are perched a pair of goggles to aid his vision and protect his eyes in rain, sleet, wind and dust. He's wearing leather gloves too. His movements are fluid and expert as he shifts one lever then another, movements carried out without the gripman actually looking at the levers. He is continually studying the road for prospective passengers, turns and stops.

Denizens of our fair city appreciate the central role of the gripman in ensuring a safe and comfortable ride. But did you know that he can get the tram to its top speed – 13 miles per hour – in just a few seconds, and, conversely, bring the tram to a halt 'on a sixpence'? He has not one, but two brakes operated by levers; one applied to the wheels using cast iron shoes, while the other lowers blocks of hardwood directly onto the tracks.

I'll wager you don't really know what's going on under the road surface to propel the tram along. Well, you may lack the interest, after all the important thing is to get where you want to go isn't it? For your edification: through the slot in the roadway the grip operates as a clamp, attaching and detaching to and from the moving cable. The bottom half of the clamp is always fixed in position and the gripman lowers or raises the top half vertically to either grip the cable or release it: throwing his grip lever forward to release, pulling it back towards him to attach – an endless series of movements repeated over and over each day. Strong arms. I've learnt from speaking to the gripmen that at most stops, particularly on straight sections, they don't need to 'throw the cable'. By releasing pressure on the cable, but not enough to eject it from the clamp completely, the gripman can allow it to 'run free' within the two jaws of the clamp. Thus it becomes a straightforward matter to release the brakes and re-grab the cable to set off again.

I've been on trams once or twice when they've stalled going round a curve, the gripman having thrown the rope to get around without snagging. Everyone had to climb out and push the tram around, a highly embarrassing event. It had its funny side – watching men in bowler hats huffing and puffing as they push the stalled tram round the corner – but was incredibly annoying and tiresome for those involved. These stalls are usually the result of not enough momentum, a steep incline, or a very strong head wind, and some trams are just too overloaded in peak hour.

I hadn't had to wait long for the tram on the street. The service runs every two minutes and this tram is remarkably uncrowded, giving me views all around. The dummy can carry up to 20 people sitting on its bench seats. As we travel, passengers can hail the tram from anywhere in the street, and as the gripman slows the tram, some of these passengers board while the tram is still moving by jumping on the board at the foot of the benches and allowing the gripman to maintain forward momentum. This seems to be a minor and unspoken art form perfected between the tramway men and their passengers.

There is a leather cord hanging from the tram's ceiling, connected to a bell, that passengers can pull to indicate to the driver they wish to stop. But in the dummy car, most passengers tell the driver where they want to get off. One man in a dark suit and top hat says to the gripman, 'this is mine, up on the next corner', and the gripman slows and stops the tram to let the passenger disembark. Other passengers simply say to the gripman, 'this will do', and he either stops the tram to let them off, or they step off while it's still moving. There are major stops on the route: outside theatres, sports grounds, railway stations, big stores and major intersections, and some stops have rain shelters. Otherwise it's an open tram route that can be boarded and disembarked wherever someone hails the tram or signals they want to get off. So, if you live on a major street you can be literally dropped at your front door, as Clapp had promised.

We are now approaching the corner of Gertrude and Smith Streets, which presents a singular challenge to the tramway men. Not only is the corner extremely tight, the most severe corner on the system, it is situated at the drop of a hill. I watch as the gripman concentrates on the turn. He has the levers in his hands now and is making a series of adjustments – as they take the corner the tram lurches to the left and he calls out, 'Mind the curve!' No-one falls out of the tram on this occasion but it has happened. In 1888 there is a coroner's inquiry into the death of a man who tumbles off a cable tram at this intersection. The coroner concludes that the man was drunk and that neither the MTOC nor its staff were at fault.

The gripman is forbidden to speak to passengers but this rule is honoured more in the breach than the observance. The gripmen are known to whistle, hum and occasionally sing from their perch in the very middle of the open dummy. Conversations with passengers often occur depending on the character and inclination of the gripman. At the Birmingham Hotel stop a number of passengers board the tram, most heading for the tram car. One man, sporting a bowler hat, jumps onto the dummy car and greets the gripman with 'g'day Paddy, old son!' 'Paddy' is intent on the restart of the tram so not until we are down the road a bit does he turn to Mr Bowler Hat and reply with 'good morning Frank', and a conversation takes off between them – almost exclusively focused on football. Many of the city's gripmen have, or had, another life every Saturday playing football. These tall, strong men often play in the ruck, where the action is brutal; elbows, knees, knuckles and fists are part of the ruckman's armoury and integral to his role as team enforcer. A gripman can go to work on Friday with a full set of teeth, and return on Sunday with a toothless grin.

Frank wants to know how Paddy's team, Collingwood, is going to fare on the weekend when they take on Melbourne. 'I've got a lot riding on this game Paddy, put a few quid down at reasonable odds. Tell me I'm not dreaming. You'll give it to those toffs won't you?' Paddy stares out at the road ahead and from the corner of his mouth asks Frank how much exactly has he got on the game. Frank tells him that he's put up three guineas with the local tote and he will triple his money if the Magpies win. Paddy lets at a low whistle and says, 'You must be a flash character Frank to have that much lying around.' Frank laughs nervously. He's a short, sweaty man, with that look of quiet desperation common to gamblers who can't actually afford to gamble. 'Now come on Paddy', Frank continues, 'those Redlegs are a bunch of cream puffs, knock them over will you. The old one-and-two. They don't call you the Flying Elbow for nothing Paddy! Give them some hack and whack will you. I'll be there at the cricket ground, standing room I expect, big crowd no doubt for this one, real grudge match.'

The tram is about to negotiate the turn into Alexander Parade and Paddy once more calls out, 'Mind the curve!', as he juggles the tram around the corner at speed. We all lurch to one side momentarily before the tram rights itself and heads up the hill to Clifton Hill. Along this block Frank stands up preparing to get down. There's no formal stop but Paddy clearly knows where Frank wants to get off. He slows the tram allowing Frank to step clear, which he does with a short jump. As the tram pulls away Frank waves to Paddy as he crosses the road, and yells, 'Sharpen those elbows Paddy!' Paddy's eyes are fixed on the road ahead.

On our way up the hill empty plots of land are interspersed with two-storey brick houses, recently built. The most prominent feature in the landscape is the church spire. The roads are broad and mostly empty away from town but there are the occasional carts and buggies, horses, hansom cabs, bicycles, other trams heading to the city, and pedestrians. I notice again that walkers cross wherever they like, and others walk down the middle of the road careless of danger until they are honked or belled out of the way. The gripman has a gong that sends out a note of clear resonance, a pleasing timbre. When I caught the tram earlier in Bourke Street the whole city clanged and echoed with the bells and gongs of the trams.

At the Clifton Hill terminus I step down to help the crew shunt the tram. The cable trams can only be run one way, with the dummy car leading, so must be separately shunted at each end of the line. Usually this works fine, with the dummy shunted onto the opposite track on the first shunt to take up its lead position, followed by the tram car shunted on the second shunt across and behind the dummy. But today there's a strong wind blowing up from the bay and I help the crew push the tram car a few feet forward to be hooked up to the dummy. After, I stand for a minute next to Paddy, who towers over me. He's a giant of a man. He mutters 'thanks' and re-enters the tram to drive it back to the city.

*

Just a few years before in February 1888 our Paddy was on strike. The trammies' grievances included long hours, low wages, irregular meal times and unfair treatment. The cable trams might have been a favourite employment destination but the work came with a cost. The MTOC had interpreted section 62 of the Act to mean they could work their employees 60 hours a week on a regular basis, and overtime pay appears to have been largely unpaid. It was reported by *The Age* that after three days the strike began to collapse – the company was sacking strikers and replacing them with new staff – with over 200 tram workers losing their jobs.

A Royal Commission into working conditions on the trams was not held until a decade later, by which time the Depression of the 1890s had decimated the union movement across the country. Jack Cranston reports the Commission finding that from the onset of the Depression, 'there appears to be an ever recurring desire on the part of the company to reduce the men's wages...'.

Francis Clapp remained staunchly anti-union throughout his reign, a stance that was in part the result of his heritage, with its focus on individualism and entrepreneurship. But his position put him at odds with the general development of industrial relations in the colony and later the country. In good years, Clapp's employees generally worked less hours than their counterparts in other jurisdictions and for higher wages. J. D. Keating points out that in the general turn down of the 1890s, when wages across the board were being reduced, including for workers of the MTOC, Clapp slashed his own salary by the same proportion. Regardless of such acts of *noblesse oblige*, Clapp's antediluvian stand on unions was eventually overturned in 1913 with the formation of the Australian Tramways Employees Association (ATEA).

Somehow Paddy survived the sackings in 1888 and kept his job.

14. Central Park on the Number 5

I'm looking at one of the photographs I mentioned earlier that is over 60 years old. In it two figures are sitting on swings next to each other. One is in her twenties and the other is about five. They are staring at each other these two – the five year old looking to his right and the young woman to her left – and the only word that adequately describes the look on their faces is adoration. I'm trying to work out where this photo was taken and by whom. There is a park in the background and a building of some sort. My mother is wearing a floral dress with shoulder straps, while I'm in shorts and a shirt with vertical stripes. We both wear sandals. Must be a warm day. I have blond hair that waves at the front while my mother has her black hair down. She's wearing sunglasses, her fingernails and toenails are painted, and she looks kind of Parisian. For once she has not been captured with a cigarette in her hand or mouth, a common motif in photos of her. I'm holding on to the swing chains with both hands while she is sitting with her arms wrapped around those of her own swing.

This framed photo has been on my mantelpiece for years. I have an idea now where it was taken. I think it's at a park we used to visit on our tram trips around town, out east in Malvern. What tram is that? Ah yes, route 5. Why did we go out there and who or what did we visit? Ok, off we go down memory tram.

The route 5 to East Malvern is a lovely tram journey to take. The 5 is a combination of histories: the cable tram network from the 1880s, the Prahran and Malvern Tramways Trust (PMTT) in 1910, and the M&MTB in 1929. It's a little over 12 kilometres and takes its time winding through Melbourne south from the city and then out to the eastern suburbs. Riding the 5 will add another journey to my list, I may find the park in that photo, and on the way, will visit my old friend Ralph who is seriously ill in a Malvern hospital. As we go I remember my mother and I in a W tram on this route, sitting in the drop-down centre section on a wooden seat, with the canvas weather blinds up, soaking up the world passing.

The wooden seats were hard but at least they were straight. Today's tram is a D1 class, the class, as I said earlier, imported from Germany in the early 2000s. I now don't really mind the look of the tram, but the seating to be honest is sub-par. Many of the seats force the passenger to sit with their legs angled away from their hips, towards the aisle of the tram. It is the kind of design mistake that the manufacturers of the city's cable and W class trams would never have made, the result apparently of a flaw in the tram's structure. By the end of the journey my back will be aching.

I've picked up the 5 in Swanston Street, sharing it and St Kilda Road with a bundle of routes. Did I mention that the tram operator claims that this stretch is the busiest tram corridor in the world? There are many claims made about our system, including that we have more tram track laid – 250 kilometres – than any other network, which appears to be true, but doesn't take into account that most cities with tram networks are far more compact than ours. What is truly amazing is that our system carries over 200 million passengers a year.

At St Kilda Junction the 5 turns left up Queens Way and then crosses Chapel Street into Dandenong Road, where it has its own exclusive way in the centre of the wide boulevard. Mature elms line the track on both sides, their branches creating a green tunnel through which the tram glides. Out the front of the tram I can see that the tram's power lines are strung on metal poles that have elaborate scroll work on their sides and which are placed in the centre of the thoroughfare, at odds with the usual practice of curb poles. The elms aren't the original plantings - there were different trees here 100 years ago. The proposal to remove the road's colonnade of mature pine trees in the early 20th century was met with local resistance, which ultimately failed, and the trees were cut down.

The tram now takes a left, curving turn into Wattletree Road and enters the suburb of Malvern. Early Spring, the wattles are in full bloom, and the architecture is a mix of Victorian and later styles. I'm in the midst of the middle-class territory of the city's east, and the houses, as we travel further, become gradually larger and more refined. Many of them sit behind high walls. There are few people walking the streets. When I get down at the Cabrini hospital stop I notice that the smoke haze which has hung over the city for days has thickened. The air carries the distinct odour of burnt eucalyptus, in this city of shorter winters and longer bushfire seasons.

When I get to the nursing station on Ralph's floor the duty nurse tells me his room number and says that he is asleep and unlikely to wake up. In a day or two he will be moved to hospice care. I haven't seen Ralph for a few months and the last time I did he was fit and well so his sudden decline from liver disease has been a shock. I find the room and sure enough he is fast asleep, so I pull up a chair and wait. There are various lines entering and exiting his body and I think how easy it would be for them to come loose if he turns in his sleep. Ralph is perhaps my oldest friend from high school days and we are seriously a chalk and cheese couple. I don't know how it came about. He has always loved cars, boats, and gambling – never much into reading or introspection – and he's wealthy, owning a string of properties across the city and the peninsula. My one marriage compares to his four, I don't own a car while he has a garage full of them, he likes to holiday at Lake Como or St Moritz and I go to Ko Samui. Something about it works; his exuberance to my reticence, his ability to take me out of myself, his endless sociability which I always marvel at and secretly admire. There are no tram stories about Ralph.

As he sleeps I think about how Ralph knew and liked my mother, who he invariably addressed as 'Mrs G'. They both loved telling stories – yarns that were clearly embroidered accounts of their days, or people they knew – and I was often, in these moments that took place in the kitchen as my mother prepared the evening meal, relegated to the position of chief listener. I didn't mind. We were living deep in the outer suburbs by then and I was drifting out of my mother's orbit and into the world of sport and more sport.

When my mother died 20 years ago Ralph came to the funeral. He was the only one of my friends there that day to appear to be genuinely upset. In fact, he was outwardly more distressed than I was. Not that I wasn't suffering, but I had entered a kind of numbed state from the moment I heard she had passed. People spoke to me and I answered, but it was if I was speaking from somewhere deep underwater. But Ralph was visibly upset, so much so that some of the funeral attendees, who had not seen me since I was a toddler, assumed that Ralph was her son, and came across to give their condolences to him. He didn't disabuse them, but stood there thanking them for coming.

Ralph continues to sleep. His breath is laboured and every now and again his body jerks about – short spasms that quickly subside. After a few minutes of sitting there I'm wondering what the point is. He doesn't know I'm here and isn't going to wake up. I go back to the nursing station. I say I've heard that hearing is one of the last of the senses to go. If I talk to Ralph is there any chance he could be hearing me? The nurse encourages me to talk to him and for as long as I wish. It's quite possible he could hear you, she says, and anyway it will be good for you to do it.

I start off scratchily, not really knowing what to say. Then certain memories come back, from our days at school, various adventures and misadventures, events I haven't thought about in decades. After a while I'm speaking without any restraint, telling him all the things that bothered me about him – his loudness, self-regard, his endless plans and schemes that came to nothing. But also all the good things about him that I admire and envy – his self-confidence, his lack of fear, his joyfulness. I remembered him saying once, after several bottles of red, that he was so in love with the world that he wanted to eat it – to taste every morsel of reality, to have it all glowing inside him. I tell him that he's been a generous spirit, constant and forgiving, a nutcase for sure, an egotist, a dreamer, restless and driven. I tell him that I love him and that I can't believe he still has a luxuriant head of hair – silver now but abundant. I pat the hair gently and leave.

I take the elevator back down to ground level and wander into the street. Outside the air has cleared under the effect of a southerly wind up from the bay. I board the next tram heading east. I have this heavy feeling as if a stone has been dropped into my stomach.

We arrive at the terminus where Wattletree Road crosses Burke Road. It's a simple terminus, just a shunt with shops on one side and the park on the other. In over 100 years no-one has thought to extend the 5 the short distance down Wattletree Road to Waverley Road, so everyone living in that block has to walk up to Burke Road to catch the tram. The network is full of these anomalies. Just back from the terminus is a block of red brick flats, or should I say, there used to be such a building. I'm standing in front of another structure that occupies the site of the former flats. It's built in that indeterminate-modernist style that speaks to money and little else.

Before she moved to the nursing home my Aunt Bea, my father's sister, lived here, and occasionally my mother and I would drop in on her for a visit. Was it Bea who took the photo of my mother and I on the swing? I wander across the road into Central Park, still full of my visit to Ralph, and not really seeing much. I get out my phone. There I read that the 19 acre park was laid out in 1908 and has one the oldest conservatories in the state. It's one of the gems of the city's parklands, which dot the city like islands of sanity and repose. Trams connect us citizens to our beautiful parks: Wattle Park and Royal Park, Edinburgh Gardens and Carlton Gardens, Fawkner Park and Queens Park, Caulfield Park and the Botanical Gardens, to name just a few.

As I walk I recall my mother and I in this park on a warm spring day. I go across the oval to the playground on the other side but the old playground with its swings has been demolished and replaced. I turn around and there's the glass conservatory, a 'hot house' she called it, nearby. That's the structure in the background of the photo I'm sure.

I see us here – we go into the conservatory which is full of flowers called orchids, she tells me, and they are of all different varieties and in bloom. The colours are exuberant and their shapes resemble strange insect-like creatures. They are a bit too animal-like, too real, as if they are about to bite me, or consume me. The glass house is rather humid and there is a rich earth smell, as if someone has been sick. I hold my mother's hand, which is cool and smooth. She turns to someone behind us and says it's time to go.

*

Medical update. Some of you have been asking about my health – no doubt concerned that I may not be able to complete this master work before my demise. Dear reader, thank you for your concern, which I can assure you I share in abundance. Well, Dr Bun has completed another round of tests and reviews and he is, quote, 'reasonably satisfied' with the results. Meaning I'm not dying yet. No guarantees. It is, and I wasn't aware of this fact, a slow to medium growth tumour, which apparently is good news. I'm to call him immediately if I get a sudden onset of symptoms. Not just a headache which I should expect, but severe migraine, dizziness, sweats and so on and so forth. Otherwise see you in three months. I was glad to leave his rooms. Always the poorer.

15. At the Workshops

Today I'm visiting the MTOC's workshops in Nicholson Street North Fitzroy. The workshops comprise three shops – the iron shop, the wood shop and the paint shop. It's here that the MTOC has been building its tram-sets for the last four years. After the original purchase of 20 tram-sets from New York to run the Richmond line in 1885 all the trams have been constructed in Melbourne using local materials and labour. In a short clutch of years Clapp's teams have manufactured hundreds of trams for the new system and they are truly works of art. Today I want to see how they are put together. I'm meeting the site manager Harry, who has agreed to let me in for a short visit to two of the shops, the wood shop and the paint shop. He says that the iron shop, which produces the undercarriages, wheels, grilles and the grip mechanisms is off bounds to visitors due to the risk of injury. But he says, I will be fine in the other two, provided 'none of the workers decides to clobber you with a plane or stab you with a paint brush', a comment delivered in such a dead-pan way that I'm unsure what I've let myself in for.

We enter the wood shop and I'm immediately struck by the powerful smell of new cut wood. The workshop has an enormously high cantilevered roof, which has a wide clerestory on the south side allowing a smooth even light to flood the space. Several teams of men are at work on different stages of production. On the left hand wall are a series of shelves that hold wooden pieces of different sizes and shapes. The floor is covered in wood shavings and there are offcuts lying here and there in piles. There is a line of work bays adjacent to the shelving and here I see some long bench seats for tram cars in the making. Work benches are covered in planes, sandpaper rolls, drills, hammers and vices.

The men work together on each car, and right in front of me in the centre of the shop four men are at work constructing a dummy car. They're dressed in overalls and work aprons and have their sleeves rolled up and none of them are smoking, it being forbidden in the shop. They look up briefly when Harry and I enter but quickly get back to work when they realise I'm not an official from head office. The dummy being put together is sitting on a wooden stand so that the men can work at the right height. One chap is planing, another is sandpapering and the others are slotting the rear struts that hold the dummy roof into place. They are working quickly and there's hardly any talking going on, which surprises me, but then Clapp's MTOC is renowned for efficiency and working to tight deadlines, so idle chatter is probably frowned upon here. Clapp is lucky to have such skilled workers at his disposal. These men are the cream of the carriage-making business, capable, well paid and reliable. Clapp has been smart too – the workforce needed for his omnibus company has largely transferred over to the MTOC, including the carpenters. Wooden coaches have been hand-made in the city for 40 years, for both private and public use, and it's an industry with a tradition of fine workmanship and products that last decades.

I'm looking at the internal struts on the dummy and marvelling at their artistry. Not content with a simple rectangular block, the designers have called for the struts to be lathed, so that they rise elegantly with grooving on each edge and a slight tapering. The bench seats, made of grained wood, which face outwards, are slanted so that they don't puddle in the rain and wonderfully curved to fit any backside. The dummy roof is also made as a curved canopy, with the pagoda-like 'top-knot' sticking up like a hat – this is the chimney for the oil lamp underneath. Behind this dummy car there are several others also in various stages of production. On my right there's a dummy that is sitting on the iron undercarriage. It's been brought into the shop from the iron shop next door on rails that go deep into the building. It looks like it's complete – all the iron fretwork and the grip mechanism are there – so will soon, I imagine, be wheeled over to the paint shop. I can also see at the back of the shop a tram-car in the final stage of construction. The builders are using Australian woods, mainly Tasmanian mountain ash, Queensland maple and blackwood.

As we wander down to the rear of the shop Harry tells me that when cars and dummys are put together with their undercarriages they are 'damned heavy things'. The dummies weigh nearly three tons, while the cars weigh in at two and a half tons. We're standing now next to a just completed tram-car. It has eight windows on each side, which have wooden shutters that can be pulled up, sliding doors at either end of curved doorways, two windows at the front and long bench seats facing in on both sides. The platforms at either end each have a curved verandah over them, while the roof itself has a clerestory running the length of the roof. The tram-cars carrying capacity is supposed to be 56 people, but I've seen this rule breached more times than not. What I haven't ever noticed is that every tram-car has its own brakes situated at the end of each platform that can be operated by the conductor in an emergency. People can sit in the dummy – a popular place to perch oneself on a sunny day – but no-one is allowed to stand in front of the gripman or on the sides. The gripman has to have a clear view ahead so this part of the rule is observed, but the sides no-standing rule just shows that some rules are there to be broken. I notice that the undercarriage of the car has iron springs sitting right above each of the four wheels. I would have really liked to see the iron shop at work.

Harry is now guiding me over to the paint shop. I can tell he's getting a bit restless with this visitor with too many questions, and sure enough as we enter the shop he says that I will have to be quick – he's got the bosses coming down from Bourke Street and he needs to prepare for them.

The minute I enter the paint shop I'm assailed by a different smell entirely – pungent paint fumes. There's a lot of open windows and the doors too are wide open but the smell is overpowering and I grab my handkerchief to mitigate the effect, an action Harry finds amusing. Here there are teams working on the tram-sets completed by shops one and two. As I wander round I forget the smell and stare in wonder at the beautiful workings in progress. The painting team all wear smocks which are covered in splodges of paint in every colour imaginable. They mix their own paint here Harry tells me, so that there's a high standard to the quality and consistency of the paints applied to the trams. This shop is even quieter than the wood shop, with barely a word being uttered. Everyone is intent on what they are doing, concentrating on their paint-work, and rarely looking up.

As I've noted, the cable trams are colour coded by route. There's red for Brunswick, Victoria Bridge, Prahran and Northcote; green for North Melbourne, South Melbourne and St Kilda Beach; blue for Richmond and Nicholson Street; white for Port Melbourne and Brighton Road; brown for West Melbourne and Windsor-Esplanade; yellow for Toorak and North Fitzroy. The route colours are the dominant colour of the tram, including the top-knot. But the destination colours are complemented in each tram by other colours. The roofs and lower panel are white, there's lovely scroll work in different shades, bordering lines on panels, iron-work given colourful touches and the lettering is brilliantly done – clear, concise and perfectly aligned. All the trams tell you where they are going both by colour and the painted destinations. Here's a tram-car with the top panel almost finished – it reads, 'Rathdowne, Lygon & Swanston Sts & St. K...', done in yellow lettering on a green background. The concave lower panel is inscribed with large letters that read, 'NORTH CARLTON & ST KILDA'. The dummy also gets its share of the written word, with routes and destinations.

The visual cohesion for each tram is provided not by paint but by varnish. The grained woods of seats and other areas are strikingly rendered with layers of varnish, which is then polished to a deep sheen. Lustrous. The fresh varnish does really hit the nose though! The painters are also responsible for labelling each tram with the rules that apply to passengers. On the upper inside panels there's,

'Please close up and make room for others', 'Passengers must not stand on front or side of Dummy', and 'Passengers hold on while rounding curves'. On the doorway to the tram-car is the notice, 'No Smoking'.

Harry is hurrying me out. He's got to meet the bigwigs from town. A pity. Once I got used to the smell I was enchanted by the work being done here. There's a finished tram-set near the entrance. It's a beautiful object in anyone's language. I really like the contrast between the open dummy and the enclosed car, but most of all is the sense that the whole structure, its amenity, pattern, shape and colour is designed to sing. How wonderful to think they will still be singing long after I've departed from this earth.

16. Grand Junction

I'm catching a tram from Queens Road through the disaster that is the modern St Kilda Junction, after an uneventful tram ride. The original St Kilda Junction was one of the city's finest, if not its greatest. Eight roads intersected here, with traffic in all directions – trams, buggies, cars, trucks, people. Three hotels faced the Junction, dozens of businesses, shops and over 150 residential houses. All of this was demolished in the late 1960s and early '70s to make way for roads. This act of vandalism had its apogee with the destruction of the Grand Junction Hotel in 1973. The hotel was a marvel. Situated on the south side of the intersection and opened in 1889 the hotel was designed in a V-shape at the corner of two roads (think the Flatiron Building in New York and you have the idea). Neo-classical, multistorey, it sported a tall tower at its front corner with an enormous flagpole, where the St Kilda Football Club's flag was flown when the club was victorious.

The building was one of the city's grandest creations, a rival to the CBD's Coffee House in Collins Street, also destroyed by Whelan the Wrecker in 1973. It housed numerous parlours and sitting rooms, bars, baths, guest rooms with grand pianos, stables at the rear, and a roof top promenade for viewing the city and the bay. The building's tower had an enormous gas fuelled light, replete with reflectors, that lit up the night sky.

The Grand Junction flew the Saints' flag for a reason. Just down the road is the Junction Oval, first established in 1856, and still standing. Football started here in 1870 and it became the home of the St Kilda Football Club for almost 100 years. Fitzroy Football Club later played here for a couple of decades until the mid-1980s and when I lived in Grey Street in St Kilda I used to wander down here to watch the Roy boys play. (Incidentally, Clapp lived in Grey Street in the 1870s, where one of his four daughters was born. But did he go to the footy?) It was really something in the 1980s to witness Bernie 'Super-boot' Quinlan destroy the opposition with his massive and accurate kicking. Tall and powerful, he could have been a gripman in the old days.

I do remember the Junction as it was. Peel back the decades and I'm sitting in the back seat of my parents' car. Am I six, seven? Somewhere around there. I lean forward with my elbows splayed, resting my arms on the back of their front bench seat. The car is stopped at the lights and my father has just pointed out to me the signal box on the upper part of the building across the road and the ladder leading up to it. Inside the box I can see the shadowed form of the signal man, who is operating the points and traffic lights for the busy intersection. The signal box and its ladder look rickety and I worry that the whole thing might topple over into the intersection. The signalman manages the flow of trams and traffic using levers and a set of buttons, which operate the points that determine the direction the trams will travel in. Over 100 trams cross every hour during the peak, so the signalman has to be on his toes. Many, many changes of the points. Get it wrong and your tram sails off to the wrong suburb.

The day is hot, the windows of the Holden are down and the trundle of the passing W trams fills the car. My father has straight, brown hair that shines with brylcream, while my mother wears a floral dress and is smoking and blowing the smoke out the window. My father is so proud of this new car, the first car in our family, and recently acquired. We are headed out somewhere special for lunch on a Sunday, the day that will come to be allotted for trips in the car – to the beach at Aspendale, to the hills, down the coast – taking with us a blanket or towels to sit on, a basket full of food and a thermos of coffee. This new alternative to public transport. My parents are very young, both of them lithe and fresh in early adulthood, with acres of world and life ahead. Are they pleased to be in the car at the Junction with each other, with their son leaning between them?

17. The Language of Route 58

Route 58 is a meld of two routes: in 2017 it replaced in its entirety route 55 from West Coburg to the Domain Interchange and combined it with the southern leg of route 8 from the Domain to Toorak. Thus, the 8 disappeared and with it a tangible trace of my city jaunts with my mother.

Today, courtesy of my pin drop, I've joined the 58 to West Coburg at its stop under the Flinders Street viaduct, on the upper side of which trains travel to and fro between Flinders Street Station and Southern Cross. The viaduct is supported by a series of arches faced in dark red brick, and as the trains pass overhead they make a huge noise that rattles those below. Cars, buses, people and trams flow in all directions under the viaduct, towards Market Street in the north and across the river to the south. Against one of the red brick walls a group of people have established a camp with bedding and belongings strewn along the pavement. A kelpie is running around the group barking excitedly. More and more people are homeless as the housing crisis worsens. Yes, most livable city five years in a row, unless you are on the starvation wage of the dole.

The driver sounds the bell and the tram heads north up Market Street. It does a hard left half way up into Flinders Lane, then a hard right into William Street. Since 2019 the trams have been powered by renewables, but before that it was the electricity supplied by the coal-fired power stations of the Latrobe Valley. War hero, engineer extraordinaire and creator of the SEC John Monash would've loved the advent of renewables. The street is a 21st century canyon of glass, concrete and steel, leavened here and there by architectural survivors from the 19th century. A view of William Street would not be complete though without the sighting of 'black crows' (a.k.a, the lawyers in their gowns), who regularly prowl this end of the city, and it being lunchtime there are numerous 'murders' of them, busily heading to local eateries.

The tram is passing the Flagstaff Gardens, where in the 1840s the colonial authorities erected a flagstaff to signal to ships in the bay. A black metal ball was hauled up the flagpole every day by rope and then dropped on the stroke of midday. Set your watches folks! We stop at the Queen Victoria Market where a large number of people climb aboard with shopping trolleys, backpacks and assorted bags, and then head towards Flemington Road along Peel Street, passing one of the city's earliest extant hotels, the 1863 Victoria Hotel. The tram turns into the wide avenue of Flemington Road with its row of hospitals. At the Royal Children's Hospital stop there are pictures of cuddly animals for the kids arriving at the hospital by tram.

Now, for me, the truly interesting part of the journey. Before I get into the history of the 58 let me introduce you to the topography the tram is about to traverse – the biggest park in inner Melbourne. At 450 acres, Royal Park is an immense lung for the city, composed of expanses of grass and bushland – native grasses, acacias, eucalypts, casuarinas, wetlands. Some elderly red gums are hundreds of years old, and like much of the city this is Wurundjeri territory, and was their familiar living space.

Less concerned with Aboriginal living spaces, Governor La Trobe saw the value of this land, and set aside 10 square kilometres in 1850 as a park for the new city. It's been eaten at over the decades since, with various institutions gobbling up sections north and south. The Melbourne Zoo, which sits in the centre of the park, was established in 1861. During World War Two US army soldiers were camped here in their thousands. The US soldiers Walter saw fighting on his 48 tram with the Aussies no doubt would've been camped here. The buildings constructed for the US army, called Camp Pell, were converted after the war as housing for homeless families, and because of the appalling state of the facilities, renamed by them Camp Hell. The park is home to ducks, herons, hawks, parrots, honeyeaters, wrens, galahs, possums, lizards, water rats. The humans have constructed playing fields for soccer, football, baseball, cricket, netball and a vaste swathe is given over to golf. The land undulates up to Brunswick from the south and is crisscrossed with bike and walking paths.

I took this tram to work for many years when I lived in West Brunswick, and have always loved the incongruity of a city tram travelling through bushland on its own exclusive way. The tram now glides over the space of the park, through groves of casuarinas and wattle, yellow grass lands and the immense red river gums. I recall that red gums provided much of the material for the substratum for the city's cable trams, and wonder if it was sourced from here. But this route 58 tram, formerly the 55 as I said, was never a cable tram route. After many years of local agitation, an electric tram route from West Brunswick to the city was agreed upon in 1923 and work began on the line that year. By 1927 the route was complete and ran from Bell Street to the city, along the line I'm travelling. For a while the then 55 went to St Kilda beach but later terminated at the Domain interchange. Then, as I've noted, in 2017, in a move that dismayed many, the 55 was combined with the route 8 tram to Toorak to create the 58, making the journey over 18 kilometres and subjecting the route to endless delays due to traffic congestion. Short shunts – where the driver turns a late running tram around at a shunt well before the terminus, offloading all the passengers – became the order of the day, with lots of angry people waiting for the following tram, which was usually bursting at the seams. The magisterial forethought of a minister of the crown at work.

The tram trundles across Elliott Avenue and slowly makes its way past the State Netball Hockey Centre and the rear of the Zoo. It slows to walking speed as it negotiates the corner turn under the red brick railway bridge. At the stop at Royal Park Station, the tram doors open and I can hear the cries of baboons across the Zoo walls. This is a great way to come to the Zoo from the city, but it's not the first tram to do so. The 58 takes the west side of the Zoo, but originally a horse drawn tram travelled on the east side to the main entrance.

Started in 1890, the four wheeled tram was pulled by two horses, had a driver but no conductor, and ran from the corner of Gatehouse Street and Royal Parade, where it connected with the Brunswick cable tram. Passengers on the cable tram could use their fare to travel free on the horse tram. It was a very short ride, about half a mile, but it was popular. The open cross benches no doubt filled quickly on the weekends, with patrons lugging their picnic baskets and excited children. These 'feeder' horse trams were dotted around the cable system, giving patrons the option of a short ride to areas not covered by cable. The Zoo tram was one of the longest running of these until in 1923 it was destroyed by a fire deliberately lit by vandals during the crazy period of the police strike of that year. Many places across the city were trashed and shops looted. The stables, tram shed and carriages at the Zoo were all destroyed in the fire but the horses escaped.

We've crossed Park Street and have entered West Brunswick, an area I've always liked. The tram goes along Grantham Street, takes a left at Dawson, and a curving right into Melville Road, where it will continue until it hits the terminus at Bell Street. I'm thinking about lunch, and there are two places I have in mind – Mr Truong's Banh Mi shop on the corner of Hope Street, and the Filimex Authentic Sushi Bar just back from Moreland Road. What would you choose dear reader?

I'm pondering my choices when I notice a soft murmuring noise emanating from my neighbour opposite. A young bearded man has his head enveloped by large headphones. He's staring at his phone and is apparently engaged in some form of verbal exercise – there are silent pauses between the mutters, and now that I'm focused on them it's clear the mutters are the fragments of another language. He looks up from his phone and seeing the no doubt quizzical look on my face says immediately that he's sorry for the noise he must have been making. 'I forget where I am when I'm practicing', he says, 'so instead of just mouthing my responses I'm mumbling them out loud like an idiot.' This is how my conversation with Timo begins, and it's a beauty.

Timo is from Finland and he's here doing a master's degree in comparative linguistics. He's been in the city for six months and tells me that it's the biggest and 'most fabulous' city he has been to. 'I'm constantly amazed by how much is going on here, and how the city stretches for kilometre after kilometre.' Timo tells me that he chose Melbourne because of a particular professor who he wanted as a supervisor for his thesis, which focuses on acoustic phonetics and semantics. 'Yes, these are very odd bed fellows aren't they', says Timo, although I haven't made any comment. 'I'm really terrifically interested in how sound and meaning come together in different languages', he continues, 'and my professor is truly an authority in this area. But also I get to study in this wonderful city, which even has trams, my favorite form of transport.' Jackpot. I tell Timo that, depending on how he chooses to look at it, this is his lucky day, since my current project is precisely that – trams.

Our conversation oscillates between linguistics and trams. His thesis is really beyond my understanding but his discussion of the different languages he's studied over the years is entertaining. Here's someone who speaks multiple languages – Italian, Spanish, Chinese, English, and of course Finnish. He's now learning Japanese, which was the source of his mumbling earlier. He says some startling things about languages. I'll try and paraphrase part of what he says: each of the languages he's studied has its own constellation of subjects and moods so having different languages in his head, switching from one to the other, soundscape to soundscape, is like travelling from country to country. Each language is thus unique – in structures, idioms, ideas and expressions, but also (strangely) flavours and smells and sights. He's drawn to how each language apprehends the world, including the expression of emotions. Language communities, Timo says, inhabit their own understandings of the world, constructed as aural and semantic landscapes, while at the same time each language presents itself as a seemingly natural occurance, as a gift from nature to each member of the community.

Timo is mentioning John Berger, who I haven't thought about for years. He says, 'I like to consider this through a metaphor of John Berger's. Berger says we're naked at birth – a tabula rasa – and then we get clothed in a language, but so profoundly enwrapped in it so early in life that it feels exactly like a nature. When we learn, or adopt, another language this is like putting on a new set of clothes, and because it's new this language feels more of a construction, more stitched on as it were, more culture than nature. Perhaps he's right. But are the mother tongue and the learnt language both equally constructions? Or, do I retain a 'me' underneath the new clothes, an Ur language that can make these comparisons, a 'me' that originates in that tricky mother tongue that is really like a graft of language and genetics? I don't know. My thesis will hopefully work some of this out. Berger aside, what I do get is that each language creates more than its own insights and opportunities for expression. I guess what I'm talking about in the end is the connections between identity and language, and when I shift from language to language, I'm aware of these subtle shifts in my own perception of things, as if my identity itself is being a little stretched out, becoming more, what, malleable? Does that make sense?'

I say yes, although I'm really quite lost. (Only later does it occur to me to ask that if languages are so unique to themselves how is it possible to translate them, or indeed to learn another language?) But Timo is great company on this tram ride on the 58, which is now heading north in a winding path up Melville Road, past red brick churches and car repair yards. We pass an old cinema which is now an event venue, and Mr Truong's banh mi shop, outside of which there's a queue. I've told Timo that I'm getting off at Moreland Road to have lunch at 'my' Japanese cafe and he tells me that the cafe is one of his favourites. So this is how I come to have lunch with Timo at the Filimex.

We get off at Moreland Road and walk back to the cafe. Inside we order sushi rolls and dumplings from the owner, who is dressed in a blue smock and white headband. Timo shows off by ordering in Japanese and clearly part of the object of his coming to the cafe is to practise his newly acquiring language. We take a seat at the only table in the store, which abuts the glass window overlooking the pavement. A TV mounted on the wall is set to NHK Tokyo with the sound down and we watch a story about the latest tropical storm to hit the island of Honshu. On the screen is a large-scale meteorological map of the country with pulsing arrows that show the direction and path of the storm. There are scenes of upturned cars, flooded roads, bent trees, and huge sprays of water coming over sea walls.

Timo's English is better than mine – more precise and grammatically correct and perfectly articulated. But now I want to know about trams in Helsinki. Tell me a tram story Timo. He obliges by telling me about the key difference between our system and Helsinki's. Whereas Melbourne's system is designed as a hub with spokes, with all tracks, or most of them anyway, leading to the CBD, Helsinki's has a more circular pattern. 'In Melbourne if I want to stay on trams I often have to go towards the city and then out again, but in my hometown I can get around without needing to do that. We have a lot of tram routes that bisect other routes and others that go in arcs so that the city suburbs are accessible without having to go the centre. But we only have 11 lines compared to your dozens. Well, it is a much smaller city after all. Also, our trams are all very modern, whereas here you are running a lot of ancient tram stock, which I find amusing for such a rich country, but don't get me wrong I love them anyway. The people on your trams are remarkable. So many different faces and different languages, it's a boon for me. At home, it's basically always Finnish faces, Finnish language, Finnish everything. We are mostly a typical monoculture. Actually, I have a good story to tell about that.

'I was at the university at home and I came out of a long language lab session and my head was full of Spanish phrases and responses as I walked to the tram stop. When I got on the tram the strangest thing happened. I became aware of a foreign language being spoken, not just in one corner of the tram but seemingly throughout. I felt how odd that the people on this tram are all speaking this other language. Perhaps they are attending a conference, or are in a tour group. It suddenly hit me that the foreign language I was hearing was Finnish, and it was as if I was hearing it for the first time without meanings attached. Hearing your own language as a foreign language is a real shock to the system. It was truly the weirdest language I had ever heard. This sense of sound without meaning lasted no more than a minute, maybe less, before the world of meaning and context came flooding back, and I was back in the realm of my mother tongue. This was a lucky moment, I thought later, a moment when I was linguistically naked. But then I thought, in what language did I ask myself those questions on the tram just prior to realising it was Finnish I was hearing? The thing is, I couldn't remember.'

Timo and I have finished our lunch and we head out to catch our trams – he's heading north, while I will go back to the city. There's an awkward moment when the two of us signal farewell to each other with half raised arms. On the way back the scene at the Flinders Street viaduct comes back to me. Thousands of homeless people around the city, which as Timo points out is such a rich place, and somehow we can't afford to address this issue.

*

I'm thinking about these city tableaus and conversations I've been witnessing across my journeys. It seems to me more and more that the entire city, with its millions of denizens, might be some strange form of enactment, with multitudes of players, scenes and plot. That everyone is carrying their own individual narratives, their realities, concerns, fictions, but yet somehow these individual stories cohere into a whole, a city-wide narrative of place, time, people, history. The city as theatre? Maybe. But if so, who is directing the action, who designed the mise-en-scene, created the multifarious plots, and who chose the characters?

The city appears to be operating under the influence of some unseen hand that guides and shapes the ceaseless displays before me, and the ones before and the ones coming. And how is it that as each day passes I'm sensing that this complex story is reaching some form of crescendo, or final act, in which the meaning or meanings of this vast display of human actions and interactions and histories will be revealed?

Or not.

18. The Terminus

Old man Clapp is sitting in the sun in his garden at the rear of his house in South Yarra – the house he built after a life of renting. The petunias and azaleas are out and the air smells of warmth and promises. Clapp can't see his garden – he's been blind since 1908 – but he knows what it is doing at this moment in this season, what is unfolding, what it is bringing forth. Clapp feels the cat, Jezebell, at his ankles, a brief rubbing hello before it wanders off.

It's 1920, the Great War is over, and Clapp is in his 87th year. He's only been retired these last few years, having ridden the MTOC wave to its conclusion in 1916. The 30 year lease expired – you do remember he was on a lease don't you? – the company winds up, and the city, in the form of the Melbourne & Metropolitan Tramways Board (M&MTB) takes over the running of the tram system. The MTOC bequeathed to the new Board a highly trained staff, a system of standardised rolling stock, including 500 cable tram cars, and by 1920 carrying upwards of 100 million passengers a year. It's also been a profitable enterprise, rewarding shareholders, employees, councils, sundry supporting firms and businesses, and of course, Clapp himself. 'Endion', the grand house on the hill in South Yarra designed by Guyon Purchase in Gothic revival style is testament to Clapp's success.

Clapp's days are numbered – he will die on the sixth of September that year – but he has lived long enough to see his predictions about trams come to pass. You will recall how in 1883 he told the parliamentary committee that patrons would flock to the trams. Trams would be affordable, including for the working man, and provide a timely, frequent service linking the whole city. The network would be a world class public transport system and help to expand and transform the city. And it would make money. Clapp also said that one day trams would be powered by electricity. Clapp has witnessed the early rise of the electric powered tram in the eastern suburbs, and the M&MTB is inaugurated with the stated aim of electrifying the entire system. Clapp won't live to see this happen, but it must be nice to see the world evolve as you had thought it would.

There's an enticing smell of freshly baked bread wafting from the kitchen. Clapp's partner of decades, Isabella, is busy overseeing the day's bread making, and meal preparations. Isabella has given birth to seven children, four daughters and three sons, and there are now a multitude of grandchildren, whose birthdays are neatly marked on a calendar in the kitchen. One of the Clapps' sons, Harold Winthrop Clapp, inherits his father's energy and obsession with public transport, and goes on to become the Chairman of the Victoria Railways for over 30 years. Like his Dad, Harold is a massive innovator, and during his tenure he modernises and expands the railway system. The two men, father and son, are preeminent figures in the history of public transport in Victoria.

It has been a good morning. Clapp is an early riser and now heads down to the stables. He greets his two horses, and then with the help of his personal assistant, takes the rope attached to the household cow, Maisy, and walks her out of the property and into the parklands of the Domain. Here the trio wanders lazily for half an hour, the cow munching on tufts of grass, Clapp discoursing about the latest news, and in the distance the familiar screech of tram wheels on rails as the Toorak bound tram makes the turn from St Kilda Road into Domain Road.

*

Today there's a blue plaque on a wall at Endion which says that Clapp, 'Founder of the Melbourne Tramways System, lived here between 1891 and 1920.' This man of enormous energy and vision should have more than a plaque on a wall to commemorate him.

*

TRAM • 135

I'm sitting in the Rubber Duck café in Clifton Hill, trying to rustle up some sentences on my laptop. Above the barista a narrow window is set high in the wall facing Alexandra Parade. As I look up I see the pantograph of the 86 sailing west.

Before heading into the new era of electric powered trams I want to encapsulate what the cable tram era did for the city. It's proving difficult. The era of cable straddles two other eras – the period of the hansom cab in the 19th century, and the rise of the motor car in the 20th. The hansom cabbies' fears turned out to be well founded, as cable basically took over intracity travel. It was cheaper, quicker and more reliable. From 1885 cable trams ran for the next 55 years, before their complete replacement in 1940 by electric trams, and increasingly, the private car. At its peak, cable defined the city's unique public transport system, and it was transformative. The central city was now connected to the inner suburbs, whose shopping strips boomed. Real estate expanded outwards along the tram lines, creating the distinctive Victorian architecture that remains central to the city's heritage and identity. Cable boosted the economy, created thousands of jobs, increased crowd attendance at sporting venues, such as the grounds of the Victorian Football League, and played its part in the making of the city's beach culture. And it showed that the city was capable of developing world-class public infrastructure. It made us proud.

The Melbourne trammies in the cable era had, as mentioned, generally better working conditions than their cohorts in other jurisdictions, with shorter hours and more pay. But the trammies did not get their regular eight-hour day and overtime pay. As mentioned, the MTOC interpreted the Act to its advantage when calculating the week's hours of work, with the maximum of 60 hours imposed on much of the workforce, with overtime pay frequently slipping management's mind too. As I've said earlier, Clapp was ardently anti-union, a position increasingly at odds with the colony's industrial (and cultural) development, with the eight-hour day having been won by stonemasons way back in the 1850s. Tram workers' grievances led to the strike of 1888, well before the network was finished, and ended with the status quo reasserted and hundreds sacked.

The 1890s Depression compromised the working class movement across the country. It wasn't until Federation that better prospects emerged for Australian workers, including tram workers, with the creation of a national arbitration system, and the decision of Justice Higgins in the Harvester case, which established the principle of the 'living wage' in 1907. And, as mentioned, Melbourne's trammies finally had a union in 1913 – the Australian Tramways Employees Association – to act on their behalf to improve wages and conditions. The gripmen and conductors work hard and long and in the early days their wages were only just enough to support a family. But the tramways remained a sought after means of employment, and throughout the era a respected profession. In their heyday the cable trammies are a city fixture, in their identifiable (and cool) uniforms.

*

The above is all pretty clear and true, but I think it overlooks something important. With an abundance of caveats in mind, can I go purple for a minute or two? With your indulgence... .

Cable trams are a democracy on wheels. From the 1880s everyone is on board, shoulder to shoulder; the young and old, judges and politicians, pastry cooks, dock workers, shoppers, the gaslight men and dunny men, cobblers and trimmers, footy barrackers and seamstresses, the brewery men and toilers, insurance brokers and fashion store owners, the blacksmiths and apothecaries, doctors, nurses, teachers and police, the stable boys, the sex workers, immigrants and native born, the grog merchants and market gardeners, beach and theatre goers, the opium sellers, firemen and school children, drunks and businessmen and drunken businessmen. The Premier goes to Parliament by tram, as does the High Court judge to Court. The new trams are inherently political, not in a party sense, but in a deeper one, in which the experience of a democratic public of mores, styles and behaviours is developed.

Cable trams are an egalitarian mode of transport. No first or second or third class, just inside the car or outside in the dummy. The early morning shift workers have a concession on their tickets in recognition of their lower pay. The trams are gendered male by their crews, their makers, their owners, and their designers, but their customers are male and female. In this Victorian culture it is the closest that men and women who are strangers get to be bodily next to each other in public; the men in their black hats and grey caps, the women in their bonnets and floral sun hats. Shoulders and thighs, conversations and sighs... . Women and men going to the beach, to the theatre, to the football and the cricket.

Cable is therefore part of the organic life of a city centred on trams, creating a web of interactions and movements, journeys and relationships, journeys in civility and amity, keeping families and friends in touch with each other, altering the apprehension of space and time, creating a safe place for strangers to mingle and be together, raising all manner of opportunity, not least in the way people inhabit their city as an imaginative realm full of stories – stories experienced, overheard, enacted, stories connected to family and friends, lovers, moods, events.

The trams are also ostensibly race neutral. The city's Chinese population, mostly crowded around Little Bourke Street, travelled by tram around the city, to and from their market gardens, their furniture upholstery stores, their opium dens. The crews, all white, were specifically instructed to be polite to the Chinese (suggesting that their natural disposition was not to be). In any event, there's no apartheid here, no gender or race exclusions or separations, no bans on the poor. You pay you stay on, you don't pay, you're off. At the turn of the century, the city is the centre of the new nation.

I like to think about this moment in history. Here's Barton and Forrest, Deakin and Sir Isaac Isaacs all travelling the city by tram. And there's Gough Whitlam as a boy. Hi Gough! Here are the shoppers crowded onto the trams in busy Chapel Street, the children and their parents heading to the beach, the excited crowds heading to

Victoria Park, the Junction Oval, and the MCG. Here's Squizzy Taylor going through someone's pockets, while John Wren looks on amused. I like to think about the customers pouring out of the late night pubs and theatres onto the late night trams, the trams lit up by oil lamps, the yellow light ashining on the open faces, the hats making sharp angled shadows, the dark grained wood interiors glowing, the cackles and jokes, the whistling tunes and blasted songs, the trams ferrying the merry crowds back to their mansions and hovels, and the humming drone of the endlessly moving cable lulling the city to sleep.

*

Clapp passes on expeditiously, but his cable trams die slowly. The first cable tram to close was the Windsor-Esplanade route in 1925, five years after Clapp's death. When the Richmond line shut two years later crowds of people lined the streets of the city to commemorate the passing of the original cable tram. As the last cable tram trundled down Flinders Street people saluted and cheered. It was like a state funeral, but without the dour solemnity. In fact many in the crowd were no doubt drunk, falling out of the pubs along the way to farewell their tram, bearing inebriated witness to something treasured but now lost. The pub patrons of Young and Jackson filled the corner of Swanston and Flinders Streets, raising their glasses of brown ale to an icon of the city.

Nearly all the cable routes were converted to electric tramways by 1940 but a few were pulled up and not replaced. The Johnston Street Bridge line, which ran up Lygon Street through Carlton, then east along Elgin Street to Johnston Street, is defunct. The Rathdowne Street tram, which ran to Park Street North Carlton has disappeared, while the Wellington Street tram from Windsor to the Esplanade has gone. The Port Melbourne route has also gone, but the 109 tram now traverses the former railway line to Port Melbourne. The rest of the routes remain as the archaeology of the current system.

Apart from tram nuts and aficionados, the cable trams are largely forgotten by the people of the city; their routes are a piece of history, quaint and removed from contemporary relevance, gobbled by modernity. In another way, the cable tram network is still performing, still working out of sight within the city's layering of its bones, histories, stories. The tram lines follow the early settler tracks, which in turn follow the Indigenous tracks through the landscape. The streets are laid and then the next generation, or the one after, digs them back up. The materials, the earth, the rock, the stone, gravel, are redistributed over and over, moved and transplanted. Different sensibilities arise along with other needs and the landscape is moulded and remoulded. The cable trams literally leave tiny pieces of themselves: bits of cable, the red gum used to support the tunnels, broken sections of concrete, rail shavings, the mess of other parts. A cemetery of things. I don't know about you, but this raises an interesting question. The cable trams are forgotten but does their spirit carry on within the denizens of the city without their knowledge?

*

It's Saturday night the 26th of October 1940 and I'm on the very last cable tram to run. The tram is heading for Northcote and the dummy and tram car are full. Everyone is chatting away, to friends and to strangers, remembering their cable journeys in earlier years, swapping anecdotes, soaking up the atmosphere of this curious, historic event. The tram suddenly stops and a voice calls out from the street for everyone to 'look this way ladies and gentlemen'. A photographer with a camera on a tripod has set up on the street corner, with the obvious aim of recording this moment for posterity. He's calling out to everyone to hold still and to smile. He takes a number of shots, each one accompanied by a bright flash from his lamp. Finally he is satisfied, congratulates everyone, and the tram can carry on its journey.

The photo will later be published in the press, along with a story about the running of the last cable tram in the city. You can find this photo easily enough online. On the side of the dummy is a sign which says, 'To Aquarium – Exhibition Buildings'. The photo, taken with the aid of the flash lamp, has rendered the people's faces a bright white. But the crowd of people on board look happy, and they wave and cheer. The women and men in the photo are all wearing hats. There is a soldier in uniform, one man is smoking a pipe, three men sport moustaches while the rest are clean shaven. A woman has a stole draped over her right shoulder and the connie and the gripman are both there in their dark uniforms and caps. Everyone does look happy. They will be briefly famous, as the last group of passengers on the last cable tram. Also, if you look closely at the photo you can see me at the rear of the crowd. I'm that skinny guy partly obscured by those in front of him, with the weird look on his face.

INTERMISSION

What is the relationship between history and nostalgia? I have no real idea, but I suspect that the bare facts of any history do little to illuminate how people actually felt at the time and how these feelings become translated into memory. For my part, the W trams are clearly connected to childhood and my mother, and are thus imbued with a set of meanings that go beyond the workings of bogies, points and fares. For instance: Do you remember Uncle Max, the guy at the beach with the rolled up trousers and stinky pipe?

As you know, route 8 took my mother and I into town on our days out, but it also took us to Park Street, South Yarra, where we would, on occasion, get down and walk along the street to a double storey Victorian mansion. We would be let into the house by a woman in a white and black uniform. The foyer of the house was as large as our whole flat and the floor was covered I recall in geometric tiles. My mother would take me into the parlour room to wait while she went off in search of Uncle Max. This room housed an enormous grandfather clock in the corner, which sounded the hour, half hour and quarter hour with deep metal gongs. I would wait patiently standing before the clock as it ticked its way towards the quarter or half hour, and I especially liked the strikes on the hour since there usually were so many of them. Absorbed in this pastime I wouldn't notice how long my mother was away, but then she and Uncle Max would enter the parlour, the grandfather clock would be forgotten, and we'd head out into the street. Uncle Max dressed in a manner that was out of sync with the conservative trends of the 1950s – a 'bit of a dandy' was how my mother described him – and he would always appear in a colourful or two-tone suit, with a bow tie, pork pie hat and shiny brogues or spats. I have no idea what he did for a living.

We journey out of the house, my mother threading her arm through Uncle Max's, my hand in hers and we board the 8 and head into town for tea and scones, or a visit to Myers, an Italian bistro, the arcades, or further afield to Carlton and the University Cafe. Uncle Max is a talk-a-thon, full of stories, quips and the latest gossip around town, my mother laughs, she's so relaxed in his company, more so than usual and he doesn't ignore me either, asking me what I think about the football or do I like flying kites, and have I been to Luna Park. At my age Max is the only adult I've known other than my parents who looks at me while talking to me and listens to whatever nonsense comes out of my mouth. So I like him, my mother certainly does but I also wonder about him and this friendship of my mother's, given too that she never speaks to my father about these visits with Max after they occurred.

In some way, mysterious to me, I learnt not to mention them either, without any prompting from my mother, as if I could sense that it was a subject not to be entertained afterwards and when my father asked me how my day was over dinner I would mumble something inconsequential. My mother was generally a good cook but on those evenings following a visit to South Yarra she would be off her game. The dinners on these occasions were in some way perfunctory, as if they had been prepared without her usual forethought or care or even interest. Did my father notice this diminution in culinary standards? If he did he never commented on it, eating with his usual gusto, and describing, as he ate, the minutiae of his day at the office.

My mother would finish eating early and then light a cigarette.

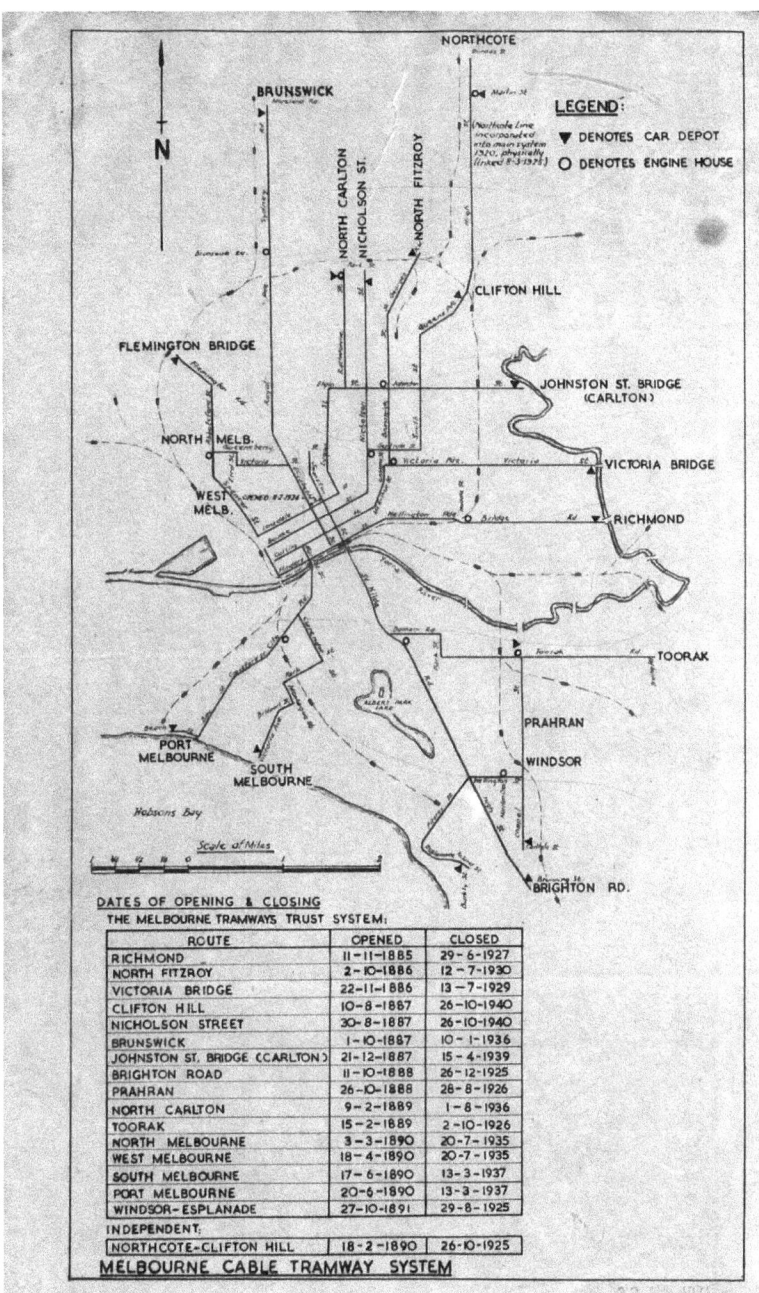

Map of Melbourne cable tram routes with route opening and closing
dates – Melbourne Tram Museum

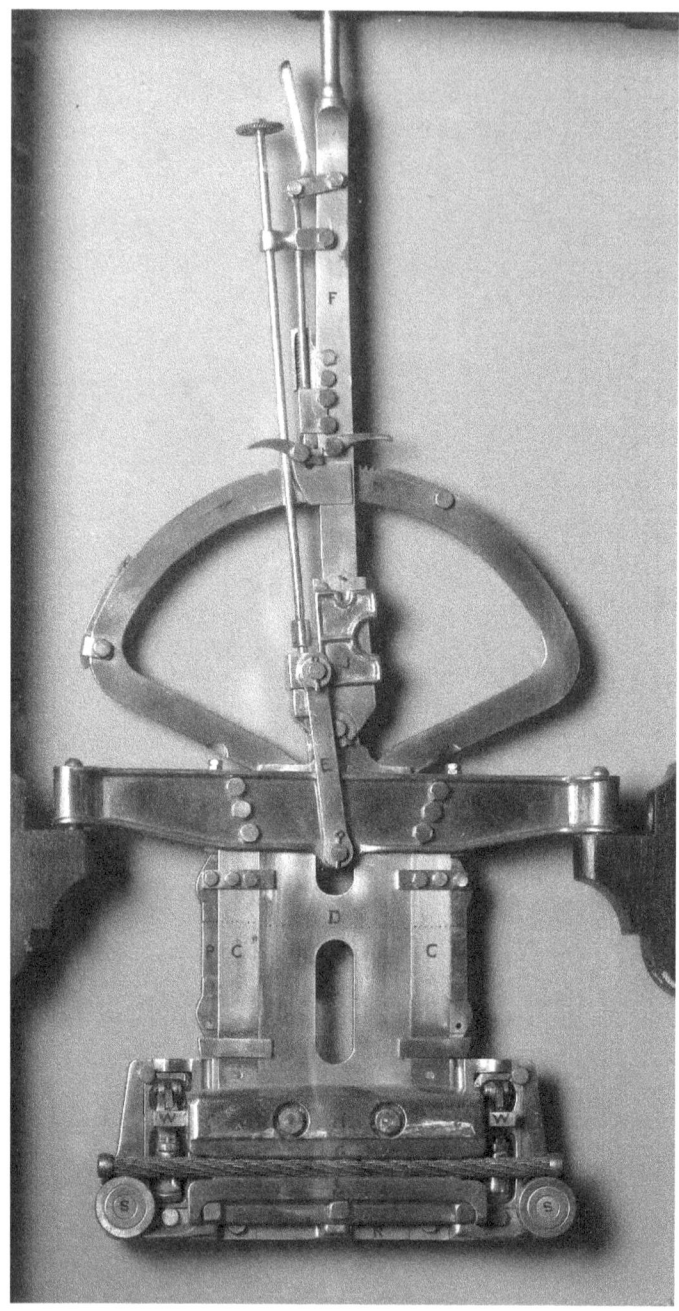

1880s Melbourne cable tram grip mechanism – Museums Victoria

Cable tram in St Kilda Road circa 1905 showing 'dummy' pulling tramcar

The Brunswick tram with long tramcar stopping near the Zoo

The last of the W class trams: city circle tram on route 35

E class tram - the return of trams built in Melbourne

19. Network Evolution

Electricity! The new dawn of an ancient power, harnessed to a multitude of purposes that have transformed the globe. While Prometheus gave us fire, it was Michael Faraday (and others) who gave us the electric motor. The electric motor got sidetracked for over 100 years by big oil for the development of the automobile, but it took off in relation to tramways and railways. Clapp could see it and so could others, including the newly minted state governments of the new Commonwealth. Electric motors that drive trams and trains are called traction motors, the essence of which is the conversion of electrical energy into mechanical energy to move the vehicle.

The same year that the Victorian Government set up the Melbourne and Metropolitan Tramways Board (M&MTB) under an Act of Parliament, it also passed legislation to establish the State Electricity Commission Victoria (SECV). This was 1918, and John Monash, war hero of the western front, would be returning to Melbourne to head up the SECV. It was largely his reputation, driving force, and intelligence that brought the state monopoly into being. The Yallourn Power Station, fuelled by brown coal, was completed by 1924, and a massive transmission line to Melbourne was finished in the same year. The SECV was empowered to take over private and council entities that ran local power stations, but not to take control of the tramway system.

The M&MTB was set up with the primary purposes of bringing to-gether all the disparate elements of the city's tramways under one roof, and to electrify the whole system. Both the M&MTB and the SECV survived as public institutions for roughly the next seven dec-ades before they were privatised in the 1990s.

I'll get back to the history of the M&MTB soon. But the early days of electricity and tramways can be likened to an evolutionary pond – so many different tram species emerged in the early 20th century that it can be confusing keeping track of them. Some species were very short-lived, others flowered and then declined, while some powered ahead. All of the survivors were to be eventually subsumed by the evolutionary giant, the M&MTB.

Bear in mind that throughout this early electric period the cable trams remained the central form of tram transport for the city, carry-ing millions of passengers a year. In the mind of the public too, the city's trams were cable trams, and closely identified as such. The elec-trics would come, but it would be a decades long transition.

Curiosities, adventures and templates. There was an electric tram in Melbourne even *before* the 20th century. In 1889, a tram began running from Box Hill to Doncaster, and it was claimed to be the first electric powered tram to run, not just in Australia, but in the southern hemisphere. It had been a curiosity brought to Melbourne from the USA for the Centennial International Exhibition in 1888. It ran along a track laid beside the Exhibition Building and was very popular with patrons, inspiring a group of local developers to buy it. The Box Hill to Doncaster tram ran from 1889 to 1896, promoted as a tourist and land boom attraction (many of the company's shareholders were land speculators). Tram Road is named in honour of the route taken up the hill by this early electric tramcar. As Robert Green shows in his histo-ry of the tramway, the project was mired in litigation and technical issues throughout its life.

The investors set up their equipment next to Bushy Creek in what is now North Box Hill and used the water from the creek for a steam engine. They had a generating dynamo, overhead wiring and the tram had two electric motors. But the power generated was frequently insufficient to get the tram up the hill so it periodically broke down. After various changes of ownership across the seven years the scheme folded. The tram shed ended up as a haven for swaggies.

So what exactly is an electric tram? In essence, an electric tram has four key features: first, the provision of direct electric current and, in the Melbourne context, by overhead wiring; next, the collection of the electricity by roof-mounted trolley pole or pantograph; third, the use of traction motors for propulsion of the tram fitted to the bogies underneath the tram car; and lastly, a control system operated by the driver to regulate the power to the engines. Of course, you need brakes too, and these are operated by hand or foot using compressed air or electricity. And what happens to the electricity itself? Like all good things it is returned to the earth, via the wheels. Neat.

The Box Hill to Doncaster tramway was a failure, but the lure of electric power was not to be deterred. The next venture into electric was in 1906. The Victorian Railways had the temerity to venture into electric tramways with the creation of a tram service from St Kilda to Brighton. Amazingly, this service lasted into the 1950s. Don't get me wrong, I like trains, but I'm of the no doubt prejudiced belief that trams are trams and trains are trains and never the twain shall meet.

Dear reader, it will take some time to unravel the electric tram story so please bear with me. Now, watch your step, we are about to enter the crowded world of tramway acronyms.

20. Trams, Trusts & Acronyms

In the years prior to, and during the First World War, and before the establishment of the M&MTB, the city saw the development of a number of individually operated tramways companies and trusts. The city was growing outwards, beyond the reach of the cable tram network, and public transport was sorely needed. Lacking coordination with one another, or any overarching city-planning, the tramways that emerged in this period served their localities with varying degrees of success, before being subsumed by big brother M&MTB. This fleet of trams was entirely powered by electricity.

NMETL: In 1906 the North Melbourne Electric Tramway and Lighting Company (NMETL) was born. The NMETL was a multipurpose private company, providing electric power for businesses, street lighting and tramways in Essendon and Flemington. The private entity built a power station in Mt Alexander Road and a tram shed that could house 28 trams, thus providing their trams with their own power. (The tram shed survives as rows 13 to 18 at Essendon Depot.) The two-man operated NMETL trams terminated adjacent to the cable system near Flemington Bridge. Two NMETL lines began on the north side of the bridge, one heading down Racecourse Road to Flemington and terminating at Maribyrnong River, while the other went up the hill along Mount Alexander Road to Keilor Road, with a branch down Puckle Street. K. S. Kings' history of the NMETL tells us that by the second year of operation the company was making a profit. The tram fleet included end-loading saloon cars and open to the elements cross-bench 'toast-racks'.

PMTT: The Prahran and Malvern Tramways Trust (PMTT) gave us the first electric tram network in the city's suburban east, and over the decade from 1910 it expanded to cover a wide arc of the east and south east suburbs. More than just a template with a few lines, the PMTT was a fully fledged tram service, creating for the eastern suburbs of the city a reliable, modern system of transport. By 1918-19 it was carrying almost 30 million passengers a year on nearly 100 trams, which ran on average every 10 minutes. The profitable PMTT has its origins in the 1907 *Prahran and Malvern Tramways Trust Act*, the outcome of sustained lobbying of the then Bent government by Prahran and Malvern Councils, in particular the Malvern Councillor, lawyer Alex Cameron. Cameron is a key figure in this development (and a man about whom I will have more to say later). He was elected Chair of the Trust and oversaw both the creation and running of the system.

The PMTT built the tram depot, offices and workshop in Coldblo Road, just off Glenferrie Road in Malvern. There's a wonderful photo in Ian Brady's history of the PMTT in which Alex Cameron is depicted standing on the stairs of the new car barn declaring the PMTT open on the 30th May 1910. A huge crowd dressed in their finest to celebrate their new community asset listen as Cameron tells them that, 'We have produced a work that will compare favourably with any tramway in any city in any country.' Big call!

The PMTT purchased electricity from the Melbourne Electrical Supply Company's Richmond power station. Like the NMETL, the PMTT established overhead wiring as the means of powering the trams. The Trust originally bought 13 single truck combination cars (by Adelaide vehicle manufacturer, Duncan and Fraser Limited). Outsourcing the construction of vehicles would remain the PMTT's principal method for most of its existence. The tramcars were in chocolate and cream livery. In 10 years the PMTT connected the suburbs of St Kilda, Caulfield, Glenhuntly, Prahran, Hawthorn, Kew, Camberwell, Malvern and Mont Albert with over 50 kilometres of track, a significant achievement in such a short period, particularly given the impacts of the war years on personnel and finances. Nearly all of the PMTT routes are still being traversed by trams today. Perhaps the most popular PMTT route was the one from Kew to St Kilda beach, which opened in 1913. Today's 16 tram follows the same route.

And the PMTT trams themselves are a fine set. So fine, that the PMTT's drop-centre model became the template for the M&MTB's famous W series. A common feature of PMTT trams is the curving body – the lower sides under the windows taper towards the chassis. It's a nice look. There are many photos online of opening days of various PMTT lines – crowds of people are swarming the trams, hanging off the running boards on both sides, which are painted with the words 'Municipal Tramways.' Notice the full stop.

HTT: The Hawthorn Tramways Trust (HTT) also owes its existence to an Act of Parliament, in 1914, and its main route was Princes Bridge to Burwood (think today's 70 route). The tram depot was built on the corner of Power Street and Riversdale Road in 1916 and the first section from Batman Avenue, along the Yarra, and out to Hawthorn opened that year. (The depot building is now the home of the Tram Museum.) Later in 1916 the line was extended out to Camberwell Junction, and then further out to Warrigal Road. These trams, also built in Adelaide, were painted in French Grey, which is a green grey, taking its inspiration from 19th century French wallpapers. Of course. Eventually the Hawthorn Trust ran out of dough and had to sell off some of its trams.

MBCTT: The most successful of the wartime trusts was the Melbourne, Brunswick and Coburg Tramways Trust (MBCTT) established under legislation in 1914, beginning operations in 1916. The main route travelled from Bakers Road in Coburg, along Sydney and Moreland Roads, then Lygon Street to the city, where it connected with the rest of the network. By 1920 nearly 200 staff and 18 trams worked out of the depot in Coburg. Financially successful, well administered, an efficient service, with good wages for staff, the MBCTT would provide a significant slice of the manpower, expertise and collateral taken up by the M&MTB in 1920. Also adopted by the M&MTB

were two MBCTT innovations: single journey one penny tickets, known as 'flimsies' (because they were so wafer thin), and it dispensed with centre power poles in favour of roadside poles. The Duncan and Fraser MBCTT trams were painted Dark Paris Green – a rich dark green with blue undertones – and inside had polished brass fittings, native timbers, and silver leaf. Comfortable, elegant.

FNPTT: Less successful was the 1915 Fitzroy, Northcote and Preston Tramways Trust (FNPTT). The intended route was along St Georges Road from the North Fitzroy cable tram terminus to Miller Street. A lot of work was carried out, but the first trial of the system didn't occur until after the war in January 1920, and in February of the same year the FNPTT was taken over by the M&MTB.

FTT: The Footscray Tramways Trust is a classic western suburbs story. The Council had grand plans for electric tramways for the city of Footscray, but none of them eventuated in the life of the Trust, dissolved by a Governor-in-Council order in 1920. This system was supposed to connect directly to the rest of the tram system but never did. The segregated Footscray network that eventually did emerge in 1921 under the M&MTB has always suffered as the poor child of the system, given hand-me-down trams, the oldest and slowest in the fleet, a story that continues to this day. And where did all the money allocated by Council for the network go? Well, dead men tell no tales.

The successful suburban tramways of the early 20th century and war years proved the viability and capacity of an electrically powered system. The best of the electric trams carried almost twice the passengers of a cable tram at double the speed. It was a lesson that, eventually, would not be lost on the state government.

But before I go on to explain how the M&MTB became the biggest fish in the evolutionary pond I have a tram to catch.

21. Route 16: Reveries

Today I am on the 16 tram from Kew to the city. At over 20 kilometres it is one of the longest tram routes on the system. As mentioned, route 16 runs along the PMTT route constructed over 100 years ago. Various modern iterations have occurred, most recently in 2004, when the then 16 route was amalgamated with the 69 route.

My tram today is an old Z3 class tram. As I implied earlier, the Zs are some of the oldest trams ever in use on the system, now in their fifth decade of service, bearing in mind the cable system lasted 55 years. By rights they should be dead, but trams are hard to put down, and besides, the system needs them to carry on. Today's Z is not in good shape. It's décor and fittings are worn, the seat covers are a faded green and yellow, decorated by dots and stripes. Tired. Parts of the tram's inner walls have become unhinged from their structures, and rattle as we gather speed. The exterior is dented and scraped, with a band of congealed black dirt adhering to the sides. Lovely. Do I dislike the Zs? No, as you know I appreciate them, I'm just a bit sad for them. All those journeys, all those people – can't a tram retire in dignity?

My journey today approximates three sides of a square – south from Cotham Road Kew along Glenferrie Road, around Dandenong Road into Hawthorn Road, then along Balaclava Road to St Kilda; a loop around St Kilda, then down St Kilda Road to the CBD and the University terminus in Carlton. The rolling hills of the Glenferrie tram reveal a wealthy domain of expensive private schools, mansions and churches with imposing spires. The 16 gives access to the world of old private school Melbourne, beautifully brought to life in Janet McCalman's evocation of the 69 tram circa 1934: Trinity, Xavier, Genazzano, MLC, Scotch, and later, around in St Kilda Road, Wesley and Melbourne Grammar. Over 100 years of young scholars from the quasi-gentry boarding and deboarding their tram to and from school in their distinctive uniforms, bearing with them the aspirations and dreams of their parents.

Glenferrie Road shops buzz with people and activity. The journey is slow to the point of tedious, but I'm entertained by the constant flow of people in and out of the tram. Just near the Glenferrie Station is the Railway Arcade, dating from 1910, a fine Edwardian structure. This eclectic and rambling strip which once included cinemas, billiard saloons and a motor garage owes thanks for its existence, in part, to the PMTT tram, which opened up the suburb in a similar fashion to Clapp's Chapel Street trams. We pass the Hawthorn Town Hall with its Ziegler clock tower and head up the gentle slope to Riversdale Road and down through a steep cutting to Kooyong, past the lawn tennis courts (where I remember seeing Evonne Goolagong Cawley play 50 years ago), and into the territory of the terribly wealthy – their mansions gaze at the street through a hundred windows.

A few minutes later and we are outside the Malvern Depot at Coldblo Road, the original home of the PMTT fleet. I get out and wander round the red-brick depot, a fine Federation style building, designed by the architect for the PMTT, Leonard Flannagan. It looks a bit like a Norman castle, with its corner turret and parapets. Magnificent. I imagine the crowds here for opening day over 100 years ago – everyone in their finest, a grand community event. I stand and watch as Z3s and D class trams trundle in and out. Proper tram nut.

I reboard the tram heading to the city. As I sit a woman in a vivid purple suit with white piping enters the tram and sits with her back to me in the next seat. This Malvern end of Glenferrie Road is like its Hawthorn counterpart, a long stretch of blocks densely packed with disparate businesses, with its own distinct history and ambience, but for some reason I've always preferred the Hawthorn end. An office block on the corner of Glenferrie and Dandenong Roads occupies what was once the New Malvern Theatre, the destination of Saturday tram trips with my mother to the matinees. It had an amazing neo-classical interior, and originally a proscenium arch, long gone by the time we were watching Charlton Heston, Elizabeth Taylor and other luminaries of the early 1960s. It was pulled down in 1987 after 57 years of operation.

Through the dogleg of Dandenong and Hawthorn Roads, we head west at Balaclava Road, past Jewish schools, medical centres, and bakeries. Balaclava Road morphs into Carlisle Street and here is the famous Glick's Bakery, home since the 1960s to the celebrated boiled bagels and challah breads of (now late) Mendel Glick. Several of the passengers sport yarmulkas. Hebrew is being spoken. This area, south of the Yarra River, has been home to Jews since the 1930s, and then especially after the Holocaust when tens of thousands of Jews, including Glick, migrated to Melbourne. The journey progresses, the average age of passengers drops, the tram travellers now largely young people and students, some reading text books. Atmospheres on trams are always changing.

Over St Kilda Road the tram crosses Barkly Street and heads into St Kilda, passing the National Theatre, opened in the 1920s as the 3,000 seat Victory cinema – pre-talkies! – and now a performance centre and home to the National Drama and National Dance Schools. The tram takes off round the Esplanade and there is the surprise view of the sea, a deep blue today.

The 16 tram arrives in the city and the woman in purple gets down at Flinders Street. I hop off too and cross the road to Young and Jackson and order a pint of beer. I sit at the open window and watch the crowd pass in and out of the station opposite, and the trams trundling in all directions. As I watch there's a loud clap of thunder right above us. Pretty soon a torrential downpour is making people scurry across the road to the shelter of the station, brollies are going up, and the gutters fill with water.

*

Reverie. Lost in a daydream, deep absorption or thoughtfulness, from the Old French for rejoicing, revelry, and earlier still, delirious, mad.

My mother and I are sitting at the kitchen table in the flat in Prahran. We were about to go out when an enormous thunder storm takes place, so forceful that it shakes the window panes. The rain comes drumming on the roof of the kitchen lean-to at the rear of the building. My mother says the storm will pass and gets up to collect raincoats and the umbrella. We sit for quite a while – five minutes or 50 I have no idea – without speaking, contained in our own thoughts, listening to the rumble and crash and rattle of rain on tin. Eventually it eases up and we don our rain gear and head out. I have on a round yellow plastic hat and plastic see-through raincoat, while my mother has the umbrella and her long overcoat. As we walk through the rain drenched street to the tram I jump in the puddles that have appeared on the footpath, until I'm admonished to cease and desist – I was splashing her new coat, which just the week before she and I had bought at Myers. I'd said at the time that the blue coat suited her more than the grey, but in the end she chose a kind of off-white. It didn't matter, she looked great in it – tall and thin, long legs, big hands, red lipstick, black hair cut short.

We get to the tram stop and wait in the light rain. I always like wet trams – the green trams without sliding doors are so exposed to the weather, with one side completely open, and gaps on the shuttered side, that in a storm they quickly fill with rain water. The seats nearest the doors get wet, the floorboards splashed, small puddles form from shoes and umbrellas. In these circumstances everyone crowds into the saloons at either end. Here the windows fog up with condensation making looking out impossible, but it is warm and cosy. My mother hurries us onto the tram – she was very quick when she wanted to be – and secures a couple of seats inside. Even in here the floor is wet.

The connie comes and my mother pays the fare and as she does the connie shows me a penny on his open palm, then closes his hand, reopens it, the penny is gone. What the? To complete the trick he reaches behind my ear, and surprise! finds the coin again, flicks it into the air, catches it, slaps it on the back of his hand and asks me – 'heads or tails?' I say tails – I always say tails – and he opens his hand and it's heads. My mother laughs at this performance, and the connie says the penny is mine until the next time we meet by which time he expects me to have learnt the trick. Go to Bernard's Magic Shop in the city, he says, and they will teach you how. This is the first time I've heard of Mr Bernard. All the way into the city I nag my mother to take me to Bernard's, whoever he is. She says she would 'one day' but that today we are busy.

22. A Royal Commission & an Act of Parliament

'That the whole of the Metropolitan Tramway systems (privately and publicly owned) at the earliest possible date be vested in and operated by a Municipal Tramways Trust...'.

From the Report of the Royal Commission, 1911.

More documents. I'm back in the bowels of the Parliamentary Library and I'm staring at those historic words above written over 100 years ago. The *Report of the Royal Commission appointed to Inquire into and Report upon the Railway and Tramway Systems of Melbourne and Suburbs* was tabled in the Parliament in 1911, and that sentence is the first clause of the Commission's first recommendation to Parliament. The Royal Commission made 10 recommendations regarding tramways in a report that ultimately had a massive influence on how the city's tram network developed in the 20th century.

The Commission found that the city's tram network was overcrowded and failing to meet the demands of its growing population. The network did not link up the city's urban and suburban areas, there was a continual 'piling up of cars' at the city's intersections causing delays, and the trams never travelled more than 13 miles per hour (just under 21 kph).

Electrification of the system was seen as a key to its future. 'Electric traction' would be cheaper, faster, have greater capacity, use centralised power, be better lit, and much quicker at making crossings.

Recommendation six specified that cable trams be, 'electrically converted, route by route, as extensions from the present cable termini and overcrowding of the routes necessitate, and that the conduit system be not adopted'.

The conduit system refers to a system that runs the lines that power the trams under the road surface between the rails. It had been used in other cities, but in the Commission's view it was too expensive and harder to modify and maintain. It opted, in recommendation seven, for the adoption of an overhead span wire system, the system we have to this day (and no doubt influenced by the PMTT's successful usage of overhead wiring across its sizeable network). There would be through and sectional fares (recommendation eight) a night service (recommendation nine) and, 'for the convenience of women and elderly people', a low step be provided at one end, (recommendation 10). The electric trams, riding on their electric motors, were going to be higher off the ground than the cable trams, so the step up was going to be an issue for some.

The Commission found that the only comprehensive tram system in the city was still Clapp's MTOC cable system. There were others, including electric networks, such as the ones I've listed above, and some still extant horse tramways, but in 1911 the MTOC dwarfed other tramways, with, according to the Commission, 76,295,824 passenger journeys in that year. (Passenger numbers climbed exponentially over the next decade.) The Commission was no doubt aware that the government was keen to get its hands on the MTOC. With its lease set to expire in five years, and the profits handsome, the Commission recommended that the MTOC be purchased as 'early as practicable' (recommendation four). It was not to be. Clapp had a watertight contract and his lease would hold until the end.

The Commission recommended the creation of a Municipal Tramways Trust, suggesting that it be made up of 12 members serving four year terms, nine of these elected by ratepayers from relevant councils, a Chair and two members appointed by the Minister. Interesting idea. No-one today would have the temerity to recommend that the administration of our transport system be open to democratic processes. In the end the government of the day didn't like it either, making the Melbourne & Metropolitan Tramways Board (M&MTB) an all appointed board. But, it's remarkable how much of the Commission's vision for the tramways is eventually adopted by government.

The report did sit on the shelf. When do they not? But it was dusted off in 1918 when the government finally moved to create a single entity to run the system.

I might as well do it now – pull out the relevant Act – since I'm down here, although I'm tired and the air is chilly and dank. Also, could someone do some dusting? Many of these antique volumes haven't been touched in years – decades? – and they each have a thick layer of dust on their top end.

I have before me the volume that contains the *Melbourne and Metropolitan Tramways Act* 1918. It reads okay, a bit on the wordy side at over 100 pages. But I actually do like the circumlocution of the early acts of Parliament. The formal language lends these laws some greater authority than the plain English of modern acts. They are like a puzzle that has to be worked out, with their endless clauses, sub-clauses and relative clauses.

The Act is a comprehensive template for an integrated electric tramways network for the city. First, it creates a Board to be known as the Melbourne and Metropolitan Tramways Board, to be appointed by the Governor-in-Council. In effect the Minister will appoint the seven members of the Board, including the Chair, who will be paid 1,500 pounds a year, a substantial amount in 1918 (the equivalent of over $150,000 in today's terms). The new Board is to have sweeping powers to take over, remake, construct, expand, operate and maintain the city's tram systems. All previous tramways acts are suspended, all of the Tramways Trusts dissolved, and all of the Trusts' and the MTOCs' properties will be vested in the Board, including finances and liabilities.

The new trams will be electric and the old routes converted to electric. The electricity can be bought from any municipality and from the state electricity authority when it comes into being. The Board will have the power to set tramways by-laws governing passengers, timetables, running frequency, declare offences for fare evasion, violence on trams, damage of property, offensive behaviour such as spitting or smoking, and tramways officers can make arrests. Passengers can carry 28 pounds of luggage, but not dangerous goods. (Sound familiar? Yes, same provision as for cable.) Fares will be set and displayed inside the trams, and fares can include sectional fares, through fares, single journeys and return fares and special fares on the basis of age or class – the latter harking back to workers' fares at the beginning of the cable system. But there's one group that won't have to pay a penny to ride a tram. Members of Parliament will be exempt. How nice for them!

The Board can hire and fire, set up offices, build new depots, acquire or lease lands for operations, dig up roads, insure itself against losses, issue debentures and stocks, borrow money, conduct legal proceedings, and ensure that a common seal authorise all its works. All Board employees must be paid at award rates (an illustration that Australia's unique arbitration system has already taken hold). The tramway gauge will be four feet eight and a half inches (approx. 1.43 metres – that's right, the same rail width as cable). Single track lines can be converted to double track. The trams will have flange wheels. There's plenty more like this dear reader.

In summary, the Act can be interpreted as an invitation to be bold and innovative: it creates a powerful, appointed Board, with its key figure its only full-time member, the Chair. This appointment will be crucial to the success of the new system in coming years. The move to a centralised, and centralising body to run the system for the city, in place of an array of private and public entities, is also of its time. With the First World War over, the newly federated states are signalling a stronger and more expansive role for governments across the country.

I've had enough for one day – time to surface.

*

I emerge from my dungeon of tomes into the sunlight. I'm standing at the top of the stairs that lead to the Parliament's grand façade – essentially a neo-classical Greek temple, replete with its colonnade of Doric columns and enormous pediment with sculpted mythic figures. Looking down Bourke Street from this elevated position I can just make out the Bolte Bridge in the distance. Trams are heading east and west up and down Bourke Street, as they have most of the last 140 years. Here comes something interesting. To my left chugging slowly along Spring Street comes a W class tram, one of the city circle tourist trams. I scamper down just in time to step aboard the tram among the crowd of tourists, and we head off north along Spring Street.

At Victoria Parade, we turn left, past the gardens and view of the Exhibition dome, and into Latrobe Street. The 35 is a free city circle line designed specifically for tourists, and is the last domain of the W class trams, the heart of the electric tram system for over 60 years, and as you are aware, the trams of my childhood. The passenger group is diverse with a multitude of languages being spoken. At regular intervals a good proportion disembarks, and another lot get on. It's a warm day and many look harassed and uncomfortable. After standing for a while I eventually get a seat at the front of the saloon section. (Nerd alert: It is tram number 946, which makes it originally an SW6 class tram, the class built from 1939 to 1951.) It has power-operated sliding doors, green cushioned seats, wooden interiors and doors, brass struts for the handle rail, opening windows and a curved ceiling. The brakes squeal loudly and on downward sections of the route the tram shudders to a stop. It's hard to believe the W trams were this slow, but the driver is probably under instruction not to damage his precious cargo.

Most people don't have a seat and I calculate that there must be over 100 people on the tram. The man opposite has somehow managed to fall asleep (good for you sir!) and only stirs when his partner's elbow jabs him to wake up for their stop. Behind me is the driver's compartment, and I twist around and look inside it through the glass panel. The same electric controller is there, as are many of the fittings I remember from childhood trips with my mother, when I perched at the front of the tram watching the driver at work. The driver would operate the tram with the controller handle held in his left hand, while his right hand would operate the air brakes. Today there is a black panel in the centre of the console, and I realise that this is a new braking and lighting system, which must have been recently installed – the city circle trams having been refurbished to make them safer.

Latrobe Street has taken us to the Docklands area – a precinct created in the 1990s following the demolition of the old wharves and docks. When Victoria Dock was built in the last decades of the 19th century over wetlands where people of the Kulin nation hunted and met for millenia, it was the largest dock in the world, making Melbourne the port city of the country. Millions of tons of cargo came through the dock over the 100 odd years of its operation, and it was only abandoned with the advent of containerisation. Some cargo sheds remain but 90 percent of the site has been erased, not this time by Whelan, but a new generation of city vandals, an entire chapter of the city's history which could have been preserved as a national heritage and tourist site sold off as scrap.

My father loved cars but he also had a thing for ships. I remember family outings to the docks in the early days, with my father expatiating on ship makes and origins, how they were loaded and unloaded, the produce they carried. My mother always came along on these Sunday trips but, try as she might, she invariably had that look of hers which said 'ineffably bored'. I know how she felt, but I liked being with the two of them on these strange occasions. The ships loomed over the wharves like huge metal monsters, their hulls covered in barnacles, rust and algae. The air stank of oil and sea and the wharves wobbled and shook whenever an errant wave washed under them. The sheds were massive and their dark interiors mysterious. My father liked visiting sites of industrial modernity – docks, bridges, dams, skyscrapers. I recall one holiday in the Latrobe Valley touring the power stations. He took endless photos of smokestacks and generators and the occasional one of us.

The tram proceeds into Harbour Esplanade and travels past apartments, office towers, a few boats, pine and palm trees. People are scarce and this newest part of the city has an abandoned feel to it. None of the tourists get off here. Another left into McCrae Street and we head west towards Flinders Street. Looking left I see the wonderful 25 metre sculpture of Bunjil the eagle, spirit creator of the Kulin nations. Formerly placed at the top of the city, visible from across town, it is now sited in an obscure position, a move dictated by the billion dollar Lend Lease development.

At the corner of Flinders and Spencer Streets the tram rejoins the old city. Throughout the journey the voice-over guide to the city has worked haphazardly and barely audibly; only scraps of description can be heard amongst the static. The sites the tram is travelling past are 'world class', scratch-inaudible, 'showcase', more inaudible, 'excellent', something else. Scratch, scratch, fizz, pop. No-one is taking the slightest notice of the recording. Many on board look bored, some are fanning themselves with maps, while others have their phones out. The tram passes St Paul's Cathedral, Federation Square, the arabesque Forum, Hosiery Lane. Most of the wonders of the city's history, including the docks, are ignored by the malfunctioning address system. I get off. It took an hour to go round.

Underwhelming. Route 35 – two stars!

23. Alex Cameron's M&MTB

The M&MTB comes into existence in late 1919. The First World War is over and it's time to start building. By February 1920 the M&MTB has taken over all the municipal tramways trusts, all of the operations and collateral of the MTOC, and a bunch of smaller entities, including, as noted, some horse drawn trams. The M&MTB acquires the former privately owned Clifton Hill to Northcote cable tram, which by 1920 was being operated by the local council. In 1922 the M&MTB also acquires the tramways part of the NMETL. The M&MTB is now a mega-corporation, owning and operating hundreds of trams and employing thousands of people. It's gobbled up everything in sight that looks like public transport except the railways (including their two tramlines), who are stoutly defending their territory against this new behemoth. Created with two purposes uppermost – unification and electrification – the M&MTB is immediately on the road to success, and achieves the electrification of most of the system between 1925 and 1930.

The transformation and modernisation of the city's tram network is a massive undertaking. It will take someone gifted with enormous energy, intelligence and drive to pull it off. The city by this stage is a highly complicated beast, full of competing interests, factions, disputes and outsize egos. The population is once again growing, and will reach a million people in 1930, placing further demands on public transport. The M&MTB would need a leader who can swim in waters full of circling sharks while not losing sight of the big picture.

You remember Alex Cameron? The guy who ran the PMTT and is about to inherit Clapp's cable trams and every other tram operation

172 • GREG GARDINER

in the city? The man to be known as the 'father' of the city's electric trams, who will lead the PMTT and the M&MTB for a combined quarter of a century? Yes, that guy.

There's something about people like Clapp and Cameron who are born outside the metropolis but who come to be dominant figures within it. Think Bradman and Freeman for sport, John Curtin for politics, or Derrida and Camus for philosophers, O'Keefe and Kusama for artists. Cameron was born on a sheep station, Morgiana, near Hamilton in 1864. He's the offspring of Scots migrants, members of the Victorian squattocracy, who took up their run in the early 1840s. Cameron has no intention of being a farmer though. He heads off to Melbourne where he studies law at the University of Melbourne, and is sworn in as a barrister and solicitor in 1886. He sets up in private practice, marries in 1892 in a Presbyterian church in the city, and soon enough involves himself in politics, becoming a councillor in Malvern in 1902. He's appointed to the Board of the Melbourne and Metropolitan Board of Works, which gives him an insider's role in the city's development of sewerage and waterworks and a keen understanding of the regulations governing such works. Meanwhile, like Clapp before him, he's become obsessed with tramways and is instrumental in getting the government to pass legislation establishing the PMTT. The Malvern and Prahran Councils elect him the PMTT's Chair in 1908 and he spends the next 10 years building this successful network in the eastern suburbs. As Ian Brady shows, unlike Clapp, Cameron has no aversion to the unionisation of his workforce.

In recognition of his commanding prowess in the field, the government appoints him the Chair of the M&MTB in 1919. In June that year *The Prahran Telegraph* lauded his appointment – Cameron was 'a giant', the acknowledged expert without peer in running electric trams, with 10 years experience in studying tram systems around the world.

In our city just because someone has been legislated to do something doesn't mean they automatically can or will. Vested interests are always ready to knock down any significant proposal for change.

Tram electrification was vehemently opposed for years by sections of the media, particularly *The Herald*. In his article for the Melbourne Tram Museum on Cameron, Russell Jones explains how Cameron had returned from his tour of overseas public tramway systems in 1923 convinced, as the 1911 Royal Commission had been, that overhead wiring was to be preferred to the much more expensive method of burying wires underground. Cameron's decision in this regard would set the scene for the coming struggle, which would pit him against powerful local interests keen to derail the new public monopoly.

Cameron resisted the naysayers and doomsayers. He wanted to spend the money on the trams and the infrastructure to support and run them. He wanted to create a world class tram system, just as Clapp had a generation before. In an interview in 1928 he is described as a man who 'talks and thinks trams'. (I know the feeling.) The *Melbourne & Metropolitan Tramways Act* required the M&MTB to return a proportion of surpluses to other bodies. Cameron wanted to keep the money within the M&MTB for investing in the system so he cleverly ran only small surpluses throughout his reign.

He made the M&MTB a complete tramways organisation: it made the trams, laid the track, constructed the poles and wiring, built the depots, employed all the staff and maintained and operated the whole system. The trams might be labelled by critics as 'behemoths' (which they weren't of course), but Cameron made sure the M&MTB was. He normally had the government onside, and was repeatedly appointed to head the Board until 1935, when he was unceremoniously dismissed.

Cameron is a wonderful figure in the city's history. Bon vivant, member of various clubs, reader of the classics, raconteur, golfer, fisherman and renowned for his affability and enthusiasms, he was a shortish man with a big personality. He's remembered by a number of statues around the city, annual events are held in his honour, and school children all learn about him. No, none of that is true. He is remembered solely in the name of a side street in Brunswick.

*

The great stories of modern Australia are so often immigrant stories aren't they? Like Clapp, Cameron's antecedents are important to understanding this man's drive and commitment, so I'm going to digress here a bit. A contingent of Camerons had arrived in Sydney on the government ship the *SS Boyne* as assisted migrants in 1839 – all 100 of them. The ship held nearly 300 Highlanders, nearly all of whom had 'callings' that were connected to the land; shepherds, ploughmen, farm labourers, house servants, dairy women. A few years later some of these Camerons left Sydney and trekked with their flock of sheep to the Western Districts of Victoria (then known as the District of Port Phillip).

The Camerons, as Benjamin Wilkie describes in an article in *Agricultural History,* were at the forefront of the pastoral development of 'Australia Felix', creating a community of squatters, connected to one another by family and marriage, holding vast tracts of land from the Port Phillip District into South Australia. Two-thirds of the squatters in the Western Districts were Scots. One of these holdings, established in 1842 by John and Alex Cameron, was Morgiana station. The Scots brought their culture with them and our Alex Cameron would've grown up hearing Scots Gaelic, which was still being spoken out west up to the 1880s.

Why did so many Clan Camerons from the west of Scotland end up on the other side of the world in the 1830s? Clan Cameron were an ancient clan from the Western Highlands – Jacobites and supporters of the failed campaigns of the Catholic 'Bonnie' Prince Charles, who suffered enormous losses at the battle of Culloden in 1746. Thereafter things only got worse. You recall my mother's story of the 'wicked men' who drove her family out of their traditional lands? Like my mother's kin, the MacDonalds of Skye, many of Clan Cameron of the West Highlands were driven off their lands in a phase in history known, euphemistically, as the 'clearances'. These 'clearances' targeted the Highland Scots and were a form of ethnic cleansing, driven by economic interests.

Over 70,000 Scots were expelled from Scotland over the first half of the 19ᵗʰ century – to New Zealand, Canada and Australia. For the lowland Scots, English slavers and Highland nobles who wanted their lands, the Highland clans were seen as pre-modern and dispensable. These old communities were forced to give way to modern agricultural methods, principally sheep grazing, which needed acres and acres of land for sheep but very few people to manage them. In the first phase of the clearances they were driven to the periphery of estates to take up kelp farming or fishing. In the second, they were expelled entirely – people had guns shoved in their faces and homes were burnt down. They were soon starving, indebted and without a future. Rather than pay for them to keep living, landowners offered debt cancellation on condition of assisted emigration.

Not all Highlanders were the direct subjects of expulsion – many free settlers took up the opportunities for employment and 'free' land presented by the colonies. But the clearances created a context in which emigration, assisted or unassisted, became a necessity for working people, particularly in the economic downturn of the 1830s and '40s.

I know, this seems like a serious digression from trams. But Alex Cameron's heritage is important to understanding his drive and passions. He was another one of these inspired souls brought up on a diet of hard work, with the addition of a clan history of punishment, loss, humiliation. And Cameron was a man of his clan, serving as the President of Clan Cameron in Melbourne, so he knew his history. In the successful enterprises established by Highland Scots across the Dominions there's a fair bit of 'we'll show you' at work. In the early days many of these businesses involved sheep grazing. Here's an irony. The sheep grazing industries of the New World were so efficient they put the Highland sheep farms out of business. What's that saying about revenge?

What is not ironic is that the Highlanders, so many of whom had been dispossessed of their traditional lands, arrived here and then engaged in their own acts of dispossession of First Nations Peoples.

Of course, they were not alone in this – the colony itself was founded on dispossession – but they, along with every immigrant group to this country, were the beneficiaries of the presumption of terra nullius: a land uninhabited, ripe for the taking.

24. Body Politics on Route 67

'I do love a good, long tram ride.'
'What's your favourite tram Nettie?'
'Oh, I suppose the 67. Yes, the 67. It's a very nice tram ride.'
The late Auntie Nettie, aged 97.

Today I'm taking the 67 tram to Carnegie, a classic Cameron route if ever there was one, and as Aunt Nettie says, a very nice tram ride indeed. The 67 covers the old cable tram route in the city to Brighton Road, Balaclava (1888, electrified in the mid-1920s) then runs along the route of the PMTT electric tram to Grange Road (1913) and then continues on the M&MTB extension to Carnegie (1926). Well done Alex! Route 67 runs for 12.7 kilometres and you are carried along its path by either a Z3 class tram or a B2.

I'm waiting in the wind for the tram to arrive in Swanston Street at the Collins Street stop. Opposite me on the other side of the street a busker is singing French ballads, in a throaty and emotional voice accompanied by piano accordion. It would sound great if it weren't for the competition from a heavy metal busker thrashing the soundscape up the street with electric chords and the voice of a devil. It is a long wait for the tram and the two musics are giving me a headache. When the 67 arrives it is packed. I am standing for the journey down St Kilda Road and can't see anything for the press of bodies around me. Most people, standing or sitting, are on their phones but for a brief moment through a gap in the bodies I see someone reading a book of poems by Judith Rodriguez. Old fashioned thing to do, reading a book of poetry, but no doubt very apt, given how Rodriguez's work documents our city. Poems are like mini documentaries aren't they... .

Through St Kilda Junction and I finally get a seat as St Kilda Road becomes Brighton Road, also known as Nepean Highway, a massively wide enterprise, its modern iteration the result of the same 1960s demolitions that blasted the Junction. Parts of the original 19th century streetscape persist on the east side of the road: a diverse and motley looking set of businesses. You can have your dog groomed while you are having a massage or haircut and on your way home pick up an African mask or a nice red. At Carlisle Street we pass the neo-classical St Kilda City Hall. A number 16 tram crosses the highway heading to St Kilda Beach.

Trundling along the avenue of London Plane trees, past Chapel Street, Glen Eira Road and Hotham Street we turn left and east into Glenhuntly Road, towards Carnegie. At Elsternwick railway station the tram enters another of Melbourne's great linear shopping strips. Glenhuntly Road is a major hub for the southern suburbs, with an atmosphere that is part old European, part modern Melbourne – Jewish family stores, Hungarian restaurants, clothes, shoes, sushi, hardware – you can get anything here. The street is crowded and the tram, which had thinned out, is now full. At the next stop a man in a billowing Hawaiian shirt boards and sits next to me. He's big, as am I, and it's a squeeze for both of us in the narrow seats. He fidgets and sighs. When a couple get off at the next stop he moves across to occupy the now empty seat and we can both breathe again.

I look around the tram. There's every shape and size of the human body on display. Trams collect the plain oddness and diversity of the human form don't they? Researching the cable trams I've come across a bunch of photos showing the work gangs employed to dig up the ground and lay the cable and rail. In one, taken near the intersection of Elizabeth and Flinders Streets, the men working on the project have all ceased work while their collective portrait is taken. They're wearing caps and look up from their shovels and picks with that characteristic stern look of early photographic subjects. All to a man are almost as thin as the rakes and shovels they are holding. Other photos of the era reveal a population that looks different to their modern counterparts. Faces are lean and angular, show bone structure, and bodies are slender and light. There are occasional heavy-set, and sometimes quite rotund, individuals. But from their clothes – and the cigars the men sometimes puff – these latter types are clearly members of the upper class, for whom a wide girth is a sign of success.

By contrast, today's population appears, in general, to be bigger than their forebears – taller, wider, and weightier – and this is not a value judgement but rather a matter of observation. Do trams have anything at all to do with this change in the literal body politic? Remember, in earlier times people used to walk everywhere. Apart from the wealthy indolent, who could afford the expense of private transport, ordinary folk hoofed it to wherever they needed to go. The men who built the cable network probably walked to work – did their long hours of labouring and then walked home.

Before mass transport in the late 19th century, cities and their surrounds were full of walkers. People walked to school, to work, to temple: to the football, to the pub, to the beach. They walked to their friends' houses and to their relatives'. Most people were walking because they couldn't afford a bicycle or a ride in a hansom cab, or to own a horse and buggy. Some were recreational walkers – writers out imagining their next chapter, philosophers pondering first principles, curates discussing God with themselves. Most were just ordinary folk heading off to do the necessary, and most in work would spend their day in some form of manual labour. In a city official's diary I once read from the middle of the century, the author recounts how he was required to visit Geelong for business, but lacked the means to take a horse or buggy on the 75 kilometre journey. Setting out before dawn he arrived at the sister town on Corio Bay over 20 hours later. On his journey he met many people like himself travelling in either direction by foot. Everyone doffed their hats as they passed and said 'good day'.

Clearly work now tends to be sedentary rather than manual, diets are different too, more diverse, and more processed. The advent of an affordable means of intra-city travel – the tram – meant people inevitably walked less. I'm surprised by how many people I see board the tram at one stop only to get down again two or three stops later, journeys of less than one or 200 metres. The trams made it easier for people to move about the city for all manner of purposes, but did this mean their frames were altered in the process?

My reflections on trams and the human form are interrupted by a whistle. The tram has just crossed Hawthorn Road. A man with a red bandana and open shirt is standing in the tram's stairwell. He is whistling as we go; his whistles are musically elaborate, but I can't discern if they are snatches of songs, or something he has made up. The tram is now held up by a truck parked across the road. The man in the bandana stops whistling and advises us loudly that the driver of the truck is 'a fucking idiot'. As the tram moves off the man resumes his whistling – this time a long trill that might easily have been inspired by Charlie Parker.

Glenhuntly Depot, one of the eight depots on the network, is our next stop, fronted by a double-story red-brick building with cream features. The depot is over 100 years old, one of the M&MTB's new depot additions to the system. Happy Birthday Grand Old Depot! Designed by lead architect for the M&MTB, Alan Monsbourgh, the building reflects the Classical Revival style he favoured for the many buildings he designed for the Board in the 1920s and 1930s, which included depots, workshops, signal boxes, substations and the M&MTB headquarters. When you look at M&MTB structures you are frequently looking at his inspirations. Check out the Doric columns at Camberwell depot with its colonnaded tholos (entrance porch) and in Sydney Road the Brunswick depot with its neo-Georgian facade. This guy was so talented.

Now, cast your mind across the thousands of trammies who have had their lunches or dinners in the Glenhuntly depot's canteen room, the millions of pounds, and afterwards dollars, paid in by connies at the end of their shifts, the endless number of tram shunts into and out of the sheds from five in the morning until after midnight. Tram depots sleep for only a few hours a day. These are scenes that are replicated across the network's depots. Today Glenhuntly depot houses about 50 trams running Z3 and B2 trams for the 3, 3a, 64 and 67 routes. The 78 was stolen by Kew Depot about six years ago.

At the depot stop a small contingent of inspectors, known as 'authorised officers', gets down. They are probably nice people, but the travelling public has never warmed to them. Their arrival on a tram prompts some commuters to depart the tram immediately. Today they look weary and despondent but perhaps it is just the warm day. What's it like to check mykis all day? 'Inspectors' dressed in dark green uniforms once roamed the network, with the apparent purpose of managing both the staff and the orderly running of the system, but their job wasn't really to check tickets.

It was the conductors who were the system's protection against fare evasion – like the cable connies before them, on W class trams the connies moved through the tram calling out, 'fares please!' – and knowing their tram cohorts was second nature. Unless the tram was really packed they knew who had paid, and who'd just got on. A fare evader might sit, head down, trying to avoid the gaze of the connie, pretending that they've already paid, but this stratagem rarely worked. The removal of conductors from trams in the late 1990s by the Kennett government was a turning point. The conductors lost their jobs, the tram system lost part of its soul, and machines and inspectors were introduced, one consequence of which was a significant rise in fare evasion.

We've been edging along and now head through the open boom gates of Glenhuntly railway station, and the street is offering gulab jamun, roti chanai, and dosas. Yum! I can get my beard trimmed at a hipster hair salon and sip a cocktail while I'm at it. Just as we leave the shops there is a commotion at the back of the tram. An elderly man yells at the driver that he has missed his stop because the driver did not give him time to get off. He has a long white beard and ponytail, and clutches a walking stick and bag of shopping. The driver has now pulled up the tram between stops – not exactly a legal thing to do – and the old man gets down awkwardly, cursing the driver.

The tram soon turns into Truganini Road and heads to the terminus at Koornang Road. This bit of the route was only duplicated in 1989, the last single track section of the system to be converted. At the terminus a passenger holding a UDL can and clearly drunk, goes up to the driver, who has just emerged from his cabin, and tells him that the elderly man is 'just a pest, a real damn pest', before he sways off the tram. When the driver walks past me to change ends he has a broad grin on his face. Humans.

*

I'm sitting at the kitchen table looking at Pinterest pics of old Ws. I've had the heated up lasagne from last night and I'm now delighting in a concoction of herbs that have been vitamised to a pulp – yech.

I'm thinking again about trams and bodies. There's a photo of a W tram in 1944 in Fitzroy, heading to East Preston. It's been swarmed with riders. The running boards are full of men clinging on, as is the rear of the tram, with half a dozen guys braced on the tram's bumper bar. One guy has a toe hold on the driver's step and is gripping on for dear life. All of them are grabbing what they can – stanchions, the edges of the roof – to hang on. There's one man in uniform. They are all thin, angular types. Have a look at this photo when you have a chance.

As I look through photos of Ws through to the 1970s and beyond I'm seeing that my earlier thoughts about the advent of public transport creating changes in the bodies of the city may be too simple a way of framing the issue. People on trams exhibit all the behaviours and idiosyncrasies of their era – in fashion, body shapes, postures, language. These are ephemeral communities, transitory get-togethers of a body of people, who consciously or not, are apprehending the bodies around them; reading their styles of clothes, speech, articulation, size, dialect. Think about how people arrange themselves on trams – how they sit, stand, slouch, how they board trams and get off, what they do on the tram as they travel, how they deport themselves. The bodies on trams change with the different eras – bodies in the war years, during the Depression of the 1930s, in the protest years of the 1960s, during eras of wealth and scarcity.

Trams are by their nature crowded social entities, you are in one another's space, one another's smells, waking sensibilities. Putting strangers together, body against body, elbows and knees – sitting where someone else sat, will sit – this is a change from before, from the walkers who walk at a distance, from isolation. So thinking and being your own body in this context is also, consciously or not, about an awareness of others' bodies, of similarities and differences. We are reading each other whether we wish to or not.

So, trams don't make culture per se but they participate in its construction. And to some extent the tram's body – its style, shape, smell, colour – is also a participant in this process. In the great eras of the city's trams – the cable trams, the W class trams, the new E class trams – there's also a subtle generation of emotions at work too. Good trams, trams with style, comfort, speed, generate a good ride, and this is a pleasant thing to experience. The cables and the Ws were viewed with great pride when they were introduced. Such trams occur in periods of boom, of investment in design and construction, when the city is bursting with new people, energy, money and ideas. They speak to a city with a strong sense of civitas, of a city that actually thought highly of itself and its citizens, and the standard of public works that people deserved. Happy trams.

25. Transport Wars

'WAR ON TRAMS IN COLLINS STREET'

The Herald, 5th October, 1928.

In the 10 years following his appointment as Chair of the M&MTB Alex Cameron worked at a frenetic pace to modernise, expand and rationalise Melbourne's public transport network. He was a firm believer in the necessity for the city to have a single public transport authority, and, against considerable opposition, worked assiduously to bring this into being. If Cameron had been a cricketer he would have played consistently off the front foot, driving his opponents to all points of the ground. This man was the Bradman of trams and the likes of the Royal Automobile Club of Victoria (RACV), private bus operators, *The Herald* newspaper and sundry councillors and politicians would be no match for this consummate public servant.

In his essay on the economic history of the M&MTB, Russell Jones describes how the 1920s saw the transformation of the tram system on two fronts. First, there were the ongoing conversions of cable trams to electric. By 1930 much of the system was converted, but the Great Depression curtailed the process for five years. At the same time as converting cable lines, the cable trams still running had to be maintained. Many were in a poor state and needed fixing, tracks were worn and engine houses had to be repaired. As the population of the city rose, the system was creaking under the weight of hugely expanded patronage from 1908 to 1919. Trams were severely overcrowded during peak hours, and the city was starting to experience the first traffic jams on its major roads, due in part to the rise of car ownership.

Cameron's second objective was to roll out new electric lines. The 1920s saw 20 new electric lines, or electric extensions to lines constructed across the city. Cameron's overseas tour of transport systems in 1923 combined with his already considerable knowledge of tram systems formed his vision for the city. The 1923 General Scheme, the outcome of a lengthy planning process, was the M&MTB blueprint for a modern, integrated tramways for the rapidly expanding city. By 1925 the M&MTB was Melbourne's single tramways entity, with system-wide standardised wages and conditions, the first of the W class trams on the lines, and in 1926 the Preston Workshops opened at an astronomical cost of 326,300 pounds, giving the M&MTB one of the most modern engineering workshops in the country.

At the same time, the M&MTB faced constraints. It was required to maintain the roadways on which its trams travelled, provide street lighting, contribute to city bridge construction, the removal of level crossings and corner widening. Local councils were also due a cut of M&MTB profits, and the Board was required to hold in reserve four percent of the capital cost of operations. On top of this the government in its wisdom had decreed that the M&MTB would contribute tens of thousands of pounds per annum to the state's Liquor Licensing Fund, the Fire Brigade, and the Infectious Diseases Hospital. Alex kept building. New tram depots were opened in Glenhuntly, South Melbourne and Camberwell. Old depots, such as Essendon, Coburg and Malvern depots were expanded to meet the new demands of electric. The electrical system itself had to be built for purpose or modified, with new substations opened around the city.

Our city has always been prey to smash and grab merchants. Alex fought off a gang of these in the form of unregulated private bus operators who started up in the 1920s. Paying no road taxes, following no timetables, stopping where they pleased, and digging up streets with their heavy chassis, the bus operators nevertheless had some powerful supporters who didn't like the idea of a public transport 'monopoly'. The RACV didn't want electric trams at all on some city streets, claiming, erroneously, that they would cause congestion and were a threat to safety. Overhead wiring was not popular, at least according to *The Herald* and *The Sun News-Pictorial* – 'unsightly', 'ugly', and ruining the streetscapes of Marvelous Melbourne. The electric trams were too noisy, the subject of bitter complaining, and so noisy that residents on main roads were shifting house 'to escape the constant roar of passing tram cars', said *The Sun* in February 1928, as well as creating traffic congestion around the city. In October 1929 *Smith's Weekly* described Cameron as having drawn 'a hornet's nest about his head' by defying the opposition to electrification.

This conflict in the 1920s, appropriately dubbed, the 'Transport War', saw Cameron frequently in the media defending his vision for the city, and hosing down his opponents. He gave interviews, wrote articles, invited deputations, and made his case publicly using the large quantity of data at his disposal showing unequivocally that the tram was the best form of transport for the urban area of the city. In a series of news articles published in the 1920s and early '30s, one of which he penned himself for *The Herald* in May 1924, Cameron argued, with evidence and international comparisons, for the superiority of centrally organised public tramways over private buses and motor cars on the grounds of safety, economy and contribution to civic development.

He labelled criticism of the M&MTB as 'uninformed', and spoke for the 'silent majority whose voice has been unheard'. Private buses used taxpayer funded roads, contributed nothing, needed twice their number to carry the same load as trams, while ignoring the less profitable non-peak. And cars? Trams carried four times the number of passengers with one sixth the number of vehicles, occupying just three square feet (1/3rd of a metre) of road per passenger, compared to 43 square feet (four square metres). In relation to the rise of the motor car he said: '…the motor car is not yet, and should not, in a properly organised system of street transport, be the means of travel for the average citizen.' Go Alex!

While *The Herald* generously gave Cameron the column space to defend himself and the M&MTB, throughout the 1920s it maintained its anti-tram campaign; it promoted the views of anti-tram politicians and local councillors, the private transport lobby, including the bus lobby, and some city retailers. Collins Street became a flash point in the late '20s with the move to convert the lines from cable to electric. It was a heated period of discord over public policy and the shape of the city.

It was clear the electric trams created 'noise' – Cameron readily admitted this, and detailed the M&MTB's efforts to mitigate tram noise. But the 'noise' question was ultimately less about the sound emanating from the city's new trams, and more about whose interests would determine public transport policy for the city. Would Melbourne have an integrated, functioning network of trams operating as a public utility, or would the streets of the city be dominated by private operators – by buses, cars and cabs?

Eventually the government had heard enough about the poor quality of Melbourne's bus services and decided it was time for regulation. With the introduction of a seat tax on the buses the private operators virtually disappeared overnight. They were always fly-by-nighters. Alex jumped on the opportunity this presented and, somewhat ironically, created a fleet of M&MTB buses to service those areas the trams had yet to reach. He held on against his opponents, dealt with the impact of the Depression on state finances, and worked assiduously to bring the General Scheme into reality. The voices opposed to him kept up their campaign, but Cameron had the law behind him and the public onside, who were pouring onto the city's trams in ever increasing numbers.

I know, dear reader, you've been desperate to hear what happened to the 1923 General Scheme. Weren't trams meant to cover the whole city? Yes, they were. The M&MTB plan had trams running along Bell Street in the north, along Warrigal Road in the east, on Ballarat Road out west. Trams would connect Footscray and William-stown to the city, and an entire spaghetti of routes would emerge across the suburbs to service the expanding population of the city.

Cameron achieved an enormous amount, implementing or laying the groundwork for the General Scheme's success. He won the 'Transport War', ensuring that electric trams would stay at the heart of the city's public transport system. He well deserves the title of 'father' of the the city's modern tram network, one that has lasted over a century. But the full extent of the General Scheme was never realised. There was the Depression, followed by World War Two, followed by decades of government inaction. Russell Jones argues that the financial constraints noted above were also a significant brake on the General Scheme being fully realised. Car ownership also soared. It's been a costly mistake for the city not to fully implement the Scheme when it had the chance. But don't blame Alex – he gave it everything he had.

*

But there is another very important character in our tram story. Every visionary needs someone on point. For Clapp this was his chief engineer, George Duncan. For Cameron this was T. P. Strickland, Chief Engineer of the M&MTB. Tom Percival Strickland became Chief Engineer of the new behemoth in 1921 and over the next 18 years devoted himself to the design and construction of the new system. Like Clapp and Duncan, Cameron and Strickland were a team; Cameron was the public face of the M&MTB – he took care of the Board, of strategy, politics, money, and administration. Strickland focused inwards on how the system would actually be made and work, in a seemingly endless series of knotty problems and challenges, and he was central to the development of the General Scheme. But he and Cameron were a team and all the major strategy decisons were joint ones.

In his article on Tom Strickland for the Tram Museum, Russell Jones details the mammoth task undertaken by Strickland in overseeing the development of the M&MTB network. It was Strickland who concluded, after careful analysis and against much popular opinion, that overhead wiring was the best fit for Melbourne, economically and long term. He decided, as the model for the new W trams, on the drop centre bogie trams made by South Melbourne tram makers James Moore and Sons for the PMTT. He straightened out the side curves and got rid of the quarter windows. Why? Because he wasn't in the business of making boutique trams, but a mass fleet that could be quickly and cost-effectively constructed. He chose the site for the Preston workshops, got them built in record time and reasonable cost, and at their peak had them producing nearly 80 trams a year. He replaced the all timber frame of the Moore and Sons' trams, with a mix of steel and timber, and by the time of the W3 class tram was making all steel frames – lighter and cheaper – although problems with this class did emerge later. He maintained the ageing cable fleet as the M&MTB went about replacing it, assessed and implemented the new tramways' city-wide power supply and oversaw the variations and improvements to the W class trams as they progressed. His W5 tram became the essential basis for all others up to 1956, when the Ws ceased to be made.

Clearly an extraordinary man, with prodigious talent and energy; but it pains me to tell you that he came from the harbour city, where he was born in 1875. A Sydney Grammar boy – he came from money – he took first class honours in engineering at Sydney University, and gained his Masters of Science from the prestigious McGill University in Montreal. He worked for G.E.C. in New York State as an electrical engineer, came back to Australia in 1902 as assistant engineer for NSW railways and tramways, became Chief Assistant the following year, the same year he married. Strickland was no stranger to tragedy. When he was 12 or 13 his father drowned outside the Sydney Heads (about the same age my mother lost her mother).

Strickland was not a media performer like Cameron – it wasn't his role. But he was often mentioned, and indeed celebrated, in the press in relation to significant events, milestones and various reports of the M&MTB. *The Age* praised him in January 1924 as the designer of the modern, new look, almost entirely Australian-made first two W trams, entering service on the Malvern line. *The Sun News-Pictorial* celebrated the first ride, carrying the engineer himself, of an electric tram in the CBD in January 1926. *The Argus* in the same year praised Strickland and his employees for the months of planning, preparation and work in making over the cable to the electric system, a feat 'among the best achievements in tramway conversion in Australia'. Strickland continues to be in the news in relation to tram related reports or debates through the 1930s and just before he retires in 1938, *The Age* waxes lyrical about the Strickland created Preston workshops, their 'modern, comfortable and speedy trams' reflecting the high level of skills of the engineers and artisans.

Strickland had enormous, and recognised, success before he retired from the M&MTB due to ill-health. Over 40 kilometres of new track, conversion of nearly 50 kilometres of cable lines, development of the Preston tram workshops, design and construction of over 570 trams. He died in Melbourne at 79, leaving behind his wife and his three daughters. The *Argus* carried a small one paragraph obituary announcing his demise.

I know, monuments to dead white men are out of vogue and rightly so given that they usually celebrate invaders, war mongers, slave traders or crooks. But in the M&MTB, Cameron and Strickland created a long lasting public good and they deserve some form of memorialisation in this city of forgetting.

26. An Existential Ride on the Number 57

Route 57 starts grand and ends in desolation. Nevertheless, it has a fine heritage, being composed of multiple former lines: the cable tram line from Flinders Street to the Queen Victoria Market built in 1887, the Victoria Street to Flemington Bridge cable tram line added in 1890, and then in 1906 the electric tram line from Flemington Bridge to the Maribrynong River, constructed by our old mates the NMETL. Finally, the M&MTB extended the electric line to West Maribrynong in 1940. Today it runs on ancient Z class trams out of Essendon depot – I keep getting Zs! – and which will, fingers crossed, be replaced by the new G trams in 2025. May God let me live that long.

Not a long route at under 12 kilometres, route 57 is however a storehouse of history, activity, and variation. I'm starting today at the terminus at Flinders and Elizabeth Streets' intersection. The terminus is the turning point for three lines – the 57, 59 and 19. It is usually crowded and as the trams bank up at Flinders Lane passengers try to gauge which side of the narrow platform they should be standing on. Lots of craning necks. The points before the terminus allow the trams to run straight in or turn to the right. It can get confusing for the drivers too, who have to keep tabs on who is supposed to be leaving next. Is it radio controlled now? Tram buffs will know the answer.

Since I was a child travelling the city with my mother this inter-section with its terminus has always fascinated me. This is where she and I would catch the 57 to the Royal Show each year, and for various reasons this intersection has featured in each of my life's stages. The imposing railway station building in its Edwardian free style stretches a whole city block, its tower with the enormous clock can be seen all the way up Elizabeth Street, and then there's the crossing itself: one of the only crossings in the city with a period devoted to pedestrian-only traffic, a kind of mini-Shibuya crossing if you like, and densely packed with people crossing at peak hour times. Today's brightly lit view sits in contrast with most of my earlier memories of the crossing, in which the intersection is bathed everywhere in a waning light, populated with hurrying black coats, umbrellas, slush and drizzle. A John Brack scene.

That clock. Its four faces are the biggest in the city, and they are the work of master watch and clockmaker Johann Friedrich Wilhelm 'Fritz' – yes, it's Australia mate – Ziegler. Arriving in 1883 Fritz and later his sons made public clocks for the city and around Australia for over 40 years, including Gog and Magog's fabulous timepiece in the Royal Arcade. The railway clock was unique – a master clock used to transmit the time by telegraph to dozens of railway stations across the city. Okay, enough about railways.

There are many classic photos of cable trams heading up and down Elizabeth Street. Some of these show the flooding that regularly occurred there. Underneath Elizabeth Street is the buried William's Creek, turned into a stormwater drain in the early 1880s. Without this drain the installation of the cable tram line would not have been possible. William's Creek was the city's major tributary running from the north, south to the Yarra. Before the drain, the flooding was an annual event; once a poor city denizen drowned in the flood waters. Even with drainage there were still floods after major rains. The last big flood occurred as late as 1972. I remember it well because I couldn't get on the tram to go to school. (In fact I couldn't get out of the railway station's Elizabeth Street exit, the underpass being totally submerged.) Cars were swept down the street.

A wholly man-made disaster happened in Elizabeth Street too. You know I'm in love with the city's 19th century buildings. Elizabeth

Street still has a collection of these, but some of the best were caught up in Whelan's sack of the city in the 1960s. Have a look online at photos of these buildings; the Australian Building, which was 11 storeys tall, built in Queen Anne Revival Style; the Craig, Williamson and Thomas Emporium, a famous drapery; and Fink's Building right on the corner of Elizabeth and Flinders, a nine storey grandee.

Despite the carnage, Elizabeth Street still contains an eclectic array of structures spanning the history of the city. There's the marvel of Ellerker and Kilburn's Melbourne City Building built in 1888, on the corner of Little Collins Street, an amazing pastiche of classical and baroque styles, turrets, balconies and irregularities. At the corner of Bourke and Elizabeth is the grand GPO (1861-67), a magnificent structure that should never have been sold off to a handful of fashion houses in the 1990s. The city has a recurring malaise when it comes to its heritage, as you are no doubt by now sick of me saying.

Opposite the GPO there should be a magic shop, but Bernard's Magic Shop closed after some eight decades in business, in 2017. After the connie's urging, Bernard's became a stop on my mother's and my city visits, and I was in awe of it and it seemed so strange that fully grown adults could engage in such frivolity. Did you fall for the 50 cent piece glued to the floor of the doorway? Further along the Aussie Disposals store is still selling bad army fashion to new generations. And here, on the Elizabeth and Lonsdale Street corner, sits the beautiful St Francis' Church, our state's oldest Catholic Church and surely, its most modest. Mary MacKillop was baptised here. And do you remember the Vespas, Moto Guccis and Hondas jacked up on their foot stands lining the pavement in the block of motorcycle stores? I bought my Czech bike, a 350cc Jawa two-stroke, here in the '70s. Gone too, in their place dozens of small restaurants running up to Queen Victoria Market. And over all, a forest of gargantuan skyscrapers.

My tram today is very creaky. Unlike many drivers, this driver is a stickler for the rules and sounds his bell loudly as the tram takes off from each stop. There are no automated announcements, for which

I'm grateful. The condition of the trams plying route 57 is truly underwhelming. Writing for *The Age* in 2019, Catherine Ford linked the poor behaviour she consistently witnessed on 57 trams with the state of the vehicles, saying that the 'disgraceful condition of its trams seems to actively encourage feelings, and the acting out, of despair and alienation...'. Yes, just as there can be 'happy trams' as I mentioned above, so too can there be unhappy ones, as Ford implies. Today though, the 57 is calm and orderly, neither joyous nor miserable.

We arrive at the stop for the Queen Victoria Market, looking its part as a major tourist attraction and the biggest outdoor fruit and vegetable market in the country, in spite of the encroaching office and apartment towers. Sole survivor of the three splendid CBD markets from the 19th century, it is built over the remains of thousands of people buried in the city's original cemetery. A good place for a day of the dead festival. The tram disgorges most of its entourage, and another lot pile on, carrying bags and packs bulging with fresh food and market bargains.

And we're off, heading west up Victoria Street, with West Melbourne on the south side of the tram, and North Melbourne on the right. It's all pretty much old Melbourne up here, low skyline under a big sky, and for years overlooked and neglected by developers. We pass the gigantic St Mary Star of the Sea, the odd cafe and restaurant in among motley 19th and 20th century buildings, before heading down the hill to Errol Street where we do a right turn. Here's the municipal library and the magnificent town hall with its clock tower – is that one by Fritz too? Where are the crowds to match this civic dignity? There is the faint air of a ghost town here today. Another dogleg into Queensbury Street before a right into Abbotsford Street, with the engine house on the corner, now impaled by apartments. Is this getting too traveloguey? Just wait, you're about to meet an existentialist, a rare and threatened species of our social order.

Down the slope of Abbotsford Street with its canopy of trees, past smart two storey Victorians, a block of housing commission flats in the process of being 'de-commissioned', and we arrive at Flemington

Road opposite the Children's Hospital. Most of the Vic market cohort are now off the tram, but sitting opposite me is a young guy who got on there, with his big shopping bag and shoulder bag. From the shoulder bag he takes a large volume which now sits spread on his knees. Poor man. He's reading Sartre's *Being and Nothingness*, one of the great bores of 20th century literature. No, make that of the 20th century full stop. Can it be true that anyone under 40 still reads Sartre? I'm bemused. Can I get him to talk to me about it though? Still a problem, this initiating business, given my steady-state introversion. Well, here goes, he can always ignore me.

'How are you enjoying Sartre?'

Michel – as I will come to know him soon – looks up from his tome. 'Oh, yeah, I don't know. I mean I'm not sure it's about enjoyment so much as trying to understand him. I've read him before but there are a few things I want to follow up.'

'I read him when I was about your age and I'm not sure I understood a thing. But I've always found existentialism difficult. Are you reading him for uni or just yourself?'

'Kind of both.' He tells me he majored in philosophy and across his degree developed a special interest in two areas – the ancient Greek pre-socratics and 20th century existentialism. Now he's doing his PhD on the topic of the relationship of social theory and existentialism, with a focus on social engagement and political action movements. 'I've been drawn lately to the phenomenology of Merleau-Ponty. Unlike Heidegger, and in a different way to Sartre, Merleau-Ponty sees being human as essentially embodied and social in character. Being human is being bodied – the senses are intimately involved in the business of being human – and social. If that makes sense.'

Michel is a bit shy or wary of me initially, but as he talks his enthusiasm for his subject is obvious.

'I vaguely recall Merleau-Ponty', I say, 'wasn't he involved with Sartre and Simone de Beauvoir?'

'Yes he was. Actually, I think Merleau-Ponty was in love with de Beauvoir, but she chose Sartre – anyway they were a pretty amazing trio. I think de Beauvoir was a better social theorist than Sartre, but Merleau-Ponty was the better philosopher of the three. Well, better is not the right word, more complete somehow.'

'In what way was Merleau-Ponty more complete?'

'Well, for me, his philosophy is more rigorous. His approach investigates ontology and epistemology, but also allows for other disciplines to engage with philosophy – humanism, psychology, political action.' Michel pauses here.

'Go on, I'm actually interested.'

'Okay, well, for Merleau-Ponty, and Sartre, being human is a social event – the social world is inescapable, you can't be outside your social self. Whether we like it or not, want it or not, we are drawn into the world of society with all of its responsibilities and anxieties, the whole business of necessity. Our senses are both physical and social. But it all comes with a sting – not the right word, caveat maybe? – well, it's because we shift endlessly between comprehension and ignorance, our lived experience, our memories. Our apprehension of things, ourselves, is never truly stable, it's always on the move... .'

By now the tram has swung into Racecourse Road in Flemington, gone under the massive freeway overpass and the railway bridge, over the Moonee Ponds Creek and is heading towards the racecourse and show grounds. We pass blocks of commission flats, a string of halal bakeries and East African restaurants. The tram is crowded again and stopping at every stop on the journey. I remember that it was here that I was going to get down and have lunch at a Somali restaurant I'd read about. But this conversation is too interesting.

'Can I ask you', I say, 'what got you interested in existentialism in the first place?'

'Sure. Yes, it was Sartre that got me interested. His complexity, his difference really appealed to me. It is as if existentialism was invented for people like me who find the every day language of the world a bit, you know, simple?' Michel gestures out the window of the tram and says, 'All of this that we are passing now is so often represented as mundane, predictable. We really have no real idea what we are looking at, or exactly what it is that is doing the looking. That's what I like about existentialism, its refusal to accept the world as given, or the human in the world as conventionally represented, our so-called common sense understandings of ourselves and others.'

'Wouldn't religious people have something to say about that?'

'Yes of course. The premise here though is the enlightenment version of reality, where God is a human construct, not a creator.'

The tram has been held up by some kerfuffle ahead involving trucks and buses. Now we are on the move again and passing the former Newmarket Saleyards. Cattle and sheep were sold here for almost 130 years, until it closed in the late 1980s, following 100 years of objections about noise, smells and traffic from local residents. Some things take time do they not? Back to our budding existentialist, with whom I've now exchanged names.

'So Michel, what exactly does Merleau-Ponty bring to this, and how are you relating his work to social action?'

'Ok, right – I feel like I'm giving a seminar paper. Well, so we have a paradox at work in our thinking, acting in the world as if we were in possession of eternal truths. In fact, reality is not an undying truth but a collection of perspectives and comprehensions, derived in the first place by our senses. For Merleau-Ponty reality is always phenomenological, always derived from eyes, ears, touch, sensibilities, lived experience. This does not mean there is no truth; our senses and perceptions don't open on just anything, on an arbitrary or random world. I'm intending to use his approach to explore community action movements for my PhD. By examining the world phenomenologically – that is through the study of lived experience – we can maybe get a more authentic appreciation of the everyday, and our own lives. This is also based on the existentialist idea that the familiar can be made strange. Most traditional philosophy takes the human being as a given, with an assumed set of characteristics. Existentialists ask the a priori question, what is the being that is human? What is thinking? Merleau-Ponty rejected the Cartesian separation of body and mind.'

Michel tells me he has been reading Marci Shore's account of the Maidan revolution in the Ukraine. In 2014 thousands of protestors gathered in the central Maidan in Kyiv to protest against corruption and the kleptocratic Yanukovych government. They occupied the Maidan for months, across the freezing winter, setting up tents, food stalls and kitchens, class rooms and libraries. They debated the forms of government they wanted and refused to be intimidated by the police and bands of roving government thugs, and snipers. Many of these people simply left their jobs to join the revolution and the protestors came from all walks of life. Shore interviews the participants. Many of those recorded talk about how in the midst of the revolution they felt more alive, more connected to others, more their authentic selves than they had in their lives. How the cold didn't affect them. There was a general sense of boundless energy, heightened senses and a growing fearlessness in the face of government violence, which would eventually see over 100 people shot dead in the square. 'For me', Michel says, 'it was fascinating to read how some protestors articulated their experience in terms of phenomenological theory, and were aware at the time of the interplay between theory and practice. Phenomenology was a subject they talked about – it gave some of these people a framework within which to view their social action, to understand the process of change they were undergoing both as individuals and as a group.'

'And now those same people are at war.'

'Yes, they are. I thought of going there to help by driving vans, you know, lots of people have volunteered to deliver medical grade supplies and stuff to Ukraine, but my parents convinced me not to. My Mum's family is Ukrainian and she's been really distressed since the invasion. Our relatives are in Lviv a long way from the front line but they've still had a terrible time and one of my cousins died fighting. Probably a stupid idea going there but I wanted to actually do something. Shit it's awful.'

Given this startling revelation I have a lot more questions for Michel but he tells me he's getting off soon, and true to his word in a couple of stops he does. My 101 class in existentialism is over. I wish him well in his studies, and watch as he gets off and stands at the pedestrian crossing waiting for the lights to change. Such a frail thin body, which looks like it could be dispatched into air by a strong wind, containing such big ideas, and an intensity to match.

*

Listening to Michel I've missed a couple of city icons on the route of the 57. Stop 30 will deposit you at the Epsom Road entrance to Flemington Racecourse, by the bare banks of the Maribyrnong. This is of course home to that highly self-conscious event – the 'race that stops a nation' – the Melbourne Cup. From the slopes of the old-fashioned Footscray Park, you can catch a glimpse of the horses through the trees over your picnic. At the track, it's the biggest outdoor piss-up in the country. Don't come back on the tram late on Cup Day afternoon. You will risk getting your shoes covered in vomit.

Just two stops further down at the Royal Showgrounds you might be in time for the 'Show', which has evolved from its origins in the Port Phillip Farmers' Society's ploughing matches (medals and prizes awarded for best furrows) to an all-out Agricultural show and carnival, an annual treat for all in the pre-TV and mass entertainment days, and still going.

It was a long day at the Show with my mother. I liked the wood chopping, the hall with sheep and lambs, the equestrian events. The prize cakes melted in the heat and were covered in flies. Afterwards my mother would take me to the hall with show bags where I could never make up my mind which bags to get. The tram back was full of mothers with their exhausted children, all of them clutching their bags of bounty.

*

Meander tram. We've gone through the Union Road shops, many still sporting their 19th century facades. A left into Maribyrnong Road and here comes an 82 tram from the opposite direction bound for Moonee Ponds. We're travelling down to the bridge over the Maribyrnong River, which shines blue in the bright sun. There are two teams of helmeted people in canoes on the water playing some kind of water polo with paddles and nets. They dash about with great vigour and purpose.

My mother told me a story once about dolphins appearing in the Maribyrnong. She had taken a tourist ferry from Footscray up the river one summer. The dolphins were silvery white and played at the bow, diving and shooting in the boat's wake. I remember her saying – I must have been a teenager by then – that she had just found out she was pregnant with me. Looking back on this story now it occurs to me that there's something missing. As far as I can remember my father had never referred to this river trip and in my memory of her story he doesn't rate a mention. Wasn't he there? Who was she with? Perhaps she was with her friend Irene, who I know was also pregnant at the same time as my mother.

The tram is almost at the end of the line and I'm the only one on board. The landscape is derelict. The abandoned Commonwealth Defence site covers a wide area of delapidated and crumbling buildings, disused arsenals, and weeds. But in 1940, when the tram was extended here, activity was booming on the site which already had significant heritage as a centre of explosives manufacture, with a cordite factory opened in 1912. The ADF say the site is surplus to requirements, so they are selling it off to developers, who will need HAZMAT suits to clean up all the asbestos.

27. A City's Identity: The W Series

As you know dear reader, the genesis of our beloved W class trams goes back to the formation of the M&MTB. Alex Cameron, Tom Strickland and the Board are no mugs. They aren't just going to fulfill their obligations under the Act. They are going to build something that the whole city will be proud of and which will last generations. The Ws were the second great era of the Melbourne tram.

The first element of this process was to determine the character and nature of the electric fleet. What should be the tram model for the new system? How would it be powered, how many people would it seat and in what kind of conditions? What style would they have and what colour should they be? The electric cars the M&MTB inherit are a motley bunch of contrasting styles, colours, shapes and engineering. The Board decrees a new standard electric tram for the whole system. This is the beginning of the W class trams, built across the 33 years from 1923 to 1956. Over 750 W class trams are produced, most of them constructed at the Preston workshops.

The inherited system had trams in every hue, and the M&MTB decides to standardise this too, eventually choosing the green and cream that become synonymous with the city's tram fleet. Most Melburnians did not think of their trams as 'W' trams, but as 'green' trams. It was said, possibly apocryphally, that the green colour was chosen to blend in with the trees in St. Kilda Road. Whatever, when you spied a green shape in the distance you knew that your tram was finally arriving.

The M&MTB based their design for the first W class tram, in a modified form, on the PMTT's L class trams, acquired by the M&MTB in 1921. The W's design was confirmed by the M&MTB in July 1922.

Writing for the Tram Musuem, Warren Doubleday explains how the very first cars were built by the M&MTB at workshops in North Fitzroy. Thereafter, and to speed up production, contracts were awarded to private companies for the construction of tramcars, Holden's Motor Body Builders Ltd of Adelaide and local builder James Moore and Sons. Local bogie production was augmented by an engineering company from Adelaide, while the electrical equipment was initially contracted out to General Electric (Australia) and Metropolitan Vickers (UK). Doubleday lists the types of wood to be used in construction of the tram bodies, including Tasmanian red myrtle, oregon, Queensland maple, mountain ash, blackwood, stringybark and Baltic pine.

The first two M&MTB W trams were delivered to Malvern depot in December 1923 and were reported as in service in early 1924, while the first tram to roll out of the Preston workshops wholly made there was in 1926. Tom Strickland was in charge of the whole process.

In their books on the Melbourne electric tram fleet Randall Wilson and Dale Budd (and earlier with Norman Cross), describe the Ws' many iterations, the major categories running from the original plain W class, followed by the W1, and then so on to the contemporary W8 class. The Ws are referred to as 'bogie, drop-centre cars' or 'bogie, drop-centre saloon' trams, which relates to their design: the central section of the tram is lower than the saloons at either end, which sit over the bogies. The drop-centre facilitates boarding and exiting. (If you find tram classes and makes a tad boring – how could you! – you have my permission to skip this section. For more details on tram rolling stock see the VICSIG website.)

W Class: The original. Two hundred of the Ws were built and delivered between 1923 and 1927. This is a drop-centre tram with saloons at either end, two bogies with two engines each, air brakes, beautiful timbers, and three doors with weather blinds. The drop-centre middle compartment is a smoking section, with face to back chairs. They could seat 52 people and 93 standing. Well, that was the theory. In practice, trams could be, and still are, heavily over-populated at peak times, beyond their supposed capacity. Was the connie going to do a head count?

W1: The W1 recalled the cable trams in its design, with the drop-centre reconfigured with longitudinal seats and the entire section open to the elements – perhaps nostalgically recalling the dummy cars. Just 30 were built between 1925 and 1928. They were easy to get on and off from, but pretty uncomfortable if it was raining. You could smoke in the open middle, although those who rolled their own cigarettes took the risk of their 'baccy' being blown away on a windy day. The wood-work on these is outstanding.

W2: By the late 1920s the W settles into the design that, while continually worked on, modified and improved, it will basically keep for the next 60 years. The W2 enters service in 1927 and 180 of them are built new, and with the conversion of most of the Ws and W1s giving an overall fleet of over 400 W2 trams. Regularly described as the 'backbone' of the fleet, the last W2 was withdrawn in 1987. The centre door is narrowed, and the drop-centre section converts to back to back chairs. The canvas weather blinds are back, rolled up on the loading side. Passengers sometimes took it upon themselves to pull down the centre blind when it was pissing down. Loading and off-loading was greatly improved with this design.

W3 and W4: The W3 and W4 classes were produced between 1930 and 1935. Depression trams. Only 21 were built (16 W3s and five W4s), reflecting the strapped state of public finances. The W3s were the first trams to be built with an all steel frame, which made them considerably lighter, thus cheaper to run. But by the late 1960s all W3s had been withdrawn, due in part to cracking in their frames.

W5: The W5s were the next big thing for the W class. Built between 1935 and 1939, 125 W5s (including five CW5s) were eventually running on the system. The W5s (called 'Clydes' after the controller) were wider-bodied, had more powerful motors, and the last 10 (designated SW5s) featured power-operated sliding doors to replace the open doorways - the W5s were the last tram constructed with three doors and pull-down blinds. Drivers liked the powerful engines but for some the W5s were, as they said, 'a bugger to drive', given the temperamental nature of the controller. It made for a more challenging day, finding out your vehicle was going to be one of these. Still trundling into the 1990s.

SW6 and W6: The SW6 and the W6 sorted out this controller problem for the drivers and the W6 in particular was a handsome, fast, comfortable tram much loved by travellers. With construction begun in 1939, 150 of the SW6s and W6s were in service by 1955 (120 SW6s and 30 W6s), all with power operated sliding doors, a major breakthrough in passenger comfort. The early saloons had flip over seats, and wooden double seats in the centre section. The more modern W6s ran on the Bourke Street line until the 1970s, by which time all the seating was padded in brown upholstery.

W7: The W7s, built in 1955-1956, were the last in the W series, based pretty much on the W6 except all had upholstered seats. Melbourne bums had had enough. (These beautiful trams were obviously also made to celebrate the birth of the author in 1955.) The W7s ran originally almost exclusively on the Bourke Street line, replacing the buses that had operated there, and which were long overdue for scrapping. They had noise reducing and other features that made for a more comfortable ride. Originally 70 W7s were planned, but the new Bolte government, no friend of the trams, reduced the order to 40.

Seating capacity on the Ws remained fairly stable across the classes, most commonly 52 passengers, and no lower than 48. All the W classes ran on four electric traction motors (two per bogie) except for the very short lived CW5 with only two motors. Power was collected from the overhead catenary at 600 volts DC by trolley poles, spring loaded to ensure they stayed in contact. As I've noted, the poles often had a mind of their own, especially on sharp turns at intersections. The pole would dislodge from the overhead, bang around in the wiring and the tram would come to a sudden halt. The driver would emerge to chase the dangling rope attached to the pole and reattach the pole to the wire. Embarrassing.

The motors themselves varied over the years but stuck to a basic 30kW output. They sat underneath the tram body of course, support-ed by the axles and spring frames on the truck. Like all elements of the Ws' construction they were incredibly durable and reliable, pro-vided the drivers were trained properly to operate them. All W class trams' bogies swiveled to a degree, greatly improving the navigation of curves, reducing wear and tear on the wheels and rails and the risk of derailment.

As time went by, earlier W trams were fitted out with sliding doors, and much later, in the 1980s, much of the fleet was upgraded. By then the W class are sharing the system with Z, A and B classes, and are gradually being replaced. Those upstart newcomers made of plastic and steel.

W8: In a final burst of reinvigoration, the remaining Ws were giv-en a complete makeover, including modified frames, new electrics, new wipers, and air conditioning for the drivers. Yes, for decades W drivers froze in their cabins in winter, and boiled in summer. The last Ws to run on the system outside the city circle, on routes 30, 78 and 79, were withdrawn in late 2013. Now just 12 W cars remain, servic-ing the city circle route, and designated the W8s. The rest have been sold off to private owners, museums and, occasionally, other tram operators, in Europe and America. (Elton John has a W2 tram in the grounds of his Berkshire mansion.) Restored bits and pieces have ended up in people's houses, including mine. Vale W series!

Clapp's influence can be felt in the M&MTB's W class – the same animating principle he brought to the cable trams: to combine effi-ciency and beauty. Cameron surely understood this. Bear in mind too that the much loved cable trams were still running up to 1940, exem-plars of the perfectly designed tram. The Ws, like the cable trams, were regarded in their heyday as the epitome of modernity and style, with their elaborate and expensive fittings, extensive and beautiful timbers, polished brass, leather straps, deep green upholstery and with their new width, a sense of space. Faster and bigger than the cable trams, they could convey more people around the city in better time. The later models in particular carried passengers smoothly, in great comfort – they had an air of theatre about them – and most people in the 1950s were still preferring them to the car.

Overall, we can see the development of the W series from 1923 to 1956 as a progressive evolution of the model, while retaining signal elements of the original design. The uniform green and cream colours gave the whole system an impression of cohesion and dependability. The W era trams were largely financially successful – as I've noted, Cameron and his successors were no mugs: the transition from a largely privately operated system to a public one could have fallen flat on its face. More than this, the Ws became embedded in the identity of the city itself. Tourist brochures for the city inevitably featured a picture of a W class tram. And as for my generation, when we dream of trams, they are Ws.

Well, do you want to take a ride in one?

28. How to Drive a W Class Tram

I'm standing outside the Camberwell depot in the 1970s waiting for my driver to emerge from inside. It's five o'clock in the morning, freezing and I'm wishing to God that I'd worn my longjohns. My designated driver for the morning, Ellie, appears and we head down to the sheds to pick up our tram. She mutters something about 'road six', which I assume relates to the whereabouts of the tram. It's a bit early for conversation so I just tag along grateful for the opportunity to be driven around in the cabin of a W class tram. Ellie, it turns out, is Greek-Australian, came here as a child from Athens with her parents and has been on the trams for five years, mostly as a conductor. She's one of the first wave of women to drive trams in the history of Melbourne trams, a right won after a long struggle by women trammies.

We've reached the sheds, which are massively high and covered in bird shit. Her tram, emblazoned with the number 982, is a W6 class, and it's waiting at the head of the queue in lane six. These later model Ws are true beauties, and I marvel at it, empty, before its day of carting passengers begins. Ellie now needs to prepare the tram for its day out on the roads. She tells me that in the early days of driving she was terrified of missing something and spent twice as long in prep, but that now the process is second nature. So, we confirm that the front pole is down and the rear one up – 'Obvious', she says, 'but, you know, some idiot occasionally tries to drive out with his front pole up – and I mean his.'

She walks around the tram making sure there's no damage to the body work, climbs in the cabin and turns on an array of switches – lights, compressor, line breaker. The compressor soon starts up, and I'm transported back to my childhood by that familiar sound, a kind of 'chugga chugga' noise. Ellie tests the bell, which is operated by foot, and the mirrors, then goes through the driver's door into the cabin and checks that the lights are all okay, the seats are good, and the sandboxes, which are under the seats at either end of the tram, are full. If they're not she has time to grab one of the buckets of sand lined up against the shed wall.

Sandboxes? Are the trams travelling playgrounds? Later in the journey I ask Ellie about this and she tells me that the sandboxes are connected to pipes that can pump sand onto the tracks in front of the wheels – this to avoid the tram skidding when the tracks are greasy or covered in leaves. The driver has a foot button to operate the release of the sand. So that's what those clouds of dust are that envelop a tram coming to a screaming halt.

Alright, I can feel your impatience dear reader, we're not even out of the tram shed yet. I'll speed things up. Ellie does a couple of more checks and then we are off, stopping briefly at the depot to pick up our conductor, and then doing a left turn into Riversdale Road. We are on a short run to Wattle Park before turning around and heading into the city. It's dark, it's freezing in the cabin, and Ellie and I barely fit in its confined spaces, but I'm in heaven. We roll through Camberwell Junction and then climb the first of numerous hills that will take us to the Elgar Road terminus. So, for those of you who have been following, you will know we are on a 70 route tram. But the 70 route number is really for the passengers. In front of Ellie propped against the window is a laminated run sheet, showing her the run numbers and running times for her shift. It may not look like it at times, but trams do have timetables. Ellie tells me that she had trouble keeping to her running times at first. 'There was the traffic', she says, 'the people taking forever to get on and off, but mostly it was me being so careful. I couldn't stand the thought of hitting a car or braking so hard that everyone fell over, so I was really really cautious. Now I'm fine, but I still have to work hard to keep on time. Everyone does, the running times were written years ago.'

It's still pitch black outside as we head up to Warrigal Road. Nearly the whole of the block down to Elgar Road is taken up by the massive Wattle Park, which is now owned by the M&MTB. The park is a creation of the tramways. The Hawthorn Tramways Trust bought the land – over 130 acres of then rural land – in 1915 and the park opened in 1917. Thousands of wattles were planted and a chalet built at the top of the hill. Scones and tea anyone? They held tramways picnics here and the M&MTB Band still plays here on Sundays.

But more to the point, how is Ellie actually 'driving' the tram?

Ellie is driving the tram with her hands. Her right hand controls the brake handle, and her left hand works the controller handle. If the air brakes fail she has an emergency manual brake which sits to the right of the air brake – an unwieldy thing shaped like a ship's steering wheel. We haven't picked up anyone on our way to Wattle Park so the stops have been few, but as we approach a red light Ellie slowly applies the airbrake by turning the brake handle. All through our morning together all of Ellie's stops are smooth and controlled. Unlike some drivers, Ellie is not going to throw you on your face with lurching sudden stops.

The controller is a grey box that sits on Ellie's left, and it's this that governs the power to the engines. Ellie operates a long handle on its top to pump power to the engines. She does this through a series of stages. There are small notches on the top of the controller, and she methodically moves through these clockwise to increase power to the engines. She tells me that its not like pumping petrol into a car engine. 'You have to go at a steady pace', she says 'otherwise you can wreck the motors, or the line breaker will pop the supply and you have to start all over. But you know, this tram is one of my favourites and it's easy to drive, not like some.' Ellie's movements are all practiced and fluid and she doesn't take her eyes off the road as she drives. As soon as we get to a certain speed she powers off and we are just gliding along. I'm jealous.

We arrive at the Wattle Park terminus and she and the connie greet each other. There's no cafe open to grab a coffee but the connie has brought a flask of her own. A few sleepy types board the tram, which is the only lit thing in the whole intersection. There's no chatter at this time of the morning. Given the theatre-like quality of the interior of the tram its occupants could be mistaken for a collection of lost souls waiting for godot.

An electric tram is a two headed beast that unlike a cable tram does not need to be arduously turned at each terminus. Ellie's conductor gets out of the tram and puts up the pole at what will now be the rear of the tram, and pulls down the one at the front. Ellie goes through the tram to the other end, changes the lights, checks the brakes and alters the destination board. This quaint rectangular instrument sits above the driver's head. It contains a roll of canvas material painted with multiple destinations from which to choose. Using a handle on the side of the box, Ellie scrolls through to set the destination – Princes Bridge.

Ding Ding, and we're off. It's still incredibly early and very cold. For the next four or so hours we trundle up and down the hills of Surrey Hills and Middle Camberwell – these lands of the Wurundjeri – past solid brick homes and solid brick churches, before descending to the Junction. Very few curves so far, until we reach the intersection of Riversdale and Power Streets, where the 70 does a left. The stop is next to the old Hawthorn tram depot, which is now the training school for tram drivers. 'I spent hours in there learning to stop and start a tram', says Ellie, 'and giving my trainer a heart attack. I kept feeling for a footbrake you know and we'd be heading for a crash and he'd have to reach over and grab the brake. Poor man.'

Ellie gets down from the tram and performs a strange ritual. From her pocket she produces a brass key which she inserts into a green box with a clock face, which is sitting at the stop. She waits a few moments before turning the key and then reboards the tram. She tells me that this device is meant to track the trams, and keep them to their timetables. She says that she only clocks the tram when she has time. 'Everyone runs late in peak hour, so what's the point?'

As the morning progresses the traffic increases. In the beginning we were the only thing on the road and now two hours later we are surrounded by a sea of cars. Ellie delights in berating the behaviour of drivers – 'look at this idiot!', 'no, no, you can't turn right here mate!', 'it's green guys come on!' She enjoys fanning the brakes to get everyone moving on and off the tram. I'm surprised how effective this trick is in hurrying people along. Fanning or 'airing' the brakes, as it is also known, involves a quick, short movement of the brake handle that releases a loud gush of air under the tram – a trick designed to make passengers think the tram is about to take off.

She tells me about the lingo of the tram shifts: 'earlies', such as ours, which will finish around lunch time; 'middles', which start around midday and run until about nine pm, 'lates' for shifts beginning in the afternoon and running to last tram, and 'brokens'. A 'broken' is a split shift covering both peak hours with a long gap in the middle. Ellie says she likes the brokens because she can do her shopping in the break, or go home and rest, prepare dinner, read a book, whatever. It makes sense given the working hours that trammies tend to live close to the depot.

Ellie knows her history, specifically route 70's, which is one of the oldest in the city's electric network, constructed, she tells me, in 1916 by the Hawthorn Tramways Trust and the first electric tram to run directly from the suburbs into the CBD – from Warrigal Road in Surrey Hills to the city terminus at the end of Batman Avenue at Princes Bridge. We're heading to Princes Bridge now, full load of passengers, over the Yarra and into the flat river lands of Richmond. Earlier we could glide past empty stops, but now every stop has people waiting and the going is slow. The connie is giving two bells after each stop when they are all on but Ellie always checks her mirror to make sure no-one is clinging to the running board. Tram driving is now a struggle I see – time, cars, passengers – and lo and behold I finally realise what it means to be stuck on tracks. Cars pull in from nowhere in front of the tram, put their brakes on and sit waiting to turn right, which prompts Ellie to hurl some priceless invective and stamp her foot on the bell.

Swan Street is a snail. Hard to believe an electric tram could move this slowly. When the traffic is thin Ellie has the tram flying along at speed but much of the morning is spent crawling along in the dense mass of cars. We pass Agapi and Dimmey's and Coles and the Post Office and the Rising Sun and the Greyhound and another 70 going the other way and trucks and vans and Holdens and Fords and a train going over the overpass and people at every stop now cramming into an already full tram. Stop start, stop start. We break free of the mess and cross Punt Road heading towards the river, which has been snaking its way towards the city from another angle. In Batman Avenue we run between trees overhanging the roadway beside the river. There are teams out rowing on the brown water, the sun is well and truly up and the city is fully awake. At the terminus at Swanston Street there's a rush to get off and Ellie and her connie have no time for a break so they swap ends and take off immediately and we head back the way we came. All morning up and down from Elgar to Swanston, Swanston to Elgar. Hypnotic.

Most of the time Ellie drives standing up, like so many of the other tram drivers. But on some sections of our journeys she reaches back and pulls down a small upholstered seat which is attached to the door between the saloon and the cabin. Noticing me seeing this she says that she prefers driving standing but if she does it for a whole shift her legs ache too much. 'Plus, I don't want to end up like my poor Mum with varicose veins. Ugleee!'

The bell rung by the connie is just above my head and I'm starting to get a headache. Ellie says, 'Too loud for you?' and pulls out a ticket stub from her pocket which she hands to me. 'Here', she says, 'jam this in the clacker and it will stop that racket.' I twist around and slot the stub into the mechanism and sure enough at the next bell it registers several decibels lower. Nice trick.

On the way back there are fewer customers, although the traffic is still bad so we are hardly flying along. I ask Ellie what got her interested in driving trams. She tells me it was really an accident. She'd finished university – a teaching degree – and was sitting around at home not doing much when a friend called her to say she'd got a job as a connie and that it was fun and the pay was great. Ellie was sick of having no money and not ready to take on classloads of 'screaming brats', so she applied and got the job. She thought she'd do it for six months or a year and then transfer to teaching but that was five years ago. 'Being a connie was fun but you know I wouldn't still be here if I hadn't started driving. It's much more stress than being a connie but I just love it. Some of the older trams are really hopeless but most of them are beautiful to drive. Every trip, every day is different and I really like moving people around my city you know? And I have some really good friends here now too so for me it's a great job.'

Later, Ellie tells me about her parents and how they came here from Athens in the 1950s. 'I was just a small child and so I don't remember much at all. It was after the civil war which was really bad. My parents were lefties you know, socialists, and basically the left lost, so life under the new regime was hard. So many people had died or were in prison camps or fled the country. Lots of Greeks were coming to Australia and they decided to come here too. It was a good decision for me and my brother but my parents still miss Athens.'

We're heading east towards the river again and on our left in parkland is an enormous tent, the main venue for Ashton's Circus. For some reason I hadn't noticed it before. There's an elephant being led by a clown towards the tent and a man facing the road juggling skittles. A clutch of caravans with circus folk milling around.

I ask Ellie if she has been back herself to Athens. 'Yes I've been a few times, once with my parents and then on my own. It's a different life there and when I get back here I always miss it for a few months.' I ask Ellie about the civil war which I know nothing about. 'Yeah well my Dad says it was that "bloody Churchill" who started it. Do you know that the glorious British bombed Athens after the Nazis left?

Yes the British love Homer and the poets and the cradle of democracy and the Parthenon but they really don't like Greeks themselves. They like the idea of us but not the reality – we're too messy, too democratic, says my Dad. So the British declared martial law and sent tanks and planes against us and they installed a king and that made Churchill happy. But Greeks weren't happy and the civil war lasted years, the whole country and families divided, so many people died. My Dad is right, what happened was a terrible disaster, a massive crime, but he's also stuck in the past.'

Time for a changeover. Ellie has finished the first part of her shift. We've pulled up outside the stop just before the tram depot in Riversdale Road. Waiting at the stop are the new driver and the connie, and Ellie and her connie get down. They all greet each other and Ellie heads towards the depot building for her break, which she tells me will involve strong coffee and a cigarette. She's been driving for four hours with hardly a minute off. The 982 heads towards the Junction.

Just before she enters the building Ellie turns to me and hands me a piece of folded paper. 'Here', she says, 'a souvenir of your morning.' I unfold the single sheet, which is headed 'TRAM READY FOR THE ROAD'. It's a checklist for preparing the tram, with 20 points that cover the process followed by Ellie four hours earlier. I like the final point on the list, which reads, simply, 'CONDUCTOR'. Yes driver, don't take off without your connie!

Trams trundle and people grumble. What a beautiful morning.

*

During the morning Ellie told me a story about a colleague which she said I should keep to myself. I did, for a while, in earlier drafts, but it's too good so I'm including it here. It goes like this: new driver 'Jane' has succeeded in stranding her tram in the middle of Camberwell Junction on a busy weekday morning. She has forgotten to power off the tram and has thus caused the points to change so that the tram is now about to head up the wrong road. Oh dear! Jane – not her real name for legal reasons – is sitting in the cabin frozen with panic. Cars are honking and pedestrians are staring at the immobile tram:

what can she do? Suddenly she remembers the points bar, a heavy metal stick a bit more than half a metre in length, which is used to manually operate the points by inserting the tip of the bar into a slot in the roadway, and which sits in the cabin for the most part unused and neglected.

Fortunately, Jane has not yet crossed the points and her wheels are still on the right rails. She grabs the points bar, jumps down to the track, manually changes the points and just before stepping back up into the cabin throws the bar inside, except her throw is wide and the bar sails out the open door of the cabin on the other side. There is a car right next to the tram and the points bar smashes through the window and imbeds itself in the child seat in the back. Jane can't see into the car clearly, but the outline of the child seat is obvious. For a terrible few seconds she imagines that she has committed manslaughter. Jane leans out of the cabin and realises with immense relief that the child seat is empty. The driver of the car suddenly takes off down the road before Jane can talk to them or get their details. Jane then extricates her tram from the intersection, minus the points bar.

After her shift Jane was required to fill in an incident report. She initially heads her report with the title, 'How I almost speared a child with the points bar'. Jane showed the draft to Ellie who said, 'it's fine if you never want to work on the trams again', so the title was altered to the innocuous 'How I misplaced the points bar'. In the text that followed Jane requested that she be allowed to return, permanently, to conductor duties, a request that management granted.

29. MCG Trams

Was it on the 70 or the 75 that my mother took me to the MCG for the first time? I can't remember.

It's a hot day and the tram blinds are open on all sides. We get down and walk through parkland to this immense building. As we get closer I can hear a rumbling noise which gets louder as we approach. We go through some turnstiles and walk along a long grey corridor and the noise is now waves of sound enveloping me. We reach a steep staircase and climb up. She has my hand and is helping me along. At the top of the stairs all I can see are the backs of people milling in a crowd. My mother pushes us through to the front and I can finally see what we have come for. It's a vast green space with men in white playing a game. She pushes me further so my view is now uninterrupted. We're standing in the aisle which runs down steeply to a fence. Suddenly the whole crowd is laughing. I can see a man in the middle of the ground holding a piece of wood that has been broken in two. He's holding it up for everyone to see. The players around him are laughing too. My mother is also laughing behind me. Later she tells me that the man with the bat was the Australian Wally Grout and he had just had his bat split in two by the West Indian fast bowler. I didn't understand why this was funny. Was that the point of the game, to split the bat? Adults are no doubt very peculiar in the things that interest them but I did enjoy being at the ground. There was a strong smell of sunscreen and beer and the men and women there were so relaxed standing and sitting in the sun and the West Indians amazed me. I asked my mother where the West Indians came from and she said the West Indies, but she didn't seem to know where that was. As we left the ground to catch our tram home we stopped at an ice cream van. Walking up the hill, ice cream in hand, cicadas singing.

*

I've heard a lot of stories concerning the famous ground and trams across this project. And how not? Trams have been taking people to the MCG for over 140 years. One I particularly like was told to me by a former connie, who was on duty the day of the Centenary Test match in 1977 between Australia and England. His tram was a 'Special', parked in the Wellington Parade siding waiting for the match to end. There was a massive roar in the late afternoon (Australia had won) and shortly after an enormous and excited crowd poured out of the ground. His tram headed to the first stop on its way to the city and as soon as they arrived they were besieged. Men with eskys climbed on board and piled them up to the roof.

Within a couple of minutes the tram was full to bursting, and the connie was so jammed in he couldn't move forward to collect the fares. Nevertheless he still called out 'fares!'. The passengers were drunk, they were happy, and it turns out, extremely generous. Coins and notes of all denominations flowed into the connie's bag, which was soon overflowing with cash. The money was handed to him, passed from passenger to passenger, or came flying through the air. The connie was supposed to be issuing tickets, and he did so as fast as he could, eventually issuing them, like the flying cash, into the air. Everyone was laughing, clapping and singing off key. When he paid in that evening the teller was astonished at the take – five, 10 and 20 dollar notes, coins of every description, a mountain of money. It was the one day the connie said when he was positive that the tramways made a profit.

*

FOOTBALL. The destination sign on W trams on Saturday afternoons said all it needed to say. These 'Specials' were run in addition to normal service, and in response to the fact that a huge proporation of the population would be flooding onto trams to get to, and from, the footy on the city's true holy day, Saturday: to the MCG, Princes Park, the Junction Oval and others.

My friend Trudy also tells me good MCG tram story. Trudy's parents barracked for different football teams – her father a one-eyed Essendon supporter, her mother a Melbourne fan. One Demons versus Essendon match day at the MCG her father was boasting ahead of the game, as he was wont to do, how the Dons would smash the Demons, continuing his boast as they took the tram to the ground. The Dons were well in front at half time and Trudy's Dad was already skiting about their certain victory. But in the second half Melbourne launched a comeback and ended up beating the Dons by a few points. In a state of what used to be called 'high dudgeon', he refused to travel back home with Trudy's mother, insisting that she catch a different tram to him. She did, no doubt glad to be free of his moaning. And it was a long trip, long enough she hoped, for him to have returned to his senses by the time he got home.

*

Just an update on my medical narrative. Over twelve months have passed since the initial discovery and treatment of my cancer. As you know my review several months ago went fine, but at this latest three monthly review the test results came back with some not so great news – the bugger had regrown. Not a huge amount, it is a slow-grower, but enough to get them (and me) worried. I've undergone another set of cycles of chemo, lost any remaining island of body hair, and feel utterly dejected. Nevertheless, the prospects are not all bad. Bun actually smiled the other day, saying that they had, quote, 'achieved a significant reduction in the tumour mass', and there were no secondaries. Another piece of happy news was me formally quitting my job. Thank God. Anyway, after a hiatus I'm now back on the trams, a bit dodgy on the legs but where I belong. There's a great story coming up. Come on quick, hop on. Ding Ding!

30. Love & Grief on the Number 11

Marco tells me his tram story. It's a love story set during his school days, when he would catch the tram from his boys' secondary Catholic school in the north and head home to Fitzroy. I presume he's talking about the 11 tram from Preston to the city, but I don't want to interrupt as he's pulling up some old memories. For Marco the end of the school day was the best time of day. He didn't like the school or the masters who taught there: too regimented, and at the same time, devoid of any real inquiry into the world. He's now an associate professor in archaeology and I've met him not on a tram but at a 70th birthday celebration. He's the only guy at the party wearing a tie – a bow tie at that – is articulate, intense and I like him straightaway. The hosts of the party are old friends, in both senses. It's a pleasure to listen to Marco speak.

When the bells sounded at the end of the school day, there is a mad rush by the boys to pack their bags and head out the door. (Marco is, I guess, in his late sixties, so he's probably harkening back to the 1970s.) Marco and his mates race to the tram stop and jump on the next one coming. There's a lot of shouting and joshing and bags piled high in the corner of the tram as it rolls off down St Georges Road. He's not as boisterous as some of the others, being essentially an introvert, but he shares their joy in being let out of 'gaol' again. Marco is preoccupied by some words he is trying to form, not to say to his friends, but to a person he hopes is about to get on the tram, which is now approaching the girls' Catholic college. At the stop a large group of girls is waiting and as they board the boys' behaviour noticeably shifts.

It's crowded and for these students at single sex schools this short tram journey is one of the few domains that will bring them physically close to the opposite sex; a charged atmosphere, full of laughter. Marco has been wondering for several weeks what to say to a young woman he has been unable to stop thinking about. He first saw her at the beginning of term, and while she's not on every tram he takes home, he sees her at least once or twice a week. He can't remember what he said to her on this particular day, what his opening gambit was, or even if she spoke to him first, but the initial words were kind of irrelevant he says. 'The most important thing was that I realised she wasn't unhappy to talk to me,' he says, 'and so it gradually began, our tram friendship which carried across the remainder of the year. I didn't see her over the long break – we both had family holidays – but for the first time in my life I couldn't wait for school to restart. It was the longest, most tortuous summer I ever experienced. There was no way I could see her outside school. It was all very old-fashioned then and besides I didn't even know where she lived.'

Marco goes back to school, now a senior, and soon enough the two reconnect on their way home. For some reason their trams *to* school never coincide. Marco's fears that she might ignore him turn out to be ill-founded and Anne-Marie is just as excited as he is to meet again on the number 11. 'So we start dating and pretty soon we are a couple, although being Catholic in the 1970s it's all highly circumscribed while we're at school. It didn't matter, we were happy, our parents weren't unhappy, and our relationship blossomed.'

They go to the same university, live in a share house in Carlton, and everything is fine until Marco decides to defer his next year of study to travel. Anne-Marie is impatient to finish her degree in vet science and, despite Marco's pleadings, decides that she will not join him. He tells Anne-Marie that he will be back in three months and they have a tearful farewell out at Tullamarine airport. But Marco is bitten by the travel bug and three months turns into six and by now he's on the overland track through Asia to Europe and can't stop. He writes to her continually and she writes back but as the months pass her letters become less frequent. When he turns up to the local poste restante more often than not there's nothing for him.

Marco returns 18 months after leaving. Anne-Marie has moved out of the share house and is living with her new partner, a fellow vet science student. She doesn't want to see him. 'I was devastated by this news', says Marco, 'but clearly had no right to be.' He goes back to uni, joins the public service, has various short term relationships, but is never settled. Travel has unhinged his Australian life – he views his country now as a parochial backwater – and he dreams incessantly of being immersed in other people's cultures, anywhere but his own. Marco continues, 'I was in a tram in Camberwell one day, standing in the open doorway, daydreaming as usual, when at the traffic lights a scooter pulled up next to the tram. The rider turned towards me and in that instant I recognised Anne-Marie.'

We are interrupted at this point in our conversation by a woman who walks up to Marco and puts her hand on his arm and, apologising for the interruption, tells Marco that it is getting late and she'd like to leave soon. Marco introduces me to his wife, Anne-Marie, who shakes my hand. He says to her, 'I've just been telling Gregory how we met.' Anne-Marie laughs and says that Marco shouldn't be boring me with 'that old story'. She turns and heads back inside. Marco is smiling.

It's not often a central character in a story suddenly materialises in the flesh. The universe shines on some people doesn't it dear reader. The ancient Greeks believed that Tyche, the goddess of luck and good fortune, could have a profound impact on a person's life. Marco is talking about how he and Anne-Marie made contact after their tram sighting, were eventually able to reunite, get married, have a family, and are now grandparents. And while he's talking I'm thinking about Tyche in the form of trams. What if Marco had been driven to school each day, as so many kids are these days? And what if he hadn't been on that tram that day standing in the doorway?

Marco looks up and sees Anne-Marie beckoning. He apologises and says it's time for him to wrap it up, and we say our goodbyes.

*

The following day I catch the 11 tram at the corner of Collins and Elizabeth Streets in the city – Marco's story has inspired me to take the 11 out to West Preston. The tram is crowded with city workers, taking advantage of the free city tram zone to take short rides to their favourite lunch time cafes and restaurants. I'm really undecided about this free ride business. On the one hand it encourages people back onto trams, but on the other, has led to massive overcrowding in the middle of the day.

The business folk dress predominantly in grey and black, although in the heat the men have removed their jackets. The tram heads east up the hill to Spring Street before veering diagonally left through East Melbourne, passing the back of the Parliament and its lush grounds, and across the road, the ivory swirl of the new Great Petition sculpture, celebrating the 30,000 signatures in support of women's suffrage presented to Parliament in 1891. The tram now bisects two religious realms – on the west side of Gisborne Street sits the modest St Peter's Church, which is dwarfed by St Patricks Cathedral on the east. I like spending time in St Peter's Bookroom, one of the quietest places in the city. On the corner of Victoria Parade and Gisborne Street is the secular Eastern Hill Fire Station (1893) with its 150 foot tall watchtower, which dominated the city skyline for decades. The tower with its glass lookout was staffed 24 hours a day by watchful firemen. Did the firies have to climb ten thousand stairs to get up there? No way, they went up by an electrically powered lift.

My tram is an E class tram, the newest tram in the city. Of the modern fleet the E class tram is the most satisfying. It's long and sleek, and has style in abundance. For the 'face' of the tram, the designers were apparently inspired by a city icon – the entrance to Luna Park. It's not just the comfort and styling of the tram that's impressive. It's also that after two decades of importing trams, the new E class represents a return to the city designing and manufacturing its own. The imported C and D classes, which dominated the 2000s, were essentially bought off-the-shelf from Europe without any real connection to the city, its culture and environment. With its combination of innovation and functionality the E class sits squarely in the tradition inaugurated with the city's cable trams. Clapp would be very pleased with it.

The front of the tram may resemble the gaping mouth of a fun park, but overall the tram looks to me like a long green caterpillar, wriggling its elongated body through the curving city streets. To switch metaphor for a minute, all trams are like lungs; inhaling and exhaling passengers at every stop. With its many doors and length, the E class does a great job at expediting this endless human in-and-out flow.

As we go a deep automated voice announces each stop. The tram turns from St Vincent's Plaza and heads north into Fitzroy. By Brunswick Street the suits have disappeared and the travellers are more colourful, more youthful. I spent a lot of time in Brunswick Street in the 1980s – the Blackcat cafe is still here, the Provincial pub on the corner of Johnston and Brunswick Streets, Fitzroy Nursey with its amazing gates. As we pass Mario's I'm recalling sitting there 40 years before with my then partner. Here's a strange scene. I'm dressed in a blue cheongsam, my fingernails are painted red and I've got eyeliner and mascara on. Wow, what's the story? Unconsciously, I laugh out loud at the memory and get some looks from fellow passengers. I'd borrowed the dress from the mother of a friend, who had worn it in the 1960s, and I'd also borrowed from her a blond wig and ivory cigarette holder, apparently part of her '60s party attire. This ensemble was in aid of a fancy-dress party thrown by my new girlfriend in Fitzroy, and we were sitting in Mario's the morning after. For a while there she was under the distinct apprehension that she was going out with a cross-dresser. Maybe she was... .

*

The 11 now crosses Alexandra Parade and travels into North Fitzroy, a consciously preserved and cherished zone of old Melbourne, home to impossibly priced two-storey terrace houses, public gardens with avenues of European trees (thanks to surveyor extraordinaire, Clement Hodgkinson), and very cool cafes. At the Piedimonte's supermarket stop a woman about my age gets on and sits opposite me. She's carrying several shopping bags and as she sits one of them topples over and its contents spill out. I help her retrieve the tins and veges and repack the bag. She thanks me and then we look at each other closely and recognition dawns. This is... God, who is it? I'm scrambling for a name when it suddenly pops into my head. Gina and I exchange greetings with exclamations of surprise. We had been at university together in the 1970s.

She's friendly and if it weren't for the multiple bags in the way we would probably hug each other. We had been close through university but then afterwards we both headed in different directions. I haven't seen her in decades. Gina is telling me about her children and the recent arrival of her first grandchild. She and her partner have been together for over 30 years and now have a new role in life. She shows me photos on her phone of baby Maud and I make the right noises. I never really know what to say about pics of new babies. They all look pretty much the same to me, kind of squished and pink and amorphous. This view is obviously not shared by the parents and grandparents involved who, invariably, debate how the baby clearly takes after such and such in the family.

While her partner is retired Gina is still working part-time. She tells me she trained in middle-age to become a counsellor after two decades of teaching. 'I've really loved this work', she tells me, 'and part of me is loath to give it up, but we've got enough money now, and with the baby arriving we've got plenty to do.' She goes on to explain that about 10 years ago she moved from general counselling into the area of grief counselling, and that this shift had come about after she counselled a client who was experiencing ongoing grief over the loss of a loved one. 'Her story was so compelling and my desire to help so strong that afterwards I trained to specialise in the area. She had lost both her parents in a car accident when she was in her twenties. They had died just after her first child was born and she had suppressed her grief at their loss, so that, in her words, she could be a good mum. But this approach eventually came undone as her children grew up. With her permission I wrote a paper about her story and our therapy together, so it's in the public domain.'

Gina tells me that as her client's children grew into adulthood and separate lives, the client seemed to be growing out of hers – a sense of dislocation enveloped her. Her client used a lot of images to describe this. She was like a parched and drought ridden landscape, an unwatered tree in a dying land. She lay in bed at night struggling to understand what was going on. This all came to a head when one afternoon she visited the National Gallery. Depressed, she wandered around until she came to a room hung with a series of large video screens. She stood in front of the first of the video installations. It showed a person walking towards her from some dark interior, and as they got closer they entered a wall of water, a shining waterfall, which cascaded over them, and as their body emerged from the water, the colour of the body changed from black and white to the most brilliant colour. This larger than life person had a look of utter amazement on their face, as if they had just been born or re-born.

She watched the screens as person after person went through this process – women, men, young, old. All of them approach the water wall with hesitating steps and then as they broke through their faces were transformed, some radiant and astonished, others perplexed and frightened. For reasons her client didn't articulate, this work had a powerful impact on her. She went home and cried for two days, and then she looked up her local paper and found Gina's counselling service. After six months of counselling her depression began to lift and she had begun the process of grieving for her parents. This was immensely painful for her but ultimately she was able to start functioning again.

'Bill Viola.'

'Yes, Bill Viola. Thought you'd get that. Wonderful exhibition. So, anyway that's what got me hooked on being a grief counsellor –

sometimes it takes everything I have to stick with someone. For some people grief is like a bottomless pit that sucks you down day after day. It's been rewarding but also draining so overall I'll be glad to give it up.'

The tram has been travelling along the middle of the wide expanse of St Georges Road with its car lanes, bike paths and palm trees. The 11 turns west into Miller Street and the interior of the tram is now in shadow. There is a baked look to the day. Whenever the door opens a blast of hot northern air enters the tram. While Gina has been speaking I'm remembering how much I had liked this smart, articulate woman. I'm also remembering something else about our friendship, a certain drunken evening when we had become something more than friends.

I ask Gina what's she's learned about grieving, and why it appears to be so different from person to person.

She explains there are many types of grief and ways people can grieve; the loss of a loved one, a home lost in a fire, the death of a beloved animal, the separation of a child's parents or the sudden termination of employment. Parents often grieve when their children leave home, some people grieve when a favourite tree is cut down. These can all have different intensities – usually the empty nest syndrome is not a long-lived grief because over time the parents and children develop a more adult relationship, which is better for everyone. Powerful grief can create a paradox. The loss of a loved one is completely explicable – the body of the loved one is no longer animated by life. At the same time, the disappearance of the person that animated the body can be utterly incomprehensible: where did they go? All that human energy, that life and its story evaporates, is over. And what am I without this person now?

'I had a client suffering terribly over the loss of his partner of 40 years who told me that grief slowly crept up on him like an assassin, twisting inside him like a knife, making him feel constantly at war with himself, never knowing what to do, what was right, how to feel beyond this pain in his guts. You remember the theory that we are

the sum of the narratives we tell ourselves,' she says, 'about ourselves, others, the world we inhabit? I think every grief arrives into
this individual narrative and works its way there. Of course there are
also patterns and similarities, otherwise no counsellor would be able
to help anyone. But the story of grief is embedded in the story of a
life and that's what the therapist ultimately has to work with. Am I
making sense?'

'Yes, you are. I was thinking how my reactions to my parents'
deaths differed so much, both at the time and as time has worn on.
And still goes on.'

We are now travelling north of Bell Street up Gilbert Road – the
only passengers on the tram. We pass the Angela Lombardi Pharmacy
and the Arab Baptist Church. I notice two brightly coloured parrots
flying low beside the tram. Gina has stopped talking and we are now
sitting in silence examining each other's old faces. Fifty years.

'You know Gregory', she says, 'I had a real crush on you all those
years ago. I don't think you ever noticed, or if you did you didn't let
on. I bet you're not aware of that are you? Too long ago? I thought
when we slept together – you do remember that don't you? – that it
actually meant something to both of us. But apparently not. You never contacted me afterwards or returned my calls. Why was that?
Were you embarrassed? I saw you see me once in the Union building
and look quickly away, like I was a bad dream, and then scurry off.
That's what hurt me about the whole thing. I thought it was shitty
behaviour and it changed my view of you. Look at the look on your
face, like I'm going to eat you. Don't worry old man, I'm not holding a
grudge against you, although I have to admit I've enjoyed saying that.
No, don't try to apologise. That's a mistake. I didn't grieve for you and
I've had a wonderful life. And you seem alright now as a grey emi-
nence. We were ridiculously young weren't we?'

Gina tells me her stop is coming up, collects her bags of shopping
and pushes the stop button. Despite her admonition I'm trying to say
something meaningful, but all that is comes out of my mouth is a

strangled 'sorry'. Gina either doesn't hear it or doesn't care. She gives me a final look and gets off the tram.

Great. I'm embarrassed and look hastily around the tram to see if anyone has witnessed this scene, as if having witnesses would make it worse, but there's no-one. The tram is now sliding into the terminus and I get down. There is a small park with benches and scrappy trees next to the tram stop and I wander over. It's far too hot to be sitting here so I cross the road and enter a cafe. The walls of the cafe are covered in brown and yellow striped wallpaper. Small vases of plastic blue flowers sit on the tables. I order a cold drink.

*

I had been intending to visit the Preston tram depot on the return journey but I'm too absorbed in reflecting on Gina to even notice it when we pass. The M&MTB had consolidated all their construction and maintenance works on this site back in the 1920s, and in addition to the workshops and sheds the depot boasted a ballroom, a concert hall and lecture theatre; a vibrant, self-sufficient community on the edge of the city. But I miss out on this, thinking how I don't remember seeing Gina in the Union that day, but do remember now not calling or contacting her. Clearly, I'd elided much of the episode and my behaviour from the memory banks. I know our narratives can be self-serving and that we can suppress uncomfortable truths about ourselves. What else has been elided I wonder?

31. This Connie Life

S o what's it like to be a connie on a W class tram, collecting fares all day, saying 'fares please' ad nauseam? Come with me to the 1970s and meet Andre, conductor from Glenhuntly depot who'll show me the ropes. Our number 3 tram is heading into the city from Darling Road in East Malvern, a rainy morning, cars whizzing past, passengers hurrying from stops furling in their umbrellas as they enter. We've been at this for a couple of hours and Andre has been up and down the tram collecting fares more times than I could count. He's very efficient I notice, able to distinguish between new arrivals and those who've paid. He's not loud in his pleas for fares, its more of an understatement, a necessary utterance that shouldn't disturb those reading their damp newspapers, or gazing out half-asleep. Sometimes he simply sidles up to a new fare and the passenger, becoming aware of his presence hands over the money. Very often people have their fares ready by the time he gets to them; surprisingly it's often the exact fare. Most fares are for a ticket to the city (90 cents) but some are cheaper for passengers who will disembark earlier.

The whole route is divided into sections of roughly a mile in length, and fares are charged for the number of sections travelled. This is very different to the standard fares of the cable trams of course, but the W trams cover a lot more territory and clearly the M&MTB wanted to attract people across the route on short journeys. Even so, I find it mind boggling what Andre has to do when a passenger tells him their destination as the name of a road or street or a rail station. Andre has to know the section for that destination so he can issue the correct ticket, and there are hundreds of streets and roads crossing the route into the city from Darling Road. But I never notice him miss a beat with this – he will say immediately, that's 40 cents, or 50 cents, or whatever the fare is depending on the sections to be travelled. I could never remember all that.

As the tram fills closer to town Andre has to push his way through a tram which is now standing room only. He does this without actually shoving anyone, just slipping his body between others', taking fares. There's an occasional 'good morning' to a familiar face, and indeed, many of the passengers appear to recognise Andre, who has been travelling this route for many years now. He's part of the furniture of getting to work for many people. When I ask him about this later when we are on a lay-up, he says that he's seen some regular passengers grow from pimply teenagers to office workers with briefcases.

Andre tells me that he was a chemical engineer in Romania before he migrated, but he couldn't get engineering work here – a combination of non-recognition of his overseas qualifications, and his rudimentary English at the time. So he got a job as a conductor instead, as a stopgap until he could upgrade his qualifications. He got married, had children and although he went to night school and eventually gained his certification, he kept on at the depot. He liked his colleagues, the job was well paid, and unlike his previous work the job didn't come home with him. He tried driving for a couple of years, but missed the middle of the tram and the daily sea of faces, so he reverted to being a connie. Soon he would have clocked 20 years on the job and would be getting an M&MTB award of some sort. He doubted it would be a gold watch.

Andre's conductor 'tool-kit' consists of a leather bag and a punch. The bag is slung over his shoulder on an adjustable strap and sits low on his chest. It's designed to hold a lot of coins and has a couple of compartments. The various tickets, the 'flimsies', are slotted in on one side and a coin dispenser on the other. I notice that Andre spends spare moments organising the coinage in his bag into different denominations on the dispenser – during the journey he just drops the coins into the bag. He gives me the bag to feel its weight at the end of the four hour shift and it is unbelievably heavy.

The other piece of his armoury is the ticket punch. This is not the bell-punch of the cable connies, but a simple implement designed to leave a hole, unique to that punch, on the tickets it perforates. The punched ticket will show the section for the fare and whether it was issued in-bound to the city or out-bound, all designed to allow roaming ticket inspectors to check the ticket's validity and limit fare evasion. The punch itself is a sold piece of metal with a spring between its two arms. Andre gives it to me to try on an old ticket from the floor, and I reckon my hand would be very sore at the end of a shift. He says you get used to it.

I haven't been looking at the outside world on our trips, too interested in what Andre has been doing and saying. But now, as Andre is off collecting fares, I'm more attentive. The most remarkable feature of the journey occurs when we're past the wide expanse of Caulfield Park and turn into Normanby Road. Here the tram travels along below the high embankment of the railway line, before dipping under it – the underpass so deep it must surely flood in heavy rain. Otherwise it's a neat, orderly, nothing-amazing tram ride comprising straight lines and occasional curves. Up and down we go, up and down.

Andre is not one of the 'performing' connies, who have occasionally graced W trams over the years, the ones who tell stories or whistle tunes, perform juggling acts, twirl their hats, make coins magically disappear and generally see their role as part entertainer. The M&MTB consistently tells such employees that it is not in their remit to be performers but somehow some connies just don't get the message. Malvern depot has been famous for harbouring some of these often well loved figures. But most connies are more in the Andre mould. They go about their business unobtrusively, collect the fares, remain upright in a swaying tram, keep the tram in order. It's the connie's job to make sure that people are safely on board before pulling the bell cord twice to signal the driver to go. Andre leans across customers to reach the leather cord suspended from the ceiling on

either side of the tram, checking that no-one is still on the running
board. When a passenger stands to get off at the next stop but forgets
to pull the cord Andre will pull it for them – he has a sixth sense
about this floating community that he is orchestrating. Andre's days
are generally regular and predictable, but he's had his share of adventures. Take the time in the 1950s when the tram was boarded and ex-
ited in short order by a fugitive with a policeman in hot pursuit, only
to be hailed and boarded by the same duo en route to the police station on the return leg, this time with the fugitive in handcuffs.

Back to the prosaic. Andre tells me that at the end of his shift he
will pay in his takings to the depot's revenue clerk, who will tally the
take and check it against the remaining tickets – the tickets are all
numbered and issued in lots of 100, so it's pretty straightforward.
He's only ever had the occasional discrepancy.

We're near the end of the first leg of Andre's shift (he's on a 'split'
shift) and the tram is headed to the depot. The tram's destination
board reads, 'Glenhuntly Depot', effectively warning passengers off
boarding. Andre asks if I'd like to join him for a cuppa at the depot
and I readily agree. We enter the canteen, a large room with dozens
of chairs and tables, and already full of tram workers. Andre greets
several people on our way to the tiny kiosk at one end where he orders coffee and cake for two. I look around at the now crowded room:
people are playing cards, chess, a group of women at one table are
knitting, some are reading newspapers, others books. A lot of talking's going on and the room has a convivial atmosphere, akin to a
large family gathering. Occasionally there's a shout or yelp from the
card table as someone wins a hand and in the background the inter-
mittent sound of trams passing in and out from the sheds at the rear.
The squeal of metal on metal.

Andre leads me to a table where two men are sitting with their
coffees. After introducing me to Frank and Karl, he settles with the
other two into a discussion, seemingly the resumption of their last
conversation together. It's an easy going exchange laced with humour
and it's clear that these guys are the 'politicos' of the depot. The main

topic is the recent sacking of the Whitlam government by the Governor-General, John Kerr. Three men and three different positions on the sacking entirely. After a willing back and forth on the subject they drop it, not through rancour but in the realisation that none of the three is going to convince the others.

Karl then asks Andre if he's had time to read the book he lent him by Milan Kundera. Andre pauses before he answers. 'Yes', he eventually says. 'I have read it and I enjoyed it, but you know, it also made me sad and angry. Kundera is Czech but the circumstances of communist rule in Romania are essentially the same. This book was a little too close to the bone for me. It reminded me so strongly of life under the communists – the oppression, the detentions, the sheer absurdity of day to day life under that regime and why I left. Most people have no idea how lucky they are to be born in this country. Freedom is lightly worn isn't it, when you know nothing else. I miss my homeland but I don't miss the life there.'

32. Fashionista Trams

I'm tramming into the city and working my way to the back I've finally got a seat. A young guy sits opposite in army fatigues, with pierced ears, nose and eyebrow. His pants reach to his knees and he wears paisley coloured stockings, with red shoes. Very good, I like it.

I've been thinking about fashion on trams across the eras. On trams we can't not participate in our fashion milieus, even if only unconsciously. Old photos of the cable trams in the 1880s show men wearing black, dark tailored suits with waistcoats, white shirts, high winged collars, narrow patent leather shoes, top hats and bowler hats, moustaches and fob watches, with wealthy men sporting expensive, fur-collared, overcoats. Working men wear moleskin, corduroy or cotton trousers, leather work boots, grandpa collars on work shirts, vests and soft short-brimmed caps. Women wear lighter colours, decorative long dresses, with corsets, bustles, high necklines, and tight, arm-hugging sleeves – their hats and bonnets laced and beribboned. By the 1890s the constraining bustle is largely gone. Difficult to get on and off the tram and sit with a larger-than-football sized bundle of wire and cloth attached to your bum. Notwithstanding this host of detail, the overall impression is one of formality and conformity.

Skip forward to the post World War Two period (a big skip I admit): the height of W class era 1950s, and mens' fashions are transformed, though no less conformist. Suits feature a broad, plain style with long lapels, in dark blues, browns and greys. Hat styles are fedora, trilby or porkpie; in summer, straw. Gone are the moustaches and the fob watches, replaced by clean chins and wristwatches. Ties are relatively wide, shirts white, haircuts short, and trousers baggy. In shoes, plain black and brown prevail, but you can see black and white saddle shoes, penny loafers, creepers, Oxfords. Women have dumped the corseted Victoriana, and now show their legs below the knee! They've taken up pencil and shirtwaist dresses with decorative patterns – floral, polka dots, cherry – and they are often wearing synthetic materials. Suit jackets over skirts, high heels, stockings, gloves and a hat. In the 1950s there are fewer women going to work on trams in the mornings compared to the war years, when numbers of working women peaked.

Commuters' clothing in the 1880s and 1950s was mostly Melbourne made. The globalisation of the textile industry is well underway by the 1950s, but the local industries here haven't yet gone overseas. By the time of the arrival of the E class trams in 2013 our clothes are mostly being designed and made elsewhere. Today fashion displays distinct generational differences: younger people often play with colour and style that ranges across eras – bright multicoloured pantaloons, '70s tie dye shirts, gothic revival, mini-skirts, hats of all shapes and size. But except for business commuters still dressed in suits, both men and women, most tram travellers are dressed 'ordinary': jeans, t-shirts with slogans or designer logo, plain shirts and jackets, loafers and runners. In summer, shorts, thongs, sandals, sunglasses, and loose fitting garments dominate. In winter beanies and scarves are ubiquitous, as are long coats, puffers, rain jackets. It's mainly sourced from China, Vietnam and Bangladesh and it's often cheap.

The general fashion trend on a modern tram is informality, and frequently unisex. That's a global trend too, but I like how our city still hews to its black on black style inherited from the late 19th century. Both men and women can appear in black from head to foot, like the young guy I saw the other day; he was dressed in Melbourne black, inflected in his own way – a black vinyl motorbike jacket tight-ly fitted with silver chains off the shoulders, black stovepipe pants, black Doc Martens boots, ink black hair, nose rings and ear rings.

And there's another element on today's trams not apparent in the 1950s, in what was still a dominant Anglo-Saxon culture. On a Footscray tram today you might encounter the vivid and elegant thobe, often worn by women from Sudan; on the 19 the beautifully embroidered Pakistani shalwar kameez, and on the 109 in Richmond the ao dai originating in Vietnam.

*

My mother was a 1950s fashionista. Photos of her taken at parties and evening dinners in this era show her outfitted in the latest modern designs. The restrained 1940s were gone and the new style reflected an elegant casualness that somehow my country born mother was able to capture. On our trips to town she wore three-quarter overcoats with wide lapels in winter, crew-neck cardigans, stockings and gloves and a hat I thought was silly, flat pumps, a long dress or slim pants, red lipstick and short hair. In summer, dresses like the ones mentioned above, particularly round-shouldered, cinched at the waist and floral patterned, or a bell-shaped skirt, her arms bare, sandals, toenails painted red, and a small clasp handbag. Without knowing a thing about 'chic', I always thought she looked like she belonged in the city, as if her clothes sense marked her out as someone at ease there, comfortable in its mores and style.

33. Invasion Day

It's the early 1960s and my mother and I are going to the city by tram to a protest being held by The Campaign for Nuclear Disarmament (CND). The CND rallies were held for many years every Easter. It's cold and windy and I'm wrapped in woollens, scarf and beanie, while my mother is wearing a long grey coat with black bordering at the lapels. At the rally outside the State Library I can't see a thing, but someone hoists me onto their shoulders and I get a clear view, although this doesn't actually enhance my ability to understand what is going on.

I understand that the bomb is bad and can kill us all but I don't follow the speaker's impassioned arguments. Never mind, the atmosphere is nice, people are friendly and I get to wear a badge with a symbol on it that I'm told means peace. But I don't know whose shoulders I'm on. Was my father with us, or was this Uncle Max holding me aloft, or some stranger? At the end of the rally my mother and I walk up the street and entering a laneway climb a steep set of stairs. She knocks on a door and when it is opened we enter a room bursting with noise, people, plates of spaghetti being gustily consumed, cigarette smoke, and carafes of red wine. The waiter takes our order, my mother lights a cigarette and we settle in. Protest clearly has its rewards.

But who was with us at the rally? I don't know and I can't ask any of the participants – not my mother, nor my father nor Uncle Max – because, as you've rightly guessed, they are no longer in this world.

*

It's Invasion Day and I'm on the tram to the city. People of all ages are carrying placards and flags and are dressed in the Indigenous colours of red yellow and black. At each stop we collect more like-minded people and pretty soon the tram is bursting with protestors. There's a carnival-like atmosphere on board and the entire tram seems to be talking at once – it's become a protest tram, a common event in this city of protest. Look at the forest of flags here, and imagine the scene replicated on trams all around the city, headed for the CBD.

All the tram services travelling through the city are suspended for the duration of the protest, short-shunting at the edge of the CBD, except routes like the 58 that skirt the city centre. By design or accident the city's tramways accommodate this frequent disruption – after all, street protest has been in the blood of the city since its founding; the first ones occurred in the 1840s.

I get down with the rest to the north of Parliament and now I'm walking down the middle of Bourke Street, the march filling the street and covering several blocks of the city. The crowd is vocal and enthusiastic, drums are being drummed and the chant of 'Always was, always will be Aboriginal land', echoes up through the canyon of buildings. There are hundreds of Aboriginal flags being flown, t-shirts with messages supporting Indigenous rights, banners stretching across the road. It's hot and humid and the atmosphere in the multi-racial crowd is as much one of celebration of Aboriginal people and their rights, as it is a protest that the national day marks the date of the first official day of white settlement.

The crowd arrives at the intersection of Flinders and Swanston Streets, a traditional space of sit down protest, with the clocks and dome of Flinders Street Station forming the backdrop to proceedings. The speakers' van, with its nest of loud speakers perched on steel poles, occupies the middle of the intersection. The crowd sits in a circle around the van, but only a small proportion of the crowd is able to fit in the intersection. I squeeze through the jam of bodies to a vantage point on the cathedral steps and listen to the speeches. I can't see much but I can hear it well enough. The crowd hears each speech in silence, breaking into applause at significant points in each address, and cheering at their conclusion. Sweat pours down my face.

An Aboriginal speaker is talking about the importance of history. I can't see him but I recognise the voice of long-time Indigenous activist and historian, Gary Foley. We are living, he says, in an age which neglects history, and there's a real need to understand our own history if we are to ever overcome racism and marginalisation. Foley says history is composed of three unchanging things – places, events, people – but what changes are the perspectives we bring to bear on them. A black history of the country is desperately needed to understand that Aboriginal sovereignty has never been ceded. A black history will remind us that today's protest isn't the start of something but a continuation of a decades old movement. 'Go back to William Cooper in the 1930s, go back to Charlie Perkins in the 1960s, to Faith Bandler and all the others. These are our heroes', he says, 'but they aren't anything if they are forgotten.'

After the speeches I wander up Flinders Street with the crowd to the Fitzroy Gardens. There are bands playing and food stalls and activists selling t-shirts and head bands. The gardens are full of Aboriginal people, meeting up on this site which had always been a place of gathering and ceremony before the invasion. The protest march has now transformed itself into a party, Archie Roach is playing – one of the great singer-songwriters this country has produced – and I lean back against an old tree and shut my eyes. With the party as the backdrop and the tree as my pillow, I fall into a deep sleep.

*

Dear patient reader, at various points in this long-winded saga I have mentioned the Indigenous presence in the city – how the Aboriginal tracks through this land preceded those of the white city, and my surmise that many of these modern paths, including tramways, overlaid, at least in part, those original tracks of the First Nations Peoples. But who are these Aboriginal people I've been talking about?

The first thing to say is that they still exist, despite the many best efforts of the colonisers to eradicate them.

The Kulin nation is the umbrella nation for a number of groups, two of whom are the Traditional Owners of the lands of the city of Melbourne. These two groups of Traditional Owners – the Wurundjeri and the Bunurong – have lived in this territory for thousands of years. They lived along the coast of the bay, along the Yarra River (Birrarung) and its tributaries, across the plains and the hills and the lands in-between, successful and sustainable communities with their own lore, traditions, economies and politics. The current city is divided in two, with Wurundjeri lands extending roughly from the Yarra north, including all waterways flowing into it, while the Bunurong's traditional lands are basically south of the Yarra, and follow the coast. The Wurundjeri are, in one sense, traditionally river people, while the Bunurong are salt-water people. Thus, all the trams of the city run over either Wurundjeri or Bunurong territory. Traditional Aboriginal guardianship of these lands is now recognised by the Victorian constitution, but a treaty has yet to be signed. The issue of a treaty is not just window-dressing, but goes to the core of the country's identity. The city is then, in a real sense, living in limbo, acknowledging its Aboriginal history and peoples, but as yet, failing to accord them their full rights as sovereign peoples under law. But there's some light: with the conclusion of the Yoorrook Commission report, the state is now entering into negotiations over a treaty with representatives of the First Peoples' Assembly.

Nearly all of us in our city have heard Auntie Joy Murphy Wandin, a Wurundjeri elder, perform a welcome to country, for most people in the context of AFL Grand Finals. In this traditional welcome Auntie Joy invites those visiting country to take part in what the country has to offer. Implicit in the welcome to country is the idea that those being welcomed are stepping onto someone else's land, and the welcome is the ceremony giving them permission to do so – it doesn't say you can have this land. The words of the welcome imply an ongoing traditional ownership to country that has never been ceded.

*

Trams and protest. Protest trams. Trams in protests.

I remember in the 1970s being in a big moratorium march against the Vietnam war. The authorities weren't happy with the anti-war movement and did their best to upset the planning and staging of it. One of the principal speakers received death threats before the event, and it was not clear what position the police were taking – there had been a lot of violence at anti-conscription rallies and the police were in an ugly mood. Riot police were stationed in the lanes surrounding the march route. In the event, nearly 100,000 people turned out and there was a remarkable sense of safety in those numbers. But some police weren't ready to concede control of the streets.

In Swanston Street a group of police had directed trams down the street from the north, refusing to let them short-shunt, and insisting that they carry on despite the enormous crowd in front of them covering both sides of the street and both tram lines. The trams edged forward into the crowd where they were eventually surrounded and came to a complete stop. It was after all, simply dangerous to continue. The police were furious and started yelling at the drivers to move. I remember the face of one driver sitting in his cabin as a senior sergeant berated him and ordered him to move his tram. At this point the driver folded his arms and resolutely refused to budge. The cop was apoplectic, but the driver had shut his doors and was clearly not persuadable. The protesters cheer his decision not to move, clapping their hands and the sides of the tram in approval. The driver smiles back, the hero of the moment.

As you know, we don't mind turning out for a march in this city. Moratoriums, climate action, International Women's Day, anti-nuclear marches, anti-conscription (two wars), the eight-hour day, Aboriginal land rights, farmers' protests, anti-apartheid, protests of the unemployed, against public service cuts, LGBTQIA marches, against cutting connies, and more recently, the Gaza war – the list goes on. One of the reasons our protests muster the numbers for what are always the biggest protests in the country on any issue is because of the ease with which people can get to the city. I admit trains have something to do with this too, but trams have been central in physically enabling these demonstrations of our democracy at work, carrying people to and from these frequently massive events. The trams themselves express a democratic sentiment, as I've said earlier – a one-class mode of transport, that sits and stands everyone together. Someone should write a book about it.

34. The Coup

O h Alex, Alex. What did they do to you? Unworthies, scally-wags, liars.

Alex is enjoying his morning cup of tea in his kitchen at Avoca Street South Yarra. He will have his tea and toast, his briefcase is packed and soon enough he will be on the tram to work – his destination the former MTOC building in Bourke Street, headquarters of the M&MTB since the early 1920s. It's December 1935 and there has been talk of the M&MTB relocating to a new premises. But Alex enjoys his office in the old building, with its fine mahoganies, high ceilings, and Persian carpets. In summer he works with the windows open, the street a daily soundtrack to work by, one that includes the clatter and bells of his new electric trams heading up and down the city. He often works late and in the quiet evenings, after most employees have left for the day, sometimes senses the ghosts of Clapp and Duncan.

But Alex won't be going to work today. Spread out on the kitchen table is the morning paper and in it Alex has just read that his tenure as the Chair of the M&MTB is over. He can't quite believe what he is reading. He has spent the last several minutes rereading the report to see if he has somehow misconstrued its meaning, but sure enough, at every reading the same thing is said; the government has decided to not renew his appointment, the position he has held since 1919. His wife Mary comes into the kitchen and queries why he isn't on his way to work. Alex shows her the newspaper. Mary is suddenly furious. How dare they remove him through the press, who do they think they are, that little sod Lawson, what a cowardly creature. Alex makes some calls, but all of his colleagues are as shocked as he is. It's an outrage. The Board has been blindsided by a government with its own agenda. Mary makes another pot of tea. The two of them sit in silence, their world having been upended with a few dozen words in black and white.

Later when asked by *The Argus* about the failure to reappoint him, Cameron says that, 'All I know of my retirement is what I read in the newspapers.' The Board issues a statement stating that the treatment of their Chair represents a 'grave discourtesy'. The government forges ahead, appointing a new Chair, H.H.Bell, and a new Board. The Cameron days at the M&MTB are finished. When it happens Cameron is 70 years old. He lives another five years, dying at Avoca Street South Yarra in 1940. His obituary in *The Age* in February says that Cameron was the man who oversaw revolutionary change in Melbourne's transport system, was at the forefront of the conversion to electric and that he led the fight against private enterprise which tried to derail public transport. During the 'Transport War' in the 1920s Cameron was 'daily in the limelight' fighting for the M&MTB and the development of an organised, single transport authority for the city. He succeeded but along the way made a lot of enemies.

So why did the government get rid of Cameron? We don't really know. His replacement had only recently been appointed as his deputy chair, so it's possible this was a coup d'état. The new chair was a bus lover and moved quickly to convert some cable routes to bus rather than electric. Cameron had acquired a bevy of enemies in high places over the years, mediocrities one and all, who were affronted by his intelligence and dogged pursuit of his goals, which were, remember, the implementation and articulation of what the law actually required of him.

Alex departs with style. As reported by *The Argus* in January he tells the staff of the M&MTB that it has been his privilege and pride to work with them, to see the metropolis develop a unified and harmonious public transport system, to witness that system grow to carry 172 million passengers a year, and to double its revenue. 'Melbourne', he said, 'now possessed one of the finest and most modern tramway systems in the world.'

Vale Alex Cameron!

35. Route 19: The Joyce Barry Revolution

'I don't need a penis to drive a bloody tram.'

Joyce Barry, conductor and driver.

I'm at the back of Collingwood Town Hall, it's 1975 and a major meeting of the Australian Tramway and Motor Omnibus Employees' Association (ATMOEA) is underway to determine a key agenda item – a motion to rescind a union resolution to ban women from driving trams passed almost 20 years before. (The ATMOEA succeeded the ATEA in 1934.) The Town Hall is packed with tramways workers, both men and women. A low pall of smoke hangs over the assembly. It seems that at least half the trammies are smokers and the air is acrid and dense. The atmosphere is also palpably tense as the union leaders on the dais arrive at this agenda item that has drawn everyone to the hall. Efforts to allow women to train as tram drivers were blocked by the male dominated union again as recently as 1973 when a black ban was placed on Route 70. The M&MTB had had the temerity to start training women at the Hawthorn Training School and the trainee women were spotted by a unionist driving to Wattle Park. The M&MTB had backed down and ceased training women as drivers.

But there's pressure on the union. The new Labor federal government is not happy with the ban on women drivers and neither are various women's and human rights groups. However most of the pressure is being exerted by the women trammies themselves, who have been campaigning for the right to drive since the 1950s. 'It's time!', was the campaign slogan of the recently elected Australian Labor Party (ALP) and many in the hall were no doubt feeling that it was time for the tramways union to get real and drop the ban. Nevertheless, as I stand there at the back I'm getting the distinct impression that many of the unionists are not wedded to the idea.

Leading the charge for the women and the most vocal proponent of their right to drive is Joyce Barry, who has been a conductor since the late 1940s. Joyce was one of the original 16 women chosen by the M&MTB to train as drivers back in 1956, and has been campaigning for the right ever since. While not alone in the struggle she is its key player. She is determined and unafraid, having previously called out the union leadership for its irrational and sexist views of women. As historian Margaret Bevege relates, Barry famously told the secretary of the union, Clarrie O'Shea, at the infamous 1956 meeting that resolved to ban women from driving that he was 'talking through his purse' when he claimed that allowing women drivers would cut the wages of trammies. Today, Joyce is out to right a longstanding wrong. The old union leadership, led by O'Shea, which had stubbornly opposed women drivers for decades has gone off into retirement. It's time.

The meeting is getting hectic. Voices are being raised for and against the motion before the assembly to rescind the 1956 resolution. There are interjections and boisterous exchanges around the hall, a rumble of anger. I'm looking at social change and it's clearly not straightforward. There are three speakers per side and they have been allotted just five minutes each.

Joyce Barry gets to her feet and states her case. Her argument is cogent and compelling, and the hall is mostly quiet as she makes her points. But just as she is wrapping up, a male worker interjects, telling all and sundry that driving trams is man's work, and that no woman should ever be put behind the controls of a tram. Barry turns towards the interjector and tells him that despite what he may think about the superiority of his gender, she for one didn't need a penis to drive a bloody tram, and neither she thought did anyone else.

At this there is a moment of stunned silence, followed by uproar echoing around the room, but there is an undercurrent of laughter too and I notice that some of the officials on the dais are smiling broadly. Eventually a vote is called, and while there are many nays – 267 for and 181 against – it's a clear victory for the women. Joyce Barry grabs a bunch of ballots and throws them in the air in celebration. It's an historic win. A few months later Joyce will become the first female tram driver in the country.

*

Joyce Barry was born and raised in Brunswick of Irish heritage, the sixth of seven children, and left school at 14 to work in her father's shirt and pyjama factory. Child of the Depression and war years, Joyce grew impatient with factory work under her father's tutelage. In 1941 women were employed as conductors for the first time in the tramways' history. Remember Walter's story of the woman connie who let him off paying his fare during the war years? These wartime women workers gained an historic Australian first, as the first women in a major industry to be paid male rates of pay. It wasn't open to all though. Those employed were either the wives of M&MTB employees or of active servicemen. From 1943-45 nearly one thousand women worked as conductors on the city's trams.

This arrangement didn't last long. Immediately after the war all the women were dismissed to make way for returning soldiers, a decision that the M&MTB had to reverse just two years later because of worker shortages. It was at this moment that Joyce struck out for her independence by joining the tramways. She worked most of her 35 years on the trams at Brunswick Depot. So it's an entire generation that has to pass from 1941 to 1975 before women can drive trams for the M&MTB.

The trams were a male preserve from the start, as with so many other industries in the country. Clapp's MTOC did employ women as tellers – that is, reconciling the tiny card chads collected inside the bell-punch with the conductor's daily takings. Otherwise it was men not just on the tracks but in management, engineering, on the Board, and union leadership. Writing on women's struggle to become tram drivers, Margaret Bevege locates their campaign in the context of an Australian workforce still largely based on sex-segregation. The women's victory therefore had significance that went beyond their own industry. The ATMOEA was amalgamated with other transport unions in the 1990s. The successor union, the Rail, Tram and Bus Union (RTBU) elected Luba Grigorovitch as the first ever woman secretary of the union in 2014.

*

Today I'm visiting the Brunswick Tram Depot in Sydney Road. The depot houses a plaque commemorating Joyce Barry and I'm keen to see it in situ. I knock on the office door but it's locked so I go around to the employee entrance and knock there. After explaining my reason for being there – no, I'm not family, just doing research – I'm let in and guided through a muster room and corridor to a covered area attached to the tram shed at the rear. On a purple wall opposite is the plaque to Joyce. It reads:

In memory of a pioneer
JOYCE BARRY
6 August 1922 to 9 August 2006
Melbourne's first female tram driver
Brunswick Depot – December 1975

Nice. I take a photo. I chat briefly to my guide but he's clearly busy so I head out. Pity, I would like to hang around and watch proceedings. I walk around the block to the tram shed at the rear. The street running along the tram shed is called Cameron Street, and yes, that's to honour Alex Cameron. Good work Alex, your trams are still running out of the depot you created. Like all tram sheds, this one is a wide structure, with multiple roads for housing the trams. At the entrance a large digital sign tells the drivers which number road to park their tram in at the end of their shift (in earlier days this sign was managed manually). I watch as trams enter and depart. The drivers no doubt assume I'm a tram spotter, standing there with my phone out taking pics. The rail tracks into the shed overlap and criss-cross in all directions, forming an elaborate pattern on the ground. It starts to rain lightly.

I'm tram hopping today, not on and off different route trams, just the same one – the number 19, which was one of Joyce's routes both as a connie and a driver. The 19 runs along Sydney Road, one of my favorite stretches of the city. It's a straight line of glorious sights and sounds, bursting with a collision of history and modernity, the most diverse of the city's tram streets. Crammed into a few short kilometres and held together architecturally by a largely intact set of Victorian buildings, is a fantasia of businesses, peoples and activities. Up north towards Bell Street there's a strong Arab and Turkish influence – restaurants, supermarkets and cafes, Islamic fashion, shishka cafes and clothing stores and jewellery shops. Down south between Albion Street and Brunswick Road is a mixture of bridal stores, hipster cafes and barber shops, churches, opportunity and two-dollar shops, Mediterranean groceries and Asian fusion cafes. Between Bell Street and Brunswick Road there are at least a dozen pubs, and bars are everywhere. On weekends live music pours into the street from venues. You'll see more tattoos walking the streets here than anywhere in the city. The tram is so integral to the street that it moves up and down like a familiar character in a novel.

Route 19 is of modest length at 10.2 kilometres, and it's run with B2 and D2 class trams. As I've noted, the cable tram from the city to Brunswick was established in 1887, and it terminated at Moreland Road. The M&MTB electrified the cable line across 1935-36. The 19 runs from the terminus at Flinders and Elizabeth Streets to Bakers Road in Coburg.

Along Sydney Road there are glimpses down alleyways and laneways of houses and structures built with the classic red-brown bricks made in the area. This road was originally a track to the northern goldfields and to Sydney and from the 1840s the area abounded in quarries, potteries and brickworks. The reddy-brown bricks were ubiquitous – tram structures (engine houses, depots) clothing factories (like Joyce Barry's father's pyjama factory), textile mills, food processing works, foundries – all made from local fired clay.

Merri-bek was always Indigenous, part of the Wurundjeri lands, and since the 19th century a migrant town and a working class town with working class politics, with successive waves of migrants, particularly after World War Two. Irish, Scots, Chinese, Italians, Greeks, Maltese, Turks, Lebanese, Vietnamese, Pakistanis, Iraqis – the list goes on. The shops and stores along Sydney Road bear the imprint, often as no more than faded signage, of these successive migrant waves. The latest migrants are internal – young, middle class professionals from the eastern suburbs, attracted to the area because of its unique culture. According to the locals, Brunswick is now the undisputed coffee capital, not just of the city, but the world!

I'm heading up to Bell Street in Coburg. I have in mind a falafel from the Half Moon Cafe in the Victoria Street Mall, the best falafel in the north. The street when I alight is crowded, lots of hijabs, people sitting outside chatting and coffeeing, bargain hunting in Fat Harry's Clearance Store and Foley's Mall. Just across from the mall is the wonderful Dunnes Building, built in 1891. There's a queue at the Half Moon and I have to wait. Outside a man is yelling something about socks and gesticulating wildly, but his behaviour doesn't appear to annoy anyone.

Full of falafel I'm back on the tram heading south and at Albion Street I get down and enter the Edinburgh Castle Hotel on the corner. This rabbit warren of a pub has a falling-down ambience – decrepit, walls cracking, worn carpets – hosts good and bad local musos, young families, singing groups, table tennis and solid drinkers, who surround the horseshoe bar with their pints of Guinness and local brews. Built originally in 1854 with a major renovation in 1939, it's the oldest extant pub in Brunswick, with all the other pubs of the 1850s having been demolished and/or rebuilt in successive decades. The survivors from that era include the Retreat, the Cornish Arms, the Sarah Sands, the Woodlands, the Duke of Edinburgh and the Post Office. There's more folks. Take a wander down Sydney Road and sample some of them.

Well, I've had my pint and I'm feeling fine. Let's see. Sydney Road also has its share of ghosts, grand buildings squandered for little benefit other than the pockets of developers. We pass an ALDI, formerly the Empire Theatre built in 1912 and the first theatre in Brunswick to show 'talkies'. There was the Padua Theatre built in 1937, one of the city's great art deco buildings, with a foyer to die for, and the pre-talkie Lyric Theatre, now home to the Brunswick Club.

And whose business just happened to inhabit Sydney Road? I look up at just the right moment as we head down the hill and there it is – the old sign from our old mate, Whelan the Wrecker. It was the habit of locals to drop into Whelan's yard to check out the latest goodies that had been 'rescued' from his demolitions – beautiful window frames, ironwork, pilasters, mahogany doors, elaborate brickwork, friezes, you name it and Whelan took it. No doubt there are still homes around Brunswick with fancy bits and pieces of the city's heritage taking pride of place.

We're now passing Sparta Place, with its wonderful bust of Leonidas, the Greek hero at Thermopylae. Merri-bek and Sparta are sister cities and many of the Greeks who settled here from the Peloponnese were like Ellie's parents, who fled the country after the civil war.

The street is now decidedly bridal, bridal, bridal. Local companies make and sell their own designs, an industry started by Italian dressmakers in the 1980s. The mannequins in the store fronts are draped in the most elaborate and sparkling wedding dresses, whites and creams dominant. There's a cafe specifically for the 'after-fitting'.

Apologies dear patient reader, this is sounding like a travelogue. But I can't leave Brunswick without mentioning its 19th century churches, which until the rise of the apartment boom, were the tallest buildings in the area. There's the Gothic Wesleyan Church built in 1872, the Uniting Church, and St Ambrose Catholic Church. Naturally, fewer churches than pubs. The trams of Brunswick and Coburg took people to church, to the pub, to work, for shopping, to the football, to the city. It's no surprise that the area boomed in the 1880s when it became possible to get around cheaply and quickly from the south to the north and vice versa.

Trundling past the Brunswick Town Hall I notice the name Miss R. E. Yon painted in large letters on the upper story of a shop. I find out that Miss Yon's grandfather came to the colony in the gold rush and later became a tobacco farmer in Wangaratta. Miss Yon became a dressmaker, and this was her shop from 1917 to 1937, the year she died aged in her early fifties. A city with so many working lives lived and worked along tram lines.

At the Barkly Square stop a long queue curls out of the Green Refectory Cafe into the street. This intersection is so crowded it's like a mini Flinders and Elizabeth, and the tram stop sees dozens of people hopping on and off. A woman in a black burqa boards the tram, followed by a woman in white and pink cosplay. As the tram exits Brunswick, Sydney Road broadens out into the expanse of Royal Parade, and on both sides a profusion of trees, gardens and fields. Princes Park is densely dotted with joggers, dogs and their owners, and practicing sports teams.

The tram is in Parkville and the Melbourne University zone. I get off at the stop near Grattan Street and wander the University grounds. It's amazing, the mass of new buildings, both modernist and post-modernist icons to the new learning, that have sprung up here, and I hardly recognise my alma mater. There is a wildly coloured and extravagant new arts building, made of concrete, steel and plastic, which makes the old sandstone arts building look quaintly provincial. I search my memory for my former self, for ancient events, for memories of friends and colleagues, but to my annoyance nothing appears. The present is continuous and quite underwhelming. I sit in the refurbished Union hall and drink soy latte, surrounded by a garish array of restaurants. Outside I wander into a farmers' market in the Union courtyard. A man is making paella. I stare at the pieces of chorizo and chicken bubbling in the enormous pan.

Now some memories gather: I'm in a picture, comprised of my younger self and my then lover. We are sitting on grass in one of the University courtyards, I can't identify which exactly. The lover is expounding on Camus, or perhaps it's Sartre. In the bag beside my lover are two books, a heavily marked-up copy of the Iliad and a book of poetry by e. e. cummings. The intensity of the conversation is striking; it is as if what is being discussed has life and death implications. I can't recall the words clearly, but there's no mistaking the urgency and energy that is passing between us. My lover's face is glistening with articulation, our bodies are entangled, expectant, vividly alive to the biology, the fact of the other. Yes, I can now feel the cool autumn air of that day and the smell of the newly cut grass. The lovers suddenly get up and head towards a distant gate, their shoulders brushing against each other. I see how awkward is my stride from the back. What a dag.

I walk away from the market towards the tram stop. I'm walking the same route as I had walked – how many times, hundreds? – over 40 years before with this lover, from the Union to the tram stop.

The lovers will get to Swanston Street and catch the 19 into the city. They will sit in the open saloon section in the middle of the W class tram, rain whipping through the base of the leather shutters, it is evening and the yellow interior light of the tram is glowing on the wooden benches, the smell of rain water comes off the commuters' woollen jackets and jumpers and people's hats are dripping. They could be characters in a Brack painting, the one artist to capture the city's rain with commuters with trams, with streets and evening. They will journey to the city and get down somewhere near Bourke Street, or is it Lonsdale, and they will hurry in the rain down a side street, a small lane barely lit and then head up some flights of stairs, covered in wet footprints, and enter a room, a wide long room lit with low hanging rectangular lights, and below the lights the beautiful green of the billiards tables. And they will play some games here, one after the other, until they are tired and hungry. They will take the tram home and cook a meal with whatever is in the fridge, which isn't much, but at least there is wine in a cask, and they will drink their wine and play their music on a turntable and then go to bed.

He will wake and rise in an upstairs room in Carlton, with a window overlooking a garden, back yards and the roofs of other houses, a lemon scented gum rustling in the early autumn breeze. He will turn to his lover who is lying in bed asleep and stand there watching for some time. The bells of a church will ring out in the distance. He will have the thought that this moment is about to be lost and yet will somehow never be lost, that the contradictions of time and memory which were one of the subjects of the previous night's discussion, before they got completely drunk, are completely here before him at this instant, now in this morning, sensing that this moment already has a present, past and future, which is, and will be open to transformation, reinterpretation, and he senses now that he will leave the lover, but the lover will never be left, and he reels from the headache caused by the cheap red, as he descends the stairs to the kitchen in search of panadol.

36. Out West on the Number 82

Fell mongers, tanners, wool washers, bone grinders, slaughtermen and tallow men, soap and glue makers; the workers of the 'noxious trades' down by the Yarra, giving the city its moniker of 'Smelltown'. By the late 19th century the denizens of Melbourne had had enough. The noxious trades would be shifted and the city made clean, smelling of roses, not offal, blood, fat and entrails. But, where to for the noxious industries? What sanctuary from civilisation would take them? Who but the most destitute, the most desperate and needy would want the work?

As I mentioned back in my discussion of the cable trams, the network didn't extend to the west. Swamps, rail yards, cable length and disease were the ostensible barriers to expansion. The miasma of Footscray was an impediment to cable trams and so many things of the New World, but not to the relocation of the noxious ones. By the late 1880s the Yarra had been superseded as a dumping ground by the Maribyrnong River and on its banks sang the dirge of 100 industries pouring their excrements into the river, contaminating the air, the ground water, everything. By 1900 Footscray had one of the highest infant mortality rates in the whole country. More than one in 10 babies died in their first year. Everyone got sick – dysentery, cholera, typhoid – had shorter lives, lived without the amenities of the east.

The noxious industries joined the heavy metal and chemical industries of the west. Chromium works, foundries and engineering workshops, ammonia and formaldehyde businesses, fertiliser companies, everything bad and necessary for the city and colony to survive, to be modern, was landed here along and near the Maribyrnong. In a media report from 1887, the Maribyrnong is described as a river of waste water, full of rotting carcasses, coagulated blood products, dead horses. Sometimes the river was so steeped in shit that it stopped flowing entirely, but when it did flow it flowed red.

*

Today I'm in Leeds Street Footscray waiting for the 82 tram to arrive at the terminus. The street is crowded with shoppers. Most of the shops and stores are run by Vietnamese Australians, who came to Footscray in the late 1970s, early 1980s, many as 'boat' refugees from Vietnam, joining previous waves of post-war migrants from Italy, Greece, Macedonia, Croatia, Malta, and the rest. The late Franco Cozzo started his furniture business here, and the whole town is a demonstration of the human capacity for rebuilding and renewal. I've always liked Footscray since I lived here in the 1990s. I didn't know much about its history then and it smelt and it was often poor, but its inhabitants adhered to an older notion of egalitarianism and community that the rest of the city had seemingly abandoned. The newest wave of migrants to the west are young families from the east of the city, drawn to Yarraville in particular by its lower property values and its emergence as the city's latest 'place to be'.

Here comes a Z class tram along Leeds Street (again!). It doesn't surprise me that the oldest trams on the network are running here to the exclusion of any other class of tram. I mentioned earlier that the west always got the 'hand-me-downs' after the electric system first opened in 1921. Those trams were originally from the PMTT in the east. Cameron wanted the west to join the city's tramway system, and the General Scheme had a proposed line running to Footscray down Dynon Road. Never came to pass. Today the west is only indirectly connected to the eastern tramways through the overlap of the 82 with the 57 tram, both of which cruise along Raleigh Road in Maribyrnong.

So the 82 is a bit like its cousin the 78, the two tram routes that never venture into the CBD. Not exactly long at 9.2 kilometres, the 82 has been an important link between the suburbs of Footscray and

Moonee Ponds, where it also terminates. This Footscray-Moonee Ponds route started in 1954. It's the last surviving piece of the M&MTB western suburbs network, which had several short local lines that were shut in the 1960s.

Along with the noxious industries, the west was also traditionally home, from 1888, to the armaments industry, making bombs and bullets and the stuff that goes into firing them. This highly dangerous industry was mainly settled in the horseshoe of the Maribyrnong north of Footscray, and as I discussed in relation to route 57, the site is now abandoned. Explosive, cordite and ordnance factories were established in the early 20th century and in the Second World War these defence sites were expanded. Footscray trams were critical in getting the workforce to their factories every morning. In an unusual departure for the electric tram system, they were emblazoned with signs denoting their war-time destinations: 'Explosives Factory', 'Ordnance Factory', 'Pyrotechnic Factory', 'Ammunition Factory'. These trams filled to bursting every morning with local workers, smoking their last rollies, or pipes for the day, as they headed to the immense defence industries. The Commonwealth funded a number of line extensions during the war so that these industries could be served.

The Melbourne tramways have always 'done their bit' for war efforts, including paying in blood, as the ever reliable Russell Jones shows in his ANZAC article for the Tram Museum. Amongst the ANZACS who never came back were 86 Melbourne trammies. In World War Two the M&MTB partly converted the Preston workshops into component manufacturing for the military. Trams ran at night with blackout cowls over their headlights. The tramways were declared a protected industry, annual leave cancelled, and resignation banned (unless you joined up). The M&MTB built trenches around the network in case of air raids, offered reduced fares to those in uniform, and guaranteed reinstatement to all employees who served. This was the moment women flooded into the system as conductors. By 1944 there were 992 women working on Melbourne's trams, about one in five of the workforce.

It's actually normal for trams to run during wartime. Right now the trams are still running in Kyiv, with bombs and drones coming down any time of the day or night. You can ride a tram and hear them exploding and hope to God they are not going to land on you. Some of the trammies there have gone off to fight.

Back to the 82. I've been waiting at the terminus for my friend Kim to appear. According to my PTV app the tram won't be leaving for another seven minutes, so there's time for us to catch it. Kim's agreed to join me on the journey out to Moonee Ponds, where we will have lunch. All good, except he isn't here, and I can get fidgety about departures, or rather, the prospect of missing one. Kim finds my tram project wryly amusing. He's a creative person with diverse interests – musician, song writer, film maker, astrologer – so he understands the call of the strange. At school he was one of the guitar freaks, playing at lunchtime to groups of fellow students. Girls loved him and boys were jealous of him – long blond curls, great voice, confident, funny. He caught the 19 to school each day, his shirt hanging out of his trousers, tie askew, leather shoulder bag, peace badges on his lapels. Well, it was the '70s.

Now I spot him coming up Leeds Street, broad sun hat and tapping his way forward with a white stick which has a ball attached at the bottom so that he can feel his way down Footscray's cracked footpaths. His near-blindness doesn't stop him from getting around every day. A recognisable figure on these streets (he'd hate it if I called him a 'local identity'), and the locals always make way for him. He's coming on the trip with me for the outing and lunch despite the fact that he won't see much on the way. He's promised to tell me some tram stories. What could be better!

As I said earlier, the 82 is a real wanderer route. I've travelled it several times before today, and have always been amused at its circuitous path to Moonee Ponds in the north west. Unlike its cousin the 78, taking a straight line for its entire journey, the 82 seems to have a bee in its bonnet, heading to all points of the compass, and making endless turns. It's as if it can't make up its mind where it's heading or how to get there.

Look at this: from the southern terminus - north along Leeds Street, left into Hopkins Street (west), right into Droop Street (north-west), left into Ballarat Road (west), right into Gordon Street (north), left into River Street (west), right into Rosamond Road (north), left into Williamson Road (west), right into Wests Road (north), right into Raleigh Road (east), along Maribyrnong Road (east), left into Ascot Vale Road (north), terminus in Moonee Ponds. Reverse directions going back. My head's spinning.

Kim and I are on the tram, which is about to take off. A young guy sprawled near us with his feet on the opposite seat is asking each passenger as they get on when the 'fucking tram' is going to leave. Eventually the driver, who has left the tram to its own devices for some minutes, returns and walks the length of the tram greeting his customers. He takes no apparent offence at the young man's question, and replies calmly that the tram is leaving right now. Three stops later the young guy will get off.

We depart and slowly wind our rattling way past Pho shops, Footscray Market, immigration agencies, African cafes and ancient red brick factories which once made rope and cord interspersed with sites completely razed for apartment development with names like 'Live City', now in its 'Final Release'. The tram passes Kuz's Kebabs, 1950s flats and a soccer ground and in River Street has its own dedicated path alongside schools and sports grounds. We are now travelling in Maribrynong and turning into Rosamund Road, before the tram does a right northwards. Our route is through what appears to be spare land at the back of factories and warehouses, a scene of true desolation. Compare this treeless landscape with the wide boulevards of the city and the east. My phone map tells me we are on Wests Road, but there's no street here and no signage.

Kim and I have been chatting amiably as we go. He is the only person I've told about the cancer and the chemo and he's very solicitous, wanting to know the details of how it's all going. All good I tell him, which isn't entirely true, but I don't want our journey to be absorbed with subjects of distant or, indeed, imminent demise. It will all happen won't it, even to you dear reader.

At Raleigh Road we travel east for several kilometres, cross the Maribyrnong River, with the Anglers Tavern perched on the north bank, and enter Ascot Vale which is instantly and recognisably middle class. A 57 tram passes us going in the opposite direction. G'day 57! A turn into Ascot Vale Road takes us up to Moonee Ponds. It is extremely hot and we're both glad of the aircon in the dumpling restaurant. Kim has to readjust his bearings to the interior light, so it takes a while to be seated, but everyone treats him with respect. I've noticed this on our outings together – people don't hesitate to accommodate his disability – and it makes me less grumpy about humanity.

Over lunch Kim shares his promised stories, mostly to and from school tales, reminiscent of Marco's account of his school tram days. It seems that the thousands of students tramming to school in the city were having similar experiences. Kim recalls a couple of students who always played pontoon on his tram, always in the same seat. There were the bags stacked in the corners, crowded doorways, pushing and shoving, jokes and laughs, some absorbed in their books, others just staring vacantly out the window. Hats were grabbed off heads and thrown from saloon to saloon. He recalls the smell of wet wool on rainy days, the blistering heat in summer, the openness of the tram's configuration letting the weather flow through, how at the urging of others he occasionally played his guitar on the tram too, but some of the connies were not pleased.

He recalls one day when, so engaged in conversation, he stupidly left his guitar on the tram, and had to fetch it from the tram depot's lost property, in a room with a series of windows 'like tellers' windows in a bank', he says. 'So I was about to leave when a couple of trammies came in from their shift', he continues, 'and one of them calls, "hey maestro, give us a tune!" I remember I sat on a bench in the corner, pulled out the guitar and played them *Up on Cripple Creek*. After that, more trammies came in and demanded more music. For the next half hour or so I played songs for them until a man in a dark green uniform came in and told them that the depot "wasn't a concert hall" and to get back to work.'

Kim now switches from his own past to tell me about his great aunt. I get the sense that he has been saving this up for last. Towards the end of her life Kim occasionally visited her in her nursing home. He liked her company – she was a vibrant character and always up for a yarn. Cecily worked as a cutter and seamstress in Flinders Lane in the shmatte trade ('shmatte' – Yiddish for rag). She worked for Jewish designers and dressmakers for years, before, during and after the war. 'Cecily often told me stories about her life', says Kim, 'she was a "spinster", as unmarried women were called then and had to support herself. She really loved her work, and the other women in the business were close friends. She told me that in summer the workroom, which had about 20 women working in it, cutting, sewing, and stitching, had no aircon or cooling so the women all stripped off to their underwear as they worked.' Kim tells me that Cecily was a real fashionista, always, according to her, immaculately dressed in the latest styles. Melbourne was making its own designs then and the industry was buoyant.

'Anyway, here's the tram part of her story', says Kim. 'She always took the tram to and from work, and claimed that she never had to pay a fare in her younger years. Not once. She said it was because she was so pretty, and that every time she reached for her purse to pay the connie, one of the men on the tram would insist on paying her fare himself. This went on for years, until one day it simply stopped happening. She got a really big surprise at this turn of events. Wasn't she still adorable? She always told me this story with a laugh – yes she told it often when she was very old – and it clearly still amused her.'

Despite all the attention she got from strangers and her own declared good looks, Cecily had told Kim that marrying a man was never her intention. 'She liked working too much and her independence.

She liked going out every day to work on the tram, looking at what everyone was wearing, spending the days with the other women, and coming home to her own place. She had a small flat that sat right on the tram line. She read books in the evening and listened to the radio. She drank a glass or two of port. She did her nails and put her hair in curlers. On Fridays, she and the other women went out together, dressed as she called it "to the nines". Cecily wore red lipstick, make-up, black stockings, vibrant dresses that pinched at the waist, the works. They caught trams to different venues around town – big band clubs and dance halls – and they spent the night out, dancing, drinking and smoking. She often caught the last tram home, and fell into bed after midnight.'

I ask Kim if he was ever game enough to ask Cecily if she ever came home on one of these nights out with a companion. He says that he never did. 'Once she did let slip that she thought she had lost a precious earring one particularly raucous night, but a friend had retrieved it from the grooved floor of the tram on their way home, where it had lodged. And then she quickly changed the subject.'

37. The Major-General

After the coup that took down Alex Cameron and the rise of the anti-tramists, who would step forward to save our trams from extinction? Let's welcome to the stage the third major figure in Melbourne's tram story – the Major-General.

Robert Joseph Henry Risson was born in the small rural Queensland town of Ma Ma Creek in 1901, the year of Federation. A farmer's son, Risson studied engineering at the University of Queensland and joined the Brisbane Tramways Trust in 1923. He was a life long advocate and lover of trams. Tall, commanding and imperious, Risson served in World War Two at Tobruk, El Alamein and in New Guinea and rose to the rank of Brigadier. His engineers cleared minefields at El Alamein, and Risson was decorated for his bravery and efficiency. After the war he was made Major-General, the title he used until he was knighted Sir Robert in 1970. He returned to the Brisbane Tramways Trust before being appointed Chairman of the M&MTB in 1949, where he remained until 1970. He was long-lived, dying in Melbourne in 1992. He and his wife did not have children.

In his 2001 memorial lecture for Risson, Graeme Turnbull describes the Major-General as a man who liked uniforms and adamantly opposed relaxing the rules of dress for M&MTB employees. He wore a homburg hat to work and was a stickler for punctuality. His approach to leadership was hands on; he was both admired and feared and never one to avoid a fight. I get the sense he actually enjoyed a good dust up and was not intimidated by the likes of ministers or premiers. The word 'martinet' also comes to mind.

Unlike today's ministers and transport bureaucrats, Risson caught the tram to and from work. Drivers were never entirely happy if Risson happened to catch their tram. He would sit right behind the driver in the most forward seat in the saloon and watch their performance. In 1954 the M&MTB was criticised for overcrowding on the Toorak tram at peak hour by a member of the public in a letter to *The Age*. Risson took the Toorak tram himself at peak hour and counted the number of passengers, ascertaining that it was not, technically, overcrowded.

On one occasion, he invited the media to watch the Chairman himself climb onto the roof of a tram to demonstrate the correct way to reattach a trolley pole to the overhead wire. This followed the tragic death of a driver who'd died falling off a tram in the city trying to reattach the pole. The union had challenged the Major-General to show the correct procedure himself and Risson obliged. By today's standards it was a display that lacked sensitivity given the death of one of his employees, but it showed Risson as fearless and undaunted. But that was Risson, a sometimes cold man, who brooked no opposition.

The union did not like the Major-General, but they knew that he would honour any agreement struck with the M&MTB. For his part, Risson was a strident anti-communist, disliked the union and its leader Clarrie O'Shea, but knew that the union was a permanent feature of the industrial landscape that he would have to deal with. Nevertheless, strikes were frequent post-war, as unions across the country fought for better conditions and wages, and the tramways were no exception. The entire system was shut down in the 60 day strike of 1950, one of the longest strikes post-war. But the union was also keenly aware that Risson was a key to the survival of their jobs, as the post-war generation of politicians decided to rip up the tram lines around the country. Premier Hollway wanted to review the tramways with a view to their abandonment. The bus lobby, the car lobby, the oil lobby, all the anti-tram lobbies in the city were joining forces to rid the city of its trams. The *Herald* newspaper was in the forefront of this fight in 1950s, which echoed the 'Transport War' waged decades earlier.

Buses had run on two routes down Bourke Street since the Cameron era, and Risson wanted to replace them with trams. These routes – covering parts of today's 96 and 86 – were critical to the network expansion and long overdue. The Major-General was adamant that the buses would be replaced and he made his case loudly and publicly. Tramways, he said, were logical, efficient, economic – the best form of urban transport – and the Major-General would not countenance attempts by the city's vested interests to undermine them, let alone abolish them. He appeared on TV and gave long interviews to newspapers. He set out in detail the tramways' advantages (the general thrust of which, dear reader, you are no doubt familiar with by now). Trams carried more people, had a long life-span, were easy to maintain, were more comfortable, and unlike buses, actually made money. Risson argued on the basis of what he called 'hard economic facts'. Echoing the arguments of Cameron a generation earlier, his address to the Institute of Transport in 1955 compared trams to buses: buses broke down four times as often as trams; the M&MTB maintained roads, buses paid nothing; a tram cost 6 pence (5 cents) per mile to power, while a bus cost over 3 and a half shillings (roughly 35 cents); labour costs on buses were 50 percent higher, and so on. In modern sports parlance, he flooded the zone with data.

He was a forthright and polished media performer and utterly undeterred by criticism from *The Herald* newspaper or anyone else. Premier Bolte, the farmer from the western districts, was a man with his own cruel streak – witness the hanging of Ronald Ryan alluded to earlier – but it's pretty clear Bolte was, like the premiers that preceded him, intimidated by the military hero and in the end it was Risson who prevailed. He succeeded in converting the Bourke Street bus routes by 1956, and that same year the latest iteration of the W class tram was introduced to significant acclaim. As mentioned, these were the so-called 'quiet trams' – the W7s – with engineering features that reduced noise by a claimed 50 percent.

Risson had other wins in the 1950s, but the W7 was the last tram to be built in Melbourne for nearly two decades. Unable to dislodge the tramways, governments resorted to starvation tactics, denying the M&MTB the investment needed for expansion and renewal. Fortunately the fleet was in such good condition that it lasted into the mid-1970s when tram production restarted. The Major-General was fighting a rearguard action through much of his tenure, maintaining the fleet, cutting costs when necessary, and basically keeping on everyone's hammer to perform.

It wasn't until the 1990s that Risson was acknowledged in Parliament as the man who had saved Melbourne's trams. In 1994 the terminus at Elizabeth and Flinders Streets was named 'Sir Robert Risson Tram Terminus', and a plaque set in the pavement acknowledging his central role in preserving the system. In 2001 RMIT held the inaugural Sir Robert Risson memorial lecture, referred to above. So Risson fares better than his two tram predecessors in the remembrance stakes. Much better.

*

This project has opened up a veritable Pandora's box of memories; to wit, last night while struggling to sleep I had a sudden image of a man met decades ago.

I met Ross on a dull, rainy day as we waited for the tram in Glenferrie Road. Ross was an ex-trammie who had worked on the trams from the 1930s to the early '70s, almost 40 years of service. He had one of the most lined faces I've ever seen and his English was from another era. Ross had been a gripman in the '30s, driving trams in the dying days of cable. In 1940 he transitioned to electric, a move for which he had to retrain but never regretted. The cable trams were 'a bit of a rattle trap', according to Ross, but he enjoyed chatting to passengers and the skills involved in the job meant it was never boring. Ross said the changeover to the W trams was a revelation: they were so powerful and so commanding of the road that you felt like a general up there. He missed his interactions with the customers, but it was a 'grand job'. For a while Ross worked at his new depot as a conductor and a driver, a role, he told me, known as a 'marmalade', before eventually settling for driving full-time.

He said that in his early days being a trammie was regarded as great employment – well paid, annual leave, decent hours, uniforms – and he raised his family on that one wage. Being a tram driver had a certain social cachet. 'We were looked up to', he said, 'and so were the connies. It was a job that held respect.' But by the end of his tenure things had changed a bit – the trams were getting old, cars were everywhere, and working on the trams had lost its sheen. It was still a good job, but no-one thought much of it any more. So he was glad when he got to 65 and received the royal gong. He doesn't miss the trams. 'Retirement is beautiful', Ross told me, 'everyday a free man, and I do love my roses.'

38. Clarrie O'Shea & the Union

C larence Lyell O'Shea ('Clarrie') was sitting in his gaol cell at
Pentridge wondering what would happen next. Clarrie had
been sent to gaol by Justice John Kerr for failing to pay a $500
fine for contempt of court. Older readers will remember Justice Kerr
as the man who, as Governor-General of Australia, sacked the Labor
government of Gough Whitlam in 1975 – just six years after he'd
gaoled Clarrie. As John Merritt shows in his article for the *Canberra
Historical Journal,* Clarrie's contempt of court followed his refusal to
pay $8,100 in fines imposed on the state division of the ATMOEA. As
state secretary of the union's Victorian division Clarrie had appeared
before Kerr on charges brought under the penal clauses inserted into
arbitration awards by the federal government. The union had been
racking up fines since 1966 under these provisions over various disputes and union actions which the state government considered 'un-
authorised'.

Clarrie ignored various subpoenas to appear in court but did so
eventually in 1969. He refused to be sworn in, or to produce the union's books as demanded by the court. When he refused to pay the
fine for contempt he was arrested on the 15th May and imprisoned. A
general strike was called almost immediately in Victoria affecting
public transport, power supplies, communications and other industries. The strike spread and pretty soon hundreds of thousands of
workers were on strike across the country. I remember this moment
well because I couldn't catch the train to school and instead my father
drove me there, smoking his mini-cigars all the way. I got to school
smelling like a tobacco shop.

The right wing had overreached and now there was fear that the general strike would bring down the government. Miraculously, an anonymous donor paid both Clarrie's contempt fine, and the union's fines. Clarrie was released and became an instant hero of the industrial union movement. Not long after, he retired as secretary of the union he had served since 1947. Clarrie always maintained that ASIO had sprung him from gaol.

So, who is this Clarrie character and why is he important? Clarrie's grandparents migrated from Ireland in the 19th century and Clarrie's father, James, was born in Ballarat. The O'Sheas moved to Tasmania where Clarrie was born in 1905, the fourth of eight children, and Clarrie's father worked in the mines on the west coast. James developed lung disease so the family moved back to Victoria where they lived in a five room cottage in Richmond. Due to his lung condition, Clarrie's father was in and out of work, so Clarrie went to work at age 11, delivering the 'Labor Call' newspaper. He also worked at a grocery, a bakery and warehouses and left school at 13 – the same age my mother left school – and also took care of his younger siblings. The O'Sheas were poor by today's standards but Clarrie maintained that his childhood was a happy one. Clarrie married Edith Pomeroy in 1925 and in the same year he joined the trams as a conductor, working out of the North Melbourne Cable Tram Depot. Yes, that's right, our future labor hero was a cable conductor! (And like Ross, straddling the eras of cable and electric.) He rose through the ranks and became depot delegate for the union in 1932, federal secretary in 1942, and, the job with real power, state secretary in 1947, a position he held to 1970. Clarrie and Edith had three children.

Clarrie was Major-General Risson's nemesis for over 20 years. These two implacables were both dedicated to preserving Melbourne's trams, but they fought some bitter battles along the way. Clarrie believed that workers had the right to exercise their only real source of leverage with their employers – the right to strike. He achieved a lot for his members in terms of conditions, wages and working hours, and was involved in wider union campaigns to improve conditions. Clarrie became a communist in the early 1930s during the Depression when he saw the working class being made to pay for the follies of capital, in such actions as forced evictions, which he opposed and fought against. It's hard to believe now that so many unions, like Clarrie's, were dominated by communist leadership across the country, and the huge sense of optimism that generation had for a socialist future.

Amongst tramways stoppages in the 1950s, the longest of them all was led by Clarrie in 1950 and centred on the union's demand for more pay. As mentioned, the strike lasted 60 days but did not secure the wage rise they'd fought for. If anything this defeat made the union leadership under Clarrie more, rather than less militant. There would be more ways to skin a cat in this era of low unemployment and boom conditions, so different to the Depression years before the war. Over the decades Clarrie's union gained considerable victories for tram workers, including annual leave and sick pay entitlements, reduction in working hours from 48 hours per week to the 40 hour week (1947) and preservation of two-man operations. This latter issue was a source of major disputes across the 1950s and into the 1960s, and was at the heart of the campaigns that saw Clarrie go to prison. Essentially, the M&MTB wanted to cut costs in its bus services by introducing one man services. The union saw one man bus operations as the thin edge of the wedge, with trams to follow, and resolutely opposed the proposals throughout this period and was largely successful. One blight on Clarrie's record though concerns the union's opposition to female drivers during the term of his leadership. As we've seen, it was only after the old guard of the union retired, including Clarrie, that women won the right to be tram drivers.

Clarrie lived to a ripe old age of 83, and was apparently everyone's favorite uncle. He followed the Richmond Tigers his whole life, but then nobody's perfect. The unschooled Clarrie was a master of industrial intrigue and plotting – he fought the right wing Groupers throughout the 1950s and 1960s for control of the union and succeeded – and he was a brilliant organiser with a huge talent for bringing members along on the cause. He kept the trams as a decent place to work with decent pay into the 1970s and, like his life-long opponent Risson, he is part of that human equation that preserved the tram system for our city.

*

Twenty years after Clarrie sat in his prison cell the ATMOEA was engaged in a massive fight with the Labor government to save Melbourne's tram conductors. In 1989 the state government announced the introduction of automatic ticketing to Melbourne's trams and the end of conductors. The union responded with direct actions, including giving the public free tram rides. The government refused to bargain so on the first of January 1990 the union took drastic action, driving 250 trams into the city and parking them there. As *The Age* reported on the following day, most of these trams occupied Elizabeth Street and were banked up, end to end, for blocks of the city. Have a look at the photos of this action, it's a truly remarkable sight.

The 'blockade' as it was called, involved the drivers and connies staying with their trams throughout the 33 days the trams sat in the streets. They were supported by teams of tram workers and others who brought them food and supplies. Eventually on the 2nd of February the union and government reached a compromise. The union agreed to the new ticketing system and driver-only trams on the proviso that no conductors would be sacked, effectively allowing for natural attrition to get rid of conductors for the first time in the history of the trams in the city. I've always thought this decision was irresponsible on both the union's and the government's part. The end of any conductor role for the city's trams has meant huge losses in revenue through fare evasion, the disappearance of thousands of decent, well-paid jobs, and the compromise of tram safety. But then, dear reader, you will no doubt counter by saying I'm a tram romantic with a slim grasp on reality.

Labor lost the next election anyway, in part because of the blockade and the sense of a government no longer in control. The new Liberal government was no friend of unions. The last connie to work a shift was on 24th May 1998 (out of the Malvern Depot). The Kennett government set about dismantling public transport services, sacking 16,000 transport workers, and in 1999, privatising the tram system. The union shrank to a fraction of its former size, and the era of tram-way workers having a major influence over the running of the system was over.

Bring back the connies!

39. Public v Private: From a Z to a G

Melbourne's tram system has been unique throughout its history, in part because our trams were designed and built here. But with the rise of neo-liberal economics in the last quarter of the 20th century the impetus to create locally came under threat. This chapter is about the trams that followed the W class series, many of which you've already met on my journeys. But I will cover more detail about the models that succeed the beloved greens, and sketch the shift from public to private ownership of the system. (For more details on the current fleet see Wilson and Budd's *Destination: Waterfront City,* and the recent handbook of Aymeric Perfrement.)

Z Class: You've already seen how the W series grew in classes, and sometimes sub-classes, across its history. This fervour for classification has prevailed over time and is still applied across the current fleet. As I've noted it was almost 20 years after the last W class tram before a new tram appeared. Starving the tramways of capital eventually gave way to a realisation the system would soon fall apart if nothing was done. Enter the Z class tram, built at Dandenong by Comeng between 1975 and 1984, marking the revival of trams built in the city. An industry that had virtually disappeared was resurrected, signalling a shift in public policy – government would again invest in trams as part of the city's transport system. Much of the W fleet was getting ancient. Trams built 20 years before were in good nick, but trams from the 1920s and '30s were now 50 and 40 years old. There are only so many times you can grind the flats off a wheel before the thing has to be replaced! Still, they are remarkably enduring, the Ws, and it would be decades before they were ultimately retired.

The Z was odd though. Made of steel and plastic, with a funny bull nose and, on take off they made a strange buzzing noise that sounded like a swarm of angry bees. There are three Zs – the Z1, the Z2 and the Z3. One hundred Z1s and 15 Z2s were built between 1975 and 1979. A single unit two bogie saloon car, they could seat 48 passengers (later modified to 44), had heating for the first time and the conductor sat at a console all day. The connies looked completely bored in their new role as stationary ticket collectors. There wasn't much difference between the Z1 and Z2. They only had two automatic doors and all of them were withdrawn from service by April 2016. Forty years and millions of kilometres and millions of passengers. What value!

As you know through its appearance in these pages, the Z3 is still well in use. Built between 1979 and 1984, 115 Z3 trams were in operation at their peak, and almost 90 of the darlings are still going. The Z3 has three doors, there were changes to the brakes and body design and improved ride quality. It seated 42 people (later reduced to 40) and by 2009 all of the Z3s were fitted with air-con for the drivers. Route 82 is always a Z3 and they are scattered around the system, including routes 3 and 57. Older readers may recall the bright orange paint of the first Zs. Yes, different. The Zs are vintage trams now.

A Class: So where do you go after Z? To A of course. The A series trams were also built by Comeng in Dandenong, from 1983 to 1987. There were 28 A1 trams constructed and 42 A2s. As noted earlier, the A1s started with a trolley pole, but the A series eventually shifted to the pantograph, the first use of this system on Melbourne's electric trams. (No more climbing on roofs by the Chairman for photoshoots as he demonstrates reattaching the trolley pole.) The A1 and A2 are not a lot different except the A2 has better brakes. They are both squared ended, single unit two bogie trams, have three doors and seat 42 people. The connie console was thankfully dropped. The drivers got aircon in the mid-2000s. One of the A1s has been withdrawn, all the rest are still running. You can catch one on routes 78, 70, 64, and 48.

B Class: There were two B1 prototypes built by Comeng in 1984-85 and we are now in the realm of 'articulated' trams, that is, trams with two or more sections connected by a flexible joint. The B2s made between 1987 and 1994 were a step up in size and complexity. Originally seating 76, they were later modified to increase standing room and now have seating for 52. They have three doors, air-conditioning for the first time on the fleet, and comprise a two section articulated saloon, with three bogies, and can run on light rail. One hundred and thirty B2s were built and all are still running. To look at them they are essentially two A class units stuck together with an accordion-like joint in the middle. As mentioned, some B2s are equipped with lean seats in their centre, otherwise the seating is good. These are the workhorses of the system, the most common tram on the network – reliable, safe and can pack in the customers. Bs are run on nine city routes.

The rise of neo-liberalism throughout the west in the last quarter of the 20th century has been well documented; an ideology that rejected class compromise and sought the reassertion of an unfettered capitalism. In Australia one of the prime forms and effects of this ideology was privatisation. Public utilities, such as airlines, airports, power utilities, public banks, railways and other government-led operations were suddenly on the market to the highest bidder. Melbourne's tramways were no exception. In 1999 the tram system was handed over to two private entities under franchise agreements. It's no small irony that this development was a return of the city's tramways to an earlier era of private operation. As the private operator of Melbourne's cable trams for decades Francis Clapp would no doubt have applauded this turn of events, until he saw the fine print. There was no stipulation that new operators build trams in Melbourne, a fatal flaw in the contracts that would have horrified Clapp. The new operators weren't interested in, or required to be involved in tram building and so the tram industry resurrected in 1975 was turned overnight to dust. And so followed the importation by Yarra Trams, one of the operators, of the Alstom Citadis C class tram made at La Rochelle in France. Alstom Citadis have built and exported thousands of these around the world.

C Class: The 21st century thus begins with Melbourne's new trams being entirely sourced from overseas – the first imported trams since 1923 (just two Birney Lightweight Safety cars from the US). In 2001 and 2002 Yarra Trams imported 36 C1 trams from France. They came in batches by boat, were unloaded at Webb Dock in Port Melbourne, and transported by truck to the Preston workshops. The Citadis C1 is a three unit articulated saloon tram with a fully low floor (the first on the system), three doors and despite its length only seats 40. All of the 36 are still running. For some reason I've never liked the look of the C1, but perhaps I'm prejudiced by its provenance. C1s tend to sway around a lot too, perhaps the result of having only two bogies (and have other deficiencies that I will recount later). Well, they were kind of cheap at $100 million for the lot so what do you expect? All of the imports were modified and over time upgraded at the Preston workshops. They currently run on routes 48 and 109.

Why France? Well, the parent company of Yarra Trams is Transdev, a French transport conglomerate operating in several countries. In 2008 Yarra Trams acquired more trams from Alstom in the one of the strangest deals ever entered into by a Melbourne tram operator. Rather than purchase the trams outright, Yarra Trams decided to lease five second-hand trams that had been already running in Mulhouse, France for three years. These are the 'Bumblebee' trams, so named for their original yellow livery. Five unit articulated saloon trams, with a 100 per cent low floor, three bogies, five doors and seating for 56. They run on the 96 line, a mix of tram and light rail. The trams were due to be returned to France at the end of the four year lease. Really? Who dreamt this up? It's one thing to ship trams across the world, but then to return them just four years later?... 'Er, thanks guys, great trams, and here they are back again'. So the authorities didn't return them, deciding instead to buy them outright.

Yarra Trams are still with us, and have been operating the whole system since 2004. The other franchise, National Express Group, went bust in 2002, just a few years after entering the market. One of the downsides of privatisation is that private companies have a habit of doing precisely that – going bust. National Express are British with global transport interests. They announced on the 16th of December 2002 that they would be rescinding their contracts on, wait for it... the 23rd of December 2002! Gee, thanks Express, so nice to have had you here. Their three year stewardship of half of the city's trams must rank as the shortest tenure of any operator in the history of our state's public transport.

D Class: Before they left, National ordered Siemens Combino trams from Siemens Mobility in Düsseldorf. Siemens Mobility sold the Combino world-wide to a dozen countries. This tram became the D series, with 38 of them delivered from 2002 to 2004. This three unit, two bogie articulated tram is a low-floor tram, seats 36 and all are running. As I've noted earlier, the D Class has its critics – *Timeout* called the D class the worst trams on the network in 2021 – with criticism based on poor seating and a rough ride. In 2003 and 2004 the second batch of 21 Combinos arrived. The D2 is a five section, three bogie low floor tram which seats 58 people and all are in service. Due to structural problems, both the D1 and D2 trams underwent modifications in 2009 – causing a loss of seating. Despite the critics I like the D2 better than the D1. It can carry a lot of people. When it trundles up Elizabeth Street towards Coburg it's usually packed. It has four doors, allowing for reasonable boarding, and on a clear track it can move along at speed. Has a tendency to rattle and grind these days and some are really noisy. Catch a D2 on routes 6 or 19. Three stars for the D2!

E Class: The imported low-floor C and D class trams have non-pivoting bogies, which is tough on the condition of tracks and the bogies themselves. This issue was addressed with the next tram to appear – the E class, the first of which (the E1) arrived in 2013 and represented a return to the norm: making trams here, rather than importing them. The Es were built at the Bombardier workshops in Dandenong on a contract stipulating 50 percent local content. The bogies and propulsion systems were manufactured in Germany. So, Clapp is still way ahead on this score, with 100 percent local production. Maybe we won't return to 100 per cent local manufacture any time soon, but the new G class tram contracts stipulate 60 per cent local production, so the trend is in the right direction.

At 33 metres the E class tram is the longest on the network. Fully low-floor, its five doors can transfer dozens of passengers in and out simultaneously, with a carrying capacity of over 200 (seating for 64). Fast, with a maximum speed of 80 kmh, and powered by six 105 kw motors, the E has three sections and four bogies, each encased in a wheelbox, and two of which sit underneath the mid-section. As mentioned above, E class bogies pivot, a design that allows the tram to 'swivel' around corners and bends (much less metal on metal screeching), a return to traditional tram engineering. At over 49 tonnes it's a heavy beast with a braking system to match its weight and acceleration. There are 50 E1s and 50 E2s on the system, with the last E2 delivered in 2021. The E2s came with modifications, such as improved safety features. The driver's cabin of the E has its own door. No more pushing through a packed tram to manually change the points or fix a door! Es run on routes 11, 30, 58, 86 and 96.

As with C and D class trams, the E's low floors make tram travel possible for people with disabilities, thus marking a watershed in the city's public transport policy. For the first time a tram built in Melbourne considered people with disabilities in the tram and network design. It's only taken 130 years. However, only three lines run exclusively low-floor trams – 11, 96, and 86. Lines 5, 6, 16, 19, 48, 58, 72 and 109 have a mix, while the remainder are operated by step-up trams. On low-floor tram routes level access stops are concentrated in the CBD, with a sprinkling of accessible stops across the rest of the system. We are still a long way from a fully accessible tram network.

The General Scheme was never realised but the network has expanded over the decades, with its now 250 kilometres of track. For a wonderful representation of the growth of the city's tram routes from the early days of cable to now, see Geoff Brown's animated timeline for the Melbourne Tram Museum

@ https://www.hawthorntramdepot.org.au/papers/timeline.htm.

In their heyday, the cable trams and the W class trams gave people a sense of pride in their city. The Es are a reversion to this role played by trams in our history – functional, modern, aesthetically pleasing, and built in the city. Having survived decades of neglect and half-hearted acts of renewal, the Es show that the tram is back as a key element of the city's transport system.

The D2 marked the end of the era of wholly imported trams on the system, an era hopefully not to be repeated. The system is not in public hands. Yarra Trams is the operator and this will be the model for the foreseeable future. But as Clapp showed, private doesn't have to mean sub-standard. The operators have a new mandate from the state government to support local industry. With the city's population booming and public infrastructure rapidly ageing, billions need to be spent on new trams to restore the network to the world class system the city needs. In this context the arrival of the new G class, due for release in 2025, is a good sign. One of the planned lines for the G tram is route 82. Finally, the west will get new trams, not hand-me-downs!

Without a doubt the import period was an era of poor public transport policy, driven by a neo-liberal desire to get public transport off the state budget, to hand operation over to multi-national corporations with no connection to the city and, in short, to do the minimum required to keep the network afloat. As always, any tram is better than none, and the imports have indeed kept the system intact. However, the three great tram personages – Clapp, Cameron and Risson – would have been turning in their graves at this era's departure from tram reality.

40. Six O'Clock Closing on the Number 6

I'm sitting in the bar of the Tramway Hotel (1873) having a quiet ale. The oncologist had been adamant about ales, as in 'you are to have none'; no quiet ales, no loud ales, no any ales. Well, what's a rule for if not to be broken? I'm feeling fine, truly. This pub, like all of them, was an all male preserve back in the day, but now it's a cool, inner city hotel with vegan burgers and music on Fridays. I'm enjoying sitting here out of the heat, drinking and ruminating on days of yore. This pub in North Fitzroy has a model W tram sticking out over the doorway and rumour has it that the horse drawn trams of Clapp's MOC – remember them? – used to trot right past the hotel. Nearby the stables for those horses are still standing, heritage listed tin buildings, now used as residences.

The general ambience is not too dissimilar to the pubs of my childhood. My father would smuggle me into the front bar of hotels dotted around the city – his 'watering holes'. Sometimes we would arrive in a terrible hurry, my father anxious to get in the door before six o'clock closing time was called. In those days the city fathers ruled that there should be no drinking in pubs after six o'clock, why, I don't recall, except that the city was still in the grip of the 'wowsers', who saw alcohol as the devil's work. My father's car – his beloved car – would be parked any which way outside the pub and we would rush inside. One time after a hurried session we found that the engine was still running with the keys in the ignition.

My father would order me a sarsaparilla and two pots for himself. All the men at the bar would have multiple pots lined up in front of them and were engaged in steady deliberate drinking. A low hum attended the scene, bass masculine notes that entrenched themselves around glasses, grubby floors and unwashed walls. I think now how much these occasions with my father resembled some form of religious rite. My father was apparently happy for me to be there, but rarely spoke to me, preferring to engage with his fellow drinkers and the barman.

My childhood memories of my father are very different to those I have of my mother. Whereas memories of her are sharp, clear and too numerous to count, those of my father are few and far between, scraps really, which don't cohere into a solid picture or form. Apart from the watering hole episodes, my strongest recollections of him date from before we moved to the suburbs, when he and my mother had not yet begun their hostilities. In that phase of their marriage he worked long hours, often late into the evening, climbing the ladder of corporate success. There was the occasional holiday with both of them of course – always a driving holiday, during which I would spend the day reading in the back seat of the car. There were Sunday drives to the country, and sometimes to a drive-in theatre in the outer suburbs. But these are family memories which include my mother. I remember him at the Christmas table wearing a funny hat, and driving me to football practice, but very few occasions when it is just the two of us. No father-son holidays. The pub visits before closing time were a rare exception to this pattern. I remember as a child liking and looking up to my father but I sometimes wondered how much he liked me.

This reverie about my father has been provoked by this morning's tram journey. I'd spent the morning on tram 6 from Moreland to Glen Iris, a journey from hipster heaven to the rolling hills of the solid bourgeoisie. It's a complex set of streetscapes that the 6 traverses. There is the Taoist Tai Chi Society in Moreland Road, a Buddhist Institute near Park Street, a Greek Orthodox Church in Lygon Street, the vast Melbourne Cemetery which sprouts thousands of headstones and monuments to the dead. (As we pass I recall smoking weed in the dead of night with a friend perched on a gravestone, decades ago – such sacrilege!)

There's the old Carlton Brewery building in Swanston Street, the elegant Church of Christ just down the road and then it's the familiar passage down St Kilda Road, until we turn left and head into Prahran, past the old Mechanics Institute, now a Polytechnic. In High Street two young women, who are presumably Irish given their accents, get on and sit near me. They spend the next 10 minutes or so discussing a much unloved and detested fellow worker. I'm really impressed with their capacity for invective, as they tear strips off the reputation of their colleague. The woman in question is untrustworthy, inept, incompetent, ugly, has horrible taste in clothes, is a self-centred narcissist, and worst of all, they agree, an unmitigated liar. Also, she's always late for meetings, sits there like a princess, saying nothing, playing with her hair, which is always 'a fucking mess'. The two women continue on, competing to see who can slander their colleague in the most entertaining way, until finally there's a pause. Then one says to the other brightly, 'Other than that she's really lovely!', at which comment they both laugh uproariously.

I continue my journey out to Malvern Road, along the way passing the Harold Holt Swim Centre, named for a former prime minister who drowned at the beach in the 1960s. There were rumours at the time that he was still alive, and living in Beijing, having been abducted by a Chinese submarine.

The entire trip took over an hour and a quarter.

*

It is on the return journey that I notice the funeral home where my father's funeral had taken place many years before. He had died 20 years after my mother. On the way out I had not seen the venue, presumably because I was sitting on the other side of the tram, but in any case I had completely forgotten that this was where we had farewelled him. I remember that the day of the funeral had been hot with a gusting northerly wind. The small gathering of 20 or so souls were grateful for the home's fans that provided some relief from the oppressive heat.

My sister flew in from the far north and gave a heart-felt speech in honour of our father. She spoke with compassion and humour and it was easy to see that her connection to, and memory of him, while not uncomplicated, was warm and generous. I recall the eulogy I gave, which recounted the major milestones of his life – childhood, marriage, career, travel. I had drawn closer to my father during the long course of his dying, spending many hours and days with him at doctor's appointments, hospitals, emergency rooms, rehab care, and finally, hospice care: a rapprochement in dying as it were, although we'd never been actually estranged from one another. Our relationship was marked by recognition and lack, as if we were on the opposite sides of a bridge that we rarely crossed, but from which vantage points we could clearly see each other: both of us sharing a diffidence that made the expression of feelings, such as 'I love you', highly problematic.

My speech did reflect this recent closeness between the two of us. But although adequate, it had something of the quality of a report, factually accurate, covering each era of my father's journey through the world, but was a bit dry, too unsentimental. And, as with most eulogies for the dead mine avoided any reference to the unpalatable parts of his, and my mother's story. Certainly no mention of the role alcohol came to play in their marriage. I felt I had not adequately captured the essence of my father, had not conveyed his character, had provided only partial insights into him as a person.

This assessment became especially apparent when my son spoke on behalf of himself and my daughter. Both of them had flown in from overseas for the funeral. His eulogy was in great contrast to mine. My son spoke about their grandfather with great affection, describing a man that I only partly recognised. He spoke at length about the character of their grandfather as they'd known him, as a man who had been a consistent feature of their lives, from childhood through to adulthood. A man who was attentive, kind, approachable. A person who was a great listener, who gave good advice when it was asked for, who was dependable and always sincere. He described various outings with their grandfather; to museums, fire stations, cafes, parks and gardens, even once or twice to McDonalds (a forbidden treat). Magnum ice creams, jam donuts, hot chips. With their grandmother dying early, their grandfather had assumed a central role in their lives.

What emerged in these speeches was a view of the different character of the relationship between grandfather and grandchildren, compared to that between father and son. Maybe that's inevitable. He worked enormously long hours and was preoccupied when he wasn't working. I didn't feel jealous at my son's revelation, so much as surprised. It became clear how important my father had been in their lives, that he had provided them with critical support when it was needed, and that he was much loved. I was proud of the way my son spoke, but also couldn't help but feel a sense of loss that the man they were describing was one who I would like to have better known myself as a child.

*

My mother's funeral, which I touched on earlier, was a very different event to that of my father. She had died suddenly at the age of 66 and although she had been unwell for many years her death came as a huge shock. It wasn't just that she had died at what is considered now a relatively early age, but that I was simply unprepared for either of my parents to pass away. I gave the eulogy but I have no memory of what I said. I recall a mass of people, condolences, flowers, the didge played by an Aboriginal friend, her body in a casket looking like someone else, my father's devastation. There was something incommensurable about her death, ungraspable, unknowable. I felt like that for years about her passing.

It's really only now all these years hence, sitting here writing in the Acustico cafe, travelling on all these trams, listening to all those stories, hearing and seeing my own memories, that at least a part of this family saga is coming into some kind of clarity, that I can exercise a form of emotional reasoning that has eluded me until now.

As uncomfortable as the encounter with Gina was, listening to her talk about grief has helped. I'm still in the dark about a lot of things. I don't understand why my parents started fighting, and their descent into disharmony. I don't really understand my mother's relationship with Uncle Max.

At some point I'm going to have to consult the oracle – Aunt Bea.

41. Route 59: The Cars that Ate the City

C ars, cars, cars. The cars that ate the city of Melbourne, the cars that ate cities all over the world. In the second half of the 20th century the car had a great – and terrible – victory over public transport. Car ownership in this period doubled then trebled then went through the roof, pouring hundreds of thousands of cars onto city streets. This process transformed our city, and many other cities, which were designed for transportation by horse and cart, hansom cabs, trams, buses, and trains. Nightmare on Bourke Street! The horrors of gridlock! Emissions emissions!

Sorry dear reader, getting carried away. I will return to the car soon, but I've got a tram to catch.

*

Route 59 from Elizabeth and Flinders Streets to Airport West covers 14.7 kilometres from end to end. Like our other tram routes, route 59 has multiple antecedents. The number 59 was allocated to this route in the 1940s when the route was extended from Essendon to Essendon airport, bringing the suburb of Niddrie into the tram network. The 59 shares tracks with the 19, the 58 and the 57 before each diverges to their appointed routes. I do like those parts of the system where trams overlap, seeing trams running in close proximity, either one after the other, or crossing paths in opposite directions. Drivers waving to each other: the trams like cousins intent on their particular path within this one extended family.

Today I'm heading to Airport West on a B2 Class tram in relatively good condition given that it is at least 30 years old, and has travelled millions of kilometres. I've joined the 59 at the Children's Hospital stop. I've visited friends in the north-west occasionally but I don't really know the 59's territory. I've never lived in this part of the city, and my mother never took me on this tram route on our days out. I've done some reading before heading over here.

Down the road the tram travels under a railway bridge and a span of freeway. Next door is the freeway itself, adorned with large red metal sticks set at 45 degrees from the vertical and appearing to fall over the roadway. A 20 storey block of apartments sits cheek by jowl with the stream of cars. As we head up the hill, the Thanh Vinh Son Liem Catholic Centre, a Church of Scientology and the Laurel Hotel (1853) make interesting neighbours. At the Essendon Tram Depot we pull up, the driver gets out and a new driver boards the tram. Changeover. Along the route a sign 'Your sanctuary near the city' is plastered on the fence of one of the city's ubiquitous development sites. Did we debate this new colonisation, this transformation taking place in the heart and lungs of our metropolis?

Further on we pass a cafe which announces in tall letters that there is a 'NONNA TAKE OVER', next to which, on a large poster, an elderly Italian woman pokes her tongue out at the viewer. Nice. At the Moonee Ponds Junction the tram sits for a few minutes. The whole area has changed since I was younger. I remember a country feel, removed from the hustle and bustle of the inner suburbs. But now it seems under siege, the Junction jammed with traffic, towering buildings, noise. We're off again, diverging right into Pascoe Vale Road and here is the Queens Park with its flowers, lake and green lawns and layers of history: the 'Moonee Moonee' ponds creek ran through here brimming with eels and murnong, while the waterhole attracted waterfowl, possum and cockatoo. Aboriginal country for generations. Burke and Wills camped here in 1860 before they wandered off into the interior never to be seen again.

The tram does a large loop: up Pascoe Vale Road, before venturing west to rejoin Mt Alexander Road at Essendon Station. We enter a zone of the discreet charms of the bourgeoisie with upmarket cake shops, upmarket cafes, upmarket hair salons. Essendon, its own little pocket of wealth in the north-west. Eventually we enter Keilor Road and head towards Niddrie and the bourgeoisie disappear. 'Niddrie' was a farm, dear reader, although I don't know what was farmed on it. We've abruptly shifted from Protestant to Catholic territory (as so often happens in our city). Along Keilor Road a string of cafes with outdoor furniture sits empty.

I've been thinking about moods on trams. Trams have their own characters, while tram journeys have their own moods: party trams full of late night revellers, introspective trams of the early morning worker, chatty shopper trams, singing footy trams. Trams can change atmosphere as they go, from dull and lifeless to crowded and talkative, and back again. Today's tram journey is a case in point. From the moment I boarded, for the whole of this journey, not a single person has said a word, neither to a companion nor on their phone. Not just a quiet tram, but completely silent, as if obeying some unspoken rule against discourse. And I have to say there is something truly melancholic about this tram without voices. The passengers all seem to move warily too, with Joe Biden-like shuffling movements, as if afraid to wake some deadly monster lurking in the tram walls.

We turn right into Matthews Avenue and head north again along an exclusive way, bordered by a road on one side and a freeway on the other. There are no trees. I see hangars and buildings, and a DC3 labelled Air Nostalgia. Strung out along our left are a string of 'useful' businesses. You can do taekwondo, learn to dance, fix your car or buy a dildo here. On the right a river of cars hurtles along the freeway – 10 lanes of fire and brimstone. Eventually the tram comes to a stop at the terminus, in a landscape devoid of features, save a toilet block provided for the tram drivers. The sky out here is enormous and carved with grey streaks.

*

On the return journey down Matthews Avenue I'm the sole passenger. Time to listen to that podcast I've been saving. Yes, it is about
trams, but it's also about the car. The podcast – which is titled *The
Car and The Tortoise*, is a lecture by Melbourne sociologist Dr Susan
Green. Green specialises in the history and sociology of transportation. Her nasally voice is a bit hard on the ears, but maybe she had a
cold that day. Anyway, you don't have to listen to it do you. Here is
some of what she is saying:

'In the second half of the 20th century the car became the dominant mode of transportation in cities throughout the developed
world. It was a dramatic shift in public policy, with profound impacts
on the cities and their inhabitants. It was a shift with no socially ra-
tional basis. Enormously expensive for individuals and governments,
a massive waste of the planet's resources, creating one of the main
sources of global warming, this policy turned formerly quiet neigh-
bourhoods into hell holes of endless noise. How was something that
was so inimical to human culture, so draining of physical and financial
resources costing thousands of lives, allowed to occur? We live in a
city that defied a global trend. Around the western world, tramways
were abolished in the post-war period, usually never to be replaced.
We were lucky.

'There are now almost five and a half million private vehicles on
Victoria's roads. Roughly 20 percent of the population is under 18,
which means there's a car or truck for every single adult in the state.
In 1924 there were 70,000 private vehicles in Victoria, in a population of 1.6 million. While car ownership increased substantially after
World War Two, in 1951 only 15 percent of Melbourne workers travelled to work by car, and in 1960 one-third of households were still
car-less.

'But between 1950 and 1975 the number of vehicles quadrupled,
while the population only doubled, and by the late '70s two-thirds of
commuters travelled to work by car. By the mid-90s it was up to
three-quarters. Public transport now moves just 20 percent of com-

muters each day. So the status of public versus private as the principal means of commuter transport has completely reversed since 1951.'

Green says that Melbournians spend, on average, almost $40,000 on a new car. The total value of capital investment in Victoria's vehicle fleet is at least $10 billion. Cars don't keep their value over time because they are not engineered to last – on average about 10 years. I notice that Green's argument is, in essence, a rerun of both Cameron's and Risson's arguments from decades before. She says that the 100 new G class trams, currently being built, cost millions but will last decades. The city's cable trams lasted from 1885 to 1940, the W class trams built in the 1920s were still running in the '80s, while today's Z class trams were built in the late 1970s. Trams wear slowly, hardly ever break down, while cars require constant maintenance. Tram tracks last for decades, trams don't damage roads, and don't need expensive freeways. Car and truck usage has massive add-on costs, nearly all of which must come out of public finances. 'The toll in lives lost is in the hundreds each year', she says, 'and injuries in the thousands, many of them permanent and life changing. Trams can injure people, but the major risk to tram travellers is the car – drivers speeding past stationary trams, risking injury to people getting on and off.'

From a commuter perspective, says Green, the car doesn't compete. The E class tram's maximum capacity is 210 passengers, while most commuter cars carry one to two passengers. 'Imagine', says Green, 'an E tram full of passengers at traffic lights during peak hour with 10 cars sitting alongside it. The cars are carrying 20 people, the tram 200 in the same road space. A major reason for congestion is those millions of cars travelling around with one to two people in them. Cars are not energy efficient. Since 2019 our trams have run on 100 percent renewable energy. Cars and trucks consume about 10,000 megalitres of petrol and diesel each year in Victoria. Nearly a quarter of all greenhouse gas emissions in Victoria come from the transport sector.'

Green describes the 1950s: the last W trams are made in 1956 and while the production of motor vehicles surges, the development of trams ceases, not just in Melbourne but in cities around the world. Tramways are under pressure to disappear, from car lobbies, manufacturers, the oil industry, transport bureaucrats and lobbied politicians, who portray trams as a nuisance, as too slow, too old, too... public. Cities are obsessed with building freeways, which snake their way out into the domains of the new suburbs, far beyond the reach of tram networks. Green says that from the mid-century the car is mythologised – in film, in books and in advertising. The car says freedom, individuality, convenience. Jack Kerouac's *On the Road* is published in 1957, and becomes an instant classic celebrating the freedom and lure of car travel. In the world of Sal Paradise, the main character, it was simply cool to be on the road. Today's advertising depicts the car speeding along deserted roads, across plains, through forests and over mountains – no scenes of traffic jams, no gridlock on the city commute.

'Urban transport moves from public to private', she says, 'from efficient to inefficient, from community to individual. In our city it becomes a simple equation: five and a half million private vehicles versus 500 trams.'

In Melbourne, Dr Green says, the city's tramways survived through a combination of inertia, the city's love of trams, and the 'solid albeit uninspiring rearguard action undertaken by the leadership of the M&MTB, with the support of the union'. The Bolte government starves the trams of investment, thousands of cars pour onto the roads, but the trams do keep running. She says, 'While the car demonstrates the limits of individualism, the tram shows the innate strength of the collective. They are profoundly different in conception. The car expresses a powerful individuality, which is paradoxically ensnared in the dreams of others, as they crawl in traffic jams. By contrast, the tram creates a space for anonymity in the midst of others, who are all going in the same direction.'

Hear, hear!

42. Beyond Tram Lines

Major-General Risson might have conducted an 'uninspired' campaign to preserve the tramways, as Green contends, but he did succeed in saving them. Nevertheless, history and vested interests were on the side of the car. The rise of the car as the principal means of commuter transport transformed the city. Social and technological change remoulds society in new and unexpected ways and such changes can also have profound impacts on individuals and families. The victory of the car had a huge effect on my family. My father loved cars and my mother loved trams, or, more exactly, she loved trams and the world that they delivered, the old Melbourne of parks, gardens, shopping, galleries, cafes and Victoriana. The trams gave her freedom and connection to community, to the city. She was at home in all of this, while my father was a 'progressive' who had no trouble with Whelan's depredations of the city. He liked buildings of steel and glass and looked forward to the day when the city would be home to a network of freeways. He thought Los Angeles was wonderful with its endless circles of freeways, flyovers and ramps.

As I've said, in the mid-1960s our family moved out beyond the tramways to the south east suburbs where the car was king. Our newly minted suburban home, a triple-fronted brick veneer, had no public transport within walking distance. These suburban streets were predicated on each family having a car, the shopping had to be done by car, sports events got to by car, visiting friends by car. My travels by tram with my mother became a thing of the past partly because there were no trams anywhere near where we lived, but also because I was getting older. I drifted away from her orbit, played football, messed around with school mates, being assimiliated into that peculiar era of the post-war suburbs.

The family went everywhere by car on the weekends. But for years my mother was stuck for long hours and days at home during the week as our one car took my father to work each day. The suburban men disappeared early in the morning and returned after dark. It was so quiet out there it was as if everyone was dead. Eventually, and like millions of women in suburbs across the country, my mother had her own car too, and something of her former sense of freedom returned. She took up golf and joined various local clubs, developed new friendships and began studying at night school. This was all well and good, and she was making the best of it, but I could tell there was something wrong. Something had changed.

One consequence of our shift out to the 'burbs was that my mother and I no longer visited Uncle Max in South Yarra, and he never visited us in the new house. Max was car-less. Nothing was ever said about this turn of events by either of my parents. I only ever saw Uncle Max again when he turned up years later at my mother's funeral. As dazed as I was on that day, I have a distinct memory of him standing at the back of the funeral parlour during the service, but he slipped out before refreshments were served.

The change from inner to outer suburb seemed to suit my father. He became more approachable and relaxed as he assumed the mantle of suburban husband and father. Barbecues, mowing, car washing, pool cleaning. For all her new pursuits and friendships my mother on the other hand appeared to gradually shrink into herself. She became ebullient when drunk, but much of the time she struck me as someone who felt that she had been marooned. She worked endlessly on household chores – cooking, shopping, cleaning, dusting – but these activities gave her small satisfaction. She was cut off from extended family, her former friends, from work. The city that she had loved to go about in by tram was a distant entity rarely visited.

And then, after some years out there, my parents started to fight, a thing that had rarely happened before our move to the suburbs. They started to drink heavily. They drank, they fought and then they drank some more. They had always enjoyed a drink. As my parents gathered a circle of friends in the 1950s and early '60s they held parties in our tiny apartment where alcohol flowed, cigarettes puffed, and jazz made everyone jiggle about. They were happy occasions.

But in the shift to the suburbs the atmosphere between them changed. I had no idea what it was about but their fighting became a regular feature of our life. They were verbal battles, no-one was being bashed, but doors were slammed, voices raised to shouting, the air became at these times toxic. The drinking and the fighting was bizarre and frightening, but even then it seemed to me it was a masquerade for something else, something deeper, particularly in my mother. The more I consider what I felt in her at the time and was too frightened to admit to myself – let alone to raise with either of them – the more I sense a kind of despair, not the exhilarated despair of the artist, but the fundamental loneliness of the abandoned. Nothing in her situation was helped by me growing up and becoming a teenager with my own private interests. I'd been her mate and now I had my own mates. At 18 I moved out of the family home, and went back to the urban realm inhabited by trams.

43. Route 96: Tracks to St. Kilda

My waiting-for-the-tram book today is Han Kang's *Greek Lessons,* the plot of which centres on a man who can't see teaching Ancient Greek to a woman who can't speak. A million years ago I studied Ancient Greek at university. I spent an entire semester translating the *Bacchae* line by painful, beautiful line with my mentor G_, who later became my close friend. I think the Athenians would've 'got' the idea of tramways, if not the technology – the idea of a public transport system open to everyone, a moving architecture of utility and style.

Thinking about G_ I almost miss my tram arriving. Route 96 terminates at one end at Nicholson and Blyth Streets, East Brunswick, just opposite the Lomond Hotel (1888). The 'Lowie', as it's known by locals, is one of the pubs keeping live music alive in the city. (Personally, I prefer the Union Hotel in Brunswick, which also hosts live bands, but that's probably because the music at the Union is free.) The 96 runs for 13.9 kilometres and is one of the two routes that mix tramway with light rail. The 96 heads to St Kilda Beach, while the 109 heads to Port Melbourne.

As you're aware, the 96 route has heritage. One of the original cable tram routes, from Bourke Street in the city, up Nicholson Street to Park Street in North Fitzroy, which began in 1887. Remember when the system was finally electrified in 1940? Well, this route was then serviced by buses, not trams, and it was not until the mid 1950s that electric trams ran up Nicholson Street to Brunswick East. In 1987 with the creation of the light rail to St Kilda, the 96 was extended all the way south to Acland Street. This involved regauging the track to standard gauge, and reducing the overhead voltage from 1,500 v DC to 600 v DC. In the long struggle between tramway and railway to St Kilda the tram is, after 100 years of competition, finally victorious!

I was hoping to ride in a Bumblebee tram, the C2 class tram I talked about earlier. You recall that in a moment of delirium, the city authorities decided in 2008 to rent trams from a city on the other side of the globe. The C2 class trams only run on the 96 route and they were acquired for that very purpose. They have a bumblebee sticker at the front, the only tram in the system to identify with an animal. But today I'm out of luck as it's an E1 class tram that pulls in. Never mind, it will be a good ride.

Large tracts of land on either side of Nicholson Street in Brunswick have been cleared of all their structures to make way for new apartment blocks. A series of tall cranes stand at intervals along the road, ungainly insects that point to a leaden sky. These sites would resemble bomb sites, or the aftermath of an earthquake, were it not for the cranes and enormous billboards advertising the new developments and the private entities responsible. Nicholson Street is narrow in Brunswick, but widens significantly once it hits North Carlton. Here the street has been reconstructed, with new tram stops in the centre of the roadway. These are infinitely safer than the old ones, creating islands in the road's centre into which the tram pulls up and stops. And as mentioned they make the system accessible to people with a disability. For generations the people of the city have taken their lives into their own hands getting on and off trams in city traffic. Always look left people!

The tram passes Kebab House, a favourite haunt of mine in the 1970s, when it had a giant kebab erected over the verandah, and then the Empress Hotel on the corner of Scotchmer Street. Further down we glide past the art deco San Remo Ballroom, famous for its eclectic music events, now a wedding venue, and previously, a cycling school, a theatre and a furniture store. I have fuzzy memories of this venue as a teenager, largely centred on too much tequila and vomiting on my girlfriend's suede boots. Unforgivable. In fact she sacked me two weeks later.

After the sharp angled modernity of the Museum, we move alongside the gilded dome of the Royal Exhibition Building among its floral beds and the deep shade of the Carlton gardens. It's a grand visionary edifice earning us our only World Heritage listing. Thank you Joseph Reed, architect of wondrous edifices (the Town Hall and State Library are his too). The first meeting of the Australian parliament was held at the Exhibition Building in 1901. Less gloriously, it was the strange location of our final school exams, where we, in our thousands, went in the 1970s. I wanted to vomit there too, but somehow held it in.

The 96 heads into town, and at Bourke Street turns its back on Parliament House as it heads east. Going this way it's clear the city is comprised of a series of gentle hills. The tram proceeds down the slope to Elizabeth Street, before heading up to William Street. Here I get off, as planned, and walk up past the Supreme Court to the corner of William and Lonsdale Streets, where the Magistrates' and County Courts face each other, the two edifices celebrations in high modernity. I buy a latte from the coffee stand and sit on a concrete bench in the forecourt of the County Court, which faces onto the road. There is a sufficient gap here in the superstructure of buildings overhead to allow the sunlight to bathe half the forecourt, as the shadow line of the buildings bisects the space into dark and bright zones. As I sit there the shadow line inches its way across the space, creeping forward inexorably like the law itself... .

The courts are their own milieu. Small knots of lawyers, in black robes and white cravats, and carrying bundles of files and briefcases, gather in sometimes intense, sometimes jolly, discussion before dispersing in different directions. The police are also present in their severe dark uniforms – the men with their heads shaved, the women with hair tied back or cut short. The lawyers' gowns flap in the light breeze, their hair coiffured and luxuriant, while the police look like marathon runners, lean and sharp.

As I sip my coffee I think about my son, now living and working in New York, and who used to work some years earlier in the building opposite. We would meet occasionally right here in this forecourt. I'm thinking it is time I told both him and my daughter what has been going on with my health. My sister too. I've been reluctant to do this, to spare their feelings, I tell myself, but actually more in superstition than anything else. As if talking about illness makes it magically manifest itself, or in my case, reappear with the grim reaper in tow. Yes, there's nothing like a frightened old man.

At this moment a young woman sits down on the concrete bench and asks me if I have a light, holding out a hand with its unlit cigarette. I say sorry I don't. She then sits in silence at the end of the bench, her leg jiggling up and down. And this person, I will find out, is called Yi Ling and she is about to tell me a story. We are at opposite ends of the concrete bench but the sense of unease and nervousness in her is palpable. She is taking large gulps of air, which she is holding and then expelling slowly. After a few of these large intakes and exhales she stops her jiggling and asks if I have a court case on and if I'm waiting to go into the building behind them. I tell her I don't have a court case on and she says that I'm lucky not to have to front a magistrate and that she didn't realise how nervous she would be beforehand. There is a pause during which she pulls out her phone. 'I'm too early', she says, 'I should have timed this better so I didn't have to sit here waiting. Jesus.' I sense that she wants to talk if for no other reason than to relieve some of her anxiety. I ask her what type of hearing she is about to attend.

She tells me that she's going in for her sentencing hearing and that she is very apprehensive of the outcome. She may be sentenced to gaol but is hoping the magistrate will instead give her a community order. It's her first offence and she has been undergoing a court approved substance abuse program, while she has been on bail. She is hopeful that this will persuade the judge that she is a suitable candidate for a non-custodial sentence. She doesn't normally dress like this, her lawyer had insisted that she look smart – according to her lawyer the magistrates take your appearance into account when sentencing.

I ask her what she had done to be fronting the court in the first place. She looks at me a bit warily, and asks me if I'm with the police. 'No', I say with a laugh, 'I've been all sorts of things in my life but never a cop.' She says, 'Yeah, I guess, and no offence, but you are a bit too dishevelled to be a cop.' She says this smiling and I smile back. 'Yeah, well in answer to your question', she continues, 'I was caught stealing from cars and charged with theft. It's not normally something that would get you a gaol sentence, but they had me for a string of the same offences once they had my DNA and fingerprints. So I'm a thief. The fact that I became a thief still strikes me as incredible. I know how it all happened, but it is like a story that belongs to someone else, to a different person.

'It is strange how suddenly things happen in a life, or how they appear that way. One minute I was in a good job, had a partner, a house to live in, totally middle class. The next minute I'm on the street begging – no job, no partner, no house. I lived in my car until I sold it. I kind of slid into this chaos without seeing it.'

I ask Yi Ling – by now we've exchanged names – if she can now see what sent her into this chaos. She tells me that she and her boyfriend had been occasional heroin users, that it was a small, but enjoyable part of their life. They had good jobs in the public service, holidays overseas, were thinking of buying an apartment. But then he met someone else at a conference. She hadn't noticed anything different about him after he got back, but one night his phone was sitting on the kitchen bench while she was cooking and a text message appeared. It was blatantly sexual and at first she thought it was a joke from one of this mates, but it turned out to be real. Afterwards she wondered if he'd deliberately left the phone there, and that he didn't have the balls to tell her straight out what he'd done, and he was going to leave her for this new person. She was furious with him and when she confronted him he admitted to the affair and not long afterwards they split up. Up until this moment she had had no idea how reliant she was on the relationship with him. In the months after they split she felt okay and went on with her life. She continued to be angry with him, but the fury seemed to give her energy and she was confident she'd meet someone else.

Her next sentences are drowned out by the passing of two trams across the nearby intersection. I'm listening to her as if watching a character in a silent film. Her voice returns and I pick up that she is talking about dating other men in the aftermath of the split. She dated some guys and that was fine as far as it went – she started to see a pattern in male behaviour on these dates and it began to grate on her that they were so unoriginal and self-centred. Most of them had been taught to listen, but it struck her as an act, a kind of show piece for the modern male, along with the care taken with their choice of clothes. She started to drink more and to turn up at work with massive hangovers. 'I thought I was in charge of things', she says, 'but then I started having these terrible feelings of sadness. I was depressed and I began to truly miss my former boyfriend, like an ache that wouldn't go away, and instead of getting better it got worse. I couldn't believe the level of pain I was experiencing. I tried to get in touch with him, but he rebuffed me, told me to leave him alone, that he didn't want me in his life. He said some things to me that were truly horrible.

'It was after that that I started to seriously get into heroin. At first I was relieved that there was something that deadened the pain without leaving me with a hangover. It was bliss and the people I was with were okay. They were funny and supportive. One night a friend of mine passed out. Instead of taking her to hospital we decided to treat her ourselves, walking her around, standing in the shower with her, massaging, it took hours and hours. She was okay, but after this the group split up, and then I started doing it on my own.'

She goes on to tell me how she began her descent into addiction, the depressive episodes, her inability to focus at work, the constant need. She could, from time to time, see herself from the outside and wondered at the transformation – a certified monomaniac with wild hair, red eyes, bad teeth. Everything else in her life fell away. She lost her job, her apartment, stopped seeing her family. Her so-called friends now were dealers and a few others struggling on the edges like herself. Her bank account emptied and then suddenly she was on the street. At this point it seemed entirely logical to her to start stealing. How else was she going to live? That's when she became a thief.

I ask her why cars? Yi Ling tells me that a friend of hers showed her how to break into cars one night. 'It's not hard you know. A lot of the older models are easy to get into, sometimes they are unlocked and you wouldn't believe what people leave in their cars – money, laptops, wallets, jewellery – and on a good night we could make 500, even a thousand sometimes. Anyway, enough to get the next fix.'

She pauses in her story here and we both sit silently for a minute. She looks at her phone. Eventually she was caught one night and the court sent her off to rehab. That was nine months ago. 'I should be alright in there', she says, 'I'm clean, I've got work, I'm studying too and I never ever want to go back to that life. I remember a few months ago, I was coming back on the tram from uni where I'd just enrolled in a post-graduate course. It was one of the first days of autumn late in the afternoon and the city was bathed in this cool, yellow light. It had been raining and everything looked washed and clean. The streets were teeming with people. As we went along with the tram bells sounding the buildings and people appeared as if I was in some kind of theatre set – the light was not so much shining on them as coming from them, as if the streetscape possessed its own light source. I was looking at people's faces, all of their expressions, all of this animation. It seemed entirely to be a miracle. But then I thought that maybe the real miracle was that I was seeing all of this. My brain had switched on at that moment in a way it hadn't for years – I could feel it humming along again like it used to – I had never until that point thought of the brain as an organ that could be sick, and that it could get well. I love having my own thoughts and feelings again without the drugs. I keep having this image of an open field with this vast panorama of light all around me, the colours and shapes of things are brilliant. And other people now interest me again. I had been completely bound up in myself and now I feel incredibly lucky. I've been given a second chance and I really don't want to fuck it up.'

She has to leave. She gets up and thanks me for listening. I wish her good luck with her hearing. I watch her cross the road to the Magistrates' Court opposite. The afternoon has turned warmer, and now I get up too and head down the hill to restart my journey on the second leg of the 96.

*

I'm back on the 96 heading for St Kilda. It's another E class, so I'm out of luck with the Bumblebee again. We pass Southern Cross station with its wavy roof design, covered in the black soot of years of diesel emissions. Just before the river we pass Batman Park. There's a stop on the bridge itself and tourists pile off, take selfies and wander in the direction of the enormous casino which is about to swallow their life savings. At the Clarendon Street junction we take a right and begin our light rail trip to the beach. From City Road we travel on the former railway elevated track, a beautiful work of 19th century engineering. Through South Melbourne, with the market nearby – where my mother and I went that day with Uncle Max – and then the green lung of Albert Park, and now the track is a deep cutting, under a bridge, a glimpse of palm trees and at Middle Park a cafe in the old rail station building. We are moving fast: sports grounds, the Grand Prix track, trees and more trees. Close to St Kilda the line is hemmed in by cheap apartments and the old St Kilda station is now shops and an Irish bar. The couple who have been speaking in Bahasa next to me get off here, along with a large contingent of passengers.

Into Fitzroy Street heading east, and then the tram curves left along the Esplanade. St Kilda with its domes and palms and eclectic sea-side apartment styles and beachside baths and pavilions conjures a Californian mid-20th century glamour. The sea is a grey green today. A number 16 passes us heading to the city. A right hand turn and we enter Acland Street and slowly travel to the terminus at the Barkly Street junction. I head to a cafe for my second coffee for the day. I'm thinking about the story Yi Ling has told me. I don't think I've heard a story quite like hers in all the shared stories across this strange and wonderful project. For the first time in a long time I feel lucky. I can sense my tram story itself is coming to a close soon.

After the bitter coffee I walk up the street. The Scheherazade cafe, with its delicious latkes, is long gone, and the street in general looks lifeless. It's been modernised, with wide pavements and no atmosphere, but maybe that is because none of the local lounge lizards are up yet. Anyhow, congratulations to the city planners for another job well done on an iconic Melbourne street! I continue on to Luna Park which owes more to Coney island than California. Here's the Mr Moon entrance – as mentioned, inspiration for the face of the E class tram – and through it a riot of ghost trains, carousels, dodgem cars, stomach flipping rides and the Big Dipper beckon. I do not partake. Luna Park was run by the Phillips brothers, Leon, Herman and Harold, from 1912 to the '50s, and they also created the Palais Theatre next door, saved from destruction and development like other parts of St Kilda's nostalgic streetscapes, by local activists.

I'm now on the 'improved', somewhat forlorn pavement of Fitzroy Street and about half way along I find Leo's Spaghetti Bar, popular with Melbournians since the year after I was born. I wander inside and at a table in a dark recess in the corner are my parents. They are both smoking and studying oversize menus. I sit down on the spare chair and pick up the menu in front of me. Studying the menu is a bit redundant since we each know what we will order. I will always have the spaghetti bolognaise, my father will order the lasagne and mother the spaghetti marinara. Their cigarette packs rest on the table on either side of the glass ashtray – my mother is smoking Rothmans and my father Kent. They take long drags on their smokes. The air is thick with their fumes, but I don't appear to mind. They both look incredibly youthful – not a line on either face, their hair is luxuriant and they both have a sharpness and clarity about them that only comes with being young. My father is wearing a polo-neck shirt and he has a large silver watch on his wrist, which he occasionally refers to. My mother is in a blue cardigan, which sets off her blue eyes nicely, and a white collared shirt. The waiter comes to take the order, we order the usual, and two glasses of house wine and a milkshake. The wine and milkshake come, they light more cigarettes, and then we stare at each other. They look happy – this must be before the onset of their war – and yet they seem to want something from me. They have some expectation that is below the surface of language or expression. I look at my father, I look at my mother, and then back again. Yes, something is there, but perhaps it is just the way satisfaction is – at this point in their lives they have immeasurable years ahead. Anything could happen, to me or to them. This is that moment, they say with their eyes, when we sat in Leo's on a Saturday afternoon, with the sea air wafting in the door, tram bells clanging, and all of the nights and the days ahead of us.

44. Visiting Aunt Bea on the 109

Today I'm on the 109 heading to Box Hill. The 109 is run with C1 trams. The C1s run out of the Kew Depot and also service the 48 route to North Balwyn, and if you recall, have been known as the problem children of the network. The 109 route itself is inherently interesting, amalgamating as it does different historical tram lines, light rail and tramway, and new additions. But the imported C1 trams have had a history of derailing and their drivers have seriously disliked them. In 2019, after a third derailment, the tram union, according to *The Age,* declared the C1 'cheap as chips', the cause of endless health problems to drivers' necks and shoulders, and called for their removal from service. The tram's bogies have been shown to be set too far back from the ends, causing it to vibrate and shake, become unstable and risk derailing. As the trams pick up speed they snake at the rear affecting the ride of the passengers. Yarra Trams claim to have fixed the problems causing these issues. Bring on the G trams!

But really, driver comfort was never a priority for the various operators in the city. As mentioned, the gripmen were out in the open in all kinds of weather, subject to the endless vibrations of the cable, the W drivers stood or sat all day in the cold or heat, and some modern trams have created new sets of ergonomic problems. As we saw with Ellie, tram driving requires stamina and concentration, and a fair amount of chutzpah to deal with endless car driver madness. Maybe a bit of Zen too: going up and down the same route every day, month after month, year on year.

318 • GREG GARDINER

I've spent a lot of time riding trams for this project and I've gotten an inkling of what it's like to spend all day working on them. It's probably a lot lonelier without the connies for company, and the speed of travel is nothing like the leisurely pace of the cable trams. Despite all these obvious disadvantages I retain an almost child-like wonder at the business of tram driving: have I 'wasted all those years' – thanks Simply Red – in the bureaucracy, writing reports that inevitably end on shelves gathering dust? Was I meant to be something else, someone else? Just a thought dear reader, as my project enters the final stretch.

*

I'm heading out to Box Hill with the twin purposes of reviewing the journey and of visiting my 92 year old aunt in her nursing home. She is physically delapidated but intellectually strong and I have some serious questions for her. My parents' suburban war had lasted 10 years. It ended with a whimper rather than a bang and a peace treaty was never signed. The combatants were simply exhausted and retreated behind their respective fences within a frozen conflict. Think the two Koreas in 1953. Occasionally one or other of them would forget that hostilities had ceased, and there would be an outburst of anger, but over time even these brief flurries petered out. They were tired and getting old. They would never divorce. What was the point? Indeed, could either of my parents at the end of 10 years of conflict have been able to identify what the war was about in the first place? The arc of their marriage traced a spiral into a pit where they remained for the best part of a decade, before slowly hauling their way back to the surface, scarred and battle-worn, but nevertheless 'together'. And they became in these latter years model and loving grandparents to my children.

Did I just imagine that they had been happy before, when the tram still ruled and the car would have to wait? Clearly my mother found my father's excursions to various sites of modernity – the docks, power stations, bridges – rather tedious. The role played by her relation to Uncle Max in their marriage remained a mystery. What was its nature, and why was she so careless with our dinners on those nights following our outings with him? But in all that earlier time there was no fighting, no sudden eruptions of invective, no slamming of things.

Out in the 'burbs no-one outside the marriage would have noticed the inner disharmony that took over their life together. In public my parents were typically well behaved middle class people. They held dinner parties and pool parties, went on holidays, had numerous friends and acquaintances, none of whom, I presume, had an inkling of what went on behind suburban doors. If anyone could shed any light on all of this it is Aunt Bea. Aunt Bea is the very last member of her generation in the family still alive. She has an elephantine memory and a droll wit. Never married, but with a score of nephews and nieces, she worked for decades in the publishing business before the company she worked for was bought by overseas interests and then taken off shore. I haven't seen her in over six months and most likely I will receive a tongue lashing for my tardiness. It will be worth it.

*

The 109 route combines cable and horse drawn tram routes with the electric tram routes of later years, and adds in 1987 a light rail component to Port Melbourne along the former railway. The cable tram ran from Spencer Street to the west side of the Yarra in 1886, and the following year a horse drawn tram route was started from the river's east side, travelling up to Kew Cemetery. In 1915 a PMTT electric tramway was built running from High Street Kew to Burke Road Camberwell along Cotham Road, extending to Union Road in 1916. The M&MTB replaced cable with electric in 1929, creating the 42 tram route which ran all the way to Union Road from the city for the next six decades. Light rail was initially a separate line, route 111, but this and the 42 were amalgamated to make the 109 in 1993. In 2003 the line was extended from Union Road in Mont Albert to Box Hill.

It's a long trip from the bay to the foothills of the Dandenongs – over 19 kilometres. It also takes a long time. I can't imagine anyone in a hurry to get to Box Hill from the city choosing the tram over the express train, which takes a third of the time. On my trip from the city I test out this theory – and sure enough, I'm the only one who travels the whole distance to the terminus. (Damn, I've just given a salute to railways.)

I decide to cut the Port Melbourne leg from the journey, since I will be late for my aunt if I take it. I need to get there well before lunch which is served early. I board the 109 at the Casino stop at the river with crowds of tourists. A man at the tram stop holds a large placard that reads, 'Jesus Loves You, the Casino Loves Your Money!' When we reach the eastern edge of the city an eclectic crew have boarded – office and health workers, students, patients heading for hospitals and health centres that are located in Victoria Parade. The Parade is wide and tree lined, the foliage dense and green. The tram trundles down the gentle slope in its own exclusive way.

Over Punt Road, we enter Victoria Street Richmond under a massive sculptural gateway spanning the road in the form of a boat, homage to the Vietnamese community and the boats that brought thousands of refugees to the country in the 1970s and '80s, when the nation accepted, rather than reviled boat people. In the boat's textured sides are represented the 100 ancestral eggs of Vietnamese mythology. It seems such a short time ago that we knew the suburb as Little Saigon, but in recent years Korean, Japanese, Indian and South American restaurants have been added. Just past the rail bridge I see a mural of the 109 on a side street wall. Not bad. Around here somewhere – ah yes we're passing it now – is Thy Thy, one of the first Vietnamese restaurants in the city, opening in 1980. Run by the Ho family, Thy Thy was named after one of the Hos' two daughters and they later opened another restaurant called Tho Tho, named after their son. I ate at Thy Thy so often in the 1980s it was embarrassing. Couldn't get enough of paper rolls, pho and pork chop on rice. I'm tempted to jump off and wait until they open.

We cross Church Street, with the 78 sitting dutifully at the terminus, and arrive at a former light industrial zone before the river, now inhabited by apartments, IKEA and other home goods stores, which face their surrounds with blank walls devoid of windows. The heritage listed Little Audrey the Skipping Girl, much reconstructed and repaired, joy in a neon sign, commands the skyline briefly. My reading tells me that she was put there originally to mark a Swedish vinegar factory below. Skipping and vinegar? A skipping rhyme, I read: salt, vinegar, mustard, pepper... .

A large number of shoppers get down here. The tram crosses the river at the bridge which replaced the ferry in 1884, heads up through the cutting into Kew, and turns left up Church Street by the Kew Depot, the monumental red brick building from the 1920s. After the five-roads-meeting of Kew Junction the driver activates the track points below the old Post Office, now a cafe, to angle the tram right, into Cotham Road. Here is a long stretch of track without curves, a series of gentle hills, as Cotham Road becomes Whitehorse Road at Camberwell. I am remembering an evening in the 1980s spent on an earlier incarnation of the 109 – the 42. A W class tram, hired by a local theatre company, became the moving venue for a play, with characters boarding the tram at different points of the journey. The play was called 'Storming Mont Albert by Tram', but I can't remember the plot, only that it was played as farce. It's a blank as to who I was with that night.

The 109 arrives at the terminus in Box Hill. I walk through the crowded shopping mall. Mmm, a bowl of Lanzhou noodle soup is beckoning but I have to hurry. The nursing home is a 10 minute walk through tree-lined streets and Californian bungalows. At the crest in Albion Street I have a clear view of the Dandenong ranges to the east. A dark plume of smoke is rising from the ranges. The smoke pall has an animal like quality, as if some primeval being had awakened and was now curling itself upwards, in ever greater size and density, to the sky.

*

At the nursing home it is the hour before lunch and many of the mostly female residents are waiting patiently in the annex next to the dining room. A piano in the corner of the room is being played by a young man dressed in a tuxedo. The residents sit deep in armchairs and settees, and nod their heads – many of which are festooned with blue rinse – along with the music. A clutter of walking frames and sticks accompany the women.

My aunt is sitting in the one armchair in her room as I enter. She is dressed, as always when I visit, in an elegant dress and her neck, wrists and fingers are covered in flamboyant jewellery. Her TV is on with the sound many decibels above normal. I kiss her and draw up a chair opposite. For the next 10 or so minutes we discuss her various ailments and conditions. This part of my visits rarely varies: the discussion of her medical conditions acts as a kind of clearing house. As she tells it, many of her organs and essential components are in severe atrophy and decline: a heart condition, mobility issues and a recurring pain in her stomach, which frequently prevents her from eating. While she talks I make concerned noises meant to show sympathy and that I'm listening attentively. I've learnt from experience not to ask any follow up questions about her medical care. Our hour together can be quickly consumed by her recitation about the incompetence of the home's medical staff, and doctors in general. Only when she is satisfied of my concern for her aches and pains is she content to move on to other subjects. In the following interlude she asks me about my work and the progress of my children.

I don't mention that I've left work, have been undergoing chemotherapy, or that I've embarked on a project centred on trams; the latter she would no doubt find highly amusing. But I do tell her about the working lives of my son and daughter, or at least as much as I gleaned from my recent painful phone conversations with them. (I did inform my sister and my offspring about my condition. Each one of them was genuinely pissed off with me for not telling them about the cancer earlier. I felt guilty and kind of annoyed at the same time. At the end though I'd managed to persuade all three that things were okay, the treatment was working, and no-one needed to get on a plane anytime soon.)

Aunt Bea asks me to pour some tea which has been sitting in a silver pot under a cozy on a side table. I hand her the lukewarm cup. The thin porcelain of the cup and saucer are delicately patterned with rose images. On the wall behind my aunt are portraits and photos of family members and ancestors. I'm always struck by this gallery, particularly the earlier men, who sport moustaches in every possible shape and design. There's a photo too of Bea with my father as children. They are standing in a bare backyard, dressed in heavy woollens, both with blond curls and intense looks.

Despite, or maybe because she had no family of her own, Bea is the keeper of the family lore, my father never having shown the slightest interest in it. She finds our family history both amusing and disturbing and once told me that I was descended, on my father's side, from a long line of God botherers and military failures. But she's also alert to what she calls the 'gems of interest', ancestors who in some way broke the mould and made or did something different. One of her 'gems' is her grandmother, who grew up in Quebec. This grandmother was a Francophone Canadian, a descendant of the French Acadians, who had settled in Quebec in the early 17th century. And unlike Bea's own mother, she was a poet and storyteller. Bea had grown up hearing stories centred on her grandmother's childhood and early life in the frozen town of Quebec City, the streets of which were laid out in Bea's mind as if she had herself been born there, and not on the other side of the world. I too listened to Bea's tales about my great-grandmother often enough to consider her almost as a living relative, and her city a familiar landscape.

Aunt Bea had a tram story that I had heard more than once. Perhaps readers will recall that Bea had lived in a block of flats near the terminus of the number 5, where my mother and I would occasionally visit. My aunt never owned a car and travelled to work each day by tram. On one such morning she was sitting next to a pregnant woman in the front saloon when the woman's waters broke. As the men nearest saw what was happening they quickly fled the saloon, while Bea pulled off her overcoat and gave it to the woman, who was clearly

324 • GREG GARDINER

embarrassed, to cover herself. Apprised of the situation the driver took the tram to the next public phone on the route where he called for an ambulance.

The situation turned farcical however, when the driver took it into his head to continue in towards the city – moments later the ambulance passed them going in the opposite direction. Banging on the driver's door Aunt Bea yelled at the recalcitrant driver to stop. She paused her story here, saying that she had astonished herself with the language that came out of her mouth that morning. I've never heard Bea use a single swear word the whole time I've known her, but apparently she laid into him with every expletive in the book. The tram stopped, the ambulance arrived, and Bea helped the woman out of the tram and then re-boarded the tram – sans coat. She regretted losing the coat, which was expensive, but the story finished with her declaring that the experience on the tram was as 'close as I ever wanted to get to having a baby'.

Aunt Bea doesn't suffer from dementia, but at 92 she does have trouble remembering exactly what she has previously told me, so there can be, like the tram story, some repetition in her narratives. Regardless, she is clearly keen to pass these stories on to me. I am, she tells me, the only one of her nephews and nieces with any interest in the past.

I'm keen to ask Bea my questions but need to be careful how I go about it. Over tea she's upbraided me for not coming to see her more often and her dissatisfaction with me leads onto questions about my divorced status. She doesn't blame me for the end of my marriage, but is nevertheless concerned, that I am leading the 'reclusive life of a monk'. Why wasn't I re-partnered? It had been years now that I had been single, and did I not appreciate that men do not do well alone, particularly in old age? Eventually though we move onto safer territory. I ask her about her early memories of herself and my father. Where was the photo of the two of them behind her taken?

'Oh that was in Christchurch before we came to Australia. I grew up terrified of earthquakes in New Zealand but I loved Christchurch.

Your father and I were never that close in adulthood as you know but as children we played all the time. I have a very strong memory from a particular winter's day when it snowed and snowed – that year winter was freezing. The two of us are playing in the snow in a park square outside the house we grew up in. We've made a snowman and are throwing snowballs at each other. He's older and bigger than me and his snowballs are packed tighter so better at hitting their mark. I'm pinged on my arms and legs and painfully on my nose. I must have been six or seven at this point. Well, it sounds rough but you know all I remember is that we were laughing and carrying on like old chums.

'We were very wet and got a good hiding when we came in dripping water all over the hallway carpet.' She pauses here before continuing. 'You know it's odd but I loved that hallway – I would practice my ballet routines there, don't laugh, I know its difficult to imagine me as a ballerina – and the hallway was wide and long and while balancing on one leg I would stare at the stained glass panels in the front door, two blue and one red, with lead scroll work in the shape of flowers. The light of the winter sun glowing in the glass. Motes of dust float in the hallway. In the background I can hear my mother in the kitchen. The house only has a few rooms and I can tell from the sounds at the back that she is preparing to bake something in the wood fired oven. Oh damn, I've gone completely off track. What did you want to know about your father?'

This is my opportunity. I tell Bea that I'm trying to piece together some things from the past about my mother and father. Did she recall Uncle Max who I spent a lot of time with as a child?

'Uncle Max? Max with the cravats and swanky suits? Goodness I haven't thought about Max in years. Why on earth are you interested in that old fop?'

'Well, he and Mum were very close weren't they for a time? But then we moved to the suburbs and didn't see Uncle Max after that.'

'That's the second time you've said 'Uncle' Max. You do know he wasn't your uncle don't you?'

'Well, I suspected as much.'

'Suspected? Gregory, you are obtuse sometimes. Of course he wasn't your uncle. Your mother certainly had a thing for him, although God knows why. He wasn't interested in women that way.'

'Max was gay?'

'Yes, darling boy, Max was homosexual. What are you trying to understand? I knew there was something the moment you walked in – a certain glint in the eye you get when you want something.' I tell Bea about my memories of being out travelling around the city on trams with my mother and Max, and how these days came to a sudden end when we moved to the suburbs and I had wondered if my father had been responsible. She replies that as far as she knew he had nothing to do with it and why would he? He hadn't particularly liked Max, but he never seemed troubled by your mother's friendship with him and besides Max had no car. I ask her if my father's dislike of Max was because he was gay and she says, 'Your father had many deficiencies but being prejudiced was not among them. No, I don't know why your mother stopped seeing Max, but then, she rarely confided in me after you moved to the sticks. Perhaps Max was a schoolgirl crush she grew out of, or she realised he was, as you put it, gay? I really don't know. Your mother was a simple girl from the country – sorry Gregory, but it's true – and your father was not the most demonstrative of men. I loved my brother dearly but he was often a hard man to like – not aloof or arrogant, he was always polite and could be quite charming, but it was as if he lived in a large house and only ever visited one or two of its rooms, the rest were shuttered, never to be explored. Max was different, outgoing and flamboyant – a real show pony to be frank – but he probably listened to your mother, entertained and confided in her, talents your father didn't possess.'

Aunt Bea sips her tea and then slowly puts her cup back in its saucer. She stares at me for a minute and then says, 'So what is this all about young Gregory? You didn't honestly think your mother was having an affair did you? Goodness gracious, by the look on your face you did! Well, well, life continues to surprise.' She's smiling and half chuckling as she says this and once again I feel in her presence half a century younger – but not in a way that I mind.

Bea tells me she knew my parents fought bitterly for years and that she had worried about me and my sister often, but when she approached my father about it he told her it was none of her business. I ask her what she thought they were fighting about. She says she has no idea. 'Don't all married couples fight?', she says. 'At least in my day all the married women reported to me privately the horrors of their married life, but then in public they were all happy contented housewives. Glad I never did it. Such hypocrisy.' She pauses then continues, 'What you should appreciate young man is that despite their troubles both of your parents loved you. Although besotted might be the better word. I've never seen my brother so over the moon as when you were born – he couldn't stop grinning. Yes he was a bit of a closed shop, emotionally bottled up, but there was never any doubt how proud he was of you. You were a light to both your parents. You do understand that don't you?'

It's not usual for Bea to praise my father like this. The strain in their adult relationship was a subject that I knew well, much of it from Bea's perspective given that my father rarely talked to me about family history or relationships. Bea always maintained that she made my father uncomfortable, not just with her forthright views, but because of how unfairly her parents had treated her. Bea was dux of her school while my father had barely scraped through final year. Despite this it was my father who was supported to go to university, while she was not. This rankled with her and according to my mother, was the source of Bea's disenchantment with my father. Bea eventually put herself through an arts course while working and then went into publishing, becoming renowned for her great 'eye' for local literature, and publishing several successful authors, including a Miles Franklin winner.

Bea is giving me another one of her searching looks. 'There's something else, isn't there, that you're not talking about,' she says. I demur, telling her that everything is fine and that I'm just chasing some old memories. She considers this for a moment and then with the slightest of shrugs, a kind of turning of the page, begins the process of preparing herself for lunch. Nursing homes – preparing for lunch, for dinner, for bed.

A gong sounds in the distance, the signal the meal is about to be served. My aunt tells me she has something for me before I go. I help her out of the armchair and she walks unsteadily to the other side of the room to a chest of drawers from which she takes a bundle of papers. 'Have you got a bag?', she asks, holding out the bundle to me in both hands. 'I wanted you to have these.' She explains that they are some of her grandmother's poems and short stories and also some old papers of my father's that she'd kept after he died.

I put the papers in my bag and help Bea with her walker. We stroll slowly down to the dining room, where I leave her at her usual table with three other women, who greet me enthusiastically. I had forgotten to kiss her goodbye in her room, and now it is too late. She dislikes public shows of affection.

*

Are we, dear reader, destined to be like our parents? We're definitely shaped by them. They give us our DNA, raise us from birth, and, if we're lucky, infuse our beings with care and love, those great stabilisers of the universe. But the DNA they share with us also has the DNA of thousands of others embedded in it, and we grow up with other people – siblings, cousins, friends, uncles, aunts – who can also be important in how we turn out.

As interesting a question is how well do we know our parents? There's an assumption that in growing up with them we get the whole unvarnished picture, and in some respects this has to be true. But we also forget that they are often very young when they have us, not actually fully formed adults themselves. And, we are having an impact on them too – our very existence changes their lives in ways they couldn't imagine before they had us – so the shaping is working in two directions. Our parents are imagined by us as ever the same, but actually, they are evolving, and the strange thing is, they keep evolving even after they die.

Aunt Bea has added another layer to the family saga and in a way she's re-written one of the chapters. My concerns about Uncle Max and the role he played in my mother's life, and by extension mine, have been allayed. In hindsight I had nothing to worry about – Max was great and had a special place in my mother's heart, but he was never a threat to the marriage. Uncle Max was a friend to me and his disappearance from our family life stung, not least because it was never explained. Clearly my mother missed him too and his absence perhaps contributed to her gathering depression.

The poems by my great grandmother will be interesting but I'm more intrigued about these 'papers of your father's' Aunt Bea has given me. I wonder what's in them?

What was my parents' war about? I still have no idea. One day it started and then 10 years later it was over. As Bea said, who knows what goes on in a marriage? They are opaque relationships, yet full of prescribed norms and behaviours, so imbued with convention that even the participants can struggle to define what they are doing. One thing I know, and where Bea was wrong, is that my mother was never 'simple'. From the country yes, lacking complexity, no.

And my father? Bea was right. He was an old stick in so many ways and typical I suppose of many men of his era. But I now understand that his affection for me was expressed differently to my mother's. I recall now that he drove me everywhere; to school, football and cricket practice, friends' houses, the station, the movies. He watched every game of local sport I ever played and cheered me on, attended every sports night, father-son night, parent-teacher evenings. And I was his helper – car-washing, lawn mowing, painting walls. These were his versions of hugs, of familiarity and love.

I look forward to meeting all these ghosts from the past in the bureau of the afterlife, which I'm told is run by angelic public servants, who serve endless cups of tea and scones. And, of course, running around with my mother in a heavenly W class tram... .

EPILOGUE: 2040

It's 2040 and I'm riding on a trackless tram down Bell Street Preston heading east towards Heidelberg. The tram is part of the new network of Trackless Rapid Transport (TRT) trams, built by the government over the last eight years. I'm enjoying the ride – it's smooth, fast and safe – and we are making great time in our own dedicated lane at 80 kmh. The tram's interior is very comfortable, spacious and for once, the décor is actually pleasant to be in. We glide on rubber wheels, there are no tracks, obviously, and no overhead wiring. The tram's batteries are recharged overnight and at major stops along the way. The T class trams can carry over 180 passengers, and run across a tram network now twice the size of the old one, with plans for further expansion. We have returned to the vision of Alex Cameron's M&MTB 100 years before, of a greatly expanded network to service the suburbs of the growing city. Remember the General Scheme? Congrats Alex! And, oh yes, another important point – all these trams are run by Melbourne Tramways (MT), the government owned corporation that now also controls the trams still running on the older system.

How did this happen, I hear you asking? In 2030 the city reached 6.5 million people, which was great, no problem with people, but along with 6.5 million people came 6.5 million cars. One day in March of that year the city reached deadlock, not just gridlock but a total cessation of movement across the road system. People sat in the cars for hours and hours, and some people ran out of petrol (not all cars had converted to electric) and couldn't move, compounding the gridlock. By evening the city was in a full on crisis – people left their cars

331 • GREG GARDINER

in the street to get home by foot – and a state of emergency was declared. Eventually the mess was cleared up, and a range of measures introduced, including odd and even number plate driving days, to get things moving again. But the jig was up on cars as the main means of urban transport. For city travel, the heralded electric car was as much a failure as the petrol car. There were simply too many cars for a liveable city, or indeed any city to cope with, and we had long ago become a city for cars not people. No matter how many freeways or tunnels were built, or roads widened, the city was car-full. It was an expensive and throughly predictable outcome.

It was then that the government looked at alternatives, and TRT came into its own. It had been piloted in the 2020s and had been quite a success, which governments then ignored. But TRT was cheaper than other solutions – it didn't require rail or overhead wiring, it could run on existing roadways, it was cheaper than other systems to run, and it could be constructed in a handful of years. Not since the miraculous Francis Clapp have we witnessed a network up and running so quickly.

The conductor comes down the tram to my seat and I pay my fare (her fare reader deducting from my bio-account). We chat for a few minutes. She's more than just a fare collector, having a wealth of information about what's happening in the city and its history, and is the vehicle's digital and safety officer. I'm going all the way to the terminus in Box Hill via Doncaster – the tram originates at Sydney Road Coburg – and it is no small irony to think that 150 years after the failed experiment of the Doncaster to Box Hill tram these two suburbs are finally linked by a functioning tramway. All the over one thousand trams on the system are now two-person operations and this has almost eliminated the fare evasion which was costing the government tens of millions in lost revenue a year.

But there's a problem isn't there… . How the hell is this guy still alive in 2040?

Thanks to the genius of gene editing my cancer is not just in remission but completely eliminated from my body – the cancer cells have been destroyed, and moreover will never come back. In fact, cancer is now in 2040 a disease of the past, and largely forgotten like other diseases that have melted into history. But gene editing didn't stop at my cancer. The medicos set about fixing problems with my heart, liver and kidneys. My enlarged prostate was rebored and rejuvenated, and my bladder now functions normally so I'm not going to the loo five times a night. Believe it or not I have head hair too and I look like a sprightly 70 year old, not the approaching 90 years I've been on the planet. And, I've lived long enough to see the tram system finally taking its place again at the heart of our urban transport system, a thing I could never have envisaged when I first began this story 20 years ago.

I travel around the network, to all points of the compass, at least a few times a week, when I'm not playing tennis or hiking in the hills. I carry in my wallet a photo of me and my mother, a black and white photo taken about 1960. I found it just recently, amongst a set taken around that time, while clearing out a cupboard. I've got no doubt now that these were taken by 'Uncle' Max on one of our days out with him. They all record a very particular moment in time – my time, my mother's time, the times. In it she and I are sitting on a wooden bench seat in the middle compartment of a W class tram. We stare smiling at the camera and appear to be sharing in the same private joke, or if not a joke, then the simple pleasure of each others' company, heading out into town for who knows what adventure.

Dear reader, do one thing for me – keep tramming!

BIBLIOGRAPHY

Primary Sources

The Melbourne Tramway and Omnibus Company's Act 1883 (Vic).
Melbourne and Metropolitan Tramways Act 1918 (Vic).
State Electricity Commission Act 1920 (Vic).

Victoria, Report from the Select Committee of the Legislative Assembly upon the Melbourne Tramway and Omnibus Company's Bill together with the proceedings of the Committee and Minutes of Evidence, *Report* (1882).

Victoria, Royal Commission appointed to Inquire into and Report upon the Railway and Tramway Systems of Melbourne and Suburbs, *Report* (1911).

Museums of History NSW – MHNSW Boyne 2 Jan 1839, Assisted immigrants (digital) shipping lists, Item No: [4/4780] Ship: Boyne, Series: NRS-53B, Reel no. 2654. (Accessed 2024).

Network tram journeys undertaken by author – 2019, 2022, 2023.

The Clapp Memorial – Record of the Clapp Family in America, 1876. Compiler Ebenezer Clapp, Committee of Publication: Otis Clapp, David Clapp, William Blake Trask, David Clapp & Son Publishers, Boston.

Books, articles and websites

Bailey, A. R. (2024) *St Kilda Junction signal box operation,* Melbourne Tram Museum, hawthorntramdepot.org.au., originally published in 1966 as 'The Signal Box Helps Get Them Home', *MMTB News July/August,* vol. 3 no. 6.

Berger, John (1972) *Ways of Seeing,* Penguin Books.

Bevege, Margaret (1980) 'Women's Struggle to become Tram Drivers in Melbourne 1956-75', in *Women, Class and History* (ed. E. Windschuttle), Fontana, pp. 437-452.

Bowie, David (1972) *The Rise and Fall of Ziggy Stardust and the Spiders from Mars,* RCA Records.

Brittanica (2024) 'Highland Clearances – Scottish History', *Brittanica,* Accessed 2024.

Broome, Richard et al., (2016) *Remembering Melbourne 1850-1960,* Royal Historical Society of Victoria Inc.

Brown, Geoff (2018) 'Melbourne's Cable Tram System: Was it the Largest?', *The Bellcord,* Journal of the Melbourne Tram Museum, no. 39, September, pp. 1-3.

__ (2019) 'Introducing low-floor trams to Melbourne', *The Bellcord,* Journal of the Melbourne Tram Museum, no. 41, March, pp. 1-4.

__ (2019) 'Birth of a Tramways Titan', *The Bellcord,* Journal of the Melbourne Tram Museum, no. 43, September, pp. 1-4.

__ (2024) *Timeline of Melbourne's tramway network,* Melbourne Tram Museum, https://www.hawthorntramdepot.org.au/papers/timeline.htm#.

Budd, Dale & Randall Wilson (1998) *Melbourne's Marvellous Trams,* University of New South Wales.

City of Stonnington (2012) *Chapel Street Precinct – Heritage Precinct Citation,* Assessed by J. Statham, City of Stonnington.

Codognotto, Kathleen (1992) *History of children's services in the Western Region: regulating Footscray mothers – the Tweddle Baby Hospital and the Plunket System,* Crow Collection Association.

Cooper, Ross (2006) *Eleanor Towzey (Nellie) Stewart (1858-1931),* Australian Dictionary of Biography, https://adb.anu.edu.au/biography/stewart-eleanor-towzey-nellie-8663.

Cranston, Jack (1988) *The Melbourne Cable Trams 1885-1940,* Craftsman Publishing.

Crash, Liz (2024) *Swamp, Meat, Salt,* https://lizcrash.com/underfoot/track2/.

Cross, N., D. Budd & R. Wilson (2001) *Destination City: Melbourne's Electric Trams,* Fifth Edition, Transit Australia Publishing.

Davison, Graeme (2004) *Car Wars: How the Car Won our Hearts and Conquered our Cities,* Allen and Unwin.

de Lacy Lowe (2001) *See Melbourne by Tram,* New Holland Publishers (Australia) Pty Ltd.

Doubleday, Warren (2023) *Building the W class tram,* Melbourne Tram Museum, https://www.hawthorntramdepot.org.au/papers/wclassbuild.htm.

Elliott, Emory (2025) *The Legacy of Puritanism,* National Humanities Center, Divining America, Teacherserve.

Fiddian, Marc (1993) *Clang, Clang, Clang: A study of Melbourne's tramways,* Pakenham Gazette.

__ (2024) *Tram Route 72,* BookPOD.

Fielding, Marcus (2016) *Sir Robert Joseph Risson (1901-1992),* Australian Dictionary of Biography, https://adb.anu.edu.au/biography/risson-sir-robert-joseph-17250.

Finnegan, William (2015) *Barbarian Days: A Surfing Life,* Penguin Press.

Ford, Catherine (2019) 'Despair, hatred and fear on the tram route from hell', *The Age,* Nine Entertainment, 13 October.

Green, Robert (1989) *The First Electric Road – A history of the Box Hill and Doncaster tramway,* John Mason Press, East Brighton.

Grishin, Sasha (2023) *Cecil John Brack (1920-1999),* Australian Dictionary of Biography, https://adb.anu.edu.au/biography/brack-cecil-john-32399.

Han, Kang (2023) *Greek Lessons,* Trans. D. Smith and E. Yae Won, Hogarth, London/NewYork.

Harvey, David (2007) *A Brief History of Neoliberalism,* Oxford University Press.

Heritage Victoria (2024) 'Heritage Place – Morgiana Woolshed', *Heritage Victoria,* Study no. 458.

Hindsight (2012) 'Cap #4074: the Joyce Barry story', ABC Radio National, 2 September, https://www.abc.net.au/listen/programs/hindsight/cap-234074/4208670.

HISTORY.com (2009) *The Puritans,* A & E Television Networks.

Hone, J. Ann (2006) *Francis Boardman Clapp (1833-1920),* Australian Dictionary of Biography, https://adb.anu.edu.au/biography/clapp-francis-boardman-3209.

Johnstone, Rose (2021) 'Melbourne's trams ranked from best to worst', *Time-out,* Time Out Group Plc.

Jones, Noelle & Mal Rowe (2023) 'Glenhuntly Depot: 100 years old', *The Bellcord,* Journal of the Melbourne Tram Museum, no. 59, September, pp. 7-16.

Jones, Noelle (2024) "Wee Alick' McNaught: head track oiler,' *The Bellcord,* Journal of the Melbourne Tram Museum, no. 64, December, pp. 10-15.

Jones, Russell (2002) *Francis Boardman Clapp: transport entrepreneur,* Melbourne Tram Museum, hawthorntramdepot.org.au.

__ (2002) *George Smith Duncan: tramway engineer,* Melbourne Tram Museum, https://www.trammuseum.org.au/papers/duncan.htm.

__ (2003) *Melbourne tramways: union vs management,* Melbourne Tram Museum, hawthorntramdepot.org.au.

__ (2004) *Fares Please! An Economic History of the Melbourne & Metropolitan Tramways Board,* Melbourne Tram Museum, https://www.hawthorntramdepot.org.au/papers/ecohist/ecohist0.htm.

__ (2009) *Joyce Barry: Grassroots advocate for equal opportunity,* Melbourne Tram Museum, hawthorntramdepot.org.au.

__ (2009) *Alex Cameron: father of Melbourne's electric trams,* Melbourne Tram Museum, hawthorntramdepot.org.au.

__ (2014) *T. P. Strickland: designer of the W class tram,* Melbourne Tram Museum, https://www.hawthorntramdepot.org.au/papers/strickland.htm.

__ (2015) *Tramway ANZACS,* Melbourne Tram Museum, hawthorntramdepot.org.au.

__ (2024) 'Why W?,' *The Bellcord,* Journal of the Melbourne Tram Museum, no. 62, June, pp. 17-18.

Keating, John D. (1996) *Mind the Curve! – A History Of The Cable Trams,* Transit Australia Publishing, Sydney.

Keenan, David (1985) *Melbourne Tramways,* Transit Press, Sans Souci.

Kernot, William Charles (2024) *Cable trams: how they work,* Melbourne Tram Museum, hawthorntramdepot.org.au, originally published in 1888 as *The Melbourne Tramways*, republished in J. Cranston (1988) *The Melbourne Cable Trams 1885-1940,* Craftsman Publishing.

Kerouac, Jack (2007) *On The Road,* Viking Penguin.

Kings, K.S. (2016) *A Short History of The North Melbourne Electric Tramway & Lighting Company Limited,* Tramway Publications, Nunawading.

Kundera, Milan (1984) *The Unbearable Lightness of Being,* Faber & Faber, London.

May, Andrew (2008) 'Baths and Bathing', *emelbourne – the city past and present*, University of Melbourne, https://www.emelbourne.net.au/biogs/EM00162b.htm.

McCalman, Janet (2006) *On The World of the Sixty-nine Tram,* Melbourne University Press, Carlton.

__ (2024) 'Diseases and Epidemics', *eMelbourne – the city past and present,* The University of Melbourne.

Melbourne Tram Museum (2024) *Melbourne and Metropolitan Tramways Board W5 Class No 774,* Melbourne Tram Museum, https://www.hawthorntramdepot.org.au/trams/mmtb774.htm.

Merleau-Ponty, Maurice (2012) *Phenomenology of Perception,* Trans. D. A. Landes, New York: Routledge.

Merrett, Bronwen (1994) 'Melbourne's Tramways: The First 50 Years', *Ancestor,* vol. 22 no. 4, pp. 11-12.

Merritt, John (2007) 'The Trade Union Leader Who Went to Gaol', *Canberra Historical Journal,* no. 59, pp. 8-15.

Monash University (2023) *Caulfield-Rowville Trackless Rapid Transit*, Monash University, https://www.monash.edu/industry/caulfield-rowville-trackless-rapid-transit.

Murphy Wandin, Aunty Joy (2016) *Welcome to country: A Traditional Aboriginal Ceremony*, Lisa Kennedy – Illustrator, Walker Books Australia Pty Ltd.

Old Treasury Building (2024) *On The Road: The Omnibus*, Old Treasury Building, oldtreasurybuilding.org.au.

O'Neill, Aaron (2014) 'Infant mortality rate (under one year old) in Australia from 1870 to 2020', *Statista,* 9 August.

Perfrement, Aymeric (2023) *Trams of Melbourne: The Ultimate Handbook,* IngramSpark.

__ (2018) *Why Melbourne's Tram Network is the most Successful in the World: The World's Biggest and Longest Serving Tram Network,* Aymeric Perfrement.

Premier of Victoria (2024) 'G Class Trams: Developed With, Built By, And Made For Victorians', *media release,* 8 November, https://www.premier.vic.gov.au/g-class-trams-developed-built-and-made-victorians.

Prouty, Florence Newell (1941) *History of the Town of Holden 1667-1941,* The Stubbs Press, Worcester.

Rice, Franklin (1904) *Systematic History Fund – Vital Records of Holden, Massachusetts to the end of the year 1849,* Stanhope Press, Boston.

Risson, R. J. H. (1955) *Address to the Victorian Branch of the Institute of Transport,* in D. Budd & R. Wilson (1998) *Melbourne's Marvellous Trams,* University of New South Wales, pp. 90-96.

Rodriguez, Judith (2016) *Flares,* Melbourne Shakespeare Society.

Rosenthal, Lesley S. (2000) *Shmatte Mazel,* Video – YouTube, https://www.youtube.com/playlist?list=PLtwrFqFmlRRCGU4XmzjqaJvMShg6W9Cm0.

Sartre, Jean-Paul (1984) *Being and Nothingness: An Essay on Phenomenological Ontology,* Trans. H. E. Barnes, New York: Washington Square Press.

Stewart, Terry (2017) *The Highland Clearances,* historic-uk, https://www.historic-uk.com/HistoryUK/HistoryofScotland/The-Highland-Clearances/.

Thomson, Kathleen (2006) *Alexander Cameron (1864-1940),* Australian Dictionary of Biography, https://adb.anu.edu.au/biography/cameron-alexander-5471.

Turnbull, Graeme (2001) *The Sir Robert Risson era: an enduring legacy,* Melbourne Tram Museum, hawthorntramdepot.org.au.

Rowe, Mal (2017) *Electrolysis: the destructive by-product of electric traction,* Melbourne Tram Museum, https://www.hawthorntramdepot.org.au/papers/electrolysis.htm.

Rymill, Peter (2006) *Alexander Cameron 1810-1881,* Australian Dictionary of Biography, https://adb.anu.edu.au/biography/cameron-alexander-12833.

Shore, Marci (2017) *The Ukrainian Night: An Intimate History of Revolution,* Yale University Press.

The Mornington Cable Car (2018) *Technical,* Dunedin Heritage Light Rail Trust, https://dunedincablecars.co.nz/technical.html.

The Scottish History Society (2024) 'The Highland Clearances', *The Scottish History Society,* scottishhistorysociety.com.

VICSIG (2025) *Tram,* Vicsig, https://vicsig.net/index.php?page=about.

Victorian Aboriginal Heritage Council (2021) *Boundary Variations Consideration June 2021,* Victorian Aboriginal Heritage Council, https://www.aboriginalheritagecouncil.vic.gov.au/boundary-variations-consideration-june-2021.

Viola, Bill (2007) *Ocean without a shore,* Exhibition - National Gallery of Victoria (2009), https://www.ngv.vic.gov.au/explore/collection/work/87110/.

Wikipedia (2024) 'Luna Park, Melbourne', *Wikipedia,* https://en.wikipedia.org/wiki/Luna_Park,_Melbourne.

Wilkie, Benjamin (2017) 'Family Networks and the Australian Pastoral Industry: A Case Study of the Port Phillip District and Victoria in the Late Nineteeth Century', *Agricultural History,* vol. 91 no. 1, pp. 78-95.

Wilson, Randall & Dale Budd (2014) *Destination Waterfront City: A Guide To Melbourne's Trams,* Transit Australia Publishing.

__ (2014) *The Melbourne Tram Book,* University of New South Wales.

Yarra Trams (2025) *Home page - Yarra Trams,* Yarra Journey Makers - Transdev Australia & John Holland, https://yarratrams.com.au/.

Newspapers

Byrne, Bridie (2015) 'Melbourne's inner west was at the forefront of ammunition production, producing all the bullets for the first Australian Imperial Force', *The Herald-Sun,* 3 April, Nationwide News Pty Ltd.

Cameron, Alex (1924) 'City Traffic Problem – The Case for the Tramways Board', *The Herald,* The Herald and Weekly Times Ltd., 29 May, p. 4.

Carey, Adam (2012) 'Passengers, drivers at risk in 'cheap as chips' trams', *The Age,* Nine Entertainment, 4 August.

Hansen, Brian (1955) 'Risson smiles on Bourke st. – 'Sneak' trams pick up lost time', *The Argus,* The Argus Pty Ltd., 29 June, p. 5.

Hope, Z. and T. Papworth (2019) '"Cheap as chips" Kew tram's off-the-rails history revealed', *The Age,* Nine Entertainment, 7 October.

Nicholas, Josh (2025) 'Tourists, watercolours and the sad, still star: sketching the route 35 tram showed me a Melbourne I had never really noticed', *The Guardian,* Guardian News & Media Ltd., 22 March.

Shmith, Michael (2011) 'Long way from hot metal: the changing face of newspapers', *The Age,* Nine Entertainment, 31 May.

State Political Reporter (1954) 'Risson's Job In Balance', *The Herald,* The Herald and Weekly Times Ltd., 23 April, p. 3.

The Age (1885) 'The Richmond Cable Tramway', *The Age,* David Syme and Co Ltd., 4 November, p. 4.

__ (1885) 'The Richmond Tramway', *The Age,* David Syme and Co Ltd., 30 November, p. 6.

__ (1887) 'The Brunswick Tramway', *The Age,* David Syme and Co Ltd., 21 July, p. 7.

__ (1887) 'Melbourne Tramway And Omnibus Company. Annual Meeting of Shareholders', *The Age,* David Syme and Co Ltd., 31 August, p. 5.

__ (1888) 'The Tramway Strike. Progress of Negotiations: Accessions To The Company's Strength – Mass Meeting At The Trades Hall', *The Age,* David Syme and Co Ltd., 17 February, p. 5.

__ (1888) 'The Royal Sanitary Commission', *The Age,* David Syme and Co Ltd., 4 July, p. 11.

__ (1924) 'New Tram Cars. Designed And Built in Victoria – Two in Service on Malvern Line', *The Age,* David Syme and Co Ltd., 4 January, p. 6.

__ (1928) 'Tram Noises – Board's Many Experiments', *The Age,* David Syme and Co Ltd., 22 May, p. 14.

__ (1938) 'Tramway Workshops', *The Age,* David Syme and Co Ltd., 23 June, p. 15.

__ (1940) 'Obituary - Mr. Alex Cameron', *The Age,* David Syme and Co Ltd., 24 February, p. 24.

__ (1954) 'Mr. Risson's Tram Ride', *The Age – Letters to the Editor,* David Syme and Co Ltd., 28 August, p. 2.

__ (1954) 'Chairman Defends Trams as Best', *The Age,* David Syme and Co Ltd., 28 October, p. 8.

__ (1990) 'Rebel drivers block the city with trams', *The Age,* David Syme and Co Ltd., 2 January.

The Argus (1869) 'The Melbourne Omnibus Company', *The Argus,* The Argus Pty Ltd., 22 February, p. 6.

__ (1885) 'Commencement of New Tramway Lines', *The Argus,* The Argus Pty Ltd., 11 August, p. 6.

__ (1885) 'Laying The Richmond Tramway Cable', *The Argus,* The Argus Pty Ltd., 24 October, p. 13.

__ (1897) 'Saltwater River Pollution', *The Argus,* The Argus Pty Ltd., 6 September, p. 3.

__ (1923) 'Street Transport', *The Argus,* The Argus Pty Ltd., 26 September, p. 8.

__ (1926) 'Tramway Conversion – Intricate Preliminary Work', *The Argus,* The Argus Pty Ltd., 4 January, p. 11.

__ (1926) 'Victoria Parade Trams. Centre Reserves Favoured.', *The Argus,* The Argus Pty Ltd., 1 April, p. 13.

__ (1928) 'Tramways Strike. Non-Punishment of Men.', *The Argus,* The Argus Pty Ltd., 12 April, p. 15.

__ (1934) 'Mr. Cameron in Defence of his Trams', *The Argus,* The Argus Pty Ltd., 20 July, p. 9.

__ (1934) 'Why Trams are Preferred to Trolley Buses – Board's Reply to Automobile Club', *The Argus,* The Argus Pty Ltd., 21 July, p. 9.

__ (1936) 'Clan Cameron Has a Real Scotch Night', *The Argus,* The Argus Pty Ltd., 8 December, p. 3.

__ (1936) 'Mr. Cameron Retires – Not Told Officially Of Replacement', *The Argus,* The Argus Pty Ltd., 1 January, p. 6.

The Herald (1924) 'Relieving Traffic Congestion – Tram Board to Help – Report Promised', *The Herald,* The Herald and Weekly Times Ltd., 17 April, p. 7.

__ (1924) 'Buses And Trams – Mr Cameron's View: One Controlling Body', *The Herald,* The Herald and Weekly Times Ltd., 10 July, p. 5.

__ (1928) 'Mr Cameron Angry – Objects to The Herald Conducting Noise Tests', *The Herald,* The Herald and Weekly Times Ltd., 9 May, p. 1.

__ (1928) 'War On Trams In Collins Street', *The Herald,* The Herald and Weekly Times Ltd., 5 October, p. 6.

__ (1929) 'Obstacles To All Night Trams – Mr. Cameron's Side', *The Herald,* The Herald and Weekly Times Ltd., 20 July, p. 4.

__ (1935) 'New Tram Chairman – Successor To Mr Cameron', *The Herald,* The Herald and Weekly Times Ltd., 7 December, p. 2.

__ (1954) 'Stagger hours, says tramways' chief', *The Herald,* The Herald and Weekly Times Ltd., 8 November, p. 5.

The Independent (1887) 'The Report on the Sanitary Condition of Footscray', *The Independent,* 9 July, p. 3.

__ (1887) 'Out in a Gondola – At Low Water', *The Independent,* 27 August, p. 3.

The Prahran Telegraph (1919) 'The Tramway Board – The New Chairman: Mr. A. Cameron Appointed', *The Prahran Telegraph,* Aubrey Brotherton Publisher, 28 June, p. 5.

__ (1926) 'Wood Blocking in High Street Prahran', *The Prahran Telegraph,* Aubrey Brotherton Publisher, 26 February, p. 5.

The Sun News-Pictorial (1926) 'First Electric Tram Ran Through Melbourne Streets Yesterday on 12-Mile Route – New Tram Run', *The Sun News-Pictorial,* The Herald and Weekly Times Ltd., 25 January, p. 3.

__ (1928) 'Noisy Electric Trams: Some Information for Mr. Cameron', *The Sun News-Pictorial,* The Herald and Weekly Times Ltd., 3 February, p. 21.

__ (1954) 'Risson: "Folly To Scrap The Tram"', *The Sun News-Pictorial,* The Herald and Weekly Times Ltd., 5 July, p. 11.

The Toowoomba Chronicle and Queensland Advertiser (1869) 'Melbourne Omnibus Company – From the Daily Telegraph', *The Toowoomba Chronicle and Queensland Advertiser,* Toowoomba Newspapers Ltd., 17 April, p. 4.

Valent, Dani (2023) 'An old Victoria Street Vietnamese favourite springs back', *The Age,* Nine Entertainment, 4 August.

Warwick Daily News (1942) 'Thrilling Chase – Kangaroos in Melbourne Suburbs', *Warwick Daily News,* The Warwick Newspaper Pty Ltd., p. 4.

ACKNOWLEDGEMENTS

Any book is a collective human effort if for no other reason than it includes the patience shown by family and friends in the face of the author's ongoing obsession with their love-child. To my family – Ed, Thea, Alex, Jude, Kay, and Michael - I thank you for your support and forbearance.

To my partner Sue Rechter I thank you for your loving support, your reading and commenting upon multiple drafts, wonderful editing and faith in the project.

Several friends acted as readers and provided valuable feedback. I thank Pamie Fung, Helen Collins, Trudy McLauchlan, and Kim Bessant for their insights, corrections and suggestions. I also want to thank Paul Godfree, Peter Yates, Wendy Burnett, Joanne Linsdell, Jane Baldwin, Colin Meredith and Toni Lechte. Thank you Dr Thea Gardiner for your excellent proofing work.

Special thanks to the staff and volunteers at the Melbourne Tram Museum. Thanks to Warren Doubleday, Geoff Brown and Mal Rowe for patiently answering my questions, and to Brian Weedon. The museum is a must visit for anyone interested in Melbourne tram history. My visits to the museum had particular resonance, as this was the building in which I was taught how to drive a W class tram 50 years ago.

Thank you to Gail Oliver and the Talbot Writers' Group for your great company and shared literary adventures. To the staff at Acustico cafe in Brunswick thanks for keeping me fueled with good coffee. I was delighted when Mike Maka agreed to the use of his Sydney Road tram mural as the cover of this book. Thank you Mike!

I wish to remember and acknowledge my late friend Gerald Fitzgerald for his teaching, mentorship and friendship of over forty years, and without whom this book would not have been written.

This book was composed and written on the traditional lands of the Kulin Nation.

Finally, I want to recognise and thank Melbourne's tramway workers and officials for making this system what it is today: the network is successful because of the endless labour and love that has gone into its creation and ongoing service to the people of this city by generations of 'trammies'. We are profoundly lucky to have such a unique system in our lives.

ABOUT THE AUTHOR

Former tram driver, Greg Gardiner, worked out of Camberwell depot in the 1970s. He has a PhD in Classics, lectured in classics and theatre studies, and was a research fellow in the Centre for Australian Indigenous Studies, Monash University. For a decade he was the head of research in the Victorian Parliament's Library Research Service, before serving as executive officer for parliamentary committees. His published research covers a wide range of subjects, including Indigenous criminal justice, Victorian politics and history, climate change and disability services. Greg is married with two children and is now a grandfather.